LAKE CHAD

Katsina

KANO

MAIDUGURI

A

R.Benue

**FRENCH
EQUATORIAL AFRICA**

Road ———

Railway +++++

*Many towns, esp. in north,
omitted for clarity*

Ogoja

Bansara

**BRITISH
CAMEROONS**

bakaliki

Ikom

Bamenda

Mamfe

Calabar

FRENCH CAMEROONS

ron

obo

Rio del Rey

Kumba

Cameroon Mountain

ebunsha

Buea

100 miles

ta Isabel

Victoria

DO PO

STEAL ME A DUCHESS

WILLIAM MUTCH

Steal me a Duchess

Woodmarch

Endpaper maps © William Mutch

First published in Great Britain in 2001 by
Woodmarch Productions
Craigdhu, Kinnesswood, KY13 9HX

ISBN 0 9540170 0 5

Jacket design by Jim Proudfoot
Printed and bound in Great Britain by Ritchie of Edinburgh.
www.ritchieprint.co.uk

AUTHOR'S NOTE

The fact a real Italian ship, the *Duchessa d'Aosta*, was forcibly taken from Santa Isabel in 1942 by a civilian group composed mainly of Colonial Service officers from Nigeria, acting with SOE, makes it all the more important to state that this book is fiction, about – if you will – a one-time sister ship, the *Duchessa di Lucca*. The characters here are all fictitious and any resemblance to actual people, living or deceased, is entirely coincidental and unintentioned.

In contrast, the spectacular forests of Uronigbe, with the diamond-clear Jamieson River, delightful Sapoba and its local people, were very much fact, still remembered by the author with great pleasure.

The references to the Kinmont Willie raid are based on Sir Walter Scott's *Minstrelsy of the Scottish Border* (1801) and on George MacDonald Fraser's book *The Steel Bonnets* (Pan Books 1971). The cutting-out of the *Duchessa d'Aosta* is described in *Secret Agent* by David Stafford (BBC 2000).

William Mutch
Edinburgh
December 2000

CHAPTER ONE

MAY 1940

The bright morning sunshine sparkled on the ship's white upperworks and on the blazing red and green of her funnel as she cleared Table Bay. Glittering ripples of light reflecting from the wavelets flickered along the immaculate black paint of her hull. It was Tuesday the 21st of May 1940 and the smart ship was the *Duchessa di Lucca*, homeward bound to Italy after discharging cargo and picking up passengers in Cape Town.

Capitano Mattia Palma came from a family of seafarers going back certainly five hundred years and he himself had been a deep-sea sailor for more than forty. In his cups he would sometimes boast that a Palma ancestor had sailed with Marco Polo in the Venetian war against the Genoese in 1298, an assertion that could not be readily checked but was never challenged; he had such an air, it seemed quite likely. Home was a small village between Monfalcone and Trieste, where the extended family of Palmas, brothers and cousins, close and far removed, almost cornered the maritime market; they built ships, crewed them, chandlered them, commanded them – cargo, passenger, naval, the lot.

As he stood on his bridge Mattia Palma looked every inch a sailor, stocky in build with a commanding eye and dark hair tinged with grey that showed more in his neatly trimmed goatee beard than on his head. For the past eighteen years he had been voyaging around Africa, mostly from Trieste and Genoa to the Cape and sometimes as far as Lourenço Marques in Portuguese East, for the last eight years as captain. He had been fortunate to be given command of the *Duchessa* immediately after her refit at Trieste in 1930. It was surprising the owners had gone ahead with that major investment, given the economic blizzard at the time, but they had done so and he must have been in their good books, for he was given the command. He and the *Duchessa* had been sailing the West Coast ever since.

Mattia Palma was content; he had a good ship and a good crew, six officers, all Italian, and twenty-nine men of whom nineteen were Italian, four were Portuguese and six were lascars signed on in Port Elizabeth a couple of trips back. The *Duchessa di Lucca* was a handsome vessel of more than eight thousand tons, extensively refitted in 1930 by the builders, Stabilimento Tecnico Triestino, including most attractive passenger cabins and saloons. She was registered at the Italian port of Trieste and owned by Africa Triestino Società Anonima di Navigazione which operated the ship as a passenger and cargo carrier on the Africa run.

A notable feature of the ship were her four lattice masts supporting the derricks, with which cargo could be handled by the crew, where dockside cranes were not available. Although there were cabins for fourteen passengers, there were only five aboard this trip, three Italian businessmen returning home from the Cape and two government officers on leave from Portuguese East Africa. The war in Europe made sea travel unattractively hazardous and booking on an Italian ship was, for people of many nationalities, an added and unnecessary gamble although the country was officially still neutral. In addition to that, (although Mattia would be reluctant to admit the disadvantage) the *Duchessa* was slower than the larger liners on the run and had to stop further up the west coast of Africa to pick up cargo, so it would be six weeks before she was due to dock at home in Italy.

The departure from Cape Town was unremarkable, as befitted a workaday ship, homeward bound. The captain was pleased to be clear of the tiresome complications of the port – agents, customs, health officials and all their bureaucracy. God be praised, now Table Mountain was fading astern, they could settle down to the comforting routine of shipboard life for the nine-day run to Banana, the port in the Belgian Congo, at the mouth of the great Congo River, where they were to pick up the main cargo. Then the 25-day voyage to Genoa, with the short break at Las Palmas on Gran Canaria to take on oil fuel, the cheapest and most convenient oil-station on their voyage.

Once the pilot had been dropped and the main engine had settled to the regular cruising rhythm on the course to the north, Palma had time to reconsider the radio news of the shattering events unfolding in Europe. It looked as though Europe would be a different place when they reached the Mediterranean in six weeks. The phoney war had rudely ended and the German blitzkrieg was ripping across France. Nevertheless – the Captain pursed his lips at his thought and gave an eloquent little private shrug – it was Germany's war, not Italy's, so let them get on with it. Yugoslavia, now that would be different; all Trieste and indeed every thinking person in Italy knew that Il Duce and Count Ciano were correct in asserting that the natural resources of the Balkans were essential for the expansion of Italian industry. He wouldn't be surprised if Italy soon made a move in the Balkans. However, the important thing now was that the *Duchessa* was at sea and they could settle down for the trip home. Germany's war in France was far away and looked as though it might well be over by the time they docked in Genoa.

By the third day the lazy pattern was well established. The weather was pleasant. In the delightful art nouveau surroundings of the *Duchessa*'s saloons, the passengers had relaxed into the gentle round of drinks, meals and peaceful occupations such as reading and bridge, which is the hope of every ship's officer for passengers. Wagers on the distance run each day were their greatest excitement.

As far as the voyage itself was concerned, the run north to the Congo River was uneventful and on the morning of Thursday the 30th of May they moored alongside the main wharf at Banana. The news from Europe, however, was anything but uneventful and Captain Palma was expecting severe problems. Banana was a Belgian colonial port and the defeated Belgian army at home had capitulated to the Germans on the 28th, only two days before. The Belgian king, as commander-in-chief, had surrendered with his troops but a government-in-exile was being set up, apparently drawing great support from the colonial administration in the Congo.

The mood of the Belgian port officials in Banana was a confusion of intense distress, patriotism, deep anxiety for families at home and bitter hatred towards Germany. Palma and his officers soon

3

found that the attitude towards Germany spilled over to at least coolness towards Italy and Italians. Mussolini had signed the Berlin-Rome Axis treaty and his approval of Hitler's attack in France was common knowledge; indeed the cynical opinion was widely held that Italy would declare war when it best suited Mussolini and when there was not much fighting left to be done.

In view of the chaos following the defeat of their country and the possible alignment of Italy with the loathsome Germans, Belgian officials clearly regarded loading cargo on the *Duchessa di Lucca* as a matter of no importance whatever. Nevertheless the ship's first officer and the owners' local agents pressed relentlessly for speedy action and their efforts were successful. The full cargo was waiting on the quayside and, within four hours of docking, it was filling the holds. All day and every day that week the cranes were busy feeding cargo steadily into the ship. In torrid heat the crew and African wharfies toiled to the endless exhortations of the first mate who was aware both of the anxiety of his captain and of the stream of wireless messages from the owners urging them to complete loading and get to sea. As a result of these efforts, the full cargo was on board by the morning of Friday June 7th and the *Duchessa* sailed immediately.

The ship's hatches were still being battened down when they cleared the Congo River. It was then, while they were still within sight of land, that the wireless signal reached them from the owners instructing Palma to steam at full speed northwards. No reason was given for this order which took them off the main shipping route but the crew were relieved to be out of the fiery heat of Banana port, away from the mosquitoes, the clamour of the dock cranes and, best of all, away from the hostility and bitterness of the Belgians.

Three days later and almost seven hundred nautical miles to the north, when the ship was approaching the Spanish island of Fernando Po just before midnight on the 10th of June, the officer of the watch woke Captain Palma with the first of a series of comfort-shattering radio signals. Mussolini had declared war on both Great Britain and France, and Italian troops were engaged in the invasion of France across the Alpine passes. Led by the elite Alpini Divisions, invincible Fascist forces under the inspired command of Il Duce had joined their stalwart German allies in the glorious Axis struggle against the reactionary powers, that undoubtedly would result in an early and magnificent victory over France and England.

4

The first radiogram was quickly followed by another from the Ministero Marittimo giving general instructions to Italian ships in the South Atlantic: although the war was expected to be short, since France and England would not be able to resist combined Italian and German might, all Italian ships should avoid contact with enemy naval vessels, notably the squadron of British light forces believed to be operating out of Freetown in Sierra Leone, and should avoid the territorial waters and harbours of all British, Belgian and French colonies in Africa.

Only twenty minutes later another radio signal, a priority one, came from the Africa Triestino owners. Since there was no possibility of the Italian vessel making an uninterrupted passage into the Mediterranean as long as the British fleet was operating out of the naval base at Gibraltar, the *Duchessa di Lucca* was to proceed to the neutral port of Santa Isabel on Fernando Po and await further instructions. Captain Palma immediately executed that order and eight hours later he brought the ship carefully into the harbour on the north coast of Fernando Po.

Il Duce, however, had made a sad miscalculation: the war was not short, as he had predicted. Admittedly, France capitulated to the Axis forces in a matter of days (although Italian troops contributed little or nothing) but Britain hung on stubbornly. Dreary days dragged into weeks, and weeks into frustrating months. News of the late summer's air battles over southern England filtered down to the *Duchessa's* crew, news which, even in Rome Radio's well expurgated form, did nothing for the men's morale. This was followed in succeeding months by disturbing accounts of war in the Italian colonies of Abyssinia and Cyrenaica where things were certainly not going in Italy's favour.

In soul-sapping tedium, the *Duchessa di Lucca* was stuck, apparently for the long war's duration, in the miserable open roadstead of Santa Isabel on the neutral Spanish island.

CHAPTER TWO

DECEMBER 1941

Oberst Otto Eichel of 9 Fallschirmjäger-Gruppe plotted the new position on his map and was well pleased with progress. Over the past three weeks his convoy of vehicles had driven south from Tripoli, skirting the Hamádah-al-Hamrá, past Birak, through the Fezzan to Marzák and yesterday through the Passe de Korizo. Tonight they were safely camped on the west flank of the mountain Pic Toussidé, the western rampart of the Tibesti Highlands in the central Sahara. He had successfully brought his unit of paratroopers more than half way to the target, from the Mediterranean to beyond the midpoint of the desert. It was Day -14, two weeks before the attack and he reckoned they had more than a day in hand.

Junkers 52 transport planes had made the rendezvous with petrol, water, food and some spares, so now he could give the men a rest day to catch up on sleep and prepare for the final leg of a thousand kilometres to Maiduguri in northern Nigeria. The column had circled round Tummo oasis on the frontier between Libya and French Niger, and there was no reason to think they had been spotted, so the Colonel now believed there was a fair chance they could get south to Lake Chad without the British being alerted. Much depended on the enemy in Nigeria believing that the Sahara was an obstacle the Germans could not cross with a fighting force. Colonel Eichel intended to shatter that misapprehension. His unit was small but in action it would pack a heavy punch that would combine with the larger operation further south. His present independent command fitted into a strategic plan of enormous potential. In any event, he was enjoying the desert environment. These Tibesti Highlands were glorious.

He studied the map with care. They must keep well to the east of the main camel route by Bilma and Dibbéla, avoiding all contact with local people until they reached Chad. Thereafter, entering Nigeria between Bosso and Geidam, there would be no question of secrecy; they would shoot their way through any opposition and head straight for Maiduguri, creating as much mayhem and panic as possible, in order to draw British attention and forces away from Nigeria's southern provinces. Their attack in the north would pull the enemy off-balance and ensure success for the main effort.

His men, all paratrooper veterans of Crete, were in high spirits. For a month they had trained in Libya's Hamádah-al-Hamrá to gain desert experience before starting on the operation, learning to use the sun compass for navigation and ironing out the routine problems of Saharan travel. They were a crack unit and things were going according to plan.

The Colonel folded away the map, quietly content but not complacent.

'*So weit, so gut,*' he murmured to himself. And here was Gefreiter Prüm with the evening brew and the special treat he had ordered.

'*Kaffee mit Schnaps heute Abend, Herr Oberst.*'

*   *

Only thirty miles north of the *Duchessa di Lucca*'s anchorage was the steamy mangrove coast of the African mainland. The country was Nigeria, vast in extent and immensely diverse in climate, vegetation and people. It embraced hundreds of tribes, kingdoms and emirates, but the broad racial groups coincided with the divisions imposed by the two great rivers, the Niger and the Benue. The dry savannas of the north were dominated by the Hausa people and the nomadic Fulani with their prodigious herds of humped cattle. The southwest was occupied by the Yoruba and related tribes, including those of Benin. The wet southeast was predominantly Ibo, densely populated, over-crowded.

7

This Babel was part of the British Empire, a protectorate but entirely an African country. It was governed by so-called "indirect rule" which left intact the local structure of emirs, chiefs, kings and councils as native authorities, with a tiny cadre of white officers as advisers. Lagos, the crowded seaport in the extreme southwest, was the capital. In the nineteenth century Lagos had been the crucial base in the suppression of the slave trade to America but now it was the centre of both thriving commerce and government.

The car carrying Christopher Wickham, a Senior District Officer in the Nigerian administration of Britain's Colonial Service, swept smoothly up the drive between beds of orange African lilies and well-trimmed lawns, and drew up quietly in the shaded archway forming the entrance to Government House. The Nigerian driver ran round to open the door at Chris' elbow. Flanking the sides of the porch were lines of large earthenware pots with West Africa's standard set of potted plants, the common magenta bougainvillaea, vermilion hibiscus and the dismal variegated croton. It flashed through Chris' mind, as it had how often before, that the colour-clash of the purple and vermilion was outrageous but classic Africa. Even the Governor's gardeners stuck to the well tried favourites.

Chris was puzzled and wary as he stepped from the back of the car but nonetheless glad to be out of it; at half-past four the heat of the tropical afternoon was past but the leather seats were sticky and the metal box oppressive. After driving to Ibadan he had come down to Lagos by train to save petrol, now scarce after two years of war: it was the very end of December 1941. Wickham was jaded after the rail journey from Ibadan; it was only one hundred miles but the train averaged a mere seventeen miles an hour. It was thoughtful of the Governor to have sent his car to pick him up at Lagos station in Ebutta Metta but, for the life of him, he could not imagine what justified the invitation or rather – let's face it – the order to come. True, he had been Sir John's junior ADO when the old man was Resident in Oyo Province, but that was years ago, before the knighthood and governorship, and certainly failed to warrant this call from the blue. They had not even exchanged letters since then; the difference in rank made correspondence inappropriate when postings had taken their careers apart.

Chris wakened to the fact he was still standing by the car and now here was a young man coming to greet him, presumably His

Excellency's aide. What a soft posting that would be: a thought instantly rejected in the realisation that it involved living in Lagos and missing all the fun of the real country, in the villages and the bush. The ADC was tall, fair and fresh-complexioned, in his very early twenties: probably first tour – hard luck to be stuck in the Secretariat.

'Good afternoon, Mr Wickham. I'm Robin Kitchener, HE's ADC. Sir John asked me to watch for the car to welcome you and see you have everything you need. He and Lady Robertson hope you will be able to stay overnight. You have your kit with you? Good. This is Sunday, the guest's steward boy who will look after you.' A slim young Yoruba man in white drill uniform put his hands behind his back and made a little bobbing bow, with a friendly smile.

'Welcome, sah,' he said and began to unload Chris' bag from the back of the car. Royal hospitality, Chris thought: a personal steward for a visitor.

The wide reception hall the two officers stepped into had a polished mahogany floor, looking almost black after the glare of sunshine outside, and plain white walls. A handsome Persian rug showed well against the dark wood. Two finely carved iroko panels decorated the walls, flanking a vase of pink orchids on the mahogany hall table. The shade and the breeze from the electric ceiling fan were gloriously welcome but time to enjoy them was lost as the peace was shattered by a tall white man in his mid-fifties erupting from the inner part of the house.

'Tigger!' he shouted. 'Great to see you again after these long years', as he came forward to pump Chris' hand.

'And you, Your Excellency', Chris replied formally, while grinning with natural pleasure at meeting his old boss again.

There was an age difference of nearly twenty years between the two men. Sir John Robertson, the Governor-General of the tiny Lagos Colony and the huge Protectorate of Nigeria, was over six feet tall, slim, dark-haired and slightly greying. In the sticky hot climate of Lagos, only a little north of the equator, he was sensibly dressed for off-duty comfort, in a short-sleeved white shirt, Bermuda shorts of native-spun cotton and leather flip-flop Hausa sandals on bare feet. In dress at least, the man had not changed from the one Chris had known in Oyo ten years before. In spite of spending his whole working life in tropical Africa, his complexion was pale but his bearing was unquestionably that of a man who kept himself fit, his movements

9

decisive and vigorous. After public schooling at Fettes College in Edinburgh, he went up to Oxford where he gained a First in Greats in 1912. Thereafter he had spent his whole career in the Nigerian administration, apart from war service in Palestine and France and four years as Governor of a smaller African colony. Prior to that first governorship, he had been Resident of Oyo Province in Western Nigeria, a hundred miles north of Lagos. It was there the newly appointed Christopher Wickham had worked as his junior and where the two men had come to know each other well.

In the period of his service John Robertson had seen enormous change in the country, from the end of tribal raiding for slaves to the beginnings of a modern, settled and prosperous country, now a British protectorate but destined, he guessed, to become an independent nation state in a few decades. His first appointment to Nigeria had been only fifteen years after the Benin Massacre in 1897 when eight Europeans of a trading mission and two hundred and forty native carriers were killed in an ambush. When the British troops had entered Benin City in retaliation two months later they had found an avenue of four hundred rotting corpses of people crucified in an attempt to appease the ju-ju gods and keep Britain out. Good administration over the past thirty years had made things very different now. He could look back on his service with huge pleasure, especially the early days as a District Officer. Those were wonderful times in the bush, when he was master of his own district, in close touch with the local people whom he liked, dealing with their real problems – water supplies, land disputes, feuds, thieving, occasional murder – living a life shorn of almost every luxury, but one that provided great satisfaction.

Now he was Governor, for goodness sake, in charge not of a district or a province but of the whole country, the chief executive responsible for the administration of thirty-odd million people with only some twelve hundred officers to run everything, ports, railway, water, police, judiciary, prisons, forestry, agriculture, treasury, the whole civil administration. He had been forced to learn the art of delegating – not easy after his early one-man-band experience – but in a sense delegation made life more difficult because it introduced an unreality and left one wondering if the required action was being taken out in the bush, down on the Cross River or six hundred miles away to the north on the Saharan fringes in Katsina.

Now he was immeasurably more powerful, in a sense far less well informed and apparently less in control of events; and the war was making things much more complicated. Many of his young officers were away, into the army, or on war-related duties, and others still were fidgeting to go, although it was well recognised that keeping the place peaceful by good civil administration was worth a division of the army. But there were virtually no new appointments, and the depleted staff had much reduced leave, which raised medical problems for Europeans kept longer than was healthy in Nigeria's trying tropical climate. Changes! Young Kitchener there had no real knowledge of the country, infinitely less than he had had at the same age when he spent twenty days a month in bush, trekking from village to village, talking to the local chiefs and elders, and hearing cases as visiting magistrate. That was how to take the pulse of local society: in contrast all Robin knew was Lagos and the Governor's office.

But here was "Tigger" Wickham, reminding him of the golden times in Oyo when he was Resident. Tigger was the best young DO he ever had: vigorous, full of good sense and judgment, never shirking responsibility, spoke Yoruba with such flair that the court benches were filled with joyous laughter as the local people showed their agreement with the wisdom of this young magistrate who not only saw through the feeble excuses of the accused but was able to dismiss them with apt and witty idiom. And Olivia thought the world of him. That strand of reminiscence reminded him of his two sons whom Tigger had befriended and entertained at Oyo. He shied away from the bleak topic and hoped Tigger's coming would not be too painful for Olivia as a reminder of the boys. Tigger looked sharp and fit. Oh God, he would need to be, in view of the letter in his desk drawer and the job he had to give the man. Why had he sent for Tigger? It would have been so much easier to send someone he held in lower regard. But the Service did not work that way. He felt like a Valkyrie, choosing who should be slain in battle.

'Tigger! Great to see you again after these long years.' And after Chris' formal response, Sir John went on, 'Thank you. Now you have made your number with the ceremonial title; once a day is sufficient from someone I have known as long as you.'

Christopher Wickham had carried his nickname from a tender age; its derivation was simple but now known to few of the people who used it. When just beginning to read as a small boy, he had seen a large and lurid street poster advertising a prize fight between "Gunboat" Smith and "Tiger" Wickham. He was fascinated at seeing his family name in bold red type and imagined himself a fighter, in the army, in India, in all kinds of deeds of derring-do. Inspired by make-believe heroism, he insisted on adopting the fighter's title, but unfortunately his reading skill was inadequate and he mispronounced the prefix as "Tigger". The name was then used occasionally within the family, to humour the child, but he took it to his prep school and thereafter it was a fixture, carried by his peers to public school and thence to university.

Wickham completed his schooling with a sound academic record and a well developed flair for rugby. At Oxford as a fresher he played for his college fifteen, in his second year regularly for the University at stand-off and in his final year gained his England cap. The England selectors and the press then bemoaned the fact this natural play-maker was joining the Colonial Service, thereby depriving England of his considerable and apparently still developing talent.

Thereafter he played his life as a stand-off half, a natural play-maker, incisive, energetic and wholehearted. He was fair-haired and fair-skinned, of medium height and robust build. His colleagues enjoyed working with him; juniors found they were given both responsibility and backing, their successes publicly acknowledged, their shortcomings criticised in private. The training he had received under John Robertson in Oyo Province reinforced the disciplined self-confidence gained from a good degree, a Blue and an international rugby cap; as a result, when he was transferred on promotion to Benin Division, he felt able to be somewhat avant-garde. While many of his peers in other provinces stood slightly aloof from officers in other services and certainly from the native rulers, Chris Wickham met these at least halfway and developed strong friendships with many.

Some eyebrows were raised initially when Chris began playing tennis with the Bini king, the Oba Ewuare, and more when he invited him to the Club for snooker, a game at which the Oba shone, having devoted much of his time at Cambridge to it. Currently no African was among the forty-odd members of the Club but these moves, although mildly unpopular as advanced notions always tend to be, paid dividends in the stability and administration of an important district which had a reputation for trouble, so his stewardship was

12

solidly successful. Chris' relations with the Benin Resident, his immediate senior officer, were perhaps the exception, certainly very different from those he had had with John Robertson in Oyo. Robert Fitzroy Grenville-Fletcher held far right-wing opinions that did not countenance the acceptance of either technical service officers or the African in friendship. In fact the Resident was unsure of himself, something of a bully and secretly jealous of his junior's success in a difficult charge.

Sir John called for tea to be brought to his study, an airy room on the upper floor of the house, with pleasant views over the garden down to the sea. Lagos is a sandbar island shielding a swampy lagoon. For hundreds of miles the west coast of the African continent is devoid of natural harbours and the sheltered area behind the island was the best available, although far from ideal and notoriously tricky to enter over the shallow bar. In this cramped and sticky town a sea view and openness to the sea breeze were the most prized amenities: not surprisingly, the Governor's private study afforded both. Here the two men proceeded to catch up with the events of the past several years. Each knew the official moves made by the other but the more important personal details were unknown. Chris answered enquiries about his wife and young son, separated from him by the war and apparently condemned so to continue in a life of rented houses and grandparents. Was Lady Robertson well and with him here in Lagos? And what about the boys? Sir John frowned and gazed at the glittering sea.

'Adam has been a PoW since June last year when the 51st Division was forced to surrender at St Valéry. And young James was posted missing two weeks ago. He was shot down when his squadron was making a sweep over northern France. He joined the University Air Squadron, you know, and went straight into the RAF from there.'

Chris was dismayed at having opened a bitterly painful subject in such a casual way. He had been close to Adam and James when they were boys, back in Oyo. The Robertson parents must be racked with anxiety; they would be devastated if James had indeed been killed.

'Good Lord! I hadn't heard about Adam. I am frightfully sorry. Lady Robertson ...'

'Yes. It has hit Olivia very hard, I am afraid. Marooned out here seems to increase the worry because being far away from the

13

events gives one a sense of helplessness. That's quite illogical of course, because one would be just as helpless in London or Bognor. It is very upsetting and worrying anyway. We just have to hope for news he's a prisoner.'

Chris was trying to say sympathetic things when Sir John gathered himself.

'Thank you, Tigger, but look here. Let me be frank, I haven't brought you here to talk about my family problems or to chat over old times in Oyo. I have a job for you, away from Benin, a tough job that you may dislike just as I dislike giving it to you. Nevertheless I believe you are the best man for it and I want you to take it on, although it is far removed even from the varied roles the Colonial Service always demands.' From the desk he took a letter and an attached paper. 'Please read that and you will see what is being asked.'

Chris was glad of the change of subject and took the paper offered to him.

20th October 1941

Sir John Robertson, KBE,
Government House, Lagos, Nigeria.

STRICTLY CONFIDENTIAL

Dear Sir John,

I am reliably informed that the
Duchessa di Lucca, an Italian merchantman
with a valuable cargo, is skulking out
the war in an unfortified harbour on the
northern shore of Fernando Po Island, a
few miles south of your Nigerian coast.
Since the island, once British territory,
is now Spanish, the Admiralty tells me
the Royal Navy is unable to take
possession of the ship save at risk of it
being construed as an act of war against
Spain. This latter must be avoided at all
costs but it is highly desirable that the
enemy vessel and especially its cargo
should become available promptly to this
country for the better conduct of the war
against the Axis. I enclose a paper
giving details of the ship's construction.

15

Since the Navy is unable to act, I trust that an operation may be devised and mounted at an early date by civilian officers from your colony to cut out the Duchess of Lucca and bring her to British waters in such a way that the armed forces of the Crown are not involved, thus avoiding the Foreign Office's scruples concerning the Spanish reaction. Since the Navy's Nelson touch is denied us, we must revert to the Drake tradition. Pray put this work in hand forthwith.

To aid the required result, I have arranged for two men of our Commando forces who are experienced in this type of warfare to come to Lagos. They will report to you personally for their further orders. I trust that your colleagues may put their experience to good use, although their profile should be kept low, so that there is no sign of our armed forces' involvement.

Under no circumstances should the British Consul on Fernando Po be consulted or involved in any way concerning the operation.

I shall not require accounts of progress, nor a reply to this. You will understand this is a <u>private</u> letter, not on the correspondence files of either the Colonial Office or the F.O. The recovery of the ship, when it is achieved, must be clearly the result of private citizens' initiative and will be a matter of which His Majesty's Government will have had no prior knowledge whatever.

I wish your people all success.

With kind regards,

Winston S. Churchill

Chris took less than two minutes to read the letter but then he went through it again, this time more slowly.

'So that is the signature of the great man. But I am not sure I like the backhanded compliment of being the best person for what the Navy obviously regards as piracy, Sir'

To himself, Chris thought this is going to be damned difficult. Steal a damned great steamship! It's probably not just difficult: it's bloody well impossible. Why pick me? And, skimming back over the letter in his hand, he said:

'It certainly won't be easy to carry it off. But the Prime Minister leaves us no real space for debate: "Pray put this work in hand forthwith" simply assumes it is going to happen. So I suppose we had better get on with it. Right, Sir. Though on the face of it, it looks stark impossible.' The plight of the Governor's sons, fresh in Chris' memory, appeared to leave him no room for manoeuvre or procrastination.

'You are a good man to take it like that,' Sir John said, on impulse shaking Chris' hand. 'I must admit I don't like asking anyone to take on a task I wouldn't even know how to tackle myself.'

Inwardly he thought the chances of success in stealing an eight thousand ton ship anchored or tied up in harbour, against an enemy crew and without the Spanish authorities intervening, were extremely remote. Churchill's orders were sending men to internment, at best, and he himself was the guilty instrument of that. He felt bad about it. This was a poisoned chalice he was handing over. The war was bloody! Adam gone: James lost: now Tigger!

'There would be hell to pay if you were caught by the Spaniards so, whatever you do and whoever you take, you simply must not get caught.'

'Who can I take?' Chris enquired, 'Apart from these two soldiers the PM refers to.'

'You will pick your own team, though I have no idea how many you will need; as few as possible is probably wise. You had better keep the letter, to show to your chaps. Obviously tight security is essential so only your team should be allowed to know anything about it. I need hardly remind you to say nothing in front of the servants.' After a moment Sir John continued, 'Let me have a list of your team by telegram, with the length of time you envisage people being required and I shall personally approve local leave for each without reason being stated. That should avoid questions being asked that might threaten security. I expect you will take mostly Admin. Service men. Best to keep it in the family, don't you think?'

Chris had nodded his agreement with most of the Governor's suggestions but he drew up sharply at the last.

'I am not sure that's wise or even possible, Sir. After all, we are likely to need a lot of technical skills more familiar to other services than the Admin.'

Sir John mumbled reluctant acceptance while Chris went on:

'In any event, my first choice for this kind of job would be Peter Thorburn; he is now Forest Officer, Benin, you know. You may remember we played rugger together when we were up at Oxford; he played scrum-half in the Varsity team in my final year when we both got our Blues. We even played against each other at Twickenham in the Calcutta Cup match! He is the best scrum-half I ever played with – we think the same way and he's my best pal here. And, come to think of it, I am pretty sure he speaks good Italian, which could be a bonus. I would want to have Peter with me on this show, if he will come.'

'Naturally.' Sir John nodded understandingly. 'But keep the party to our service as much as possible. Of course, you won't want to take any Nigerians. By-the-by, the two Commando men mentioned in the PM's letter have arrived in the ship that came in last week. Not officers, unfortunately: two NCOs. The Army's looking after them in the local barracks, *pro tem.* They know nothing of the task we have, of course.'

Chris felt that Sir John's outdated prejudices about school ties, black men and the right types were in serious danger of making a difficult task well nigh impossible. If the job had to be done, he had no wish to be boxed in with regard to the choice of his companions even before the essential tasks and skills had been identified. However much he liked him and owed him, Sir John was showing both his age and the fact he was a true Edwardian, or even a Victorian, in his assumed divisions of the world. It was a near certainty such patrician attitudes would not survive the turmoil of the present war. Nevertheless it seemed unnecessarily churlish to deny bluntly the Governor's expectations in the choice of the team, so he let them lie. The thought of the war, however, reminded him of another slant to the problem.

'There is one aspect of security, Sir, that may be especially difficult. Hilda Fletcher.'

'Blast! Yes.' said the Governor slowly. 'Good thinking. That had escaped me. I am afraid you'll have to work the scheme without the knowledge of your Resident, which won't be at all easy.'

One of the results of the Treaty of Versailles in 1919 was that the German colony of Kamerun, immediately to the east of Nigeria, was forfeited. Subsequently in 1922, by decree of the League of Nations, it was divided into two, roughly on a north-south line, the west part being mandated to Great Britain and run virtually as part of Nigeria, and the eastern part mandated to France to be run with Equatorial Africa. Although the Cameroons administration was British and almost indistinguishable from the Protectorate of Nigeria, some of the old German firms and German families remained. Economically the place had good potential; the soils were fertile, timber and plantation crops, especially bananas, offered excellent export opportunities, and the range of altitude meant that living conditions for Europeans could be most attractive. Cameroon Mountain rises to over 13,000 feet and much of the high spinal ridge of the country gives places such as Bamenda a climate providing strawberries and cream twelve months in the year.

Some of the Germans who remained in Cameroons after its loss, however, did not stay on simply for the climate or the strawberries. There was a core who held the vision of the country returning to German sovereignty, an ideal sharpened to clear expectation by the emergence of Hitler as German Chancellor. Baron Ludwig von Ehrwald was unshaken in this belief and in his loyalty to the Fatherland. Born the third son of an old East Prussian family, he left home in 1908 for Kamerun colony where he built a fine house in Buea on the side of the mountain, as well as owning land near Bamenda, and began farming both coffee and cattle.

While on home leave three years later von Ehrwald married the daughter of a neighbouring Junkers landowner and children were born in succeeding years, two sons, Helmut and Klaus, and a girl, Hilda. In 1914 Ludwig and others tried unsuccessfully to mount a military campaign in West Africa to match the highly effective one in German East but it came to nothing and he was captured. With both his brothers killed in France, Ludwig succeeded to the title but after the war it made financial sense for him to remain in Kamerun, now mandated to Britain as Cameroons, where farming and business seemed likely to be more profitable than landownership in Europe. His children returned to Germany for their education in the twenties and early thirties and for them the emergence of National Socialism provided the creed that offered the dazzling prospect of Germany regaining control of its colonies. All became fervent Nazis.

By 1936 Helmut was in Germany, an officer in the SS. Klaus had returned to their African estates, under Party instructions in line with the official but clandestine policy of harnessing the services of all expatriate Germans to the advancement of the Third Reich; he was to assist his father with the creation of a resistance cell in preparation for war against the mandate-holding powers, France and Britain, for the return of Cameroons to Germany and for the annexation of Nigeria.

Late in that same year Hilda was married to Robert Grenville-Fletcher, the Senior District Officer in the Bamenda District of Cameroons, who had just been promoted and appointed Resident, Benin. Thus, by 1941, she was by marriage a British citizen, although undeclared a staunch Nazi. Grenville-Fletcher, inherently unsure of himself, was well endowed intellectually and a perfect stickler for the minutiae of regulations. He was infatuated by his beautiful wife and was essentially at her service, although having given a guarantee at the beginning of the war concerning her loyalty to the British Crown. The problem Chris faced was that Robert Fletcher was his immediate senior officer who could demand a full explanation of his every move. Hilda Fletcher, albeit a closet-Nazi, was now First Lady in the province where the preparations would have to be made for an illegal, if highly patriotic, operation.

'You will simply have to be especially careful about security,' said Sir John, 'and you had better think up some cover story to account for the preparatory meetings of your team. There's nothing wrong with Grenville-Fletcher, of course, but you should not take him into your confidence on this subject, in view of his wife's family connection.'

The two men continued to talk through the project and possible means of surmounting the difficulties. Petrol was in short supply, so the Governor promised to provide authority for Chris to draw additional rations to enable the team, still to be chosen, to travel. They talked around the major issue of sea transport, without which no

21

operation could be mounted; possible vessels were few and the final choice would have to wait for expert analysis.

The setting sun and rapid darkening signalled it was time for bath, drinks and dinner. Sir John had put together a slim file of background papers with relevant information about the ship and the island harbour, which he handed over. The subject was then dropped.

On the way to his room Chris was intercepted by Robin Kitchener, the assiduous ADC, to tell him that dinner at Government House would be black tie, as Chris had expected. In fact Sunday had already laid out black trousers, soft white shirt, black tie, white mess jacket (monkey jacket or bum-freezer colloquially), green cummer-bund, this being the uniform colour for all Nigerian service officers, and mosquito boots. The steward boy had arranged these expertly on and beside the bed in such a way it appeared that an already dressed but completely deflated Chris Wickham was lying there, waiting to be materialised when he came fresh from his bath. Sunday stood ready with a small whisky in a half-pint tumbler and a bottle of water, dewy from the fridge.

'Whisky, sah?' Chris felt he deserved it more than usual, considering the task before him.

Chris met Olivia Robertson before dinner. She was a slender, handsome woman with auburn hair, something over fifty, of an Anglo-Irish family. As a girl she had lived for fox hunting and was an expert horsewoman; for her, northern Nigeria had been a complete delight, Lagos was just tolerable. Chris was saddened to see she had faded from the vivacious woman he had known and admired when they last met ten years before. On speaking to her he realised the main cause was deep anxiety for her sons who, given her husband's inevitable preoccupation with his heavy job, had been her interest and delight. He tried to imagine what the effect might be on him were something similar to happen to Phillipa and young William.

Lady Robertson claimed Chris as her neighbour at dinner; their friendship went back to the start of his service and they had plenty to talk about. In former times she had learned to rely on her husband's ADC, then in his early twenties, in helping off duty to entertain her two wild young sons. She was glad to meet him again, although knowing nothing of the real reason for him being invited to Government House. Over the years she had learned to accept that some confidential affairs were not disclosed to her and she liked it that way; it meant that, if there was a leak, she could not be the source and her husband could not be blamed for tittle-tattle. She was simply glad to see Chris again after these years. In spite of her husband's fears, she did not allow his arrival to upset her on account of Adam being shut up in a prison camp and James being posted missing. Olivia felt herself relaxing under the spell of Chris' talk. Their reminiscences of Oyo brought Adam closer, warmly and cheerfully rather than in the bleak anxiety of an unknown and fearful Stalag somewhere in wintry Germany, and James lived again in her mind instead of the gnawing griping picture of a smoke spiral and searing flame. Surprisingly, Chris sitting next to her at dinner was a reassurance, a staunch link with good times past, perhaps a talisman for their return.

Sir John watched with dismay the warmth of the meeting of his wife and Tigger. It was obvious it was lifting Olivia from the depression caused by the fate of her sons. Ordinarily that would have been welcome, marvellous, but Olivia did not know what lay ahead of the young district officer. Tigger was a special friend to her and their meeting now was refreshing and deepening his value. Her anguish would be that much deeper, far sharper, if Tigger were now to be lost as well as James, and Adam a prisoner. Tigger's chance of success, even of survival, was remote: an amateur group trying to steal the Italian ship, taking on a task denied to the Royal Navy.

He could not dodge the demand from Churchill. Presumably in London's eyes the vague chance of success justified the probable loss of the men: his men, his friend Tigger. He squirmed in his chair and replied quite fatuously to his neighbour's polite conversation. The Spanish authorities would hold the attack to be piracy – even the Prime Minister's letter admitted as much. Tigger had used the word also. And under Spanish law piracy was a capital offence.

Apart from Robin Kitchener, the other guests were senior army officers. Their presence was too good to miss: Chris traded on it to arrange that the two soldiers in Lagos barracks be given orders and army transport to Benin City to report to the Forest Officer there in seven days' time. He reckoned he needed at least a week to return to the City and begin to devise a plan for stealing a ship in a foreign country but getting the two professionals to his own base was an obvious first move. Urgent questions and ideas continually swimming into his mind quite took the edge off his appetite and threatened to interrupt his conversation with his hostess. Chris struggled to keep his end up in the talk and observe the social graces: after all, it was Government House, his first visit, and the food was excellent.

Nevertheless this was a hell of a task he was landed with. To steal a ship. A big ship, eight thousand tons. Could it be done? Without being caught? There was the rub! If they were caught, it would be his responsibility, Tigger Wickham's fault. Not like just fumbling a pass at Twickers. A fumble now and chaps would go to prison. Even worse? How does Spanish law deal with piracy? Shooting? Hanging? No! My God! The garrotte! Chris shuddered, in spite of the heat, and firmly forced his thoughts on to other lines. He made up his mind to take time off tomorrow, no matter how pressing was business, to have a swim at Victoria beach: sea surf was a luxury Benin could not provide. In a couple of days it would be 1942: he wondered what the New Year would bring.

CHAPTER THREE

Both Peter Thorburn's parents belonged to the Scottish Borders, from families in the textile trade. Peter's father was employed by a famous international firm that had mills in the west of Scotland and in Italy, manufacturing cotton and silk material. Soon after the birth of his son, he was appointed to a managerial post in the firm's north Italy subsidiary. Thus it came about that Peter spent several of his childhood years in the family home on the outskirts of Turin, the centre of the company's overseas operations and, almost inevitably with local maids and neighbours' children, he grew up bilingual in English and Italian. When he was eight, however, it was decided he should return to Scotland and he went to live at his grandparents' home in Edinburgh where he went to school and university.

The whole of Peter's schooling was at George Heriot's Hospital, a school founded in the early seventeenth century by the Scots goldsmith who was court financier to King James VI in Edinburgh and later in London. Heriot's was a boys' day school of high academic standing, especially in science, and outstanding for its production of fine rugby players. Beginning to play rugby at eight years of age, Peter was cast, because of his small size, in the role of scrum-half. The choice was a happy one, however arbitrary by the master, since it found the boy's natural talent and he proceeded to make scrum-half play something of an art-form. His speed of decision, quick hands and accurate long service were soon recognised as exceptional; "Wee Pete" made a name for himself and scored considerable success for his teams through his whole career at Heriot's.

After leaving school, Peter attended Edinburgh University to study forestry. As usual in Scotland, his rugby loyalty remained with his old school, however, not with the university, and it was as a member of Heriot's FP Club he was given a Scottish trial and then gained a Scottish cap, playing against Wales and Ireland in his final year at Edinburgh.

It was the golden age of amateur rugby. The Heriot's FP team were all former pupils of the school and inevitably some had played together for ten years, from junior classes to the sixth form. The concentration of boys' schools in Edinburgh – George Watson's, Loretto, Royal High, Daniel Stewart's, Melville College, the Academy – all strongly committed to rugby, provided intense local rivalries and ensured that competition and standards were high. And if that should have been insufficient, there were lurking only a few miles to the south the hard men of the Border teams, Jedforest, Gala, Melrose and Hawick, for whom rugby epitomised local pride and sense of place. Nevertheless it was a game and truly amateur; Peter had his studies and the exams to pass. His weekends in term-time were free for rugby but the vacations in summer and at Easter were almost filled with study tours of forest visits and surveys, and then permission was required to play a game, even an international. The diminutive Professor of Forestry feigned reluctance to release Peter from his practical course obligations; clamping the monocle to his eye (he was ex-Indian Forest Service and played the part for all his worth), he expressed surprise at the very suggestion.

'A game of rugby football? What? Well, I recall when I was in the Chittagong Hill Tracts getting leave from my Chief Conservator to play polo for the IFS against the Poona Light Horse. They had won the Inter-Regimental Tournament the previous season, don't ye know, ...' And so on and on. From the start Peter's permission was fully assured because the professor longed to be able to say, in his London club, 'One of my men plays for Scotland, don't ye know, ...', which would give him the necessary opening to repeat, for the *n*th time, the story of his polo match against the Poona Light Horse. (He never gave the score.)

On graduating BSc Forestry, Peter's first preference, as for most of his classmates, was to join the prestigious Colonial Forest Service; in this he was successful, being appointed to the Nigerian Forest Department. At that time the Colonial Office required all its trainee Assistant Conservators to attend a year's postgraduate course at the Imperial Forestry Institute in Oxford before taking up their appointments. For Peter it proved to be a pleasant interlude that added little to his technical knowledge and prepared him scarcely at all for his subsequent work in West Africa, being largely theoretical and based on Indian conditions. Nevertheless it was an extremely enjoyable year, providing excellent opportunity for rugby and the basis of lasting friendships. For its part, Oxford welcomed the arrival of a scrum-half who had already gained an international cap, so Peter found himself playing regularly for the university, winning his Blue and teaming up with a stand-off called Tigger Wickham, then a final year undergraduate. Their training, discussion of tactics and devastatingly successful play together laid the foundation for a close alliance.

Talk of Peter's impending career in the Colonial Service sowed the idea of a similar move by Chris Wickham, which indeed he followed a year later. For the moment, however, all was rugger, with the highlights of the season the Cambridge match, which Oxford won, and the Calcutta Cup when Chris and Pete found themselves on opposing sides, Chris winning his first England cap and Peter his third for Scotland. These games forged a comradeship to endure a lifetime even if their careers had been in separate continents.

The service the two men joined was remarkable in at least two vital aspects: its efficiency and integrity. In Nigeria the staffing averaged one European official of all grades and departments to about twenty thousand of the population, so the administration had the merit of being frugal financially. Better expressions of its value were its achievements and their acceptability to the African man-in-the-village. In the first half of the twentieth century, West Africa was in the process of changing from a mosaic of local feudal despotisms to something more modern, which Britain, perhaps naively, assumed should be parliamentary democracy. However naive the assumption, the benevolent and incorruptible bureaucracy of British colonial rule suited well enough for the period of evolution. There were already some Nigerian political activists, well reported in the Lagos daily press, who advocated the complete removal of British rule and everything associated with it, but most people, for the present at least, placed more value on the provision of good public services. Communities wanted access to good water, health and education, safe movement, the rule of law, the avoidance of tribal violence, freedom from the worst excesses of black-magic terror and, on these standards, the Colonial Service scored very highly indeed. The fact the tiny administration was backed only by a small and normally unarmed police force was a measure of its popularity. Lord Lugard was credited with saying that, under British rule, a maiden could travel with a dozen eggs the five hundred miles from Sokoto to Maiduguri and all arrive intact. That summed it up pretty well.

The effectiveness and popularity of the Colonial Service administration rested fundamentally on its complete integrity. On joining the Service, Peter and his colleagues were addressed by the senior civil servant and doyen of the Colonial Office in London:

'You will find there are local people, and there will be increasing numbers of them, who could do your job adequately from the technical point of view; the sole justification for your appointment and continuing employment is your integrity'.

The rule was that an officer did not accept any gift; in that rule the threshold of value was zero. The only apparent relaxation was when strict observance would have caused offence where it was local custom to provide hospitality to a visitor; there the Service stipulated that a trivial gift of food might be accepted, provided it was balanced by returning a present of at least equal value. So it was that Peter might well receive a chicken from the village head where he stopped overnight, but invariably sent back a tin of bully beef; sometimes he regretted the exchange, believing his host had the tastier meal. No whisper of purchased favour was ever heard; throughout the country, the integrity of the officers of the Colonial Service was recognised. Their standing in the eyes of the local people was thus assured and, with it, respect for the law they represented and enforced.

The small cadre and the high calibre of the Colonial Service provided the conditions for operating an effective "old boy net". Each officer knew a good proportion of his colleagues across the whole country and was at least on nodding terms with almost all, When a member of the "net" asked for action, response was usually prompt and generous, since one could be sure his request would not be trivial. It was a small, well balanced and very strong team.

Peter and Chris Wickham, although both working in Nigeria, saw little of one another in the early years of their service, apart from a couple of local leaves. Then chance, operating through the whims of their respective chiefs early in 1939, decided they should both be posted to Benin. Each was delighted at the challenge of his new job, with the prospect gilded by the bonus of having his old team-mate on the same station.

Peter was clear that, as Forest Officer in Benin Division, he had the best charge he could ever wish: fifteen hundred square miles of reserved forest, rich in mahoganies and other high value timber trees, with the task of completing management plans to ensure their sustained yield in perpetuity, a fast developing timber trade presently based on the unreserved forest that was open to destructive farming, a large staff of keen and competent rangers and forest guards, a forest research station with all kinds of interesting trials and experiments; this was a huge responsibility, for which he was well trained and fitted. Benin was the plum job; Peter knew it and wished for no other. Off-duty he played golf on the Club's completely flat nine-hole course and he was highly attached to games of poker-dice and liar-dice, being quite the best player in the Club, which was saying something because the membership included three Irish Fathers, any of whom could take money off nine people out of ten prior to Peter's arrival.

The Forest Office in Benin City was a long, single storey building in the Old Fort, with whitewashed mud-brick walls, concrete floor and corrugated iron roof, set in a patch of sparse grass and dust. The office comprised a row of small rooms opening off the wide veranda. Windows on the two sides were set with diamond-mesh expanded metal to allow through draughts and protection against casual theft. Good ventilation was prized, since the temperature in Benin was in the mid- to high-nineties Fahrenheit throughout the year, with constantly high humidity, and air-conditioning was unknown. It was a shabby, dusty building that would not have impressed a casual observer – had there been one – as being the administrative centre for the region's fastest growing industry and principal revenue provider.

Peter's office was, in fact, a survivor of the fort built nearly fifty years before to house the British garrison, although the fort's perimeter wall had long since been levelled to its foundations and an abundance of ornamental trees had been planted in its place for shade and blossom. A line of fine Cassia nodosa occupied the narrow space between the office and the street, their pale green foliage and festoons of pink flowers, like rose-coloured laburnums, keeping the worst of the sun from one side of the building and making this a favoured place for market friends to meet. Through the ever open windows of the office there floated in the constant hubbub of the African street, full-voiced talking often pierced by shrieks of unrestrained laughter.

In the late afternoon, a week after the dinner party at Government House, a desert-yellow fifteen-hundredweight truck drove into the forest office compound. The driver was a Hausa private of the Nigerian Regiment and the passengers two white men, one a sergeant, the other a corporal. All three were red with dust, blotched with sweat and vastly thirsty, for they had driven for six hours on a laterite earth road heavily corrugated and potholed. The three hundred mile journey from Lagos had taken two days and the men were sore, stiff and weary from the endless vibration in the stiffly sprung truck. They stretched as they came out and tried to beat the worst of the dust from their uniforms. The two NCOs had orders to report to Peter Thorburn.

Leaving the driver by his vehicle, the NCOs pulled on green berets and strode quickly to the office and into welcome shade. A powerfully built black man dressed in slightly bleached green uniform shorts and shirt, with green puttees and a bright scarlet sash, rose to meet them from his seat on the veranda. His manner was confident and commanding, reminding the visitors of their own regimental sergeant-major, but riveting their attention were the facial scars criss-crossing the Chief Ranger's cheeks, a legacy of the ceremonial cutting soon after his birth. For some reason, Corporal Graham immediately thought of tattoo parlours back in Blackpool. After a quiet greeting and enquiry about their journey, Chief Ranger Eweka led the soldiers along the veranda to Peter Thorburn's room.

By now Sergeant James Armstrong was feeling the effects of long separation from the security and comfort of his unit and he had only half an ear for the Chief Ranger. What would this man Thorburn be like, the latest of those they had to report to? "Detached for special duty in West Africa", the Colonel had said. It sounded OK at the time but we've been travelling for bloody weeks now and never a definite bloody word about what we have to do. Cooped up in the ship; lousy transit barracks in Lagos; two days on the boneshaking bloody road. God, it's hot! I feel filthy. Wonder what the lads are doing at home: probably on an exercise sweating to the top of Ben Nevis and back, the Colonel's favourite. Not sweating as much as us. But the worst of it is we're in the dark: the operation, the target, every bloody thing in the air. Worst of all, not knowing about the new CO or anyone else for the job, apart from Rob Graham who is OK. Heaven help us if this man Thorburn is a twit, assuming he really is the leader! Thorburn's a Border's name so maybe he's a Borderer, which is something.

Eweka stepped aside at an open door and signed the two white men in. The office they entered was extremely plain. Bare concrete floor, whitewashed walls, a couple of green steel filing cabinets, a wall safe, two unvarnished wooden tables, one covered with maps, the other serving as a desk with four wooden filing trays and a shoal of manila files, three upright chairs and on the wall a framed photograph of the King and Queen (Standard issue, Government offices for the use of) all with a film of red dust blown in from the street: Armstrong registered it all in a single glance, along with the remarkable fact there were three little brown lizards motionless and without visible means of support on the wall ahead of him. A small wiry man with a cheerful grin was rising from his chair behind the desk. He was dressed in the usual informal office rig, open-necked white shirt with short sleeves, khaki drill shorts and calf-length khaki stockings. The two Commando NCOs came to a halt and stood smartly to attention.

'Sergeant Armstrong and Corporal Graham, posted from X Commando, Sir. We have orders to report to Mr Thorburn at the Forest Office here, Sir.'

'That's me, Sergeant. Peter Thorburn. I'm glad you've made it. I expect the road down from Owo was as hellish as usual and you need something to drink.'

Peter shook hands with each man and shouted 'Messenger! Ask Ranger Eweka to close up the office now.' And to the sergeant, 'We open at seven in the morning and close at two here. Just waited to see you in. Let's go back to the house right away.' To himself he thought, 'This man Armstrong's built like a great prop-forward! Tough as boots. He speaks like a Borderer but luckily he's younger than me or I might have met him at the Melrose Sevens or playing Gala. I'd rather play with him than against him.'

Jimmy Armstrong was twenty-two years old, a native of Langholm, just north of the Scottish Border, the son of a small hill farmer. He was dark-haired and thickset, having great upper body strength. At his local school he was remembered as "wild, aye up to some prank and a gey lad for the lasses". From an early age he was notably hardy. Five days a week, in all weathers, he walked the two and a half miles to and from school, joining the families from other farms in a stream which taught both robust independence and tolerance. On Sundays the walk was repeated, this day to the Kirk, in the company of his elder sister and their parents. At all times of the year, when not at school, he was on the hill with his father at the sheep, doing a man's job from the age of twelve, learning to work a dog, lamb the ewes and help with the gathering and the clipping. Hill farming was hard in the nineteen-thirties and the Armstrong household was not well off; but it was a contented family and the boy had a good education based on solid schooling and deep experience of the working countryside.

Late in 1938, the Armstrongs, father and son, had a fierce disagreement about the long term management of the farm. Believing the farmhouse was too small for both of them and seeing that war was coming, James had left home to join the King's Own Scottish Borderers. As a soldier he had been at first a tormenting mixture to his superiors: an excellent shot (aided by long experience on the farm of shooting rabbits with a pump-action Winchester .22), good at field craft and showing abundant initiative, but liable to "blot his copybook" by minor indiscipline that was triggered either by incipient boredom or ridicule of some essential military requirement such as whitewashing the kerbstones outside the guardroom. Herr Hitler and the Wehrmacht came to his rescue in the nick of time. The formation of the Commandos in 1940 provided the opportunity for raiding incursions on the enemy coastline. That this was the man's natural métier was perhaps scarcely surprising; the Armstrongs perfected this type of warfare in the 1500s, operating from their Hermitage stronghold in Liddesdale against all comers, Scots or English, essentially for Armstrong profit and to secure the Debatable Land for themselves. Jimmy was a born Border reiver, perhaps a throwback to formidable Johnny Armstrong, with qualities the Commandos valued highly, which accounted for the sergeant's stripes, even if the KOSBs earlier had doubts. He had been at first reluctant to accept the idea of the West African operation since it would take him away from the unit just when real fire-fights were promising to develop in France or nearby, but the Colonel had assured him this was no soft option and the prospects of action were high. When told it was a two-man operation and he could choose his OR companion from the volunteers, he chose Corporal Graham.

Robert Graham was from Cockermouth in Cumberland, the son of a small shopkeeper in the town. At the local school he was a steady worker, never outstanding at lessons but well liked by teachers and quietly popular with his mates. After school and at weekends he helped his father in the grocery business, making bicycle deliveries round the town and tidying the shop. Fortunately, as it turned out, he also spent time on and in Bassenthwaite Lake, learning to swim strongly and to sail a dinghy. The warlike behaviour of Hitler in 1937 confirmed Mr Graham, senior, in his view that the 1914-18 business would have to be repeated. His reiterated warnings on this subject led directly to son Robert signing on as a Territorial, so that late in 1939 he went to France. The German blitzkrieg ended that episode with the Dunkirk evacuation when he was forced to swim, after the ship he was in was bombed, but he was picked up by the crew of a small yacht and worked his passage to Dover by helping with the sails and the auxiliary motor. Physically the corporal was average height, wiry and hard, although he appeared almost puny beside the burly sergeant. Importantly, however, Rob was quietly versatile, steady and utterly reliable, qualities that had quickly gained him his corporal's stripes in the Commando. Intuitively Sergeant Armstrong recognised the great value of Rob's solid dependability, the foil to his own flair and élan.

A wash and several thirst-breaking cups of tea awaited them at Peter's house. Armstrong enquired tactfully but urgently whether Peter was to be their commander for the coming operation, whatever that was to be. The crucial importance of the attitude and competence of the boss weighed heavily with the sergeant and desperately he wanted to end that uncertainty.

'Not me,' Peter replied, 'but I'm to be in on the job and down at Sapoba this evening you will meet Tigger Wickham who is the boss. He is the District Officer here and a long-time friend of mine. He's a topping chap and you'll like him.'

'Where's this place Sapoba then, Sir?'

'It's thirty-odd miles south of here, Corporal. We thought Benin City would be too public to keep you out of sight and maintain security while we plan and prepare. So the idea is we should drive down to Sapoba now and we can take the place over as the base for the operation. It's private – belongs to my Forest Department. If we get away right now, we have daylight for the run. Driving in the dark on these earth roads is not fun.'

The army driver, now relieved of the soldiers' baggage, was told to take his truck back to Ibadan next day and the party piled into Peter's Ford V8 kit-car, a pick-up truck on the back of which an open-sided wooden body had been built locally. The Ford was well-laden; the three white men on the bench seat in the front, Peter's steward boy and cook in the back, with the NCOs' bulky kit, Peter's tin trunk, the kitchen box, two boxes of food, three camp beds and bed rolls, an open box with bottles of water, the boys' luggage, Peter's dog and a basket-work bird cage containing three hens. Their host's remark that the rest-house was well equipped so loads were fewer than usual meant little to the visitors; what more could have been taken?

Soon after leaving Peter's house, in a broad avenue of flowering trees screening the bungalows and villas of the senior officers in the Benin administration, they passed a policeman in khaki uniform, armed with a Lee-Enfield rifle. He stood smartly at ease at the entrance gate of a large house set in an extensive and particularly well tended garden. On the opposite side of the gate was a sentry-box, where a large book lay open on a shelf. As the soldiers were obviously intrigued, Peter explained.

'That is the Resident's house. He is Robert Grenville-Fletcher. Pretty stuffed-up and pompous; I am glad he's not my boss, though he is the top chap in the province. He is a stickler for regulations, especially those supporting his own position and appearance. With luck, you won't meet him – in fact we are going down to this place Sapoba precisely so that you needn't.'

'The sentry-box? Well, it houses a book that everyone who comes to Benin is expected to sign. It's really a carry-over from the old society practice of newcomers leaving visiting cards on neighbours. Signing is supposed to show a polite greeting and acknowledgement that the Resident is the boss hereabouts; in return he will invite you to tea or drinks. Out-of-date pompous stuff and nonsense in my view, but of course I signed when I arrived, just to keep the peace.'

Clear of the town, there were few vehicles on the road. A couple of times they met a "mammy wagon", a three-ton truck with a locally made wooden body and cab, carrying a mixed load of perhaps eight tons of goods and twenty people perched on top. The biblical texts painted above the windscreens were ironically appropriate: "God help us" or "Pray hard – always pray". Peter pointed out the lethal potential of the single-track bridges with low parapets when, as had happened, two mammy-wagons approaching a bridge from opposite sides raced to cross first and met in head-on collision. The cabs were usually built with no door on the driver's side, the better – it was said cynically – for the captains to abandon ship when they realised disaster was inevitable.

Although vehicles were few, there were plenty of people on foot, the great majority being women and children. The women walked tall, graceful and straight, many carrying a sleeping baby strapped to their back in their wrap-around gown. Everyone walked barefoot and almost all carried something on their head, a gourd of water, a cloth bundle, a piece of firewood, a book. The predominant colour of the women's clothes was indigo but most little children were comfortably naked. At the approach of the car, people turned away a few paces in order to escape the worst of the dense cloud of red dust spewing out like a smoke screen behind.

'The RSM would like them,' Rob remarked. 'Chest out, chin in, no slouching. Even the small kids carry something on their heads, supposing it's only for fun, but the mothers never seem to overload them.'

The countryside was flat and the road arrow-straight. For the first dozen miles it ran through farmland, with occasional tiny villages of mud-walled and palm-thatched houses.

'Overwhelmingly this is a farming community, most of the people subsistence farmers,' Peter said. 'Apart from some trading in rubber and palm oil, people don't handle much cash, but that's not to say they are really poor. It's a caring society and no one goes hungry.'

The farm crops appeared haphazard and untidy to the men familiar with Dumfries-shire and Cumberland but the villages they passed were ordered and clean, each with its school set in a fenced playground, most with a mission church. For his companions' interest Peter identified maize, cassava, yams, plantains and the scattering of oil palms.

'The palm fruits provide Nigeria's main export, the basis of our margarine and soap at home,' he said, 'and also the people's main cooking oil. It's nutritious, too, which is a good thing because they can't keep cattle beasts here in the south on account of sleeping sickness.'

35

Increasingly the farms gave way to forest, the trees crowding in, so that the car drove through a tunnel of deep green. The wall of vegetation rose from the very edge of the road, the view into the forest not extending two yards. They crossed a bridge of arched steel girders, like a miniature version of Sydney harbour's, seemingly incongruous in that untamed environment, allowing a view, the first for five miles, over a stretch of water.

'It looks like the "great grey green greasy Limpopo River, all set about with fever trees",' Rob quoted.

'In fact it's the Ossiomo River,' said Peter, 'but all the rest is pretty well true, certainly Kipling's python and crocodile, and there are still some forest elephants in Benin Division, though not in this part, so you could say there must be an Elephant's Child too.'

Here they turned east off the main road that ran on to the port of Sapele, into a side road through dense forest. Half an hour later, in the brief gloaming, they turned into the entrance of a wide clearing. There was just light enough to read a painted board announcing:

SAPOBA FOREST RESEARCH
STATION and REST-HOUSE.

They had arrived at their base. A car stood at the door of a large white bungalow and, as Peter drew up behind it, two white men and a black man in steward's uniform came from the house to greet them.

'Hello, Peter.' Chris then introduced himself to the soldiers. 'I am Chris Wickham, usually known as Tigger to my friends, so please call me that. Welcome to Sapoba. You really are especially welcome because I am mighty relieved to have two experienced professionals for the job that has been handed to me.' He looked at the sergeant's stripes on the khaki shirt. 'You must be James Armstrong.'

'Aye, that's right, Sir. Jimmy Armstrong; usually known as Cracker, Sir.' First impressions of his new CO were guardedly optimistic, although the notion of having a civilian CO was quite extraordinary. It would take a lot of getting used to.

'And you must be Corporal Robert Graham. How do you like to be known? Is it Bob, or what?'

'No, Sir. I always get Rob.'

Chris shook hands and said, 'And this is my assistant, Steven Lister,' introducing the tall man who accompanied him. 'Leave the loads to the boys. They will cope. Everyone inside. You chaps must be half-dead if you have driven down from Ondo today, so let's have a gin, baths and chop.' And in a shout to his steward, 'Jimoh! Pass gin before you bring in these masters' loads.'

The house they entered was single-storeyed, the walls whitewashed inside and out, the roof of corrugated iron under a thick palm thatch; the "pan" was to keep out the wet, the thatch to insulate the metal from baking sun. The roof projected several feet beyond the wall-heads to create deep eaves and provide cool shade in the heat of the day. The front door opened directly into a large living room, the full width of the house, with windows on three sides. It was now cheerfully lit by two pressure-paraffin lamps on tall wooden stands. To the right was a handsome refectory table, with chairs for ten or a dozen, and a long sideboard, while to the left were easy chairs cushioned in white native-spun cotton, grouped round two low coffee tables. The floor was dark mahogany, almost purple, brightened by some gaudy woven raphia mats. The furniture was mostly African walnut, golden with irregular dark streaks. The only ornaments were two locally carved ebony heads on the sideboard and a heavy brass mask hanging on the wall. There were no curtains and, in place of glass, the wide window openings were hung at night with roller blinds of finely split bamboo that allowed air to circulate but kept out the larger insects.

Beyond the main living room, the house rambled on in a comfortable and informal way. There was an office-*cum*-laboratory and a string of bedrooms opening off a long wide veranda. The house had grown like Topsy, with rooms added over the years as demand arose. Kitchen and servants' quarters were somewhere round the back. It had all been built to the designs of successive local forest officers, an airy comfortable house for equatorial living. It was ideal as the base camp for the party.

When the steward brought glasses on a tray with angostura bitters, a bottle of gin and a bottle of water, Chris went on, 'One of the penalties of the war is that beer has become almost unobtainable and whisky is severely rationed. To make matters worse, the gin comes from South Africa. I hope you can drink pink gin; it's about all there is.'

When everyone was served and they had toasted good health and future success all round, Chris proposed, and everyone agreed, that all talk of the forthcoming operation should be postponed until

37

morning, so that the evening could be given over to baths, dinner, recovery from their journey and getting to know one another.

Although Steven Lister's background did not emerge in the evening's conversation, he was in fact the younger son of the Earl of Pickering. His schooling was Eton and Oxford where he gained a Second at the House; Steve himself was wont to say his education then began. He joined the 1928 expedition to the upper Brahmaputra and in the following year signed as a crewman on a Salvesen whaling ship working out of South Georgia. His father's death forced him to face the fact his elder brother would be unable to provide the allowance that had made possible the globe-trotting life-style; he would have to earn his living. With the wealth of his varied experience, he was a strong candidate for appointment to the Colonial Service, an employment which appealed to him as the next best life to the adventures he had been living. He was appointed to the Administrative Service in Nigeria, a job he thoroughly enjoyed and did well. Being a late entrant as a result of his wide travels after university, he was junior in rank for his age; although he was Chris Wickham's assistant, they were about the same age. The two men got on particularly well together. Steve was a good man to have around when there was a tough task on hand. In both the technical and administrative services there was a premium on self-motivation; Nigeria was no place for men who would wait until they received instructions for every action. Although Chris was clearly the leader in Benin Division, Steve did not require him as a supervisor. Armstrong and Graham took to him immediately.

Altogether the soldiers felt things were looking brighter than at any time since the Colonel's briefing when they volunteered more than six weeks previously.

CHAPTER FOUR

The magnificent rain forests of Benin grew on a bed of pure white quartz sand, several hundred feet thick, at the western fringe of the great delta of the River Niger, an area almost completely flat and only a little above sea level. By 1941 large areas of the forest were legally protected reserves and, under British administration of the Forest Department, were managed with natural regeneration to ensure perpetual yield, although ownership remained with the local council the Benin Native Authority, under the Oba, the king of Benin.

The intense tropical sunlight and abundant rainfall sustained an impressive and complex forest structure: above a layer of evergreen shrubs were three complete canopies of trees, the highest at more than a hundred and twenty feet from the ground. Projecting above that top canopy were the giant emergent trees, mahoganies, agba, iroko, obeche and silk cotton, 150 to 180 feet tall, with stems six feet or even more in diameter, most with wide spread buttresses at the base. Very, very occasionally there was a giant of giants, a mahogany with trunk fifteen feet diameter, its existence puzzling the botanical historians, perhaps the rare relic of some previous forest cut down by farmers eight hundred or a thousand years earlier. This was one of the richest forests in the world, rich in timber, incredibly rich in wildlife and superbly diverse ecologically.

Through one of the finest parts of the forest, called Uronigbe, there flowed the Jamieson River in a shallow gentle valley. The stream welled up strongly, fully formed, from the underlying sand and flowed sedately, clean and pure, without variation in the course of the year. With the whole valley and banks of the river clothed in dense forest, there was no mud or debris in the water coming from its filter bed of white sand; there was no village on the upper reaches of the stream to pollute it.

Five miles downstream from the source of the Jamieson a large clearing had been cut in the forest to make space for the forest research station and its rest-house. It was a secluded place with the simple whitewashed bungalow built of sun-dried brick, set a hundred yards back from the river bank on a low bluff. Twenty years before, gardens and a tree nursery had been created, a tennis lawn sown and an avenue of avocado pears planted. Just below the house a considerable plantation of Hydnocarpus trees was established to provide chaulmugra oil for the treatment of leprosy in West African hospitals, a product of the silvicultural research for which Sapoba had been built. Groves of oranges, limes, different kinds of bananas, paw-paws, guavas and coffee were planted as trials, their success making the rest-house a favourite place for forest officers to visit. Before the war a European research officer had worked here full time, with trained African personnel, but staff shortage caused by the war now left the place without resident researchers. The furnishing of the house was not elaborate. The designs were simple but the timber for each piece was the choicest the craftsman could find in a forest of fine timbers: figured mahogany, flared African walnut, rare ripple-grain guarea. As it may be with fine wines, so it appeared that from Benin, supplier of some of the world's finest timbers, the best never reached the market. The sanitation at Sapoba was dry but the thunderbox was of figured mahogany as beautiful as any that graced a drawing room in Europe.

The principal attraction of Sapoba, however, was the safe swimming in the Jamieson River. One could lie on the diving board at the end of the short canoe pier and look down through the crystal water to the sparkling sand twenty feet below, to the shoals of triangular angel fish darting and jerking in cream and black unison in the watery green sunlight. A crumb dropped in would bring a storm of the little creatures to fight over virtually nothing, providing endless peaceful amusement, until the sun's heat made it even more attractive to dive in and join the fish, to swim gently in the cool clear clean water. The contrast with Benin's red dust and sticky heat could not have been more vivid. Sapoba's seclusion and the abundant accommodation appeared to make it the ideal place for the team to

40

meet and for the NCOs to keep out of sight for the security of the operation they had to prepare.

At six o'clock next morning the steward boys brought mugs of tea and slices of the local green oranges to the sleeping men. Breakfast introduced the soldiers to one of the Epicurean delights of the place. The resident hunter at Sapoba had shot a duiker during the night, so the party had wild antelope liver and kidneys fried with their eggs, one of the culinary masterpieces of Africa, a fry beyond the experience of those who know only domestic animals. After breakfast, chairs and a small table were carried out to the shade under the avocado trees, where they could speak without being overheard, and planning began. Chris opened the session in a serious tone; the others listened intently.

'What is said here must remain completely confidential to ourselves, unless I give specific clearance. Strict security will be essential for the success of the operation we must now plan. It is our own safety that will be at stake.' He paused to allow that truth to be taken in, and then continued.

'A week ago in Lagos the Governor gave me responsibility for organising and leading an operation to steal an eight thousand ton Italian merchant ship in harbour on the Spanish island of Fernando Po. The ship is called the *Duchessa di Lucca*. I accepted the job and I hope you chaps will join me, though it is fair to point out it will not be at all easy.' He paused and looked round the four faces with their pursed lips and wide eyes. 'The best way to begin is for you to read this letter that is, in a way, my authority and sets out the terms for the job to be done.'

The men leaned close together to read the Prime Minister's letter Chris had put on the table in front of Cracker Armstrong. He was the first to speak.

'I'm glad I came,' he grinned. And the others joined in:
'Please count me in.'
'Yes, I am with you.'   ....   'Sure.'

Chris was encouraged by the readiness of the responses, although he never expected his close friends to refuse him and, realistically, Armstrong and Graham had little choice at this late stage; nevertheless it was good to see their evident enthusiasm. He grinned at them and then went on, somewhat solemnly;

'About this operation, we know *What* – the *Duchess of Lucca* is the target; and we know *Where* – Santa Isabel on Fernando Po. But

41

we do not know *Who* or *How*. We lack information. Until we have proper understanding of the position at Santa Isabel we cannot go blundering over there hoping to steal a ship. Britain is not at war with Spain and nothing we do must change that, as the Prime Minister's letter makes clear. The Spanish authorities will be protecting the ship since it is in their harbour and we simply must not get caught in the act. The object of meeting this morning is to begin to list the information and skills we need, and define the conditions for a successful theft. How do we go about stealing a ship?'

As he stopped speaking, the thoughts of the other four men raced away tangentially and then focused on different aspects of the complexity facing them. For Rob Graham the word "ship", within a milli-second, conjured the whining scream of the Junkers 87 diving on the rescue ship at Dunkirk.

Peter tried to recall the tonnage of the Elder Dempster liners on the Lagos-Liverpool run but realised he had no proper idea and gave up.

Cracker Armstrong was thanking his stars that the new boss had his feet planted on the ground, showing every good sense by insisting the operation was set on a base of sound information; his fears of finding himself serving under an amateur who breenged in on hope and bloody heroics were lifting with everything Chris said. It was a huge relief to know what the job was and to be reassured about the basically competent attitude of the CO.

Steve Lister thought of the whaler out of South Georgia and imagined how big an eight thousand tonner would be. The tone of the Prime Minister's letter tickled his sense of humour:

'I like that instruction, "Steal me a Duchess". It sounds like the command of a high-handed Ruretanian aristocrat!'

There was general laughter but the boss was speaking again, now more briskly as he moved from intangible principle to something practical.

'We can best begin with a brain-storming session, everyone chucking in ideas we can sort out and discuss in depth later. Steve, will you please act as secretary?'

'Sure, Tigger.'

'What we want is a list of the information we need and how to gather it, and a list of the skills we shall need in the party, with suggestions who, from our acquaintance, might best provide them.'

42

Steve Lister scribbled as ideas flowed, at first slowly, then furiously as early suggestions provoked others. Forty minutes later he wrote out a fair copy of the results.

NEED TO KNOW

Is the ship anchored off-shore in the harbour, or tied up to the quay?

If the ship was on passage when Italy came into the war, where had the ship been and where bound?

What crew are on board? Are there still passengers?

Is there an armed guard on the ship? Are there Spanish police on the quay nearby? Or Spanish naval ships in harbour?

How long to raise steam? After we storm the ship, what has to be done before we can sail?

Could the ship be towed out of harbour, instead of sailing under its own power from the start?

Where do we sail the *Duchess* to after the lift?

What speed will the *Duchess* do? Will there be enough fuel for our voyage? (If the ship has been there since Italy entered the war, they must have used a lot of fuel for electricity and so on.)

What minimum crew do we need?

What is the cargo? Churchill calls it "valuable".

When do we go in? Day and time? If in the dark, what about moonrise? What about the state of the tide?

NEED TO FIND

A vessel to take the party to Fernando Po (with a crew to bring it back).

A ship's captain and navigator for the return trip of the *Duchess*.

A ship's engineer and a radio operator.

A linguist - Italian and Spanish.

Admiralty charts for the Bight of Biafra and the whole Nigerian coast.

Weapons (What will we need?)

43

'We can't even begin unless we have a ship or launch to take us out there,' said Steve, with blunt logic. 'Not to mention a captain to bring us back.'

'We may have progress on that,' said Chris. 'The captain was the obvious person for me to begin thinking about, especially since he might know of a vessel to carry us out to the island. Peter has suggested a man called Panda Moore of the Marine Department at Port Harcourt. He is the port superintendent and pilot there.'

Someone asked, 'Why is he called Panda?'

'He has white hair and jet black beetling eyebrows,' Peter answered, with a smile.

'The staff list,' Chris continued, 'shows he is a fully ticketed ship's captain and could well be the man we want, so I wired the Governor to invite Moore here today, without giving reasons or the target. Unfortunately the road from PH to here is not easy – must be about two hundred miles and there is the ferry across the Niger River at Onitsha, so he may be quite late. I just hope he can make it.'

Chris said he had also asked the Governor to send the Admiralty charts for the whole coast and they should arrive any day.

Steve recalled swapping stories with a foreman in the Public Works Department over a drink in the Benin Club. 'Do you know him: Eddie Hudson? Interesting man from Northumberland; he's a bit like me, a rolling stone, been around in queer places. He told me he was an inshore fisherman as a teenager, became a deep-water fisherman and then graduated to big ships until he was laid off in the 1930 slump; that was when he turned to maintenance jobs on-shore and became some kind of clerk-of-works: hence his present job in the PWD, I suppose. But I am pretty sure he was a ship's engineer for several years. If he has the experience, he might suit us quite well as the sort of chap who will turn his hand to anything in a crisis. And he is close at hand in Benin. He is certainly worth vetting, Tigger.'

Chris knew of Hudson, although admitted he had not discovered the marine engineering connection. He said he would contact him immediately he returned to the city. Jobs to be done were piling up.

In further discussion Peter mentioned his own knowledge of Italian, which he said modestly was "pretty good" and thought he could "get by" in Spanish. He also recalled "Clapper" Bell, the Education Officer in Ondo, whom he had known on his previous tour.

44

'Clapper is a great linguist, Tigger, and very much an Italian specialist as far as Europe is concerned, because last tour he hoped he might be useful in Intelligence for PoWs and so on in the event of war with Italy. Of course I am not sure about his knowledge of Spanish, but it seems a fair bet he may have some of that also, since the languages are related'.

The *"Need-to-find"* column was filling up satisfactorily but the *"Need-to-Know"* was a blank. Chris was depressed.

'Captain Moore and Hudson, or whoever comes as engineer, can probably answer the questions about the ship's performance well enough but we must have information on where she is lying, who is on board, whether there are local guards and so on.'

Peter wondered if they could find someone who had been in Santa Isabel recently.

'Either that or we shall have to send someone over on a reconnaissance,' Steve suggested.

'However the enquiries or the recce are made,' Chris replied, 'We dare not attract attention to our interest in the ship. I don't see how one of us could go over to look for ourselves: the Spanish would smell a rat in a minute.'

Discussion of the topic went on for most of the morning, with suggestions ranging from the unconvincing to the impossible. The men had talked themselves virtually into silence when the sound of an approaching car held their attention. A small saloon came slowly into the compound and stopped in the shade. From it a large man emerged, dressed in a blue shirt, matching blue shorts and dark blue stockings. His silvery white hair and bushy black eyebrows left no doubt this was "Panda" Moore. Chris walked across to meet him, surprised the man had been able to arrive so early in the day.

'You must be Captain Moore. I am Chris Wickham. I am glad you have been able to make it to this meeting. And you seem to have made the trip from Port Harcourt in remarkably quick time. Come and meet the others.'

'Good to meet you, Chris. You must call me Panda: everybody does. I'm glad to find this place without a hitch. Got a signal from HE in Lagos, so I guessed this must be a top priority, though I don't know why. By good fortune there was a John Holt ship leaving PH to pick up deck cargo of logs at Sapele, so I hitched a passage, saving me a long drive. Damned sight easier than coming by road round by Onitsha and Asaba. I borrowed this little car from the UAC shipping agent at Sapele.'

Cracker Armstrong marvelled at the close-knit community of Brits "on the West Coast". They were few and responded immediately to a request from another of the community; the system depended on no one making a request for anything trivial, never "crying wolf"; the net was never intrusive but instantly supportive if there was real trouble which could be relieved.

John Moore was born in 1892 at Kirkwall on Orkney and went to sea at fourteen, to the hard life of a boy on a square-rigged ship and later as a full member of the crew. By 1914 he was third mate on a cargo liner on the Far East run, Shanghai to London. His ship was torpedoed in 1916 and he served on a Q-ship against U-boats at the end of the war. Since the Q-ship deliberately offered herself as a target in order to create an opportunity to attack the submarine with concealed guns, it was far from being a soft option. He later gained his master's and extra-master's tickets, and captained one of Elder Dempster's cargo ships until she was laid up in the economic freeze after 1930 when he found himself "on the beach". Through contacts in his old firm in 1933 he was successful in finding employment in the Marine Department in Nigeria, being posted initially as Port Officer at Victoria, then emerging as a banana port serving the plantations in the Cameroons. Even by that time, at the early age of forty-two, his hair was pure white and the Panda nickname was inevitable. Now almost fifty, he was a large jovial man, red-faced and slightly corpulent; his present rig was typical, always trim, in every sense a commanding officer, he radiated reliability.

Succinctly Chris outlined the project, stated the objective and gave Panda the Prime Minister's letter and its attachments, plus Steve's *Need-to-Know* and *Need-to-Find* lists. In the silence while the captain read the papers, pink gins were dispensed as a preliminary to lunch.

After taking a first sip, Panda said, 'Damned difficult to succeed if the Spaniards don't want us to remove the ship. Maybe more difficult than you realise, although you put your finger on the key point here, where you say "How long to raise steam?" Since the ship has been in harbour for months, they will be running generators and so forth on a donkey engine and the main boilers will be cold. From this note in the Lloyd's Register, "180 lb boiler pressure" my guess is these are Scotch boilers, not tubed ones, so they will have to be warmed up slowly from cold, otherwise they would crack. I expect a "Chiefy" would ask for a day's warning to raise steam for the main engines. I doubt if it could be done in less than twelve hours, and all that time we would be in harbour, with the Spaniards asking what the hell is going on, please pay your port dues or something even more awkward. Raising steam cannot be kept secret. Getting a steam ship under way is not like using a car's self-starter and engaging first gear. It takes time.'

What Captain Moore said strengthened the fears Chris had suffered ever since Sir John gave him responsibility for the operation a week earlier: their chances of sailing the ship away from the port without the Spanish authorities interfering appeared almost nil. He faced leading the party on a hiding to nothing. He made a face and asked about the other questions. Panda replied briskly:

'Well, I expect I can find some vessel to take us to Santa Isabel, although the choice is not wide. I can certainly navigate the *Duchess* back to Victoria or PH or Lagos or wherever. That is no problem. Given that the engines turn over normally, I would expect such a ship would do 7 or 8 knots. That's rather slow. It means Lagos would be about fifty-five or sixty hours steaming, say two and a half days.'

'How many crew would we need?'

'Well, the regular crew would probably be five officers and about twenty other hands - maybe a few more as stewards and an extra cook since they have some passengers – but we could scrape by with a skeleton crew of eight or nine men for a short trip if everyone takes a turn.'

'That's not so bad. We can raise that number easily.'

'That answers some of the points on your *Need-to-Know* list but it leaves the question whether the ship is tied up at the quay or at anchor. I'm pretty sure she is too big to tie up at Santa Isabel and she will be lying off-shore. That may slightly ease the problem of raising steam without the Spaniards interfering and we could surely find out where she is anchored by casual questioning of ships' officers who have called at the port recently, without alerting them to the reason for our interest. Nonetheless she has been there so long, it may be a devil of a job to raise the anchor in the usual way or to loose a mooring cable. You had best be prepared to cut the chain with an explosive

47

charge – that is, if you want to leave in a hurry. And we are still ignorant about the number of crew and maybe passengers on board. Right now, I don't see how we can get that information.'

Since the same point had already stumped the rest of the party, there was no ready response to the captain's statement and there was relief when Chris suggested lunch.

'Public Works Department should have some explosives for blasting so we'd better ask Tom Leach. The important and encouraging thing, Captain,' he said, 'is that you have been saying what "we" will do and not do, so it seems you are willing to sign on for the party'.

'Oh, of course,' Panda said jovially. 'I couldn't let you chaps go wandering around the Bight of Benin all on your own like a tart in Piccadilly. You might get lost.' They all laughed and went in to lunch.

Chris and Peter were the last to leave the shade of the trees. Chris spoke seriously to his friend.

'It's all very well taking a positive line and joking about the operation, that it will all come right on the night, but I am far from lighthearted right now. The whole show could go horribly wrong, Peter, and I have a guilty feeling I may be leading you all into disaster. I want us to succeed but I am aware there is a cliff edge that represents discovery by the Spanish people. That would mean capture and charges of piracy.'

'Cheer up, Tigger! We are joining with our eyes open about the risks. We know damned well it is not a picnic and we all intend to keep on the uphill side of the cliff edge. You have a big plus in these two soldiers who are obviously first class chaps for training us up for this job. We don't need to rush things. We can take our time to get properly prepared, a couple of weeks – more if it's needed to collect the information about the ship. After all, she has been there for a year and a half, and another week or two is not going to make much difference. You will have a willing team and a winning team when it comes to the bit. Come on. Lunch.'

'I suppose you're right, Peter, but I hope Mr Churchill has weighed the odds accurately because we are the stakes and I have to recruit the chaps to come.'

The two Commandos were told lunch would be chicken and they remembered three hens as travelling companions. Sleeping sickness in cattle meant that, outside the large towns on the railway

48

which brought animals from the north, beef and mutton were not generally available in the south and, apart from occasional wild animals such as antelope and a large grass-eating rodent called cutting-grass, the main meat was chicken.

'At weekends the traditional lunch dishes are ground nut stew, palm oil chop and chicken curry. Today we are having a ground nut. To start with we'll have avocado pears. You have probably never had them but we think they are rather good with Worcester sauce. I hope you like them.'

Served with yam cakes and green beans, the ground nut stew was delicious. Cracker Armstrong and Rob Graham perceived that their hosts, as a result of living in the small communities of stations, some much smaller than Benin, were pleased to have new guests so they might show off the country's specialities, however modest. In fact the visitors, fresh from the restrictions of wartime Britain, were genuinely delighted with the food and praised it highly. The meal finished with local fruit salad of guavas, paw-paw, oranges and red forest bananas.

It was a thoroughly successful meal, good food, and good talk that began the essential process of cementing into a unit men who came from quite different backgrounds and had a natural hesitancy towards the others in view of the operation ahead. The talk ranged widely, from Shanghai to South Georgia, with common experiences found on the way. The grocer's lad and the earl's son discovered a common passion for the Lake District and the North Pennine hills where each had scrambled and cycled as a boy. Rob Graham also found common cause with Panda Moore after the captain had asked about Dunkirk and had with modesty swapped the account of his own Q-ship being shelled by a U-boat in 1918. Cracker's bond with Peter was immeasurably strengthened when he heard Peter had been in the Heriot's FP side which beat Hawick in a final of the Melrose Sevens (though why a Herioter should be endeared to a Langholm man on the basis of Hawick losing a rugby match several years before required an understanding of the Scottish Borders well beyond the others present). Chris was pleased at the liveliness of the chatter.

They were still sitting with empty coffee cups in the heavy heat of the afternoon when talk was halted by the noise of an approaching car. It turned out to be a large, chauffeur-driven Mercedes, causing Chris to exclaim:

'Good God, it's the bloody Resident. What the hell has brought him here?' And he went on urgently in a low tone, 'Not a word or hint about this operation. And don't give away that you two, Cracker, Rob, are in the Army. Thank goodness you have those borrowed shirts without your badges; I'll explain later.' And with that he rose and went to meet Grenville-Fletcher as he left his car.

Peter suggested, 'You had better let on you are timber men, wanting to buy mahogany logs. I'll put in any technical details but the Resident knows less about timber than you do so no worries.'

From the back of the car came a fleshy man of some fifty years. His plump cheeks, thick neck and generous waist suggested Grenville-Fletcher was fond of his food and took inadequate exercise. Unusually for a Saturday afternoon, he was dressed in a fawn palm-beach suit and was wearing a collar and tie; that might have been *de rigeur* for a secretariat meeting but was distinctly over-kill for a leisure day in the country with the afternoon temperature in the mid-nineties. Although the car he left was already in the shade, he carried a pith helmet; with accuracy Steve Lister perceived it was there, not as a guard against sunstroke, but as part of a uniform to protect the bearer's position, like a bowler hat in the City or a topper at Ascot. The whole rig was intended to make his audience feel inferior; 'He just looks bloody silly; it's a wonder he isn't wearing his damned sword and feathery hat,' was Steve's unspoken comment. Chris' greeting and enquiry if the Resident had had lunch were studiously ignored.

'Wickham, I want a word. I looked for you at the District Office this morning but was surprised to hear that, with Mr Lister, you had left Benin yesterday before office closing time to come down here. The extraordinary local leave you appear to have applied for to His Excellency the Governor has been approved but, I would remind you, it has not yet started. I take it you are aware by now that Saturday morning is a working day; I believe I have every right to expect to find you at your desk, not holidaying elsewhere in the Province.'

Chris managed to stem the flow: 'I know we work on Saturday mornings, Sir, and I can confirm that Steve Lister and I were working today. This is, after all, part of my district, Sir.'

The Resident ignored this reply to what was, after all, a trivial charge and, coming to the nub of the concern that had been sufficient to bring him a long way on a hot day, went on:

'I do not understand why your application for local leave should have bypassed me and been approved directly by His Excellency. That was irregular, Wickham, and I want to know why. It was a slight and subverted my authority in the Province. And now you have absented yourself from your station, while not on approved leave, to hold some kind of meeting I have not been told about.'

Grenville-Fletcher now appeared to have a collar one size too small for his neck. He had been genuinely puzzled earlier in the week by the granting of local leave by the Governor: why had the application not come to him? Why had his prerogative been ignored? He had said as much to his wife two days before and she had reinforced his determination not to allow his position to be weakened. Sitting alone in the back of the hot car for forty miles driving down from Benin City had allowed his anger to blossom and the slight to multiply gloriously. He did not wait for any reply but spoke again, now in a voice that addressed the whole company.

'And just what is this meeting? It is my impression my own officers are engaged in something underhand, something which has been deliberately withheld from me and thus contrary to Colonial Regulations, "an irregular meeting prejudicial to good order". Lister, I am disappointed to find you are involved in this.'

It was apparent to every member of the party that Robert Grenville-Fletcher was beyond normal reasoning; he wanted Chris Wickham's head on a plate. Steve Lister sought to divert some of the fire away from Chris and had the particular concern that, in answer to these wild suspicions of subversion, Chris might offer the cover story he had mentioned earlier in the day, that the meeting was to plan a cricket festival. With the Resident in his present mood, such a weak tale would instantly be seen to be false and would make matters far worse. The last words gave Steve the opening he needed:

'It is Saturday afternoon, Sir, and we are here at Peter Thorburn's invitation to take lunch and later to swim. I assure you that any fears you may have that this meeting is in some way disloyal or that it undermines your position as the Resident and our senior officer are entirely groundless.' To himself Steve was thinking: Good grief, I am beginning to sound as pompous as the old blighter himself.

Perceiving what Steve was about, Panda said, 'Just so, Sir. May I introduce myself? Captain John Moore, Marine Department. I

51

have just driven up from Sapele for the day. Luncheon and a swim later, you know.'

Peter felt the onus was now upon him to explain the presence of the other two whom the Resident had not met.

'Good afternoon, Resident,' he said, 'May I introduce Mr James Armstrong and Mr Robert Graham who are staying at Sapoba at present?'

Robert Grenville-Fletcher did not offer to shake hands. These two did not appear to be men he would wish to associate with. Sartorially neither soldier scored high marks. In order to avoid wearing their own shirts with badges of rank, they had, at Tigger's suggestion, borrowed from their hosts. Rob's was all unbuttoned for coolness and not tucked into his shorts. Cracker was wearing a bush jacket of Steve's; he was greatly taken with the practicality of the garment but nothing could hide the fact it was made for a man with a chest some six inches smaller than the wearer. More important than their scruffy appearance, Peter's words "staying at Sapoba at present" caught the Resident's attention: Sapoba was in his province. Here was yet another breach of etiquette, if not something more sinister. He turned abruptly back to Chris.

'Wickham. Who are these men? They look thoroughly undesirable people to be associating with my officers. What are they doing here in my Province? I did not ask for them to come to Benin and I don't believe they have signed my book. You have a lot of explaining to do. There are things going ....'

He got no further before an explosive interruption. James Armstrong had heard enough. This man who was neither his CO nor his RSM, not even an officer, just a bloody civie, was being rude to him, rude about his pal Rob Graham's turn-out and, forby, he was being bloody rude to Tigger who was his current boss and therefore "one of us".

'Wud ye have me sign your wee buik in the sentry box?' he thundered, his face flushed with an anger that automatically broadened his Langholm accent. 'Ye must be bloody well joking. When the Armstrongs leave their calling card, ye may be sure it isna an invitation to afternin tea.'

'Look here, my man. My name is Grenville-Fletcher and I am....'

'Look you, yourself, Sunshine. Not by any stretch am I "your man", so you can drop that for a start. As for you being a f****** Fletcher, I can tell you the last time the Fletchers came to Liddesdale, we Armstrongs hanged seeven of them from the walls of the Hermitage. Awaw ye go in your fancy motor-cawr. Ye're bloody well no wanted here. So just bugger off.'

Cracker, having said his say, did not wait to be answered but, turning on his heel, strode away, which was, in fact, the most effective thing he could have done. The effect of the outburst on the company was mixed. Steve was suppressing a grin as he enjoyed the clash; Cracker had spoken with the authority of a lineage at least as long as the Grenville-Fletchers' – or his own, for that matter – and was the clear winner on the day. Panda and Rob were cheering silently, on the basis that the man had it coming to him and what Cracker had said had probably needed saying for years past. Peter and Chris were shocked at the bluntness of the verbal assault, however justified the flare-up, and realised that disciplinary rockets were probably inevitable and coming their way.

Robert Grenville-Fletcher recognised that his standing had suffered fatal wounds; nothing he could say now could retrieve his position. No one had ever spoken to him in that fashion. He felt humiliated and his cunning enemy had removed himself so that he was not even available for imprecations, which might at least have been a solace to voice, however futile. The only thing he could do was retire with as much dignity as he could muster, so he did as Cracker had instructed him and retreated to his Mercedes that had been a present from his father-in-law in 1938 and was for him a very potent and comforting status-symbol. Leaving the room, he announced haughtily that they would hear a great deal more about this in the future. The driver closed the door on his damaged master and the big car swept out of the compound.

CHAPTER FIVE

For a few moments there was stunned silence. In that brief interval Sergeant Armstrong re-entered the room and stood at attention facing Chris.

'I am very sorry, Sir. I should never have spoken like that; I just saw red when he went on at you. I'm feared I've spoiled the operation by attracting attention instead of keeping low as you asked, Sir.'

'Thank you, Sergeant,' said Chris, 'but what you said to the bloody Resident has needed saying for years. Relax and sit down. In any event, Cracker, the real culprits are the Governor and myself. I see now, it was asking for trouble to fix special local leave in the way we did; given his touchiness about position, prerogatives and the drill laid down in Colonial Regulations, the old blighter was bound to be made suspicious when an application didn't go across his desk.'

'Yes, I'm sure you're right, Tigger,' Steve agreed, 'That's what brought the old buffer down here.'

'Nonetheless, Steve, the Sergeant's outburst saved me from making a fool of myself by trying to sell that thin cover story about a cricket festival, which would have been worse than useless; telling that would have simply reinforced his suspicions.' Turning to the soldiers, he continued, 'What I hadn't got round to telling you was that the Resident's wife is a German and almost certainly a devoted Nazi. Because of that the Governor decided no word about the operation should go to Grenville-Fletcher. So don't blame yourself; I attracted his attention and I am responsible for what happened.'

'Do you know,' Steve said reflectively, 'I believe we have come out of the difficult patch rather well, apart from Tigger and myself having a rocket on Monday. And that rocket can hardly be for more than keeping bad company, lunching with you chaps who wear scruffy shirts. G-F knows nothing about our operation and he does not know that Cracker and Rob are army types. The real secrets are still secure, at least at our end, although I do agree with you, Tigger, the Governor should have thought of a less conspicuous way for granting leave.' And from a base of well-balanced personal confidence he added, 'What an unhappy chap the Resident is! He is so unsure of himself and so anxious to be reassured we all know he is the whole cheese. He does love Colonial Regulations and, incredibly for someone so senior, quite genuinely believes they must always be obeyed. Perhaps his nanny or his ma spanked him too much when he was a babe. Or perhaps not enough.'

At this point Panda said he must really be getting back to return his borrowed car to Sapele. Chris and he agreed a simple code to enable them to communicate by telegram without the messages being instantly understood by other people and attracting more attention. The port of departure and the date were the main variables. Panda promised to get busy arranging a suitable vessel for transport and to enquire from any officers of ships that had called at Santa Isabel where the *Duchess* was lying.

'As I see it, we certainly cannot be ready to leave in less than about ten days,' Chris said, 'and right now I can't see how even that would be possible in view of the lack of information on those key unknowns.'

With that, Panda left, 'to look for a ship to go pirating,' he said. The rest had a swim to wash away the dregs of a tiresome afternoon.

Dinner was mainly a silent meal, each man going over the events of the day and weighing the plus and minus points. Chris was listing in his mind the actions needed to obtain hard information and where to look for the further recruits he needed.

One important matter had not yet been considered: weapons. Chris hoped the *Duchess* might be captured without resorting to severe violence but the operation had to be planned on the assumption that the Italian crew would be armed and would put up a fight. He asked Cracker what weapons, if any, the Commandos had brought with them and was told each had a 9mm Sten gun and their Commando knives. Peter had his Mannlicher .256 carbine and Steve a Winchester 300. Chris had access to the Benin police .303 Lee-Enfields, the standard British army rifle. There was no shortage of rifles. In Lagos the Governor had sanctioned the release to the soldiers of two thousand rounds of 9mm ammunition for the Stens. Since none of the others had seen the machine-pistol, Cracker brought his from the bedroom. The demonstration of the ultra-simple gun broke the gloom, by bringing a harsh reminder of potential danger in a project that had become farcical during the afternoon.

Cracker took up a point Panda had made at lunchtime. 'The captain said there would probably be an Italian crew of more than thirty, it being a cargo-passenger ship. Assuming they are still all there, that's an awful lot for only seven or eight of us to take on, Sir, especially if they are spread out around the ship. If we achieve complete tactical surprise and catch them in their beds, that would help, but even so they may be in a dozen different places, in cabins and so on. Then there may be passengers as well, although the ship has been at Saint Isabel for eighteen months or so, and I don't know whether they would still be on board or gone to stay ashore. All in all, I think we should aim to have eighteen or twenty men, boss, to be on the safe side.'

'H'm. That is more than I thought, because I was reckoning on the minimum to sail the ship and had not allowed sufficient for fighting. I take your point, Cracker.'

'There's another thing, Boss,' the sergeant went on, encouraged by the CO's response. 'Rifles are not much use for close fighting, going into a small cabin and so on. They are clumsy and have the disadvantage they have to be reloaded by working the bolt. The Stens are much handier but we have only the two. I think we should try to get some revolvers, Sir. The army in Lagos should be able to let us have some, if possible enough for most of the party. Could you pull some strings? Two or three rifles at most should be enough to handle any longer range shooting needed, anything more than point blank. Rob and I can arrange some weapons training here for the party before we go. Ideally, of course, we should achieve complete surprise, sneak aboard and into each cabin in turn, put a knife to each man's throat or cosh him, tie him up and gag him to keep him quiet, so that the ship is taken in complete silence. Back home, that is what the Colonel would order and expect. 'S'that right, Rob? Mind you, it wouldn't be easy, even for a well trained Commando group.'

Cracker's description had a sobering effect. It impressed on them all that the operation was not simply a matter of taking over a foreign ship, something requiring knowledge of engines and navigation. It would involve capturing and silencing a party of men – an unknown number – who would presumably resist, perhaps violently. What were the "rules of engagement"? How violent could any of them afford to be, given that they were civilians who would be facing, and perhaps fighting, foreigners on foreign territory? If someone was injured or killed the legal position looked black, especially if they failed to get the ship away, which – they must face it – was a possibility, and they ended up in a Spanish prison. Chris recalled using the word "piracy" when speaking to Sir John when he first read Churchill's letter. The exploits of Drake on the Spanish Main before 1600 were good exciting stuff, guaranteed to set a schoolboy's blood coursing faster and his mind running on his hero "slung atween the roundshot, listening for the drum and dreaming all the time of Plymouth Hoe". But the actual prospect of piracy raised a host of legal and moral problems. Morgan might have dropped the captured crew over the side – "made them walk the plank" was the phrase – but that could not be done to the Italian crew of the *Duchessa di Lucca*.

'When we have taken the ship,' Rob asked telepathically, 'what happens to the Eytie crew? Do we take them with us back to Lagos or wherever, or do we put them ashore? They'll be a damned nuisance if we take them along, but possibly they would rather come than be put ashore completely destitute in a foreign country until the end of the war.'

Chris was silent for a little. 'Frankly, I still have to think that through and I shall have to brief everyone on it before we go. Before that I hope to know more about the number of crew and passengers. Meantime I accept Cracker's point about the need for pistols rather than lots of rifles and I shall try to raise some.'

All talk was then stopped when sound and lights announced the arrival of another car: each man silently prayed it was not the Resident returning for another round, which seemed most likely.

'This hideaway is about as secluded as Piccadilly Circus', Steve said, echoing the thoughts of others.

The car stopped at the front door of the house in the light cast by the Tilley lamps. It was revealed as not the grey Mercedes but a dark red American Ford V8 saloon, large, very showy and sporting a grinning chromium grill. Steve and Chris simultaneously announced with incredulity that their visitor was the Oba. The Nigerian driver nipped out smartly from behind the wheel to open the rear door and allow the king of Benin to alight. Chris went out to greet him. No visitor had been expected and a prediction the Oba would call would have seemed almost as far-fetched as the Archbishop of Canterbury. Technically Chris, Steve and Peter were all advisers to the Benin Native Authority and legally the whole forest, with the rest-house and research station, was owned by the Oba who headed the BNA, but Peter reckoned it was probably the first occasion he or any predecessor had called at Sapoba. What prompted the visit?

'Christopher,' the Oba gave equal weight to the three syllables, 'I hoped I might find you still here with your friends. May I come in? Mr Thorburn, what a charming place you have here; I have often heard of Sapoba but this is the first time I have ventured in.'

The Oba was a well built man in his late thirties, above average height, with handsome and lively features. Like most Nigerians he was clean-shaven. He was dressed in an extremely loose gown, made of rose pink cotton, cut with such wide sleeve openings they could be thrown on his shoulders to increase ventilation in severe heat. The neck of the gown was decorated with numerous parallel lines of gold thread, contrasting handsomely with the material and with his dark brown skin. Trousers of the same pink cotton showed beneath his robe and he wore a matching little pillbox hat which also had the lines of gold thread decoration. He quickly set his hosts at ease and established the informality of the visit, saying:

'Since I have invited myself here, I thought it best to bring a peace-offering as a contribution to the evening. I hope it will be acceptable'.

And from a small bag he produced a bottle of Johnny Walker Black Label whisky. He made a crack about a Cambridge man daring into a stronghold of Oxford and, when introduced to Graham and Armstrong, spoke freely and sensibly about hill sheep farming in Britain, contrasting it with the style of agriculture in Benin. At his suggestion, they sat at the dining table; 'It avoids having to raise our voices to talk across the room.'

The Bini king was born at Freetown in Sierra Leone where his father and family had been exiled for several years following the British occupation of the kingdom. The chance location of exile had far-reaching consequences, determining, amongst other things, where young Ewuare would go to school. Freetown society, heavily influenced by the values of freed slave families returned from America, set high store on education as offering the best means of advancement in the world. This was the environment in which the boy was raised and which set his standards. When his father was given permission to return to Benin, the boy stayed on to complete his schooling and from there he went to university in Britain.

Ewuare was not his father's eldest son but it was in Bini tradition he should be chosen to become Oba, the Council shrewdly deciding that formal education and familiarity with the white man's world would be useful attributes in the current circumstances. The Oba well appreciated the folly of his father's high-handed attitude to the British in 1897 and the fact that prior to that the kingdom had become decadent to an extraordinary degree. Now he was intent upon restoring the country's fortunes. Nevertheless he deeply resented the mindless destruction of the artistic wealth of his country by the invading troops. Bronzes, sculptures, paintings, all were ruined or looted by soldiery who had not even valued what they stole, creating a cultural desert when they left.

The Oba, however, chose not to show his resentment, preferring to advance Benin's cause quietly by creating conditions for the steady development of education and the economy. British rule, following pillage, had brought new advantages and he was intent on milking the system as much as possible. Not that it would go on for ever. His time at Cambridge had made him quite aware of the likely progression to independence; the Congress Party in India was pressing for it now for their country and the changes that had begun to affect the British Empire might be impossible to stop. Nigeria – and Benin as part of it – was a protectorate, not a British colony, and there were no white voters or white landowners to resist an advance to independence. Ewuare was biding his time. Meanwhile his relationship with Chris Wickham and the others was quite genuine; he knew their integrity was above reproach and their administration exemplary, so he used it to the full. Chris at least was aware of this, especially from his leisure activities with the Oba, although Peter was not, being immersed in the technical matters of forest management and having much less direct contact with the king.

When glasses, soda and water had been produced and all were served, the Oba called his driver and spoke seriously to him in Bini. The driver left with the steward.

'I have ensured that our conversation will not be listened to by the servants. What I have to say, Christopher, is for you and your colleagues. Please hear me out because I have things to say of deep interest and importance to us all, which is why I thought it best to drive here all the way from Benin this evening in person instead of sending a messenger.'

'First I should tell the two soldiers,' at which there were sharp intakes of breath round the table, because the fact they were in the army had not been mentioned when they were introduced, 'some facts about Bini institutions. You others know already but the background will help them understand what I have to say'.

He then explained that, for most of the nineteenth century, Benin had been the most powerful and wealthiest state in this part of Africa. Initially its power was militarily genuine but latterly it depended on enemies believing that ju-ju magic rendered Bini soldiers invulnerable, so making Benin's victory inevitable; so strong was the acceptance of this that actual fighting became unnecessary. In fact, Bini success and its oracle relied basically on an extremely efficient intelligence system, like the Greek oracle at Delphi. The Benin empire had crashed in 1897 because its leaders had become complacent and, very stupidly, had offended the British Empire at its strongest and most arrogant. After the conflict Benin City was completely destroyed, including the royal palace, and all its art and wealth were lost.

'Surprisingly, however,' the Oba went on, 'the British administration left the social structure intact and they overlooked the intelligence organisation. Most of the senior family chiefs who now sit on the council, the Igba-rahero, were the young warriors who faced the British troops in 1897 and, not unnaturally, they aim to restore their family fortunes as best they can. For commercial success, espionage and intelligence are just as useful as they ever were for war. The key intelligence organisation in Benin is the Igboni Society, a secret society that is a cross between the masons and MI5. The Society gives me hard information about most of what happens in southern Nigeria faster than news reaches the Governor. I have agents in every department of government and all the big commercial firms as well. The placing of Igboni agents is not left to chance; bright young men are placed deliberately in positions where they may be able to provide information. So much for the explanation of circumstances; now to detail.'

The story gripped Armstrong's and Graham's full attention.

'That is a fair description, Oba,' Chris said appreciatively, 'But even I did not realise what a central place the Society held.'

'Christopher. Two weeks ago the Governor ordered you to Lagos and you stayed overnight at Government House. That visit was unusual and I wondered why. A week later two soldiers from the elite Commandos came to Benin wearing their green berets and from Mr. Thorburn's garden boy I heard they were to take part in an operation to be led by Christopher Wickham.

'Before the soldiers' arrival, I heard from a District Office clerk you had telegraphed the Governor seeking to recruit a senior seafaring man, Captain Moore from Port Harcourt, and you asked the Governor to send sea charts of the Nigerian coast, including the whole Bight of Biafra. Therefore I deduce the secret operation is amphibious. Since you could not want to re-invade Nigeria, you must be going elsewhere. The only island in the Bight of Biafra is Fernando Po. You could not attempt an invasion of the island with these forces of a few men, so what is there on Fernando Po that might be a target for a dozen or so men? Perhaps Captain Moore is to be required, not to navigate the party to Fernando Po, but after the operation. What is there at Fernando Po, not available for purchase – and the Spaniards would sell their grandmothers if they could make a profit on the deal – worth stealing, vulnerable to a dozen men and capable of being sailed back to Nigeria?

'In short, I have come to the conclusion that you are intending to attack a ship, an Italian ship, in which I also am very interested. That is why I have taken the unusual step of coming down here in person to speak to you in private.'

The Oba paused reflectively, chin in hand, and with a little grin looked expectantly at Chris. The latter could only hitch uncomfortably in his chair. It was Peter who spoke.

'That, Tigger, was a very fast ball. I suggest you kick for touch!'

'Yes; fair enough,' said Chris, with a wry smile, 'There's no choice. It seems our security was completely flawed. In fact, it didn't exist.'

'Do not be disappointed, Christopher. In the Society, only I have all the pieces of the jig-saw puzzle and I do not share my deductions with others. Furthermore, by joining our information and resources we may achieve far more and achieve it more quickly. More quickly may be extremely important, as you will hear.'

The Oba had their full attention but he kept them waiting by suggesting they fill their glasses.

'As I have said already, the senior families in Benin are anxious to recover the wealth they lost as a result of the disastrous war with Britain forty years ago and they are achieving it unobtrusively by education and trade. Some good commercial opportunities have been quite neglected by the well-known European firms. Young Joshua Oshodin – you know his father in the council, Christopher, – has made several short visits to Santa Isabel for trading purposes. Since the beginning of the war in Europe the world price of rubber has risen steeply. Rubber grows well on Fernando Po but the Spanish authorities operate a government buying monopoly that pays the farmers only a fraction of the world price. Oshodin can afford to buy island rubber well above the official Spanish price – so the farmers are keen to sell to him – and still make a big profit selling it in Nigeria at the open market price, provided they can smuggle it off the island. All that is by-the-way but it explains how he has come to bring in some intelligence on Santa Isabel. He returned to Benin only a few days ago.

'What is important to me is his report on the Italian *Duchess* ship. When he returned, Joshua told me that many crates were being loaded on the ship. What the cases contained, I do not know, but new loading suggests that the ship may be intending to sail somewhere soon. Local people expect it to leave very soon. Hence my coming to meet you tonight, to discover if we can co-operate.'

'Loading?' Steve and others flung the word back at the Oba. A stream of questions followed – How many? – How big? – Where from? – none of which the Oba could answer.

'I think you must really speak to Joshua Oshodin himself,' he said. 'More than that, I believe there would be advantage in taking him with you to the island, since he has contacts there and, as an

African, he is much less conspicuous than one of you, where there are few white men.'

For some minutes the discussion was brisk, people pointing out items of the required information that could be gained by such a move. Understandably, Chris was reluctant to commit himself finally to making Joshua Oshodin a full member of the party to cut out the ship without first meeting him to judge how he would fit in, although the advantages listed by the Oba were obvious; he summed things up by saying:

'I would certainly like very much to talk to Joshua Oshodin as soon as I can, Oba, if you could make that possible. And if he would agree to come with us as a member of the party, I am sure it would be a great help.'

'Excellent; that is settled then. If you are to be at home in Benin tomorrow, Christopher, I shall arrange for him to call.' Times were agreed and the conversation moved on.

'There is another matter,' said the Oba. 'Since we are collaborating on Fernando Po, I shall give you some up-to-the-minute information I received only late this afternoon. It may be significant to you in your official capacity as District Officer, Christopher. Soon after lunch today, while the Resident was absent from home, a white man arrived at the Residency. It appears he knows Mrs. Grenville-Fletcher very well. Although she told the servants he was a friend of her husband's from England, they spoke entirely in a language the servants did not understand, which I deduce to be German, since that is her native tongue. Could it be the Resident's brother-in-law, do you suppose?' he asked innocently. 'I leave the matter with you, Christopher, because I have neither direct knowledge nor power in it. As I think you would say at home, "A nod is as good as a wink"!'

Chris, Steve and Peter were speechless at this news. The thought that the Grenville-Fletchers were possibly entertaining a German while the countries were at war was a stunner. Could this be true? What were the implications? The immediate comment came from Cracker Armstrong in his slow vernacular.

'Man, you're a caution, Oba. And you ken whit's whit.'

Honest respect glowed in Cracker's smile. 'If you ever need a Scottish agent for your MI5 Society, just let me know. I'd offer to join you the noo but I'm tied up for the present in the army,' he said with a laugh.

63

'Thank you, Sergeant Armstrong. I shall remember that, in case I need you,' the Oba said, smiling. 'For instance, do they distil whisky in your part of Scotland?'

'Unfortunately, no. Not locally. At least, not officially,' said Cracker who was not the slightest awed or artificially deferential towards him. 'If you don't mind my asking, how do you become Oba? Does it go father to son, or do you get elected to it?'

Ewuare explained that the Bini constitution required the succession to be filled by the man the council judged most suitable from half-a-dozen princely families. 'Sometimes that may be the son of the previous oba but, on the other hand, his sons may be too young, or feeble, or in some other way unsuitable.'

'That's a good system,' said Cracker seriously, as if a specialist in constitutional law. 'In the old days the Armstrongs worked the same sort of arrangement for choosing their leader for reiving – that's to say for raiding – but it was aye an Armstrong, of course.'

The Oba laughed loudly at this solemn comparison and slapped his knee hard with his open palm. 'You are my kind of man, James Armstrong. I am glad we agree on how to choose a leader.' Turning to Chris, he continued, 'Talking of the succession of obas, Christopher, have you heard the prediction there will soon be an *Oba-nofua*? That means a white oba,' he explained to the others. 'Some of my people are very upset by the forecast. Over the past week, each night, there has been drumming, originating in Eastern Provinces I suppose, coupled with rumours of a great army coming from the east, bringing a white ruler. Neither the Igboni Society nor any of my other intelligence contacts have picked up anything more. I do not know what to make of it. I guess it is simply an idle rumour but the unfortunate thing is that many people think there must be some truth in it, which is a threat to our established order. You are not seeking my job, are you, Christopher?' he said jocularly.

Chris and Steve expressed complete ignorance of the rumour but did not make light of it. The Oba pointed out another aspect; people were making the assumption, not unreasonably, that a white king could be imposed only by the present white administration, so there was already the beginning of a groundswell of anti-British feeling in the city. Very seriously he went on;

'Benin needs stability and steady economic development, not instability and violence, I am sure you agree. If you can discover the source of the rumour and counter it, you will make a useful contribution to the good of the province, Christopher. I fear some hotheads may do something stupid.'

The district administrators promised to make strict enquiries at once in neighbouring provinces and to report back to the Oba as soon as there were replies. They knew how quickly rumours could spread and what damage could be done by crowds moved by mass hysteria. Cracker and Rob were intrigued by the reference to news being spread by drumming.

'Does it work like morse code?' Rob asked.

The Oba replied this was not so. 'There are basically two kinds of drumming. The languages of this part of Africa are tonal, so that a simple little word like "ada" has three or four totally different meanings, depending on whether the two syllables have the same tone, or the second one rises or falls, or rises briefly and then falls. Vowels and their tones play a much greater part in Bini or Yoruba than they do in European languages, so much so that a good drummer can imitate speech almost exactly by using a stick on a small drum whose skin tension can be changed instantly by squeezing the side strings under his arm. Such a drum really does talk but it can be heard only over short distances. Big drums to be heard miles away cannot transmit words like a telegram but they can convey themes and during the drumming the ju-ju man, much ridiculed by Europeans, may receive a more exact message by telepathy to fill out the theme. I cannot do it myself but I know those who can; it works, however far-fetched it may seem to Europeans.'

The explanation was intriguing but threw no light on the validity or source of the rumours of a white king coming to power. Steve speculated that, since the message came from some distance, the prediction might apply to provinces other than Benin and to other paramount chiefs. This was a new slant the Oba had not considered, his Bini advisers having used their vernacular words *"oba-nofua"* The subject died from lack of hard information.

'I must leave now,' said the Oba, rising. He asked about their immediate plans, Chris replying that he thought Steve, Peter and he would have to abandon their weekend at Sapoba to return early next day to Benin City. Peter said he could leave the soldiers in the good care of the local forest guard, Agbontaen, who could show them around. The Oba said he knew the Agbontaen family and went on to make arrangements to meet Chris the next day in Benin. Then, summoning his driver, he left.

The king's news about the ship loading new cargo caused a fury of conversation among the men and clearly forced a radical change on the pace of their preparations, from a careful reconnaissance and build-up to a race against the timetable of some unknown person who was apparently making the target ready for sea. Where could she be going? Surely it could not be an attempt to run the blockade through the Straits of Gibraltar? Surely anywhere in Spain would do, maybe Cadiz? Or Spanish Morocco? But no! that would not allow goods to get back to Italy. And what was in the crates? Almost every question would depend on what Joshua Oshodin had to say tomorrow. Could he have been mistaken and cargo was being unloaded?

How soon could the operation be mounted? They needed several additional men, as well as Oshodin, Hudson and Clapper Bell, assuming they would all be available, to make up the minimum crew envisaged by Panda and Cracker. Chris wrote out a list of things to be done, people-to-see for the next day and on Monday. It meant abandoning the previous plan for a slack Sunday and he asked Steve and Peter to join him by sharing the jobs in Benin and elsewhere next day. He suggested Peter might try to recruit the Ondo education officer, Bell; if he could contact Bell by telephone from Benin City, always difficult and unreliable, they might arrange to meet halfway and thus cut down on the driving. Chris and Steve would have to meet Oshodin.

'If Oshodin's description confirms the Oba's impression about the loading, we must instantly get on to Panda to arrange transport out. We would look bloody silly if we got out to Fernando Po and found the *Duchess* had already sailed.'

Steve interrupted this line of thought. 'But what about this stranger at the Residency? Should that not take priority over the Duchess operation? Could it possibly be Hilda's brother? I assumed he would be interned – must have been if he was in Nigeria or Cameroons. Could he have been interned in French Cameroons and they have let him out? That needs instant action, Tigger, surely?'

Chris agreed it must be followed up but he was inclined to dismiss the report on the score that Grenville-Fletcher, although undoubtedly a pompous ass, was above all a zealous civil servant and would not be so stupid as lay himself open to a charge of harbouring an enemy national; surely it must be some quite innocent visitor, albeit one who spoke German to Hilda.

'When I took on the operation from the Governor to cut out the ship I thought it was going to be damned difficult. But that was before I knew about the complications,' Chris said ruefully.

In the welter of their discussion, only Cracker Armstrong considered a passing remark made by the Oba; he had referred to the Italian ship "in which I also am very interested". He was not only interested but very well informed and Cracker recalled the army training principle, "Information is half the battle". Why should an African chief, even a very senior one, have such a lively concern for the movement of an Italian ship that he would drive at night for a secret meeting with the group at Sapoba? He did not voice his question but tucked it away for later consideration.

Plans for Sunday were finalised. Up at five-thirty. Breakfast at six with the cars loaded. Leave at six-thirty for Benin. Peter's steward boy and the cook's mate were to remain at Sapoba to look after the two soldiers. Peter summoned the rest-house caretaker and sent him, late though it was, to the Forest Guard's house in the nearby village with orders Agbontaen was to parade at the house at six-fifteen next morning.

The NCOs were then given instructions about their health; to take their anti-malaria pills without fail; drink no water unless filtered and boiled; long trousers and long-sleeved shirts after sundown to reduce mosquito and sand-fly bites; wear a hat and no sun-bathing in the heat of the day, since they were still too pale; don't walk barefoot outside in case of jiggers, and so on. The two men were inclined to demur at this mollycoddling.

'I need you in good health and top training for this job,' Chris said, 'not a couple of invalids. You are no use to me if you go down with malaria or dengue fever. And if you neglect simple precautions it is only too easy to get sick in this part of the country. It wasn't called The White Man's Grave for nothing.'

Rob was much more anxious about spiders and was relieved to hear there was none dangerous to human beings in West Africa, although scorpions were another thing entirely.

'What about these lizards that can walk on the ceiling? I worry if they may drop on me and they are poisonous.'

He was reassured geckos scarcely ever fell, were certainly not poisonous and were very helpful in eating mosquitos.

Cracker was concerned about snakes. Peter laid a bet he would not see one. 'There are plenty in the forest but they sense you coming and get out of your way. If you do see one, leave it alone and keep away from it because most are poisonous and a few have a bite that is lethal in next to no-time. If by any chance you find one in the house or nearby, call the boys and they will deal with it. Snakes are another good reason for not going around barefoot.'

They finished the Oba's whisky and headed for bed. As they prepared to turn in, Chris ruefully reminded Peter of their lunchtime conversation.

'You said we could take our time, a few weeks if necessary, to prepare the attack. Now, only a few hours later, that leisurely plan has gone down the tube. We are being forced to hurry, and that goes right against my instincts, given the risks involved.'

Chris was torn with doubt. The task the Governor gave him had been bad enough: truth to tell, it had looked damned nearly impossible, but now they were being jockeyed into doing the job hastily which was bound to increase the risks. To make matters worse, the operation was dragging in his friends – Peter, Steve and probably others – who were joining no doubt out of loyalty, perhaps in misplaced confidence in his abilities as a leader. Armstrong and Graham also. He was responsible for them. He would be responsible for taking them all into an impossible situation, into an operation that looked doomed from the start.

CHAPTER SIX

When Robert Grenville-Fletcher reached home he was angry, injured, foul-tempered. He felt injured because the Scotchman had insulted him in front of his own subordinate officers. He was angry with Lister because he was sure the man was amused at his discomfiture and, knowing he was of an aristocratic family, he wanted to impress him, not be ridiculed. Angry with Thorburn because the crude Scotchman and his ill-dressed companion were apparently Thorburn's friends, or acquaintances at least. Angry most of all with Wickham; he was reluctant to admit it but Wickham was good at his job, perhaps even achieving more in Benin District than he, Robert, was doing. Wickham was more friendly with the Oba than he should be; and he had been called to visit the Governor in Lagos, behind Grenville-Fletcher's back, probably making that very comparison and devising something to his Resident's disadvantage. He was also angry with the Governor, if it came to that; HE had never given Grenville-Fletcher the recognition he was due. Finally, he was angry with himself that he had not immediately asserted his authority when the damned Scotchman had spoken to him like that; now he rehearsed the withering comments that would have reduced his opponent to speechlessness and shown who was boss.

The car journey passed quickly with these richly resentful thoughts filling his head. Cracker Armstrong's outburst, quite fortuitously, was to have a profound effect on events because it conditioned the Resident's outraged mind to depart from his normal well-regulated behaviour. It unhinged him.

The Residency was designed with the dining room the only public room on the ground floor, convenient for serving food from the kitchen which was a separate building, and the lounge and bedrooms on the upper floor to catch the breeze, both levels having wide verandas for shade. When Robert walked into the lounge he was surprised to see a man, whom he took to be a stranger, sitting talking to Hilda.

Hearing Robert behind him, the man rose, stood to attention and gave a slight bow.

'*Guten Tag, Robert. Kennst Du mich noch?*'

Robert realised who it was in the instant the man began to speak. He strode across the room, shook hands with his wife's brother Klaus and welcomed him enthusiastically to their home. His greeting was entirely unfeigned because he had always liked Klaus; now it came spontaneously into his head to compare his brother-in-law very favourably with the objectionable bunch of ill-disciplined characters he had left at Sapoba.

Only in the middle of the family small-talk that followed did it occur to Robert that there was something amiss or at least urgently in need of explanation.

'Klaus, how is it that you are here, at liberty, a German national of military age? Were you not interned in French Cameroon at Duala?'

Klaus laughed and explained that in 1939 he had indeed been caught and interned there owing to the fact he had been prevented from returning home by a landslide blocking the road. He had spent nearly a year in the small camp but, after the fall of France and the establishment of the Vichy government, custody had become so lax as to be a joke. No doubt there was a division of opinion among the French officers between those who were loyal to Marshal Pétain and had an eye to a future with Germany supreme, and on the other hand those who wanted alignment with General de Gaulle.

Klaus had made his plans carefully and succeeded not only in escaping from the camp, which was easy, but also in crossing from French to British territory, where, on the family's Bamenda property, he had made arrangements long before the declaration of war so that he might remain in hiding. In accord with Berlin's orders for the establishment of a resistance cell, he had built a small bush-house in woodland on a high ridge. The base was well stocked with tinned food

70

where he could look after himself, and there was a short-wave radio receiver and other equipment. It was all ready waiting for him when he crossed the border and he had been living there for the past ten months. The local families were completely loyal to him, having been Ehrwald employees for more than thirty years, and they were well paid to remain quiet. No doubt the place could have been located from the air but aircraft were very few and none was looking for him. It was as snug as a mountain hut in Bavaria or the Hartz, he said, set in the elfin woodland, up around two thousand metres elevation.

'But Robert, Klaus has brought stupendous news.' Hilda was wide-eyed with excitement.

Brother and sister were closely alike, tall and fair in complexion. Hilda was fine featured and carried herself with a confidence amounting to arrogance, a demeanour that – given her native country was Britain's wartime enemy – was not admired in local white society. Nor was she popular with Nigerians, since her treatment of servants was overbearing and her general attitude blatantly racist. Hilda's position, however, as the wife of the senior government official allowed her to escape the penalties of such faults which would have fallen hard upon others. Some of her neighbours ignored the offences in the interest of supposed social recognition and most saw there was little they could do other than avoid the Grenville-Fletchers as much as possible. In truth, in a small station there was little that could be done; the local senior officer and the channel of communication to higher authority were both the Resident who was hypersensitive to any failure to accord his wife the deference due to the station's first lady. This fact polarised attitudes and exacerbated a situation that was bound to be difficult in a war. For her part, Hilda was insensitive to the issues, her behaviour set by prejudices taken from her parents and the stereotypes of her education in Germany. She was also jealous lest Robert should turn to another woman (which he never dared do) and watched him like a panther for any slippage from Ehrwald standards. They had no children.

Klaus too was lean and handsome. It was easy to see that his confident manner would disarm enquiry as he crossed the country from Cameroons to Benin. He had travelled by motorcycle, uncomfortably but quickly and surprisingly unobtrusive. Simply acting the part of a British Colonial Service officer had indeed enabled him to avoid detection as an alien; he spoke good English and

71

Nigerians simply took it for granted that a white man must be British
– unless he proved on closer inspection to be from one of the Swiss or
French trading companies. Only a rigorous check with passports
would have detected his identity. He had even passed the police sentry
on the Residency gate by putting on a bold front and telling the man
he had an appointment with Mrs Grenville-Fletcher.

Robert was in a dilemma. On the one hand he knew he should
be reaching for the telephone right now to call the police and require
Klaus' arrest. The man was his brother-in-law but unquestionably he
was a German and therefore his country's enemy. The action of the
well-disciplined civil servant was to arrange for him to be interned. On
the other hand this was Hilda's brother; Hilda would be furious if he,
Robert, was the instrument of her brother's removal. He wanted to
avoid her disapproval, which secretly he likened to that of Medusa. He
always wanted to please her. And he genuinely liked Klaus, liked his
standards and admired his disciplined effectiveness, recognising
qualities he knew privately he did not himself possess. There could be
no harm in waiting a little. What did Hilda mean by "stupendous news"?

'What is the great news, Klaus?'

'Three days ago in Bamenda, I received by short wave radio
my orders from the Führer. Germany is going to take over Nigeria. I
have come here because I want to ensure my sister and you are safe
during the campaign and, more than that, because I want you, Robert,
to join the winning side. Make no mistake, brother-in-law, Germany
will win, both here in West Africa and in the main struggle against
Russia. Russian Bolshevism is the real enemy, not only of Germany
but of all who hold dear European culture and heritage. Germany will
win that vital struggle, be very clear about that.' In a confidential tone
he went on, 'You do not belong among those of the English who are
resisting the Führer and who are set to lose. Germany has no
fundamental quarrel with England. We should be on the same side to
rid the world of Bolshevics and Jews and to establish the rule of high
standards, the traditional standards of both German society and
English society. You are family, Robert, a von Ehrwald by marriage.
Join me now and your future is assured.'

Robert was shocked into silence. Confidently, Klaus went on:

'Hilda, you know the top end of the estate up in the Highlands
was virtually uninhabited. That is where my base is, with my
Widerstands-Korps – how do you say it? – my resistance group.'

His sister remembered the area well: 'Yes. There were ribbons of lovely alpine meadow and woodland like the pictures in the book of Hans Andersen's fairy stories.'

Klaus explained that since their escape from French custody, he and his lieutenants had been busy recruiting local Kamerun men and training them up as a fighting force. There had been no difficulty in keeping out of the way of the British. They were few and most of their civil officers were in the towns.

'Furthermore many people in the *Kamerun-Gebiet* prefer German rule to British and they have a great love of secrecy. We Germans understand the African's preference for the stability of authoritarian rule rather than the uncertainty of so-called democracy that is quite foreign to African tradition and instinct.

'Now I have a force of six-hundred trained riflemen who are a firmly disciplined fighting force, or will be as soon as they get their equipment, for we have had to train them with only a handful of Mausers. They will be a formidable *Abteilung*, disciplined as only a German can discipline blacks, and can use their rifles well. With those men as the spearhead, I shall launch the campaign.'

Klaus then described in detail the operations and objectives. Success would bear heavily on the outcome of General Rommel's attack in the Nile delta and then on the Middle East.

'But rifles, you say?' Robert asked. 'How can you supply weapons for such operations?'

'Germany has supplied them, as Berlin promised. They were sent out from the Reich long ago and are now about to be delivered. The British navy's inspection of neutral vessels for contraband leaving South America for Africa could not be strict. And before they arrive, my troops will have secured the area and we shall then have all the arms we need, delivered by the *Duchessa*.

'We are going to start a blaze, there is no doubt of that. My six-hundred will be the spark for a revolution that will spread like wildfire and will consume the whole British power.'

'There is also a part for us to play in this,' Hilda said excitedly. 'Tell Robert what is proposed, Klaus.'

'The Führer has ordered that a new administration will be put in power, to run the country, using such British officers as swear allegiance to Germany. In view of the alternative, I expect sufficient will do so for our needs. I have the responsibility for selecting the senior men and I want you, Robert, to take over as Gauleiter in place of the present Governor-General. As Gauleiter you will decide the acceptability and posting of all officers and will make all decrees, acting in the name of the Führer. You have the essential experience we need, Robert. Join the winning side and take the top job. You and Hilda deserve the recognition.'

The outline Klaus von Ehrwald gave matched closely Robert Grenville-Fletcher's own concept of how Nigeria should be governed. The fact that Klaus had said almost nothing apart from the proposal he, Robert, should be in charge was no matter; his imagination filled in the blanks in such a way Robert agreed wholeheartedly with the vision. Legislative Council was a gigantic waste of time, as was the tin-pot Igba-rahero council here in Benin. The whole idea of indirect rule which was British government policy for the country was a farce. Talk-talk-talk and the ridiculous notion that in this way black people could be prepared for independence. Independence! They would not be fit to govern themselves for centuries. Germany was right in that respect. The country needed clear direction: he could give that, by God! What Klaus had said about Bolshevism being the deadly enemy was correct: Germany was serving the whole of civilised society in fighting Russia, and Britain should be helping in that, not hindering. Britain had gone to war to support Poland, but that was long finished now. Honour was satisfied; there was no point hanging on in an entirely new strategic situation, with Germany fighting Russia, the communist regime that was totally opposed to British interests and instincts. The British government must surely, even now, be looking for an easy way to reverse things. To change sides was logical, far-sighted, really a duty. He could help by giving the lead here in Nigeria. He could give firm government, keeping the country non-communist, where it was undoubtedly slipping with the present lax attitudes. He would begin by disciplining the fatuous daily papers in Lagos, that were so endlessly troublesome, and were, in fact, incipiently Bolshevic. Hilda would enjoy being the wife of the Governor-General and she would grace the position beautifully.

In his thoughts, Robert had seized on the attractiveness of the trivia, choosing to ignore the fact that these were wholly dependent upon the basic assumption he was not going to pick up the telephone to call the police to arrest Klaus. His mind dallied with the improvements he could make when he had policy in his own hand.

Cracker Armstrong's outburst and the gnawing resentment at Chris Wickham had their final effect. The moment for phoning passed.

Robert failed to realise that Klaus, behind the encouraging smile, was quite ready to squeeze the trigger of the short-barrelled Luger, fitted with a silencer, the butt of which was in the hand under the bush jacket lying loose on his knee. Had he rejected the temptation to be Gauleiter and reached for the telephone, Robert would have died there and then, and Hilda would have immediately accepted that his death at her brother's hand was necessary for the Party and the Fatherland. So much for their marital affection, Heil Hitler!

*   *

Forest Guard Agbontaen took very seriously the instructions he received from Peter on Sunday morning at sun-up, just before Chris, Steve and Peter left for Benin City. He was a small man, only 5 feet 3 inches, with a smooth round face. He had an excellent secondary school record, before gaining good results at the forest training college; although he did not know it, he had been marked by Peter Thorburn as likely to warrant early promotion to forester and probably later to ranger. Like all educated Binis, he spoke excellent English. Bini is such an incredibly difficult language that, in contrast, few Europeans learn to speak it.

The forest guard's orders were to accompany the two NCOs whenever they went out, to look after them and answer their questions to the best of his ability; it was a pleasant change from the routine of measuring cut timber for the assessment of royalty payments and ensuring that trees were not being cut illegally. Chris and Peter knew better than to expect the Commandos to remain indoors indefinitely; the inevitable boredom would sap their morale or, worse, induce a belligerency towards the project and its leaders. Better to give them freedom and a well-informed guide to guard against costly mistakes made in ignorance of the country.

Cracker and Rob arranged that Agbontaen should return to the rest-house around eight o'clock on the Sunday morning to join them as their guide on a walk. The men were suffering from lack of exercise, a surfeit of driving and long periods of loitering about in

75

ships and transit camps. They looked forward to a brisk march round Sapoba, partly for keeping fit but also for the interest of a new place. It turned out to be an extraordinary walk, far from brisk because it was interrupted every few yards by their desire to stop for an explanation of things utterly new to them. Both were countrymen and each tried to relate what he was seeing for the first time in this tropical rain forest to the place he knew, in Lake District and Liddesdale. Great trees – why do they have these buttresses? How do you know the different kinds when you can't even see the leaves? Is this where we get mahogany for furniture at home? Termite mounds – climbing palms like coils of barbed wire with thorns two inches long – a giant snail more than a foot long (You say you can eat it in stew? I don't fancy that for dinner, Rob) – Hornbills (Just like the Guinness advert, Rob) – a flock of a hundred or more swallowtail butterflies sunning themselves on a muddy patch of ground: every turn in the path brought something fresh, stimulating another question. They were interested visitors and Agbontaen a good guide, proud of his place, glad to show it to appreciative visitors.

For the visitors, the forest itself – the Bush – dominated everything. They had no view of it: they were within it, of it. The path they walked was a sinuous crack in the greenery. To leave it for a single step meant using a machete to hack a way through the close stems of lush vegetation. Seedlings, poles, ginger plants, deep green figs and aspidistras, great ropes of lianes, giant buttressed trees: all were in random profusion, webbed together by spiders, buzzing with sweat bees. This was one of nature's world wonders and the men from Cumbria and the treeless Borders were mightily impressed. Puzzled, Rob remarked on the fact the earth was bare under this mass of vegetation, without dead leaves, twigs or even a fallen tree stem, so Agbontaen showed him the dark brown mushroom-shaped nests of the termites that ate dead leaves and wastes of all kinds immediately they fell. The idea of rapid recycling sharpened the men's appreciation of the place: it was not a "timeless forest" but dynamic, living, almost frighteningly engulfing.

As they walked, Rob asked, 'What would be the animal I heard barking during the night, like a little terrier dog? It barked fifteen times, very quick like, then a gap and it barked again twelve or thirteen, then ten, then nine, eight, seven, right down to one, It fairly kept me awake, 'cos I started counting and after a minute or two it began all over again.'

Agbontaen laughed. 'We call it *akwa-wa-wa* and in English tree-bear. I think Mr Thorburn says its proper name is hyrax. It is a very little animal, only one foot long, but it has big claws that make it fit to grip the bark of trees for climbing. A few minutes ago, you ask how a man can name a tree without he can see the leaves and I show you different kinds of bark. There is a story about this and *akwa-wa-wa*.' And walking on some distance, he stopped by a middle-size tree with rough, dark-brown bark and sharp buttresses that extended far above their heads.

'This is the story my granny tell me. One day, long, long ago, Leopard was walking quietly through the bush at night, hunting for something to eat because he was very hungry. So he was happy to catch *akwa-wa-wa*, the little tree-bear, on the ground. *Akwa-wa-wa* had just climbed down one tree where he had been eating fruits and he was crossing to climb the next. Leopard was just going to kill and eat the little bear when *akwa-wa-wa* shouted:

' "Stop, Leopard! Do you know what you are doing, threatening me? I am stronger than you. You better be careful, my friend."

' "Stronger than me, little bear? Don't be so stupid. You are very small," said Leopard who was puzzled by this boast.

' "I am so strong, Leopard, I can even make trees bleed. Can you do that?"

'Leopard could not but he said, "I don't believe you are strong so to make a tree bleed. Show me and prove it, otherwise I go eat you."

'Now this was the tree they were near, an *akume* tree that botanists call Pterocarpus, and when *akwa-wa-wa* dug his claws into the bark and cut it like this' – and Agbontaen cut into the white inner bark a little with his machete – 'so then much bright blood-red juice flowed from the wound.'

' "You see," said *akwa-wa-wa*, "blood even from a tree. Now you know how strong I am, Leopard. So let me go before I get really angry."

'Leopard was very impressed and wanted to avoid trouble in future, so he said, "Please, Mr *Akwa-wa-wa*, in future you go tell me when you come down a tree so I may take a different path and keep out of your way."

' "Very well, Leopard," said the little tree-bear. "When I am climbing down a tree, I go shout loud to let you know."

'And from that time to this, *akwa-wa-wa* always barks:

"Leopard, I come down, down, down, down, down;
I come down, down, down, down;
I come down, down, down;
I come down, down;
I'm DOWN."

Then he runs across to the next tree and climbs out of reach. And of course the white inner bark of every *akume* tree bleeds red blood whenever it is cut.'

'It's a great story,' Rob said. 'Like a private version of the *Just So Stories* we read at school.'

'Is the wood useful?' asked the ever-earthy Cracker Armstrong.

'Oh, yes,' he was assured, as they walked on. 'It is hard and is not eaten by termites. It is used for making canoes and for spades, and the wood chips are sold in all our markets for dyeing cloth; it makes a beautiful deep red colour.'

The path passed close to an area where big trees were being cut and the sound of singing led them down a track to a small clearing. Here was a line of logs four or five feet in diameter, each over twenty feet long, cut from the felled trunk. The felling gang, wearing only shorts and straw hats – no shoes – were busy converting one log from the round to a square baulk. Eight men each side were chopping great notches on the top side of the log, eight axes coming down with a single "chunk" in unison, then eight from the opposing team – "chunk", sweat pouring from lean brown bodies that glittered in the harsh sunlight. The air was filled with the bitter smell of freshly cut mahogany wood. A drummer and two young acolytes provided the beat and the chant which Agbontaen explained coyly was "for men only". The logs would be hauled to the river and floated down to the port of Sapele. It gave them a glimpse of the industry of Benin.

Cracker asked if Agbontaen knew where the hunter had shot the duiker they had enjoyed at breakfast the day before. He could not say but on the return towards the rest-house their way took them through Sapoba Camp, the small thatched village housing the forest workers, and they stopped at the hunter's house. Two women were pounding cassava in a two-foot high wooden mortar, using long wooden pestles that thudded in turn into the white powder; a flock of little naked children screamed excitedly at the sight of the white visitors and ran giggling indoors.

On the guard's greeting, one of the women went into the mud-walled house and brought out her husband. The man had no English and the translation of his complicated description of where he shot the little antelope was meaningless; interest was instantly revived, however, when he went indoors and returned with his gun. The soldiers, whatever thought they had given to the shooting, were utterly unprepared for the Dane gun he carried. It was a smooth-bore muzzle-loader, with a barrel five feet long and three-quarters of an inch in bore. The hunter showed them his black gunpowder and demonstrated the flint lock by which it was fired. It was an eye-opener to find that the Nigerian was confined by law to using technology two centuries old.

'It would be good fun to go out hunting with him,' Cracker said to Agbontaen, 'but I would not want to be near when he fired that old thing. It would be more danger to the man who fires it than to the target.'

Translation was not required for their final entertainment, as the hunter mimed the whole sequence of actions in loading the gun, lighting the acetylene lamp he had had on his headband, calling up the antelope with a bleat, just like a lamb at home, and finally firing. "Bang!" he said, in any language. It was a great diversion.

'Aren't you glad you came?' Cracker asked rhetorically, as he and Rob went back for lunch.

Sunday lunch was curried chicken with a bewildering number of extremely tasty side dishes; "small chop" the steward called them, from shredded red chillies to paw-paw and fried plantains. They enjoyed it thoroughly but in the moist heat found it induced sleep and they fell naturally into the common habit of the siesta.

In the cool of the late afternoon they went for a swim. The lowering sun showed the Jamieson River at its most beautiful. The air was warm and the water deliciously refreshing. Great trees arched branches against the deep blue sky and squadrons of huge fruit bats flew over, all on exactly the same straight course, thousands upon thousands, steadily and continuously for more than half-an-hour, all travelling from their roost to some feeding site miles distant in this vast forest. The cicadas shrilled as the soldiers sat silent on the little canoe pier, hypnotised by the perfect peace and majesty of the scene, stunned by the magnitude of the flight of bats.

While they sat, a raft of logs came stealing round a bend in the river, each log roped to its neighbours to form a wooden worm, flexibly taking the gentle bends in the river. The raft flowed with the slow current, silently gliding downstream perhaps a couple of miles in the hour, guided now and again by the thrust of a pole from one of three or four men, towards some distant timber depot and the ships at Sapele. They passed, each raftsman giving a countryman's quiet friendly greeting to the soldier strangers, just as a boatman on a placid evening on the Essex coast or a shepherd coming off Skiddaw or the hill above Langholm would nod to strangers in their place.

The gentleness of the greeting from the raft-men touched Rob deeply, more so because of the idyllic setting. The contrast between this and usual army life was startling.

'The country folk here are really nice, these chaps on the raft, this forest man Agbontaen, the hunter and his wife. They're not what I expected black people to be like in Africa. I dunno, I thought they would be wild and uncivilised savages. That Ranger Eweka at Peter's office in Benin might have been a sergeant-major back home, 'cept for his cut-up face. And the Oba is a real gent, seems he was at Cambridge, from what he was saying. It's not what I expected.'

'Aye. You're right, Rob. We're bloody lucky to be here on this trip. There's maybe going to be a little fire-fight to get hold of this Duchess-ship, that's what we've come out for. And we've got this holiday as a bonus. There's good food, our own servants to cook and serve at table, fill the bath, wash the clothes – never had that in the Kosbies. We've a country house to ourselves as a billet, private swimming river, hunting if we want it, our own gardens stocked with the very best of fruit: I don't believe the Duke of Buccleuch has it so good. I'll bet the Colonel doesn't have a billet the like of this. So far it's an OK posting. Enjoy it while you can, lad!'

It was an instruction from his sergeant that Corporal Graham fully accepted.

The need to slap at a biting mosquito broke the spell, reminding them of the need to retreat to the house and change for the evening. But Sapoba had one final surprise. As they walked up to the house in the night's stillness, sparks of light appeared in the bushes and over the ground. In a matter of minutes ten million fireflies lit themselves up, pulsating little greenish golden points of brightness, like a carpet of stars between the river and the house. It was a sight of exquisite beauty beyond the imagination of the men. Africa was turning on the style, weaving a web that would entangle these two soldiers, although they did not yet know it, for their whole lives.

CHAPTER SEVEN

On Monday morning the Resident had an official engagement at Ekehuan, a large village twenty miles southwest of Benin City. He had been invited by the Irish fathers to open a new Catholic school serving the Ekehuan district; it was not an important function and he was not a churchy man, but it pleased him to be seen acting as "lord of the manor". With his mind in a turmoil over the extraordinary proposal from Klaus, he did not go to the office at seven o'clock, which was his usual drill, but instead ordered his car for eight at the house and told his driver to go directly to Ekehuan, in good time for the opening ceremony at the school.

Alone in the back of the Mercedes, he thought further about Klaus' proposals. These were frightfully dangerous. But the prize! My God, what a prize! To be Governor-General of the country, of all West Africa if he played his cards skilfully. Won't bother opening any more Catholic Mission schools after this. Finally fix that blighter Christopher Wickham, that is a certainty. He has had it now. Wonder who those two ruffians were with him at Sapoba on Saturday: Scotchmen, or Scotsmen or whatever they call themselves, presumably with Thorburn the forestry man; he's Scotch also. They're all damned uncouth rough types, don't dress properly and undisciplined. That's one thing about the Ehrwalds – in fact all the Germans – they are disciplined. Admire that. Discipline, that's what this country needs. Lacking in Britain too; can't do anything about Britain but I can sort out this place. I shall enforce discipline when I take over. The natives will appreciate that. Come to think of it, whether they appreciate it or not, there will be no more softness, no more commuted sentences, no more indirect rule. I shall say what happens and anyone who steps out of line will get the chop. I'll begin by taking proper control of the press and radio. Damned clever thinking by Klaus to set the Ibos against the Hausas; if he gets that lot started the take-over is assured. Everything depends on the delivery of the rifles. German efficiency again in getting them sent to Fernando Po for the Italian *Duchess* ship to deliver. They are well organised, say what you like. Klaus will go back the day after tomorrow to Cameroons to start the whole show.

In his thoughts Grenville-Fletcher was far away: with Klaus in the Cameroons; with Hilda in Government House; taking the salute at a parade on the Marina in Lagos. The road to Ekehuan did not register at all.

There had been normal traffic on the road for the first few miles out of the City. Then it had thinned. As they passed through the village of Iguome, the driver registered the surprising fact there was not a person to be seen on the street or around the houses. Two miles farther on they rounded a bend and there was a tree across the road. It was not a huge tree but enough to block the road. It was half-past-eight.

The driver, subconsciously warned by the unnatural quietness of the last village, sat behind the wheel and peered about him suspiciously. Grenville-Fletcher, having observed nothing in his reverie, regarded it simply as a naturally fallen tree. Affronted at this interruption to his schedule, he stepped out of the car so that, at closer range, he might glare at the obstruction, as if "Residential" fury might clear the branches and trunk that were in his way.

From behind the car three men slipped silently from the dense undergrowth at the roadside. One wore a short cloak and an elaborately carved wooden head-mask, grotesquely painted in black and yellow ochre; the others were naked to the waist, their bodies glistened with oil. Without a word, each half-naked man gripped one of Grenville-Fletcher's arms and, seizing him also by the waistband of his trousers, ran him, loudly protesting, into the forest. The masked man signalled unmistakably to the driver and, in Bini, said:

'Go now, quick as fire,' adding 'or I will ju-ju you, one time'.

From such an authority the driver needed no second telling; quickly he reversed the car into a three-point turn and drove back towards the city at high speed.

Completely indifferent to the Resident's protests, the two men ran and half-dragged Grenville-Fletcher for two or three hundred yards into the forest until he found himself facing a small, smooth-barked tree. His arms were pulled round the stem and his wrists quickly tied together. In two seconds more his shirt was ripped open and a single thrust with a knife cut the waistband of his trousers which fell to his ankles. The third man, now unmasked, then spoke in English. He was known to the Resident who had seen him regularly at council meetings.

'Mr. Grenville-Fletcher, you will now answer my questions quickly and correctly. I tell you not to shake the tree because you will make things even more uncomfortable for yourself.' To the Resident's protests he added, 'I tell you for sure, my friend, you will answer all my questions. You go tell me everything I ask. Every man tied to an ogeime tree always answers questions.'

At a sign from him, one of the other men slashed some branches from the tree, above the Resident's head. Large ants poured from the hollow tubes of the cut branches, alarmed at the attack on their home and intent on defending it. With the first few vicious bites, each drawing blood, Robert Grenville-Fletcher jerked involuntarily and shook the tree, which he had been advised not to do; the shaking signalled to the ant colony that heavy reinforcements were required to resist an attack. Ten thousand soldiers answered the call.

*   *

Monday was a day Chris Wickham would remember in sharp detail for the rest of his life. The action began at the breakfast table when Chris summoned his cook at half-past six, to that man's surprise, and instructed him to intercept the Residency cook at market and bring him to the district office. Chris wanted independent information as to whether there was a visitor at the Residency. It was universal practice for cooks of European employers to go to market each morning, as much to meet their friends as under the necessity of shopping; there was no doubt the two cooks would meet. Chris' normal working day opened at seven o'clock at the office with the usual review of impending court cases and routine administration.

All through this, which Chris could run almost on auto-pilot, he thought of the successes and failures of the previous day. With the Oba's help he had met Joshua Oshodin, reputed to have recent knowledge of Santa Isabel. He was a young man of about twenty years, whom Chris recognised immediately as intelligent, shrewd and having an agenda of his own or, more likely, of his family. The two men saw that their interests coincided; on the evidence of Joshua's observations of the Italian ship, Chris was clear, independently of the Oba's pressure, there was a strong case for the young Nigerian coming to Fernando Po, so long as he agreed to obey orders for the benefit of the main party. He made the point there could be no diversion to allow Joshua to negotiate private trade deals for rubber or any other product and that he must accept orders from Chris as the leader of the party, which Joshua readily agreed. Chris had the impression that he had been well primed by the Oba, which was itself encouraging as implying a prior endorsement of Chris' terms by local higher authority. Joshua would come to Fernando Po.

As Panda had predicted, the *Duchessa di Lucca* was anchored off-shore, a few hundred yards from the beach in the middle of the mile-wide Santa Isabel bay, immediately in front of the town and quite close to the shore that must shelve very steeply. Joshua had seen packing cases being trans-shipped from a South American freighter anchored nearby and friends told him this work had been going on for two days. Both ships were working the cargo with their own derricks and winches, loading the cases into and out of small boats that plied between them. The cases appeared quite heavy but were small, although Joshua was uncertain about the size because he had not been looking at the ships particularly and only took notice of the operation when his rubber-trading contact had commented on the fact the Italian ship, having been there for more than a year, now looked surprisingly active and perhaps was soon going to sea. The Fernando Po man and he had considered whether there was any advantage for them to be made from this burst of activity by the Italians but had decided with regret that there was none; they had observed the ship casually, not as their primary interest, Joshua apologised. The contact had remarked, however, the curious fact that the captain of the Italian ship very seldom came ashore, not even to go to mass at the cathedral as the remaining crew did regularly; it was curious. There was at least one passenger still aboard, because he and the ship's officers were seen daily on deck under an awning rigged to provide shade. Joshua saw them clearly because the ship was only two hundred yards from the beach.

Chris asked Joshua about the presence of Spanish soldiers or armed police. The Nigerian was unsure about soldiers but said there were many policía, garde, customsmen and so on, all in brightly coloured uniforms, green, purple, pink – he did not know which were which – and all usually carrying arms, some rifles, most pistols. There were no Spanish naval vessels during Joshua's visit and there did not appear to be any special interest in the anchored ships; Joshua felt there was more concentration on preventing the smuggling of rubber but agreed with a laugh that was because he had a guilty conscience about that activity. One surprise for Chris was Joshua's news that most Africans on the island understood English quite well, in spite of it being a Spanish colony, a legacy of long-past British occupation.

Chris felt pleased at the recruitment of Joshua Oshodin: an intelligent and observant young man. As a bonus, he was a lively character with a sense of humour, who could be an entertaining companion if he overcame a diffidence as the only Nigerian in the party. Nevertheless Chris admitted to himself that Joshua's inclusion could well create difficulties; some people recruited for the operation might not be as liberal as himself and could regard Joshua as a second-class member, as a black man. On balance, however, he would be an asset because his knowledge and contacts were vital for success.

Joshua's feelings after the interview were twisted like the stem of a fig tree. It was his father's wish – and obviously the Oba's also — that he should join Mr Wickham in a secret journey to Santa Isabel. He knew the centre of interest was the Italian ship he had seen there on his two previous visits; that was obvious from the white man's questions, and his news the ship was taking in boxes from the other ship in the harbour had excited Mr Wickham. The Oba had told his father this knowledge and Joshua's local contacts would give him special value and standing as a member of the group for an operation there. That was good but there was another side to that membership. It was a group of white men. He would be alone, one African among all these Europeans. How would they treat him? He was nervous, fearful of being treated like a servant; already defensive anger was rising in him at the very thought an Oshodin should be so regarded but at the same time mindful of his father's wishes and conscious of his lack of years.

86

With Joshua in this troubled state of mind, the two Oshodins, father and son, presented themselves at the palace to report to the Oba. Half-an-hour later a much more determined young man emerged, having been instructed by the Oba himself on the opportunities the operation presented and his duties in it. His father and the king had reminded him of the leadership exercised by his family in Benin's history, to stiffen his self-confidence. He was as strong as any white man; he had the advantage of knowing more about Santa Isabel and the Italian ship than any of them, because he had been there. This was a war expedition and he was an Oshodin, of the war-chief's family. The clinching argument to stiffen his resolve was the Oba's reminder of the Bini tradition:

'As war chiefs, your ancestors never came back empty-handed. They either died in battle or – far more often – took over their enemy's country with its inhabitants as slaves and wives. We do not require you to do either of those on this expedition but I am confident you have power to do just as much for your family tradition and for Benin as any of your grandfathers. Be strong! Wickham, leader of this party, is a good man and will treat you well. I am sure of this.'

Before meeting Oshodin, Chris and Peter had succeeded in telephoning Ondo, something of a record for a Sunday morning. Nigeria's telephone system at the time was primitive and temperamental. The conversation with "Clapper" Bell had been difficult, not merely because of the need to shout most sentences twice:

'Yes, of course I shall talk to Peter, if he comes to Ondo but what is it all about? Sorry I can't come to meet him half way. I have no transport this weekend. Why can't you tell me why he's coming?' and so on.

Peter left midmorning to drive to Ondo and probably would not return until Monday afternoon. Chris had good hopes of Bell, even though he did not know him personally. His puzzlement about the reason for meeting was quite natural; it must appear quite ridiculous that Peter should be prepared to drive a long way to meet him but would not say on the phone what was the purpose of coming.

Meantime Steve had been interviewing Hudson. He came back to Chris with a mixed report. Eddie Hudson was a Tynesider, tough and thickset. The son of a Northumbrian coast fisherman, he went to sea full-time at age fifteen, although he had been in and around boats since he could toddle and had often been on short inshore fishing trips before leaving school. From inshore fishing he graduated to the distant water fishing fleet out of Grimsby and from that moved to big ships as an engineer. Eddie was cagey about his qualifications as an engineer and Steve had the impression it was the lack of certificates that contributed to the next turn in his career. Laid off in 1930, Eddie was unemployed and, with very many well-qualified engineers applying for the few vacancies, had found the sea offered no future. Instead he had married and taken work as a maintenance man ashore. A year or two later he became a clerk of works for maintenance on coastguard stations and just before the war was recruited by the Colonial Office as a foreman in the Public Works Department in Nigeria.

Steve, who had seen a few, described Eddie as a rough character who would need firm orders from someone standing no nonsense.

'I am sure Panda has met plenty Eddies in his time and will cope with him well. He agreed quite readily to come on the operation and asked what appeared to be such sensible questions about the ship's engines, I guess he will handle the situation adequately. He is outspoken and may be a tricky companion; as long as that is not allowed to create difficulties, I believe we have enough of an engineer to serve the purpose.'

On Sunday afternoon Chris and Steve had visited the Residency, ostensibly to apologise for the previous day's upset at Sapoba, in an attempt to divert further inquisitiveness concerning the operation by smoothing Grenville-Fletcher's ruffled feathers. More importantly, their purpose was to investigate whether a German visitor was present. They felt quite unable to confront their Resident and question him directly about the man, since to do so would inevitably imply that Grenville-Fletcher was traitorously hiding an enemy. The man was undoubtedly a pompous ass but surely not more.

The Residency garden looked especially beautiful. Two Flame of the Forest trees were draped with cascades of brilliant cadmium red blossoms, far more flowers than leaves. A pink cassia made a superb contrast with the bright blue sky and beds of canna lilies were great splashes of gold against their own green and magenta leaves. The men admired the effect when they greeted their host, and congratulated him. In a land where so much of the countryside was untamed forest and the farmland was anything but neat, gardening was a hobby amounting to a passion for many British officers and standards were high. Garden boys were cheap to employ and keen to learn, and in the tropical climate results were quickly achieved. Steve and Chris found the Resident in the garden and talked as they walked there; their enthusiasm and praise for the blooms were genuine and well merited. They were not invited into the house itself.

The visit was curiously inconclusive. Quite out of character, Grenville-Fletcher had made light of the Sapoba incident, brushing aside the need for any apology from his officers. He did not offer them tea, although it was tea-time, nor a drink, saying that Hilda was unwell and unable to meet them: a touch of fever, he explained. They were sorry to hear that. They had heard the Resident and his wife had visitors the previous day. Yes, an old friend from home passed through yesterday, on leave from the Army, en route to Onitsha and Eastern Provinces, posted to some new job in Enugu; unfortunately he couldn't stay. Such a pity when old friends called for only an hour or two, whom one had not seen for years.

Dissatisfied though they were, Chris and Steve were unable to follow the affair further without blunt questioning and accusation, that would have courted direct rebuttal from their senior officer. Nevertheless both were unconvinced by the performance. The Resident appeared to be playing the part of a bluff, genial squire, quite unlike the martinet they knew him to be. He did not give the old friend in the army a name or rank, and there were no circumstantial details of his background – from school or university or whatever – just an "old friend" who, extraordinarily, was reported to have spoken fluent German. Ex-stand-off Tigger did not buy that dummy. Grenville-Fletcher was lying and not doing it well but it was not easy immediately to gather clear evidence of wrongdoing.

On Monday morning the DO's first action in his office was to send a telegram to Captain Moore at Port Harcourt, using the simple code they had arranged. News that the ship might soon be sailing forced a new urgency in the whole operation.

'LADYS HEALTH DETERIORATING FAST STOP VISIT NOW MORE URGENT THAN PREVIOUSLY THOUGHT STOP PLEASE ARRANGE PASSAGES FOR TIGGER RUGBY TEAM AND FIVE

RESERVES IE TWENTY IN ALL LEAVING
FRIDAY STOP IS SAILING FROM WICK
POSSIBLE AS THIS MORE CONVENIENT THAN
ALTERNATIVES BUT NOT ESSENTIAL STOP
OTHERWISE OBAN SATURDAY STOP
WICKHAM'

Wick was their private code name for Warri, a small seaport in the delta, southeast of Sapoba. Oban was code for Opobo, far to the east, near Calabar. From Sapoba it would be more convenient to embark at Warri than at Port Harcourt, Opobo or any other port east of the Niger delta that was two hundred miles across and lacked east-west roads. All the eastern ports would require the party to make the long road journey by Asaba and Onitsha. Sapele as the alternative was inconveniently far west for the sea voyage, although very close to Sapoba; in contrast, Opobo would require a long road journey but offered a short sea crossing. It now appeared they would have to be a larger group than was contemplated when they met at Sapoba but then they had not thought to arrange a code cover for numbers of people.

Chris had just written out the telegram for despatch when the office messenger told him his cook and another man were outside. Without hesitation or finesse, Chris proceeded to question the Resident's cook. Was madam sick?

'No Sah, she is well.'

'Is there a visitor man at the Residency?'

'Yes Sah, one man come two days ago.'

'Is he still there?'

'Yes Sah, he dae there now-now.'

'Who is this man, what place he come from?'

The cook gave a pout of pursed lips to show his inability to answer the questions but said:

'Jeremiah say he not British man, maybe he is brother of madam, same-father-same-mother.'

Chris knew the Residency steward boy was Jeremiah, the name curiously apt: he must have had plenty to complain about. There was nothing more to be gained from the cook but usefully he had confirmed rumours about the white visitor; the odds on him turning out to be Hilda's brother had shortened sharply. Certainly Hilda was not sick, as G-F had claimed, and there was a white visitor at the Residency.

'I dash you one shilling,' Chris said to him, 'so you do not say to madam we talk here. This is secret. Do you agree?' And at the cook's ready agreement, Chris said, '*Obeyivah*', meaning 'Hold out your hands' and the cook went away happy. In the light of Hilda's reputation with her servants, Chris was fairly certain his small investment raised the cook's regard for him well above the lady's and the secret would be safe.

Chris now faced the reality that his belief in the integrity of Grenville-Fletcher had been entirely misplaced; his senior officer was not merely a pompous ass, he was also a fool, a liar and probably a traitorous knave. The issue could be dodged no longer. Chris would have to confront the man with the evidence and demand a proper explanation prior to immediate action. No point in delaying. Best do it now. He walked the short distance to the Provincial Office and asked the chief clerk if the Resident was in.

'Unfortunately no, sir. We expected him this morning but he has not come to the office. I believe the Resident must have gone directly to his appointment at Ekehuan. Later this morning he is opening Father O'Malley's new school there'.

Chris checked his watch; it was now 0845. Frustrated in his effort to confront Grenville-Fletcher, he felt the need to follow up the enquiry to ensure the man had really gone to Ekehuan. On arriving back at his office, he jumped into his car and drove to the Residency, about a mile from the town centre. He did not drive in because he had no wish to interview Hilda or to alarm her brother into flight (assuming he was the visitor and still there); he would deal with him later, after the Resident himself. Stripped of his brother-in-law's protection, the risk of him escaping successfully, a white man in a black country, seemed very slight. Instead he spoke to the police constable on the gate. Had he seen the Resident this morning?

'Yes, Sah. He leave by car with the driver at 8 o'clock and he not yet return. When I come on duty early dis morning, the driver tell me he is to go to Ekehuan-side with the Resident.'

The thought came to Chris to examine the famous book in the sentry box across the gateway. There was no entry for "the old friend on his way to Enugu"; given the importance G-F attached to such etiquette, the absence of a signature was more good circumstantial evidence the friend was fictitious. Nevertheless his meeting with the Resident would have to wait his return from Ekehuan.

'When you see the Resident come back, constable, you must send word to me immediately. I shall tell the inspector to send another policeman to join you here, with a bicycle, so you can tell me "one-time" you have seen the Resident come home.'

There was apparently nothing more he could do for the moment, so he returned to the town, gave instructions to the police about the need for a second constable at the gate and before nine o'clock was back at his office handling the routine work of the Benin Division. With his mind now focused on the Grenville-Fletcher saga, the files received less than his full attention.

As he worked, the grass in front of the District Office was being cut by a gang of a dozen convicts under the supervision of a warder. The men cut the grass as closely as any mowing machine, moving across the lawn in echelon, each man wielding a langa-langa, a three-foot length of hoop-iron hammered to a cutting edge. They worked strictly in unison, with a chant reminiscent of a sea shanty, making a pleasant background to Chris' work. At the end of each swathe across the lawn, the men chatted and laughed amongst themselves and with their guard. Chris was conscious he had sent most of them to prison from his court and he wondered how much of a punishment this was; they seemed happy enough and certainly made no effort to leave their party for the open street only twenty yards away. He smiled, shrugged and went back to his reading; the convicts had fewer worries than he had.

*   *

The Ninth Fallschirmjäger-Gruppe was not having an easy time. They hit trouble when they came down from the stony ridges of the Tibesti into the dunes. Keeping a vehicle's momentum on the soft sand was vital: any check was almost certain to result in the rear wheels breaking through and burying themselves axle-deep. Then the men had to dig, manoeuvre the metal channels under the wheels and slowly get back to firmer ground. And when one vehicle bogged it was almost inevitable that others were checked and they bogged also.

The midday shade temperature was 48° C; the only bother was there was no shade. The going was soft and in fifteen ghastly hours of driving they had covered only 25 km.

Nevertheless Oberst Eichel was not despondent. The men were performing well; they were the very best, determined, trained. Time would be made up when the column reached harder ground.

They would have to make up the time!

*   *

The terrified driver drove the Mercedes hard away from the ambush, racing back to the town. A few minutes after nine o'clock, missing the DO by only ten minutes, the car swept past the constable at the Residency gate. Following the DO's instructions, the policeman carefully checked that the Resident was not on board and then relaxed: no action was called for.

It was part chance, part fear of the police and mainly Bini psychology that brought the driver back to the Residency. The ambush appeared to be a ju-ju matter and therefore strictly a family affair; the police had no power over ju-ju, so the driver came to the ambushed man's wife to report what had just happened. Furthermore, the driver had no wish to have more to do with the police than he could help; drivers and police were on opposite sides, so again his instinct was to go to his employer's home rather than the police barracks. He found that the cook was at market and Jeremiah was out on his own business, aware that his master was away for the morning, leaving only the "small boy" to attend to minor household chores. There was no help for the hapless driver from him.

Shaking as a result of the trauma he had experienced and with fear at the prospect of breaking the frightful news to madam, he timidly entered the house and tiptoed upstairs to the veranda where Hilda and Klaus had breakfasted, looking out over the neat lawns and the flamy blossom-laden trees. He stood silent in front of them, his face no longer its usual warm brown but the curious green that a black man goes when he is in deep shock, trying but failing to speak for fully half a minute. It was abundantly obvious to them that something extremely serious had happened but it was only with coaxing and

93

patient questioning they teased the stammered story from him. Neither the man's description of the events nor his judgment of the outcome gave grounds for optimism.

'The ju-ju man will kill the master,' he said in conclusion, wide-eyed and quivering with terror at the memory of the hideous mask and the more hideous power that lay behind it, power to will him to death even now.

Hilda instinctively clapped her hand to her mouth at this and Klaus put a strong arm round her shoulders. He spoke in German:

'Be strong! You must be strong. It may not be as bad as that. But what has happened has happened. We cannot change it. You must be strong for the Reich. Remember you are a Junkerin. The Führer expects every German man and woman to be as resolute as our soldiers on the Russian front, continuing to do our duty even when casualties are sustained. Remember also: I have my orders from the Führer and nothing must stand in the way, not even Robert's assassination, if that is what has happened. We are all in the front line: you, Robert, myself.'

The driver still stood before them, understanding not a word of what had been said. Klaus, now speaking English, asked him if he had come directly from the hold-up back to the Residency. Yes. Had he spoken to anyone about the roadblock and the seizure of his master? No, he said vehemently.

'That is good,' said Klaus encouragingly, 'Stand there and wait,' at which the man visibly relaxed. Apparently he had done the right thing coming here; it had gone better than he dared hope and he was not being given the blame.

In German Klaus then took his sister logically over the consequences of the tragedy. They had nothing to gain by going to the police. The ambush and probable assassination of Robert would be treated as a first class emergency. Police and military people would descend on the place in hordes and Klaus, if he remained, was certain to be spotted and captured, ruining Berlin's plans. Therefore he must go immediately. But he would not willingly abandon his sister. If Robert was dead, what was there for Hilda here, a von Ehrwald in a foreign and enemy country? If Robert, under stress, had talked of the plan for the revolution, Hilda would be subjected to intense questioning to reveal more and might face imprisonment.

'You cannot help Robert now. But you can help me greatly

because you are someone I can trust implicitly, and thereby you can help the Third Reich and our beloved Führer. Put your grief aside, liebe Hilda, and come with me. We shall be comrades-in-arms. That is your duty, as a von Ehrwald and a daughter of the Fatherland.'

Hilda stiffened at these words. It was not as though she felt deeply attached to Robert. Come to think about it, the marriage had been a convenience for both of them rather than a passionate love; it gave Robert a beautiful hostess for his position as Resident and also membership of a wealthy land-owning family in Germany, whose politics were close to his own; and it gave Hilda position and power as the wife of a very senior British colonial officer. Nevertheless, one had to admit, Robert was a pompous old bore without a spark of humour. She was sad if he had gone, but if he had – well – life had to go on. She did not want to be left alone, friendless in this British colonial station and, quite clearly, Klaus had to leave at once.

Against this, there was the excitement offered by her brother. Hitler had given him an important role in forging the future success of Germany in Africa and Klaus was inviting her to join him and play a part in that magnificent programme. The Kamerun Abteilung would spark the revolution among the Ibos, leading to the take-over of Nigeria and the rout of the British. The prospect dazzled her. Robert's ambush and death (she now assumed him to be dead) acquired new meaning, part of the plan, liberating her for greater things. She stood upright and looked at Klaus.

'*Was befehlst Du, mein Bruder?*' 'What are your orders, brother?'

'Excellent, Hilda. You will come with me. I am happy you have decided that. We leave immediately for the East in the Mercedes. I shall abandon the motorbike here. Pack a small tin trunk with clothes suitable for the bush, with several changes, your toilet things, a couple of towels, mosquito net, mosquito boots for evenings, your jodhpurs if they are handy. Take a camp bed if you can, but only if it causes no delay. Money. We must have petrol. Does this man have petrol coupons? No! Then does Robert keep them in his desk? We will be in deep trouble if we have no petrol. But in any event we must be out of here in fifteen minutes at the latest in order to keep ahead of those who will be coming for us. Go and pack now. We shall search for petrol coupons later. We shall want some food also, and as much drinking water as there is. And don't forget the cash.'

Klaus grabbed the driver by the arm and walked him firmly to his bedroom where he made the man hold things as the easiest way of ensuring he was kept incommunicado, while Klaus gathered his clothes together. The driver then carried cases to the car. Ten minutes sufficed for the packing. A quick search of Robert's desk produced both petrol coupons and cash in the same locked drawer; all were taken.

The puzzled trainee steward or small boy was ordered to bring all the bottles of filtered and boiled water available, two loaves of bread and two tins of bully beef. This done, he stood expectantly as the loading was completed; the driver was already behind the wheel. Hilda told the boy she was 'going out with this master' and, suiting action to the words, they left.

At the gate, following the District Officer's instruction, a police corporal had joined the constable. They looked carefully at the car as it passed and agreed the Resident was not a passenger. No action was called for. The time was nine-thirtyfive.

*   *

That same morning Agbontaen took the two soldiers along a riverside path beyond Sapoba camp to a small clearing containing two huts. On the river bank were several long logs, a great litter of wood chips and two canoes obviously in the course of construction. Three men were at work and Agbontaen explained the old man and his two sons were employed as canoe builders by the Benin Native Authority Forest Department; they were not Binis but Jekris, river people.

'They're making dug-out canoes, Cracker. Real stone-age stuff,' said Rob, going forward to look at these curiosities.

The Englishman followed the popular misconception that a "dug-out canoe" is a log crudely hollowed out on one side, blunt at both ends; so they are depicted by artists. In fact those who could make a canoe from a single log were highly skilled craftsmen and their products were robust vessels of great beauty. Working with axes and adzes on a flawless log some eighteen feet long, the builders had shaped the outside of the canoe and hollowed the interior roughly. The hollowed log had been filled with water to saturate the wood, then emptied and, when the solders arrived, had fires smouldering inside

96

throughout its length, although not to burn away the interior. In effect the green wood was being steamed so that it could be bent by gently hammering in props between the gunwales at intervals. As a result the finished canoes were considerably wider in the beam than the logs they had been cut from, with a graceful sheer at the bow. After the fire and steam treatment, the hull was finished to a thickness of three-quarters of an inch. It was a wasteful method of boat-building but, given the superabundance of the forest resource, quite a reasonable one and, far from being a clumsy hollowed-out log, the craft-built canoe was both graceful and a good load-carrier.

Rob was impressed; he knew about boats and enjoyed watching the Jekri men at work. It is always worth watching a craftsman. When the Jekris saw genuine interest, they were happy to explain, albeit mostly in sign language, and eager to take the soldiers out on the river in the finished canoe. Driven by the spear-shaped paddles, it handled well and was surprisingly fast. Initially the old man sat as steersman on the flat stern; then Rob and Cracker took turns and, much to the Jekris' surprise and delight, made a good fist of the job. It was a real holiday.

*　　　*

The Mercedes left Benin on the eastern road, heading for Agbor and Asaba where there was a ferry across the River Niger, just above its break-up into the delta. Five miles clear of Benin's outskirts, where the road was clear, nothing in sight, Klaus suddenly shouted 'Stop!' Automatically the driver obeyed. Klaus got out and looked at the rear near-side wheel. He called to the driver who left his seat and joined Klaus, finding him bent down looking intently at the wheel. As the driver bent down to do the same, Klaus straightened himself. There was a sharp crack and the driver fell, shot in the back of the head with the 9mm Luger automatic pistol.

Klaus walked quickly round to the driver's door and the car moved off fast towards Asaba, leaving the body lying in the red dust.

*　　　*

At half-past eleven news reached police headquarters in Benin City that a man's dead body lay at the roadside near Aduwawa, six miles away. The delay of more than ninety minutes in reporting the body was not unusual, particularly in view of the absence of telephones in the countryside. Those who saw the body of a dead stranger were inclined to ignore it on the principle that by reporting it they might be accused by the police of being implicated in the death in some way. In this instance a European timber agent driving into town had spotted the body and brought news of it directly to the police.

The police inspector who received the report assumed, since the body was described as being on the north verge of the road in the country, away from all houses, death was the result of a road traffic accident, a hit-and-run driver. He arranged for the body to be collected and driven directly to the public mortuary at the hospital. The drill was he should inform the District Officer, as magistrate, there had been a sudden death, cause unknown but presumably an RTA, and inform the Medical Officer that the body was coming his way. He did all this and Chris provisionally accepted the assumption of the hit-and-run road death of an unknown man.

Peter Thorburn drove into Benin soon after one o'clock, having successfully completed the trip to Ondo where he had seen George "Clapper" Bell. He stopped at his office in the old fort to have a quick check all was well, before walking the short distance to the District Office. There he was greeted by Steve and together they went into Chris' room where Peter told his friends about meeting and recruiting Clapper. It had been very successful and he got as far as 'Guess whom I met in the Club ...?', when the office messenger came in accompanied by the well dressed chief clerk from the Provincial Office, whom Chris had spoken to earlier in the day. Mr Ebue was a model civil servant.

'Forgive me coming over unannounced, Mr Wickham, but I am somewhat alarmed. I have just had a telephone conversation with Father O'Malley at Ekehuan. He says that the Resident has never arrived this morning. As I told you, he was supposed to open the new school, I believe at a quarter past ten. I am anxious in case the Resident is stranded on the road with his motor car broken down. Do you think it might be advisable to send a car towards Ekehuan to pick him up? I should be grateful if I might leave the problem with you, because of course I do not have transport available myself.'

Steve saw the concern on Chris' face, as he linked this latest news with the knowledge of Grenville-Fletcher's lying about the visitor who was possibly his German brother-in-law. Had G-F "done a runner"? Steve realised the urgent need to follow up this development and to be able to do so in some privacy. It was he who spoke.

'It is very thoughtful of you, Mr Ebue, to be concerned in case the Resident is stranded on the road. We shall take immediate action. In fact, if Mr Wickham wishes, I can go down myself by car. Thank you for coming over with that news from Father O'Malley. I suggest you should return to your office now to wait for further news, in case the Resident phones in.' While saying this, Steve was shepherding Mr Ebue to the door so that there was no opportunity for the clerk to linger.

Chris grabbed the phone and asked to be put through to the Public Works Engineer. Waiting for the call, he said to the others:

'Four and a half hours! If the road was blocked by an accident, he would have been back here long ago. If the Mercedes had broken down or had an accident, we would have heard before now. This is more serious. Hello, Tom. Tigger here. This is urgent. Have you reports about the state of the Ekehuan road this morning, anything at all unusual?' A pause. 'You have! I see. Look, I am sending Peter Thorburn down there right now with armed police. Will you please pull out all the stops and get some of your chaps there with whatever they need to clear the road? If you could go yourself and give this top priority, I would be especially glad. I am afraid there has been a very serious incident, as Peter will explain to you there. Not over the phone, you will understand. Bye for now.'

Chris turned to Peter, 'There is a tree reported across the Ekehuan road, just beyond Iguome village. My first thought when Ebue was speaking was that G-F had scarpered with his family but I know from the constable at the gate he left alone in the car this morning. This tree-thing is apparently a separate incident – nothing to do with his fibbing and the unknown visitor – and in the normal course of events we would have had G-F back here complaining like hell about the PWD's inefficiency long ago. Where is he and where is his precious car? There's no word from the police at the Residency gate so presumably he hasn't gone back there. Given his non-appearance, I think we must assume the tree was felled deliberately as a block and

99

an ambush was set for him. We must plan for the worst. Peter, will you please take your own car, with a ranger or guards – whoever you think suitable who is available right now – and pick up a couple of policemen, with rifles. I shall ring the Super now to warn him to get chaps out for you. Then get down to beyond Iguome and see if you can find G-F or whatever has happened to him. Steve and I will tackle the Residency end head-on, both the grieving widow and an escaped PoW, if that is what they are. It's always possible the Resident's failure to arrive at Ekehuan has another blameless explanation, nothing to do with the blocked road, but I think the signs are against it. Anyway, we must pick up the brother-in-law – assuming he is the visitor – right now, *quam celerrime, statim* or "one-time" as they say hereabouts.'

'Or even sooner,' Peter suggested.

While Peter hurried back on foot to the Forest Office to pick up Ranger Eweka and two forest guards, Chris and Steve drove the short distance to the police barracks to mobilise the Superintendent. Two constables and a corporal, all armed with rifles, were ordered to accompany Peter ('Goodness knows if the cartridges would fire or if the bullets would find their way through the cobwebs down the barrels', was Steve's comment). Two constables were sent as reinforcements to join the men at the Residency gate, with strict orders that no one, black or white, was to leave or enter the house or grounds until Chris or Steve came personally:

'They can hold them there safely until we know what has happened on the Ekehuan road.'

All other available men were immediately turned out to follow in police trucks towards Ekehuan. Fifteen constables, two sergeants and an African inspector left in a three-tonner; the Superintendent travelled in his own open tourer Austin with his driver and two corporals. All carried .303 rifles, except the Super who buckled on his revolver; they were ordered to be ready to tackle a terrorist group. Peter left Benin at one-forty, the police ten minutes later.

As the vehicles hurried to clear the outskirts of the city, nobody paid attention to the man quietly pedalling into town on his bicycle.

CHAPTER EIGHT

At 1.25 that afternoon Klaus and Hilda were disembarking from the ferry at Onitsha, the bustling, sprawling and incredibly noisy market town on the east bank of the Niger River, eighty-five miles east of Benin City. The Niger is one of the world's great rivers, flowing for more than two thousand miles from the highlands of Sierra Leone, through the sahelian fringes of the Sahara past Timbuktu to the vast delta of a thousand creeks, each so insignificant that for centuries the mouth of the Niger was unrecognised from seaward. But at Onitsha the river looks its part, mightily impressive and an historic trade route. The town lies immediately upstream from the point where the river, here two miles wide, breaks up into the countless distributaries of the delta. East-west road traffic crosses the north-south river trade in a district densely populated; Onitsha market was one of the great trading places of Africa. Here was the southern terminus for the fleet of the nomadic river tribe who paddled their canoes in a year-long round trip up the Niger for fourteen hundred miles to the rich fishing grounds at Timbuktu and then down with the dried catch to trade it at Onitsha for cloth and household goods. Here also the farmers of eastern Nigeria sold their palm oil to the traders who would send thousands of tons for margarine and soap to Port Sunlight at Liverpool; and down from the north came rafts with cattle and sheep to supply meat to the southern people who could not keep domestic stock because of the tse-tse flies.

For the brother and sister the drive from Benin had been an intense strain and they had no eyes for the scenery or the thriving activity. Hilda had set out from her house on an emotional wave born

101

of Klaus' high-sounding phrases about duty and the Fatherland. She had projected herself from the sticky heat of Benin City to the cool mountain grasslands of Kamerun, from the ersatz life of Mrs Grenville-Fletcher who was a mistrusted alien in a provincial colonial station, back to her privileged happy teens as Fräulein von Ehrwald at Buea and Bamenda. She visualised a heroic period ahead with Klaus when they would descend from the mountains at the head of a fighting force that would sweep all before it. But the shooting of the driver had appalled her. The dream had shattered, to be replaced by stark fear they would be caught. The shooting had surely been unnecessary. Klaus said the man knew too much and, as a nervy wreck, would have given them away if they were stopped; and in any event, he was only a black. But he was a harmless little man, almost a simpleton; look how he had stood shaking when he tried to tell her what had happened to Robert. Hilda was scared and periodically she shook with fear, although the temperature in the car was over forty degrees Celsius.

Klaus drove as fast as he dared, desperately anxious to cover the eighty miles to Asaba and the ferry quickly but fearful of a puncture. Hammering in his mind was the question: how soon would Robert's ambush be discovered? How long before the authorities went to the Residency and realised that Hilda and he had flown? Of course the servants would talk and his identity would be guessed. The authorities would soon put two and two together and would expect him to head back for Kamerun, so the police would telephone and telegraph ahead to towns on the way to order his arrest. Could they beat the traps that were sure to be set? Clearly the ferry was the first point of easy interception. How soon would Robert's ambush be discovered? And looking beyond the present race to escape arrest, if Robert was ambushed and tortured, would he reveal the plans for the German attack from *Kamerun-Gebiet*?

By fast driving, just short of reckless, he made good time to Asaba, taking just under two and a half hours. Of course there was a queue of vehicles waiting for the ferry. Those immediately in front were produce trucks. Klaus used some of the cash taken from Robert's desk to bribe the drivers so that he could move up the queue. It revolted him to have to do so: his instinct was to kick the *verdammten Nigger* out of his way and move to the front of the line, which was surely his right as a white man, but he knew it would attract attention he could not afford, so he swallowed his pride. The British were ridiculously soft, treating blacks almost as if they were equals; that was their mistake. A Syrian businessman also agreed to move back a place for some money; Klaus thought he looked like a Jew and vowed all these scum would be cleared out of the country after his take-over. He dared not try moving farther up the line because the touring car now two in front appeared to be driven by a British officer.

In all, the queuing and crossing took an hour and ten minutes, for every minute of which Klaus and Hilda expected the challenging shout that would mean that Benin's telephoned alarm had been given. Worst of all was the disembarkation at Onitsha. Would there be a police reception party at the top of the ramp? It was not only the steamy heat of the Niger valley that caused the sweat to pour.

As the Mercedes climbed slowly to the top of the steep incline from the ferry landing there was a shout, a sudden swirl of figures in the crowd of spectators and a police constable signalled Klaus to stop. This was the disaster he feared. Capture! Then, as the car came to a standstill, Klaus saw there was only one uniformed man ahead of him and knew that would be quite incapable of preventing them from driving on to Kamerun. Nothing, no-one must be allowed to stand in his way, certainly not this miserable cretin of an African constable. He eased the pistol from the side pocket of his bush jacket and flicked off the safety catch. After the strain of the drive from Benin and the tension of the ferry crossing, his nerves were twang-tight. His trigger finger was itchy to exercise power, to blow away the man with the raised hand.

Hilda saw the gun in her brother's right hand just below the sill of the open window.

'No, Klaus! Not another killing here! It won't help. Maybe we can get past without shooting him.'

'It is a trap, Hilda. They must have telephoned from Benin by now and this is the obvious place to intercept us. But the stupid English have sent only one policeman, as if he would be sufficient to stop us! There's only one.

'*Um Gottes willen, Klaus! Schiesse nicht.* For God's sake. Don't shoot, Klaus!'

The constable walked slowly from the front of the car to a point just two feet from the driver's door. The perfect position. Klaus depressed the clutch and engaged first gear ready for a fast take-off after the shooting.

103

The constable, unaware he was only a half-second from execution, saluted smartly and smiled.

'Please wait a little time, Sah. It is a thief-man, caught red-handed, Sah. At present he is resisting arrest.' And he nodded to the knot of heaving bodies ahead of the car.

As Klaus and Hilda turned to where the policeman indicated, the group parted sufficiently to reveal a young man who was well beyond the stage of resisting a loving kiss, never mind arrest.

'I will arrest the thief-man now and take him to the station, Sah. Sorry for your delay, Sah.' The constable saluted again and turned smartly. 'Clear the way there. Clear the road for this car,' he shouted, and signalled for the Mercedes to drive through.

It had been a very, very close thing. Guiltily, Klaus knew his judgment had been poor. Wisely, Hilda did not press the point. The outcome had been so absurd they could almost smile.

It was half-past one as they drove into Onitsha town and sought the Public Works Department store. There were no commercial filling stations in Nigeria. Petrol was dispensed at the PWD yard, from 44-gallon drums fitted with a hand-operated pump. They found the place: blackened, oil-soaked ground, compacted by constant traffic: another queue, shorter this time. Here was the old petrol attendant, his face wrinkled, in a shapeless khaki uniform suit; he gloried in his tin-pot power, pretending he was able to refuse service if that was his whim, brusquely demanding petrol coupons, signalling to his minions when they might, or might not, operate the precious pump. There were two stalwart young men, unofficial assistants, working the pump for pennies; they were scantily clad, ready with quips behind the old boy's back, working hard to get their feet on the ladder of advancement that one day might land them in a really good job like a petrol attendant.

Filling the car's tank, the eight gallon drum and the two cans was a time-consuming operation and, for Hilda and Klaus, a nerve-fraying one. Coupons were laboriously counted and then re-counted. Money was paid to another clerk. A receipt was hand-written, with two carbon copies. The receipt was carefully examined by the attendant ('I don't believe the old Schwein can read at all!', Klaus growled). The magic sign was given at last. The lucky minion jerked the hand pump back and forth: skoosh-skoosh-skoosh, jets of precious petrol squirted into the tank. Each minute Klaus imagined discovery. Every street cry was heart-stopping. At last the job was done. They now had fuel for nearly 500 miles, more than enough to get them to their intended destination, if they could survive that far. Meantime Hilda had bought fruit in the street, bananas, oranges, paw-paw and pineapples so that they might eat as they drove.

The country they travelled through after leaving Onitsha was far more closely settled than Benin. Towns and villages were strung along the road with only a mile or two of farmland between. It was hilly land, sometimes with evidence of heavy soil erosion caused by too frequent farm cropping and by destruction of the protective tree cover that had held the hills together. Klaus had attention only for the road, none for the scenery, prudently fighting his own impatience for higher speed in the knowledge that to break a spring on the corrugated earth road would be utter disaster. He cursed the drivers of the mammy-wagons and produce trucks trundling five or ten miles an hour slower than his own cruising speed, blaring the horn to make them pull over. There was not a relaxing minute, not an easy half mile as he fought their way eastward.

*   *

The task facing Peter when he reached the road block beyond Iguome was far from straightforward. Mammy-wagons and produce trucks had arrived there before him. Some vehicles, on finding the road barred, had turned and retreated to Benin. People had milled around. But there was no sign of the Mercedes. Nor was there immediate evidence of the Resident having been ambushed, no fallen hat, no blood, no recognisable car track or trail to follow. It might well be that the Resident, frustrated in his attempt to reach Ekehuan, had simply told his driver to take him to some other place; Peter immediately dismissed the thought since surely he would have driven either to his office or back home, both of which had been already checked and ruled out.

With Eweka and the two guards, Peter, began to search the road verges for a hundred yards on either side of the felled tree. It was in the ditch that one of the guards found two sheets of paper with neat handwriting that Peter thought was Grenville-Fletcher's. (In fact the Resident had been holding them when the car came to a stop at the tree; without thinking, he had held them when he left the car and had dropped them when he was seized.) The single words and disjointed phrases did not make sense to Peter, but memo lists seldom do to people other than the writers, and sometimes not even to them; the best he could do was to get them back to Chris for identification as soon as possible, so he scribbled a note:

> *'Is this G-F's writing? Found in ditch at the felled tree. No sign of the Mercedes here. The tree has been cut down deliberately.'*

The United Africa Company timber agent at Nikrowa, up the Osse River beyond Ekehuan had arrived at the road block just after Peter. The forest officer knew him well and asked, as a favour, if he would take the note and the sheets back to Chris at the District Office in Benin, explaining that the road had been blocked deliberately and it was possible someone had been abducted or killed.

At this point the police car and the PWD truck arrived. Peter showed the sheets to the Superintendent who agreed the probability was high the Resident had been ambushed there. He added to Peter's note by writing to Chris,

> *'Iguome villagers were frightened indoors by masked man prior to the tree felling, presumably to prevent them witnessing an illegal act. Although Mercedes car is not here, probability is strong G-F was assaulted here and abducted or perhaps assassinated.'*

The police began questioning the waiting drivers and their passengers to discover if they had seen anything that might lead to Grenville-Fletcher or his abductors.

The superintendent had previously stopped with the police truck at Iguome village. They had found all the villagers still indoors, a fact so curious as to be almost an admission of guilt, or at least of guilty knowledge. Ordered from their houses, the people had volubly and vehemently declared complete ignorance of everything. Three minutes had been sufficient to convince the Super he would gain nothing there, so he had left the inspector and a team to question the villagers thoroughly without his own distracting presence.

As soon as the PWD men had cut through the tree and rolled the log out of the way, the Superintendent took his car through, to see if the Resident might have been taken on towards Ekehuan. As he expected, he found a second tree blocking the road a mile beyond the first, which accounted for the absence of Benin-bound traffic at the main block.

Back at Iguome it was clear to the inspector both that the village people were seriously frightened and that they did not know what had happened. He was sure they had been told to remain indoors so that they could not provide any information, and they had been threatened with serious consequences from a ju-ju if they disobeyed. Eventually they admitted this but since their instructor (whether man or spirit was immaterial to the result) was hideously masked, they could give no useful description. The "thing" had come out of the bush and had ordered them into their houses: 'What else could we have done?'

Around half past two Peter and his men, reinforced by police as they were freed from questioning villagers and travellers, began to search the forest on the side of the road from which the tree had been felled. It was a slow process since the regrowth bush near the road was composed of dense tangles of climbers such as Lantana, where a man's body could lie unseen within two feet of a searcher.

It was virtually impossible to work systematically, hard though they tried. It was also difficult to maintain the rigour of the search, given the dearth of evidence that anything apart from an abduction had happened at this point.

The investigation was intensified and extended when the Superintendent and more police joined, but it was also progressively weakened by fatigue. They were working in a temperature of 95° and high humidity, sweating profusely. It was Ranger Eweka, penetrating behind the roadside climber tangles into the undisturbed forest beyond, who found Robert Grenville-Fletcher slumped at the bottom of the *ogeime* tree, his wrists still lashed together embracing the stem. He was covered with ants and appeared to be dead. Eweka called to his companions.

The small tree, known as *ogeime* to the Binis and Barteria to botanists, is common in the rain forests of Nigeria. It looks quite attractive, with smooth grey bark and fragrant white flowers, but its formidable feature is its hollow-stemmed twigs that are home to a species of vicious black ants living nowhere but in this kind of tree.

107

Any wounding or shaking of the tree induces a furious defence by the ants, a fact that had led to its use as a traditional means of torture in the forest zone.

A litter was quickly crafted from bush sticks and thin strands of forest climbers, the body was freed and carried to the waiting kit-car for transport back to Benin. The time was four-fifteen.

*   *

When the UAC timber agent brought the papers found on the Ekehuan road to Chris, the District Officer immediately recognised the handwriting as the Resident's. The circumstances convinced him that, in spite of the disappearance of the Mercedes, it was essential to persist with the search of the area around the roadblock. He must leave the police and Peter to get on with that. The fact there was no news from the policemen at the Residency gate showed him the Resident had not returned there. However, he must go to see Hilda.

Chris was just about to leave the District Office for the Residency when the Medical Officer telephoned him.

'Look here, Tigger, I have been in to see the body in the mortuary. I was told he had been killed in a road traffic accident on the Asaba road. The bit about the Asaba road may well be true, but not the RTA. The man died as a result of being shot at point blank range. He was shot in the base of the skull and, as happens when that is done, he died instantaneously. I haven't recovered the bullet yet but from the entry wound I guess it was a fairly small calibre pistol, maybe a 9mm. He was an African, height about 5 foot 6 inches, age about 30 years.'

'Killed by a pistol bullet! Are you sure, Doc?' This was staggering news; no African was licensed to hold a pistol and there was no crime on record in which such a weapon had been used. But the MO went on with more.

'That's not all, Tigger. I went through the dead man's pockets with the African police inspector and it is clear from the driving licence and other papers this was the Resident's driver. I thought you should know immediately.'

Chris could only thank the MO for telling him so promptly and he went on to warn the doctor that he had search parties looking for Grenville-Fletcher himself.

'Stick around, please, Doc, in case you are needed.' And he hung up the phone, a look of stark disbelief on his face.

'What on earth is happening, Steve?' and he told him the doctor's news. 'It looks as though we may have Peter and the police searching the wrong road. Perhaps the car was ambushed at Iguome on the Ekehuan road and then driven back through Benin City to get to the Agbor-Asaba road where the driver was shot. But why? Driving through the city was a hell of a risk; anyone might have seen the Resident being held in the car. And why kill the driver there? Hang on, though. The gang may have needed him to drive the car.'

'No! That can't be right because the Merc wasn't standing by the body on the Asaba road, so someone else could drive.'

'If the Resident was ambushed, I can't see the gang would kill the driver but leave G-F alive. It's looking pretty bleak for the boss.'

'Have you considered the other possibility,' Steve said, 'That the Resident, as part of his dis-information campaign, staged an "ambush" on the Ekehuan road, where his staff knew he should be going, told his driver to drive back to Benin to pick up Hilda and his German brother-in-law, shot the driver and now they are .. I know! It is unlikely, because, after all, that would be against Colonial Regulations. It's too far out of character for G-F and he could hardly have organised the tree-felling. You may be right. Nevertheless, we have to know why the car was driven back through town and above all where the Merc is now.'

'We must get over to the Residency right now,' said Chris, 'and weed out some of the uncertainties. Come on.'

Before they could leave the office, however, the telephone rang. The nagging fear the search was in the wrong place was reduced by the police Superintendent speaking from the Catholic Mission at Ekehuan. He told Chris the inhabitants of the village near the second roadblock had also been frightened indoors by a ju-ju man. Chris brought him up to date briefly with the MO's news and then left for the Residency.

The corporal and constable at the gate greeted them cheerfully.

'The Resident has not returned, Sah. He was not in the car when it come.'

'Do you tell me the Resident's car has returned since it left at 8 o'clock and since I visited you here?' Chris asked quietly.

109

'Oh yes, Sah. The Resident's car return about 9 o'clock with the driver alone, soon after you visit here, Sah, but the Resident was not in the car. And he was not in it when it leave again half an hour later with the Resident's lady and another white man. Since you give your order, Sah, the Resident has not been seen here, otherwise we would send you the news one time.'

Chris recalled the wording of his instruction to the policemen and he could not blame them at all for not sending him news about the car. He did blame himself, however, and said so to Steve. With the police, they drove up to the house where they found Jeremiah and the rest of the staff but, obviously, no employers. Jeremiah confirmed madam and the white visitor had left. The steward, recognising all the signs that there was serious trouble pending, showed his feelings by bullying the "small boy" mercilessly, shouting threats and calling him every derogatory name he could dream up. The small boy excitedly protested his innocence, describing what had happened and listing exactly what had been loaded into the car. They were shown the open drawer in the Resident's desk with the lock forced; Jeremiah said it had been the place his master had kept some money and tickets for petrol. The drawer where Hilda had kept the money for the cook's marketing was also empty. They heard from Jeremiah the type of clothes Hilda had taken and satisfied themselves that her husband's were intact. There was nothing to be discovered in the room previously occupied by the white man whom they deduced to be Hilda's brother.

'Bread, meat, bottles of water,' Steve said. 'They are headed on a long trip. And clearly it was Hilda and her brother only. Wherever he is, G-F was not with them in the Merc. The Ekehuan road incident must have been quite separate. We can't do more here. Let's go.'

With nothing more to be discovered in the short term, the doors of the Residency were locked and the keys removed. Leaving the police to take formal statements from the servants, Steve and Chris returned to the District Office. As they drove, Steve put together his assessment of the sequence of events.

'There must have been an ambush on the Ekehuan road about half past eight. G-F must have been made prisoner there or he may have been killed. The driver, in a complete panic, drove back like a dose of salts straight to the Residency, arriving – as we know – about

110

nine o'clock. Why did the silly man not come to us or to the police? Failing to do that cost him his life. Of course the visitor at the Residency was Hilda's brother. We don't know his name, do we? When he heard from the driver what had happened to his brother-in-law, he would realise immediately the abduction would cause intense police activity that would inevitably lead to his discovery. So he scarpered, taking his sister with him. Strange that, that Hilda should go; no "dutiful wife" touch when her husband is abducted and maybe killed. Brother must have a strong hold on her. I wonder why brother came to Benin in the first place; after all it was a hell of a risk for a German to travel so far in British territory. Anyway, they ran for it, with the driver – I saw the man often enough but I haven't a clue what his name was, just his title, "Driver"; that's rather sad, don't you think? Perhaps he objected to the abandonment of his master, or maybe brother thought he threatened their safety in some way: whatever it was, he was shot and pitched out on the road, leaving Hilda and her brother to drive on, presumably eastward.'

'Yes, I agree with that,' Chris said, squeezing the kit-car between some hand carts and a crowd of market women under the trees at the old fort. 'The two incidents were unconnected, or at least the connections were fortuitous. Hilda's brother can have had nothing to do with the ambush because it was bound to bring the Residency under hard scrutiny, not to his advantage, but he had to react to it when he heard about it. Their flight cannot have been planned; it must have been on the spur of the moment. Their packing shows that too.'

They hurried into the office, not even bothering to park the kit-car in the shade, which spoke volumes about the urgency.

'They'll be heading back to Cameroons,' Chris went on. 'That's where they were brought up, you know. Their old man had land at Buea and near Bamenda, from before the last war. We must stop them before they get there. Lucky we know the car they are in. We can get on the blower. They left about half past nine. What is it now? Good grief! Getting on for half past three. They have about six hours' start. I shall phone Charles Allison at Onitsha – there's a faint chance they may have been held up a long time at the ferry or on the road to Asaba, but that's an outside chance. The main request must go to Enugu; I suppose it should be addressed to the Chief Commissioner but that would waste time because he would simply have to send it on to the police. I shall send it to the Assistant Commissioner of Police,

111

with a copy to the Chief Comic. Steve, if I write out the telegrams, will you be a good chap and take them along yourself to P and T so that we are sure they are sent off straight away?'

Chris knew that, while the old-boy network was by far the best way of getting instant action at Onitsha, the only way to get roadblocks in place across the rest of Eastern Provinces was to go through official channels. Normally that request would have gone from the Resident or, since it was a police matter, through the Superintendent in Benin, but neither was available. He telegraphed rather than telephoned because it would almost certainly be quicker and more reliable, and because it would put the facts and the request in writing at the Enugu end, important since the Assistant Commissioner himself would probably not be in the office at this time in the afternoon. He wrote:

URGENTLY REQUEST POLICE APPREHEND WHITE MAN AND WHITE WOMAN BOTH NON-BRITISH DRIVING GREY MERCEDES SALOON CAR REGISTRATION NUMBER B472 STOP LEFT BENIN CITY 0930 TODAY BELIEVED HEADING ONITSHA AND IKOM TO CAMEROONS STOP MAN PROBABLY GERMAN NATIONAL NAME EHRWALD STOP WOMAN IS HIS SISTER MRS GRENVILLE-FLETCHER STOP MAN SHOULD BE ARRESTED AS ENEMY ALIEN AND BOTH HELD ON SUSPICION OF MURDER OF RESIDENTS AFRICAN DRIVER AT BENIN STOP MAN IS KNOWN TO BE ARMED AND IS EXTREMELY DANGEROUS STOP WICKHAM DISTRICT OFFICER BENIN

The wording of the telegram, its timing and the fact it was sent by the District Officer Benin rather than the Resident or the senior police officer all influenced the outcome.

Chris wrote the telegram at twentyfive minutes past three and, while he was phoning his opposite number at Onitsha as part of the old-boy net, Steve Lister took the forms to the Posts and Telegraph Office and demanded they be sent instantly to Enugu. Sending was timed at three-thirty and the principal one was delivered to the Police Headquarters at three-fortyfive. Had immediate action been possible there might just have been time to catch the Mercedes as it passed through the city; certainly the telegram was in ample time to intercept the fugitives before they reached the beginning of the road bottleneck at Bansara.

To get the checkpoints in place, however, was not straightforward. The duty inspector who received the telegram noted the last sentence, that the man was an enemy alien, armed, dangerous and wanted for murder. Clearly the police manning the checkpoints would have to be armed and the regulations decreed that rifles and ammunition could be issued only on the written authority of a superintendent or more senior officer. Since the telegram was addressed to the Assistant Commissioner of Police, he would be the best person to ask, although he was now off duty. The inspector acted with commendable promptness, writing a note to the Assistant Commissioner requesting authority for rifles to be issued, clipped it to the telegram and sent the papers by police motorcyclist to the Assistant Commissioner's bungalow, two miles away.

When the courier reached the house he was told the Assistant Commissioner was not at home but had left to play golf. The motorcyclist then drove to the Club on the other side of town, arriving just as the foursome was leaving the clubhouse. The police chief was not best pleased at being chased around the golf course to sign a paper that any of his superintendents could have authorised but he read the telegram carefully, signed the authorisation, urged the constable to get back to headquarters with all speed since the matter was urgent and then addressed the ball on the first tee. The constable retrieved his bike and returned to the inspector. The time was a quarter to five.

By five o'clock a road block was in place on the road entering Enugu from Onitsha, and at five-fifteen another was manned on the road leading east out of the town. The inspector had already given careful thought to the problem of arranging blocks on the alternative routes from Onitsha to Ikom that bypassed Enugu. He noted from the map that all these involved passing through Abakaliki, just over forty miles east of Enugu. He telephoned the police in Abakaliki, being fortunate in getting a clear line immediately, and told the duty-inspector there both the content of the telegram from Benin and the Police Assistant Commissioner's authority for checkpoints with armed police to be set up to intercept the fugitives. He would immediately telegraph written confirmation of the facts and decisions. His call was timed at ten minutes to five and Abakaliki responded promptly, having men at a road barrier by five-fifteen.

CHAPTER NINE

The Medical Officer pronounced Grenville-Fletcher dead on arrival at hospital at five o'clock. He estimated the time of death about six hours previously and gave the cause as heart failure brought on by shock and formic acid poisoning following myriads of ant bites. The police had made no progress with their investigation of the circumstances of the abduction or who had been responsible. The Superintendent was tied up at Ekehuan where, it seemed possible, the ambush gang might hail from or might be hiding.

Peter had thanked his men for their part on the gruelling task of searching the bush and had promptly retired for a bath and a stiff drink. He then went back to the District Office to offer Chris his help with what would be, he was sure, a difficult evening.

After making arrangements for the funeral at the British cemetery next morning, Chris drafted telegrams to the Chief Commissioner Western Province at Ibadan and to the Governor to tell them of the Resident's death. The fact that Hilda had left with her brother was going to complicate an already difficult situation. Peter came in at the tail end of a discussion between Chris and Steve on when and how to deal with G-F's effects and estate. They were interrupted by the arrival in the room of an elderly Bini whose sparse grey hair was revealed as he wiped off a little skullcap. He carried the carved and painted staff that marked him as the Palace Messenger, a senior official of the Oba's court and Igba-rahero. The fact he was seldom seen outside the palace wearing his badge of office suggested the intriguing nature of his present mission.

115

'The Oba sends greetings, Mr. Wickham, and he tells me bring this paper.' With that, the man gave a slight bow and left.

'It's very unusual for him to work outside the palace and the council,' said Chris. 'Let's see what the Oba has to say: from the delivery, I guess the letter is important.' It was hand-written by the king;

The Palace, Benin City
Monday evening

Mr C. R. Wickham
District Officer, Benin.   <u>*Personal and Private*</u>

Dear Christopher,

> *First let me express my condolences at the death of the Resident, Mr. Grenville-Fletcher.*
> *It is the circumstances of his death that prompt me to write to you now. I have acquired information of the most serious kind which I wish to convey to you urgently in person rather than in writing. Would it be convenient for you to come to the palace this evening - immediately if that suits? If you wish to bring Mr. Stephen Lister and Mr. Peter Thorburn with you please do so, as they were with us at Sapoba and I expect you will want them to know what it is that has come to my knowledge, so their coming may save time. I know Mr. Thorburn was engaged personally in the search for the Resident this afternoon and in the very disagreeable recovery of his body; I am deeply sorry that the name of Benin has been stained by what happened.*
> *I hope to see you this evening, as soon as you wish.*

Ewuare Oba.

'To say this is strange is the understatement of this incredible day,' said Chris, 'I must go at once and hear what he has to say. It is obvious he knows what happened at Ekehuan and it is my guess he knows who and why. If you chaps are fit, we should go right now. There's no point in hanging about. Then we can bring up to date my telegram to the Chief Commissioner in Ibadan. He has to be told everything in raw detail straight away.'

116

So saying, he rose and left the office, followed by Steve and Peter.

The palace was a low building constructed of mud bricks, no part over two storeys and mostly only one, with the entrance directly off the street. It comprised four or five courtyards, each devoted more or less to a single purpose: the Igba-rahero Council chamber and its associated offices formed the largest, the Oba's audience rooms and study another, the women's court a third, the staff area and so on. It was a warren and there was doubt if anyone knew all of it.

The three officers were escorted through the Council quadrangle where they attended regularly to present reports and give advice to the Native Authority, the Oba-in-Council, and went on to the small audience room where the Oba did most of his work. It was plainly furnished, a large desk of ripple-grain mahogany and desk chair to match, a low coffee table that Peter identified as rare figured guarea and four open-armed easy chairs. A long shelf ran the length of the room, carrying some fine ebony carvings and three brass heads made locally by the lost-wax process, for which Benin was famous. Nearby a stand carried the tattered remnants of some mediæval chain mail, a relic of Benin's contact with Portuguese voyagers in the fourteenth century. On one wall was a large bas-relief carving of an ancient Bini battle scene, seven or eight feet long that reminded Steve vividly of the Bayeaux tapestry; it was undoubtedly very old, probably one of the few classic pieces surviving the British destruction in 1897. On another wall was a large photograph of the quadrangle of St. Catherine's College, Cambridge. Fly screens covered the windows opening on to the courtyard and an electric fan turned on the ceiling. The room was a happy mixture of ancient and modern, reaching back into Benin's history but also showing the area's present economy, art and wealth.

The Oba was alone. He solemnly shook hands with each man and thanked them for coming so promptly. He then offered and poured small pegs of neat whisky.

'I don't want to detain you long because I know you will have a pile of things to attend to and you have already had long days of work. This has been a very bad day for us all.' He hesitated and went on, 'I shall come straight to the point.

'When we spoke together at Sapoba, I told you I was somewhat concerned about the fantastic rumours of a white oba. I

117

regarded it as a bit of a joke but warned you that some hotheads were inclined to take it as a threat to me and to the whole Benin kingdom. I became anxious lest such people might get out of hand. That is precisely what happened this morning. For reasons I did not know, Grenville-Fletcher was linked to the white oba rumour. The Resident's engagement at Ekehuan was public knowledge, of course, and its timing, and a small clique decided to get the truth out of him about the *oba-nofua* affair. In the event things went much farther than had been intended: the Resident died from the shock of the torture and the questioner got more information than he bargained for. The only partly redeeming feature is that the results of the interrogation have been revealed to me and I can pass them on to you.

'I hope I do not have to tell you, Christopher, – but nevertheless I shall say it very clearly, I had nothing whatever to do with these events. I had no prior knowledge of the plan to ambush Mr. Grenville-Fletcher. The man concerned came to me this afternoon with his story and clearly expected thanks. When I heard the bones of what he had to say, I made it my business to question him very thoroughly indeed about everything that happened and everything said, and I am satisfied I now have a full understanding.'

As Chris was about to speak, the Oba went on quickly:

'Hear me out. You shall have everything I have discovered.

'The questioner's concern, remember, was the threat supposedly posed by the white oba, whom he feared was to supplant me. So his questioning began and centred on that. Apparently the Resident, even *in extremis*, did not deny the idea. Indeed he went further, saying he was to become the *oba-nofua*, but not only of Benin; he was to become the Governor-in-Chief of all Nigeria and perhaps even more of West Africa. The torturer told me he laughed at this as obviously ridiculous, since there is already a Governor in Lagos and how could Grenville-Fletcher replace him, and there are Chief Commissioners and even other Residents who are senior to him. However Mr. Grenville-Fletcher persisted with the story and tried to bring about his release from torture by making offers of personal advancement to his captor and by volunteering more detailed information. Regrettably, he had sealed his fate by admitting that he was to be the white oba, although he did not mean king of Benin only. Thereafter, apparently, the torturer had no intention of releasing him. The additional information was of secondary interest to him, pursued only because it was probably "saleable".

'Now this particularly is what I want to repeat to you, make of it what you will. In my judgment it is far more important than Grenville-Fletcher's ambition to become head-of-state.

'The Resident insisted that an army will come from the East, which would have made him President or Governor-in-Chief had he not died. And, associated with that attack, he said the Ibos will be given arms and induced to rise in rebellion to fight the Hausa, both people being inflamed by staged incidents. He claimed that, out of this struggle, his private army from the Cameroons would rule Nigeria, sweeping away the British. When he was asked repeatedly when and where the power would come from, the Resident said rifles for his soldiers and the Ibos would be brought by a queen in a few days. What can you make of that? Is there substance in it or are these the ramblings of a dying man? If he was to rule like a king, do you suppose Mrs Grenville-Fletcher would be a queen? But I do not understand how she could bring arms and ammunition, although that appears to be what the Resident said. Equally incredibly, he said that Roman soldiers would come out of the Sahara to attack Kano and Maiduguri, and that ships would come from under the sea to attack Lagos. Submarines, obviously.'

'My God! It's far worse than I'd imagined,' Chris interjected.

'Of course I have tried to clarify the reference to "Roman soldiers", which is ridiculous, but the torturer insists that is what was said. I am assured that is so.

'What was done this morning, Christopher,' the Oba went on, 'was very wrong, obnoxious and quite illegal, but I am afraid it revealed that the Resident himself was engaged in something equally illegal. I think he was planning a revolution with his German brother-in-law. Do you agree?'

'Too bloody true,' Peter interrupted. 'He was a sneaky bastard.'

Chris nodded. 'Yes, incredible though it is at first sight, I have to accept it looks very much like it and it ties in with his extraordinary behaviour yesterday. Was it only yesterday? He lied to me about his brother-in-law being here in Benin. Steve Lister and I couldn't understand why the German should have taken the huge risk of travelling here, but perhaps it was to make some arrangements about this attack and revolution. This news is immensely important and we must pass it on. I only hope the police in Enugu have been busy and

119

have arrested Mrs. Grenville-Fletcher and her brother.'

The Oba cut in, 'I heard that they had driven away. I have also been told that the German killed the Resident's driver. That boy was the son of a friend of mine; he was a good boy and did not deserve to be killed like that. You must catch that man.'

'We are doing our best, Oba. I telegraphed Enugu with all the details. They may be in custody by now.'

'Good. But speaking about catching someone,' the Oba continued, 'In the normal way the man who ambushed and tortured the Resident would be arrested by the police and held for trial by you, Christopher, or by a higher court. In the circumstances it appears to me that would be not appropriate. Rumours about an Ibo rebellion to kill Hausa people and about an army coming from the east to kill British people would be immensely damaging. We do not want that kind of upset and even to release news that it was being planned could be socially disruptive.'

'Very true.'

'It would be bound to leak out if the man was held in the police cells,' the Oba continued. 'I questioned him on my own and, as things stand, I alone have his information.

'So I propose to hold the man responsible very securely here at the palace at least until we see how events unfold. Then we can reconsider what might happen to him. In the meantime he will not spread news of what he heard, as would happen if he went into police custody. I hope you will not try to argue for another course, Christopher. The killing of the driver and the revelation of the Resident's plans provide some justification for my reversion – at least for a short time – to the absolute rule of my ancestors.' With a smile he added, 'You never know, Christopher, I may grow to enjoy becoming an absolute monarch instead of a constitutional one, although I admit the example of your own Charles the First is a pretty strong warning against it.'

'I shall not argue, Oba. There is too much else that needs immediate action; if you have the man safe I shall be content.'

Steve spoke for the first time. 'Not *Roman* soldiers. Rommel's soldiers! I think they must be planning a raid by a motorised column coming across the desert from Tripoli: very difficult for more than a few men, but surely not impossible and, done in conjunction with a domestic uprising, potentially very effective.'

'Good thinking, Steve. I'm sure you are right. And the attack on Lagos will presumably be a submarine; it would be a torpedo attack on ships or conceivably by gunfire. It could hardly be a landing of any sort because there are enough troops in Lagos to handle anything coming from even two or three U-boats. News of all this must go immediately to the Governor so that countermeasures are taken.'

'That is my view also, which is why I asked you to come quickly,' said the Oba.

Peter snapped his fingers. 'I have it! There is the other point. The arms for the rebellion and the army will not be provided by a queen - perhaps there has been a slight misunderstanding in the translation or the torturer is unfamiliar with the grades of European aristocracy. The rifles will not come from a queen: they will come from a duchess. That is what is being loaded in the *Duchess of Lucca* now. Rifles for the private army and the rebellion will be landed somewhere on the Cameroons or Nigerian coast. And you know, the idea of whipping up Ibo resentment against the Hausas and *vice versa* is not far-fetched. It could be done and would cause vast trouble.'

'Well done, Peter. Queen : Duchess. That makes sense. But, Oba, did your prisoner say the arms for both the private army and the rising were to come from the "queen"?'

'Yes. That is what he said Grenville-Fletcher told him. I believe all the arms and ammunition are to come from there.'

'That is frightfully important because it must mean the rebel army will be relatively weak until the weapons are delivered. It puts a huge premium on capturing the ship before it discharges the cargo.'

Chris stood up. 'Oba, if there is nothing more you can tell us, please allow us to go. There is a frightful amount to be done.' He paused: 'I am very sorry your friend's son, the Resident's driver, was killed this morning; please give my condolences to his father. The torture and killing of the Resident was a crime that we can talk about later but I am grateful to you for passing on the news of the hellish plans he and his brother-in-law have been cooking up. I hope the police have caught the German by now. Whether they have been caught or not, of course it's vital we pass on your information to the Chief Commissioner in Ibadan. And that reminds me, I haven't thanked you for fixing up the meeting I had yesterday with Joshua Oshodin. He's a bright young man and we had a good talk. I asked him to come with us on the operation to Santa Isabel, although how that business will be affected by today's developments I have no idea. Anyway, please excuse us if we dash off now. There is a lot of work to attend to.'

'Of course, gentlemen. Perhaps we shall meet briefly at the funeral tomorrow. I shall be there with some senior representatives of the Council, if you think that would be appropriate. We must make a show of respect, even if we have none.'

*   *

Soon after leaving the Oba's study the three men were at Chris' house. There was urgent need to act on the Oba's revelations and to share the work load. The simplest way was to meet immediately for a meal, in local parlance "to join chop", while they decided their business. This required stewards to walk through the reservation with dishes that were then shared, making a strange combination of menus. Full though the day had been, the night appeared likely to be even busier.

Chris voiced a common thought, 'Until half an hour ago I thought we were chasing the damned Hun simply as an alien and on a charge of murder. Now we have to get him for gun-running, desert warfare, a U-boat attack, invading Nigeria and starting a bloody revolution. The man's overdoing it and becoming something of a troublemaker. But to be serious, we have to stop the bastard now.'

They were still standing in the lounge putting together the ingredients of pink gins before starting work, when the faint light of a hurricane lamp approached through the intense darkness across the lawn. It was carried by an elderly Nigerian man in shapeless khaki clothes carrying an immense staff; he was a "watch-night" and was escorting a European lady of some forty-five years. As she came into the ring of warm light spreading across the lawn from the house, she thanked the man and told him to go back and guard the house. She came briskly into the room.

'Good evening, boys. May I come in? You look as though you need that drink. I have heard the news and I know you must have had a hell of a day; you needn't tell me.'

Chris welcomed her and suggested she join them in a drink.

122

'Thank you, Tigger, may I have a teeny-little gin with lots of soda if you have it, please? Look, I know about the Resident being killed; Doc told me. And I've heard too that Hilda has run away – that's true is it? Good riddance, but I realise this whole affair must be an enormous worry and workload. Gerald is away for the night up at OPRS and it struck me that you might be able to use a secretary to help with whatever telegrams and letters you need, so I've brought a notebook and sharp pencil. You may have forgotten it but before Gerald married me I was a perfectly good secretary at home, so I am reverting to type. Apart from drinking your gin, can I help, please?'

Chris winced at the fearful pun but laughed for the first time that day:

'Helen, you are an angel and I am sure you can help. You don't know the half of it. We are just about to have a scratch meal, planning at the same time to scribble lists of jobs to be done and puzzle how to do them. Have you eaten?'

Helen Smith was the wife of the local Agricultural Officer, who was absent overnight at the Oil Palm Research Station some way north of Benin City. This evening she was sensibly dressed in a long-sleeved cotton blouse and colourful ankle-length cotton dirndl skirt over calf-length black mosquito boots. She was happily married but had plenty to worry about in her life, with a son studying medicine in Glasgow, whose digs had been bombed in the Clydeside blitz and a daughter in the Wrens working at the Admiralty in London. Her husband Gerald was a steady, unflamboyant character whose posting to Benin this tour of duty deprived Helen of one great enjoyment, her horses. Farther north, where it was possible to keep them, horses were both necessary for work in the country – especially for agricultural and forest officers – and a passion for many people, Europeans and Nigerians. In the South horses were ruled out by the tse-tse fly diseases, so Helen had time on her hands for helping people. The war had exacerbated the difficulties of living in Nigeria, particularly by preventing the import of many goods that were necessities of life. There was a premium on finding substitutes and Helen had proved herself adept at this, devising a kind of West African "Mrs. Beeton"; as the wife of an agricultural officer, she saw at first hand how local people used the great range of vegetables and other natural products which, until 1939, had not been noticed by most Europeans. Her ideas and experience in this field made her a welcome guest in the houses

123

of the young bachelors who were keen to learn her latest recipes and gardening hints. In this station where the Resident's wife was ill-fitted by instinct and origin for that type of leadership, Helen was an alternative doyenne, a role she enjoyed.

She protested she had already dined at home but she sat at table and joined at the dessert stage, her notepad and pencil ready. Chris warned her that they would be referring to some events, both past and planned, that were highly confidential; she would have to respect that.

First to be arranged was Robert Grenville-Fletcher's funeral in the morning at the British cemetery. It was desirable that notice of this should go out by hand to as many of the Europeans and leading Africans in Benin as time allowed. In life the Resident had not been a likeable man and latterly he had been plotting treason: in death no hint of that scandal or even of disharmony in the administration should be allowed to leak. Chris would have to attend the funeral and a strong turnout of the great-and-good, black and white, would be helpful. Helen undertook to get notes out to as many people as possible.

Moving aside the dishes of fruit salad and inevitable crême caramel that Nigerian cooks were happy to serve as dessert seven days a week, they spread a map and considered the flight of the Ehrwalds who would not attend the burial. Helen was able to put a name to the man whom Chris and his friends had been forced in ignorance to call "G-F's brother-in-law".

'His name is Klaus,' Helen said; 'Hilda told me so. The other brother is a colonel in the SS; Herman, I think, – no, Helmut. I never felt comfortable with Hilda, knowing her elder brother was a senior officer in the German army.'

'Thank you, Helen. I am glad to be able at least to put a name to him. But I wish we knew much more and especially how he thinks.' Chris turned to Peter. 'You know its more difficult to play opposite a complete stranger than against someone whose game you know. You cannot guess what an opponent you have not played before will do in a given situation. Will he kick for touch or use the narrow side, send up a high ball or link up with the back row; and could he be pressured into fumbling? To me, Klaus is an unknown quantity, an enigma.'

'We can be sure of one thing,' Peter replied. 'We know he is no slouch. It took nerve to travel on a motorbike all the way from the Cameroons to Benin, a German presumably passing himself off as

British on a journey of at least a couple of days. And although the flight from Benin with his sister was rushed – like having to kick when two flank forwards are about to clatter you – he has a game plan and reacts sharply. Using your analogy, Tigger, he didn't fumble.'

'Too true,' said Chris. 'They got away and they have a good car. The question is whether we can catch them. Let's look at the distances and think of the travel times.'

Helen wrote down the mileages Chris called out and then added the possible clock times the Ehrwalds might have achieved. When she finished, the page read: (*See maps at front end paper)

Benin	0	0930 am
Asaba	80 miles	1200 noon
Ferry	-	-
Onitsha	-	1.30 pm
Enugu	60 miles	3.30 pm
Abakaliki	50 miles	5.30 pm
Ikom	80 miles	9.00 pm
Mamfe	60 miles	?

'That supposes unusual good fortune at the ferry, only an hour and a half, no punctures or breakdowns like dirt in the petrol,' Chris said.

'It also implies phenomenal stamina in driving,' Peter interjected. 'I wouldn't want to drive straight from here to Ikom – far less to Mamfe – in one day. It's a hell of a timetable.'

'But just possible,' Steve pointed out, 'especially if you are running away from a murder charge and prison camp, and if your master plan for a local war depends on keeping ahead of the pursuers. To be sure of intercepting the blighter, we must allow for him getting all the lucky breaks while we get none. It is difficult to believe they could do the journey in less time than that, but we had better assume they could make the timetable and then see if we can catch them.'

'I telegraphed Enugu at three-thirty, so they may just have caught them there but I doubt it and anyway Klaus may have bypassed the town, so one cannot be certain. Surely they should be intercepted at Ikom?'

After studying the map for a minute or two longer, Steve said:

125

'Can we agree to rule out the possibility of their going by Obudu. Could they take that route?'

Peter had spent a local leave shooting in the area. 'One can just get into Cameroons that way on foot via the Obudu Plateau but it would involve at least seven days' hard trekking to reach Bamenda. Too long, surely?'

'In that case they must go through Ikom and Mamfe if Klaus is to rally his troops and get down to a rendezvous on the coast to collect the arms. From that point of view Bamenda seems much less attractive as a destination after Mamfe than Kumba and Buea. But first we must know they have been arrested. It will be hellish if they get away.'

As the meaning of what had just been said became clear, Helen's eyes widened but she did not interrupt.

The others agreed with Steve, so Helen was asked to write a telegram to the Chief Commissioner in Enugu, copied to the Police Assistant Commissioner, asking for confirmation that Klaus and Hilda had been caught and also for the reply to be copied to Chief Commissioner Western Provinces at Ibadan.

'We have been skirting round the real issue too long', said Chris. 'The Governor must be told immediately about Klaus' devilish plans for getting rifles to his private army, the Ibo rising and the attacks in the north and on Lagos harbour. The authorities must have maximum time to organise defence and counter measures. The bother is: how can we word telegrams to convey all that without starting wild rumours, pre-emptive attacks on Ibos, all kinds of trouble? In addition to that we need to know whether HE wants us to continue with the *Duchess* attack as planned or in some modified way. Sorry, Helen, you don't know what that means but you will later.'

After a moment of thought Steve said, 'Tigger, there is only one way that can be done with any success and that is for one of us to go to Ibadan or if necessary to Lagos. You are tied here as the boss since G-F was killed; you cannot go. Let me go right now and tell them the whole damned story. That will be far easier and more reliable than sending endless telegrams, and completely avoids the problem of the news leaking out. If, by evil chance, Klaus and Hilda have escaped, effective communication and co-ordination of actions will be even more important. We must know how the Duchess operation is to fit into any countermeasures against a rising. We can save a lot of time

126

if we warn the Chief Commissioner by telegram that I am leaving in an hour and want to see him in the middle of the night. That would mean countermeasures could begin at dawn tomorrow.'

The obvious good sense of this plan was agreed in two or three minutes' discussion. A counter-argument was that it would involve Steve in a round trip of over 360 miles, one way at night, if he was to be available for the preparation of the attack on the *Duchess* which, they had to assume, would be an early priority. This tiring drive would be asking for trouble and Chris made conditions. He insisted Steve should drive no further than Ondo where he could knock up a friend to chauffeur the last leg into Ibadan and he should be a passenger on the return journey.

As a first step, Peter telephoned the senior P and T officer in Benin to ensure their office would remain open throughout the night ready to accept and send some vital telegrams.

Chris drafted a telegram to Sir John Robertson in Lagos and Helen wrote out a fair copy:

TO / HE THE GOVERNOR LAGOS TOP PRIORITY BEGINS
REGRET TO INFORM YOU RESIDENT BENIN ROBERT GRENVILLE—FLETCHER DIED TODAY IN TRAGIC AND VERY SUSPICIOUS CIRCUMSTANCES STOP DEAD ON ARRIVAL HOSPITAL 1700 STOP HILDA GRENVILLE—FLETCHER AND BROTHER KLAUS EHRWALD ESCAPED FROM BENIN BELIEVED TOWARDS CAMEROONS STOP REQUEST FOR THEIR ARREST TELEGRAPHED AT 1515 HOURS TO CHIEF COMMISSIONER ENUGU AND POLICE THERE ON GROUNDS OF ENEMY ALIEN AND SUSPICION OF MURDER OF AFRICAN DRIVER STOP ARISING FROM RESIDENTS DEATH HIGHLY SENSITIVE AND SECRET INFORMATION RECEIVED AFFECTING NATIONAL SECURITY STOP THIS IS SO SENSITIVE AM SENDING STEPHEN LISTER TO IBADAN TO INFORM CHIEF COMMISSIONER AND THROUGH HIM SENIOR ARMY STOP LISTER LEAVING BENIN 2100 MONDAY VIA DO ONDO ETA IBADAN AGODI 0400 TUESDAY STOP RESPECTFULLY SUGGEST SERIOUSNESS OF INFORMATION AND NEED FOR QUICK DECISIONS YOU CONSIDER MEETING

LISTER IN IBADAN STOP HELPFUL IF CO ARMY
IBADAN PRESENT STOP ALSO THE OPERATION YOU
COMMISSIONED ME IN LAGOS WITH FRIENDS NOW
MORE VITAL AND VERY URGENT AS LISTER WILL
EXPLAIN STOP WICKHAM DO BENIN.

'Helen, please send the same to the Chief Commissioner
Ibadan, down to "0400 Tuesday stop", skip the rest and instead say,

HAVE COPIED ABOVE TO HE GOVERNOR LAGOS AND
ASKED IF HE WOULD BE ABLE TO TRAVEL TO IBADAN
IN TIME TO MEET LISTER AT IBADAN AGODI THUS
SAVING TIME AND FACILITATING DECISIONS STOP
WICKHAM DO BENIN'

Helen giggled at the thought of them asking the Governor-
General to drive a hundred miles to save a mere district officer some
extra travelling. Still, they were asking quite nicely.

Peter succeeded in getting a telephone call through to Philip
Denstone, the District Officer at Ondo. They arranged that Philip
would expect Steve around midnight and would then drive him to the
Chief Commissioner's house at Ibadan; Steve would explain the
circumstances when he arrived.

It was vital that, before Steve left for Ondo, time be found for
thinking about the information they had received and what it implied,
and also for Chris to compose the necessary report on what had
happened.

'We don't know how dependent the Cameroons force is upon
Klaus,' said Steve. 'Will it be stopped if, as we hope, Klaus has been
arrested, or are there henchmen capable of taking it forward on their
own? For instance, Klaus' and Hilda's father, the Baron Ludwig von
Ehrwald. Where is he? By all accounts he was a tough egg who made
plenty trouble as a young man in 1914, and he's not too old to make
more now. He could certainly carry on without his son, if he is not
already locked up. We must ask where he is and we must plan on the
rising going ahead with or without Klaus.'

'With the boxes of arms in the *Duchess of Lucca*,' Chris
continued, 'where will they land them? Let's look at the map again.

As I understand the Oba's version of what G-F said, the rifles are intended to arm both the Cameroons force and the Ibos. If that is so, there seems no point in landing them at Victoria or Debundscha even though they are only 35 miles from Santa Isabel, because they wouldn't serve the Ibo rebellion'.

'Come to that,' said Peter, 'surely they wouldn't want to show their hand at all with Klaus' force still in Cameroons because it would be too easily blocked in. From Victoria there is a fearsome road up to Buea, then north to Kumba and Mamfe, at least 140 miles, and only when they are beyond Ikom – 250 miles from Victoria – would they be out in the clear. The Mamfe road is a bottleneck that could be made impassable by two men and a boy. Klaus will want to get the force out to beyond Ikom without showing his hand. On the other hand, Port Harcourt is surely too far west; he could never hope to get a sizable lot of men that distance without being rumbled. Also, PH seems unlikely because it is so big; there are too many people to surprise and overpower before the rifles are delivered.'

'That's right. He wants a port outside Cameroons, handy for the Ibo people. Like Calabar, Opobo or Oron', Chris suggested.

'Opobo and Oron are the wrong side of the Cross River,' Peter pointed out. 'Extra difficulty coming from the east.'

'True. So Calabar looks the best bet; a large Ibo population where a troublemaker with a glib tongue could whip up hysteria.'

'In that case Klaus Ehrwald's men would have to leave Cameroons largely unarmed and make their way to Calabar, as they might well do in penny packets', Steve argued. 'A lot depends where their base is. If we are right about the port being Calabar or Opobo, they might go by the direct route, a short way on foot from Kumba to M'bonge to Rio del Rey. The gap between the ends of the motor roads is only 25 or 30 miles round the side of Cameroon Mountain, at most two days walking. If I was Klaus, that's the way I would send them.'

'Wait a bit', Peter interjected. 'That may give an indication of the timing. Klaus was here in Benin this morning and apparently did not intend to leave today. Even if his programme was to go tomorrow, Tuesday, he could not realistically expect to get to Bamenda or Kumba before Wednesday night. Then he tells his chaps to go to Calabar or wherever; even with good motor transport and a clear run they couldn't travel and be in position before Saturday, and I think it would be later, say Sunday or Monday at the very earliest, because they could not travel in one big party, like taking a football special. The whole point is Klaus must get them to the port for arming without raising the authorities' suspicions.'

'Yes, that's reasonable.'

'On the other hand,' Peter went on, 'if the ship is scheduled to arrive at Calabar earlier, the force having already been ordered to leave Cameroons quietly to meet it say on Thursday or Friday this week, Klaus would be going directly there, not up by Ikom and Mamfe at all. So if he is caught up the Ikom road, we have a good indication the ship is not expected before the beginning of next week at the earliest.'

Chris groaned. 'That means we may have led everyone astray by suggesting blocks be placed on the road to the Cameroons. If there is no sign of him travelling today by Enugu and Ikom, it would point to an early rendezvous at the port and there would be no point in our going to Santa Isabel. In that case, Steve, you should warn HE and the army to be ready for fireworks in the east this weekend. And since the main point of attacking Kano and Lagos would seem to be to divert our attention and forces away from the real danger, it would mean these would be very imminent – in a few hours only perhaps.'

'Have we any idea what is the army strength in this country now? Surely the regular battalions are all away in East Africa with the West African Division, leaving only training units and recent recruits.'

'Indeed', Steve said, 'if a northern attack by German desert raiders was to be effective in drawing forces from the south, especially from Eastern Provinces, it would have to be a good week before the Ibo rising. Otherwise the raid would merely have the effect of waking up the army so that it was on the alert when the trouble began locally. So let us hope Hilda and Klaus went by Ikom: then we have six or seven days minimum, probably eight or ten.'

'It's desperately important to find out from the Enugu police which route the Ehrwalds took and whether they have been arrested,' said Chris. 'Without that, no one can do more than guess at the timing of the threats. Peter, would you be so kind as to send off another signal to the Chief Comic at Enugu, asking which route they took from Onitsha? Better get them to copy the reply to the Governor in Lagos and to Ibadan, since decisions will have to be made in one of those places.'

So another telegram was drafted and sent off.

130

HH CHIEF COMMISSIONER ENUGU BEGINS URGENT IMMEDIATE ACTION STOP FOLLOWING MY TELEGRAM TIMED 1515 HOURS TODAY PLEASE INFORM GOVERNOR LAGOS BY TELEGRAM WHETHER KLAUS EHRWALD HAS BEEN ARRESTED AND WHERE STOP ALSO COPY THAT INFORMATION DIRECT TO CHIEF COMMISSIONER IBADAN BY TELEGRAM AND TO SENDER STOP ANY EVIDENCE OR INDICATION OF ROUTE TAKEN BY FUGITIVES IS URGENTLY REQUIRED ESPECIALLY WHETHER VIA ENUGU ABAKALIKI TO IKOM AND MAMFE OR OTHERWISE STOP WICKHAM DO BENIN

Helen used Chris' portable typewriter to produce two documents, a memo list to guide Steve's verbal report to the Governor and Chief Commissioner, and the preliminary written report that Chris would have to submit on the drama in and around Benin during the day. The three men contributed to the aide-memoire, the final version of each item being taken down by Helen whose eyes opened ever wider as the extent of the crisis emerged. While she produced the typed version and carbon copies, working on a cleared space at the end of the dining table, Chris retired to the other part of the room to draft his report that would be her next attention.

Through the open windows came the shrilling of the crickets and cicadas and the steady drumming from the town. And the earthy moist tropical smell of the African night.

<u>Aide-Memoire for Steve Lister</u>
                (cc for HE and HH)

1.   Question if news available on route
                taken by Klaus Ehrwald:
        a)   If <u>not</u> via Ikom, look for him
                around Calabar now and expect
                attacks on Lagos and Kano any
                time soon.
        b)   If via Ikom, expect attacks on
                Lagos and Kano about Saturday/

131

Sunday or later: put watcher
on end of Rio del Rey road
to observe possible
infiltration of Klaus force
on foot from Cameroons.

2. Warn Sahara fringe watchers and army in
north _re_ forecast German raid on Kano
area or Maiduguri. Suggest this is to be
curtain-raiser for Ibo rising; maybe 7
days ahead - Army will know what would
be the most damaging interval in
committing troops the wrong way.

3. Warn Royal Navy _re_ forecast U-boat
attack on Lagos.

4. Arms for Klaus force and intended Ibo
uprising apparently transferred to
Duchess of Lucca in Santa Isabel:
rehearse arguments why Calabar or nearby
is likely landing.

5. Authorities to prepare for rising in
coastal Ibo area: watch for rabble-
rousers and incidents to induce anti-
Hausa feeling. Ditto for anti-Ibo
incidents further north.

6. HE asked to confirm the _Duchess_ cutting-
out to go ahead. Force to be 20 men
(still need some recruits). Panda Moore
alerted. Rendezvous at Sapoba Wednesday
for briefing etc. Want revolvers and
ammunition (tho' hopefully only to
threaten Italian crew into submission):
collect these from Army at Ibadan? Has
HE any further information _re_ ship and
original 'valuable' cargo?

7. If _Duchess_ operations to proceed, need
for co-ordination with army and police
to capture Klaus force, especially the
leaders (assuming their operation goes
ahead after Klaus' capture). Any line on

Germans as potential lieutenants and on Klaus' father? Was the father interned in 1939? If so, where?

8. Our timetable:
Wed. and Thurs.- at Sapoba training and briefing. (Dangerously short?)
Fri.provisional - travel Sapoba to Warri about noon(?), embarkation and sailing time depend on Captain Moore's decisions.
Sat. and Sun. 50 hours steaming Warri to S. Isabel

Mon. - 0100 hours (?) board *Duchess*
      - about 0400 hours (?) sail
      [Alternatively drive Sapoba-Onitsha-Port Harcourt-Opobo and embark Sun.1000, sail 1200]

Mon. a.m. Try to discover from Italians where landing was intended (Calabar?) and communicate by radio to HE and army. NB: Guard against use of *Duchessa*'s radio revealing British operation to Klaus and hence loss of surprise at Calabar: necessary to agree wavelength and simple code to allow clear English morse between *Duchess* and Sir John etc.

(NB timetable depends on Capt. Moore's confirmation of the appropriate port of embarkation and on transport vessel's speed and hence adequacy of allowance of time for steaming; and on Klaus attempting the Ikom road.
Also 48 hours briefing and training at Sapoba is the bare minimum: we cannot attack earlier by cutting this.)
        Wednesday noon (maybe): arrive
        Lagos.

133

Having completed the first paper, Helen went straight on with the early pages of the interim report, the end of which Chris was still drafting in longhand. Meanwhile Peter and Steve prepared the car, checking tyres and carefully filtering petrol from cans into the tank; grit and water in the fuel were common problems and especially to be avoided on this long night drive in view of what hung upon it.

Finally Steve drove out just after nine o'clock. Chris slammed the driver's door. His final farewell was:

'Don't wrap yourself round a tree. Tell them the whole ghastly bloody story. See you at Sapoba.'

With no street lights to compete with the stars and no smog to obscure them, the Milky Way and the planets blazed in glittering intensity. These and the bright moon made driving easier than it might have been. On moonless nights the unmarked brown earth road merged with the natural colours of the bush so that a car's headlights seemed powerless. Tonight the clear road-ribbon unwound ahead of Steve and the absence of competing traffic meant he could make his own speed to minimise the vibration of the vicious corrugations of the laterite road. Occasionally eyes reflected in the headlights, antelope, maybe a leopard. Later Steve saw the curiously punctuated road-sign: "Elephants: Cross here"; as always, it intrigued him – they never forget, but can they read? Luckily none was crossing as he drove past.

Back in the house, Helen ordered tea for the three of them, preparatory to going home. Until now she had made no comment on the appalling events described in Chris' report and forecast for the next few days. She simply announced that, with two other wives whom she knew would volunteer, she intended to go to Sapoba in the morning to organise the domestic side of the training camp. In response to protests from Chris that it was not really necessary since there would be several steward boys and what would Gerald think about being abandoned, Helen said she guessed Gerald would insist on being in the party going to Fernando Po as soon as she told him men were wanted and Chris should waken up to the sheer necessity of having a catering officer at Sapoba during the week.

'Twenty men will arrive, probably with fifteen steward boys and as many cooks. A fat chance you would have of getting anything to eat apart from a tin of bully beef and you would have to open that yourself. The boys would squabble over who was the senior or just sit around and chat. Be realistic, Tigger, you need someone to take

134

charge of the commissariat because you will have plenty other things to think about.'

She turned to Peter:

'You must have tents in Forestry; you had better dig those out first thing tomorrow. Gerald will be back from OPRS early afternoon; I shall get him to pick them up at the Old Fort and we can take them down. I shall go round early morning to organise Jean and Hilary. You have had other things on your minds today so I take it you have no food arranged for the twenty hungry men you are recruiting; there can't be all that much at Sapoba apart from fruit so we girls can fix that tomorrow.'

Peter and Chris recognised they had met a power stronger than themselves and were grateful there was one thing less to organise. They thanked Helen for her timely good sense and Peter drove her home.

It had been a hell of a long day. And Steve was still driving.

CHAPTER TEN

Philip Denstone drove up the avenue of His Honour the Chief Commissioner's house at the Agodi suburb of Ibadan city just after four o'clock on Tuesday morning. The night was inky black now that the moon had set but there were encouraging lights shining in the windows, the only ones on the reservation; they suggested that the household was expecting them. It was an unusual time for visiting and Philip hoped the reception would not be too frosty. Steve was asleep; after a day of acute nervous tension, the strain of the night drive to Ondo had taken him to the limit, in spite of his earlier objections to the idea of arranging a co-driver for the latter part of the journey.

While drinking a midnight coffee in Denstone's house and during the first part of their trip together from Ondo, Steve had given Philip a resumé of the day's events at Benin, so he knew what might be facing them at Ibadan. There were several cars outside the Agodi house: a khaki-painted staff car – 'Local Army brass', he thought – and a large dark green Lanchester saloon from which Philip deduced the Governor had indeed driven up from Lagos, as Steve and Chris had rather daringly suggested. Philip gave Steve a shove to waken him.

They were met at the door, surprisingly considering the hour, by Mrs Hesket-Bramwell, the Chief Commissioner's wife, dressed in a flowery housecoat. She had felt obliged to get up to welcome the Governor forty minutes earlier and had decided to make a night of it by waiting for the rest of the party to appear. Both Steve and Philip had already met her in more normal circumstances; she greeted them in a motherly fashion, as if they were small boys who might have got

136

their feet wet and certainly needed to wash before being allowed any farther into the house for tea. They were grateful for her kindly and informal welcome, not merely for the opportunity to freshen up but for helping to defuse a potentially stressful interview. Steve in particular was acutely aware how unusual was their action in suggesting the Governor might drive from Lagos to save a junior officer the extra journey. It was a daunting business, facing the two most senior officers in the service whom they had arranged to drag from their beds in the middle of the night. Sir John Robertson settled the matter in the first five seconds.

'Don't look so worried, Lister. I know you chaps have had a bad day in Benin and I don't mind getting out of the Lagos Scratchitariat for something as important as I am sure this is. I heard you apologising to Silvia Bramwell just now – quite right for interfering with her beauty sleep. But don't apologise to me because I have a feeling you and Wickham did the right thing getting me up here. Now, what have you got?'

Steve handed over copies of the typed report from Chris and suggested that might be the best starting point. The Governor and Chief Commissioner each began reading Helen's typescript. As they finished pages they passed them on, the Governor to Robin Kitchener, his ADC, and Hesket-Bramwell to a youthful-looking Colonel Linklater who was introduced as the senior army officer in Ibadan. It amused Steve to see the play of emotions on the faces of the readers as the story unfolded for them. There were sharp intakes of breath and an occasional, 'Oh, my God'. Sir John handed over the final page and said:

'You did right to call me. I am glad I came up here to save time. Now, if the others have finished reading, there are a few things I would like you to expand on. Then I want to hear the interpretations Wickham and you put on some incidents and your own suggestions for action. After that we shall decide what orders are appropriate.'

At that, Hesket-Bramwell waved a telegram flimsy and said:

'First, you should know that Enugu has wired to say they have not arrested the German pair; that was timed at shortly before midnight. However there is a strong likelihood they drove up the Ikom road because a grey Mercedes was seen going though Abakaliki at five o'clock which is about the time they might have been expected there. Unfortunately the telephone and telegraph lines to Ikom,

137

Mamfe and so on went dead about an hour later, before a police call ordering road blocks could be sent. The fact is, we may have missed them. When this came I didn't understand the significance of the route; with Wickham's report, I now see the point.'

There followed a close question-and-answer session to fill in details of the report and to form the basis of decisions. Steve produced his aide-memoire sheets and passed carbon copies to the two senior officers. The colonel was quizzed about the distribution of troops, their strengths and mobility. Kitchener was told to send off a priority telegram immediately to Enugu demanding close pursuit of Klaus Ehrwald, wherever his trail led.

* *

The race was on. Klaus knew clearly the success of the German move in West Africa depended on his being able to elude the traps he was sure the British would set. Admittedly, at Onitsha Hilda had been correct: the policeman at the ferry had not been looking for them. So no message had come through from Benin by that time but it was bound to come and they must expect armed police at a roadblock somewhere. Friedrich and Karl, his two lieutenants, should be able to mount the operation without him, but Klaus had no intention of accepting that scenario and putting their competence to the test. So the race was on between the bungling English administration and himself. He had every confidence he would win.

By ten minutes to two o'clock in the afternoon Klaus and Hilda were clear of Onitsha on the road to Ikom, two hundred miles ahead. On the ferry, Klaus had considered the map carefully, whether to take the main road through Enugu, the regional capital of Eastern Provinces, or to take the minor roads by Awgu that would allow him to bypass the city. It needed little thought: Enugu offered the lesser risk. Time was their enemy and the Enugu route would be faster. The main problem they faced was the fact there was only a single road into Kamerun, that from Bansara through Ikom and Mamfe to the Bamenda-Kumba junction, a bottleneck with a total distance of one hundred and ten miles. That road, much of it single track, offered the easiest opportunity to stop them; one checkpoint on any part of it was

138

bound to succeed. Unless they could reach that length of road and drive some way up it ahead of a warning telegraphed from Benin, they might as well have stayed in the Residency garden.

By driving hard they succeeded in passing through Enugu at three-thirty and through Abakaliki at four-fiftyfive, half an hour before the police there were in position. The fugitives were ahead of the pack but not yet in the clear, since they had no alternative but drive that long single road to Mamfe. Two men were in a position to stop them.

Constable Enoch Ibue had been on point duty at the main junction in Abakaliki that afternoon. On completing his duty at half past five, he reported back to the station and, out of curiosity, asked what all the fuss was about. He was told: a road checkpoint, arms issued, enemy alien –

'That means a German, you bonehead man. Wanted for murder too. Nothing so exciting since Inspector Ojo got those hornets up his trousers!'

'What kind of car are they looking for?'

'Very smart car: grey Mercedes saloon.'

Enoch Ibue thought back. Slowly he became convinced that a grey Mercedes had passed him half-an-hour before he came off duty. There were not so many saloon cars; most vehicles he dealt with were trucks, kit-cars and open tourers. Five minutes later he went back to the desk and shared this conclusion with the inspector. Maybe it was not the Mercedes they were looking for but it was definitely a big grey car; there were not many around. In the end the inspector telephoned Enugu to pass on Ibue's belief the car may have passed Abakaliki before the checkpoint was manned, say at five o'clock.

The call was timed at a quarter to six, a few minutes before the Police Assistant Commissioner himself came into the station at Enugu. He had completed his nine holes and had a quick beer at the bar in the club but at the back of his mind he was concerned about the telegram from Benin and wanted to be sure the appropriate action had been taken promptly. At first reading it had riled him slightly that the request came from a district officer. Why should a DO be sending this kind of request, not only out of his province but to the police chief in another region? Why did it not come from the Resident or Benin's senior police officer? It had nagged at him that there was probably a perfectly good reason and he should make certain everything was

139

being done, because the affair sounded serious. After his beer, he returned to the station.

The Assistant Commissioner re-read the original telegram from Chris Wickham, noting especially the time the car had started from Benin, and the inspector told him about the latest call from Abakaliki. Two minutes reckoning convinced him that it was just possible for a hard driven car to reach Abakaliki by five o'clock and one must assume Constable Ibue was correct in his observation. He was a good lad to have remembered and reported it: he should be commended when this flap was over.

The police chief approved the inspector's actions but said they must assume the wanted pair had already passed all the checkpoints.

'Take the men off the Enugu checks right now but tell Abakaliki to keep theirs in position at present, although it is likely the Germans have passed. Don't worry, though, they cannot reach Ikom in time to escape a reception party there. Send a telegram now to our station in Ikom, giving my instruction they are to set up a road block with armed men to intercept this car. Repeat the information from the Benin telegram that he is an enemy alien, white, with a white woman and that they are armed. They should put up that block immediately on receipt of the telegram although the car may not arrive until morning. Add my instruction the two people are to be held on suspicion of murder and I am to be kept informed at once of all developments. Just in case these people decide to attempt an escape by the back way into Cameroons through Ogoja, Inspector, repeat that instruction to our station there and ask for a report to me if the Mercedes should arrive at Obudu.'

'Yes, Sah.'

The inspector carefully followed his senior officer's instruction and wrote out the telegram for despatch to Ikom. The P and T clerk, however, said,

'Ah-ah-ah! I am sorry. We are to disappoint you; the telegram must wait until tomorrow or until the line is repaired. All lines to Ikom went dead fifteen minutes ago. The line must be down, I think.'

*   *

140

Late on the Monday evening, while Steve Lister was driving hard up the road towards Ondo and Ibadan, Cracker Armstrong and Rob Graham were dozing in armchairs at Sapoba, quite ignorant of the excitements just to the north of them. They were beginning to think of bed when they had a surprise visit from Forest Guard Agbontaen and the hunter, Efondare. Speaking to Cracker, Agbontaen suggested he should go with the hunter to the bush: the moon was right and in every way it was a favourable time to find game. Cracker was rather half-hearted, having been almost settled on heading for bed, but the guard persuaded him. When Rob asked if they could both go, Agbontaen said only one should accompany the hunter and he pointed to Cracker. Rob was disappointed at being left out, as he watched his friend, armed with his Sten, leaving with the black hunter.

The path taken by the two men led them, after a quarter mile, back to the motor road where they turned west towards the Benin-Sapele junction. After another quarter mile walking in silence along the dusty road, Cracker was surprised to see he was approaching a large saloon car parked, without lights, at the roadside. In the moonlight he was aware that the hunter stopped, dropped on one knee and gave a brief greeting before stepping back.

It was the Oba's cultured voice that came out of the dark car.

'Good evening, Sergeant Armstrong. So you are on a hunting expedition. Please come and sit with me for a few moments. When we met before, you said that I should speak to you if I ever needed a Scottish agent.'

The interior light of the car was switched on momentarily, showing the Oba sitting alone. Cracker climbed in.

An hour later, back at the rest-house, Rob enquired if Cracker had been successful in hunting.

'Not a thing. The hunter brought me back. I think he means to go out again later on but of course I canna understand a thing the man says.'

*   *

Colonel Linklater had been in West Africa for only a few months and found it difficult to judge the severity of the threat posed by an Ibo

141

rising. He appealed to Sir John Robertson and Chief Commissioner Hesket-Bramwell for their appreciation of it, based on their combined sixty years' experience of the country. He found both took the threat very seriously. Sir John explained the background.

The roots of the trouble went a long way back. Between the fifteenth and the eighteenth century the Fulani tribe crossed the Sahara from the Middle East, into the area north of the Niger and Benue rivers. They were a hardy people, Islamic in their religion, with a way of life close to Abraham's when he left Ur. Soon after 1800 a great Islamic crusade established Fulani emirs as the rulers of the local tribes in the dry savannah region. These Hausa tribes, now Mohammedan, formed an alliance around the Sultanate of Sokoto. The emirs, malams and imams, descendants of the original Fulani emirs, were the dynamic elite of the Hausa, leading a disciplined feudal empire.

The Hausa, led by the Sultan, regarded it as their sacred duty to convert the tribes of southern Nigeria to Islam and, coinciding with British interest in trading with the south at the close of the 19th century, they sent a powerful army to attempt this, almost all cavalry. The campaign failed, not because of generalship or weaponry but because of tse-tse flies; the horses died.

The Hausa invasion, however, appeared to pose some threat to British trade in palm oil and, at the time, it provided a good enough excuse for Prime Minister Joseph Chamberlain to send in a force, nominally against the emirs but more importantly to forestall the French who were expanding aggressively in the area. The force was under the command of the remarkable Lord Lugard. He negotiated a treaty with the emirs, making the vast tract of northern Nigeria a British protectorate. This strategic treaty left the whole Hausa tribal structure intact and, with extraordinary sensitivity, permanently excluded Christian missionaries from the Muslem north. In contrast, southern Nigeria was strongly served by Christian missionary effort, much of which was devoted to the provision of excellent education, later reinforced by the state education service.

Thus it came about that for many critical years education in Hausa-land was restricted to Koranic teaching of a limited number of boys only, when in the south education was nearly universal, certainly for both boys and girls, and in some colleges to a high standard in science and crafts. As a result, southerners, on merit, gained overwhelming superiority in the public service and in technical appointments throughout the country in mining, in the railways and so on. Few things are more infuriating and calculated to cause disharmony than to see the best-paid jobs in one's country, that carry influence and power, being taken by foreigners of a different religion and culture who, adding insult to injury, send their pay out of your country to their folks back home. The Ibo people, too numerous for their limited land resources, were expansionist, versatile and highly ambitious; the Hausas loved them not at all.

A counterirritant was provided by the British army. Lugard had been impressed by the soldierly bearing of the Hausas, regarding it – rightly or wrongly – much higher than that of the Yoruba and Ibo tribes of the south. The army thereafter recruited in the north and any civil unrest in the south involved confrontation with Hausa soldiers. On both sides there was resentment, nervousness, inter-tribal fear rooted in long years of slave raiding, bad blood and thirst for revenge for some wrong, whether real or imagined. Summing up, Sir John said,

'The fact is, Linklater, the Hausa generally are proud, strongly devoted to Islam, self-righteous and secretly jealous of Ibo affluence. The Ibos are thirsty for technical education, versatile, materialistic, naturally inclined to political machination and secretly fearful of Hausa discipline and military prowess. The two peoples are not natural friends. A couple of carefully designed and well embroidered atrocities could easily set them at each others' throats in a way that would be difficult to stop and could leave the police and army seriously weakened by their own tribal attachments. The threat of a rising engineered and armed by Klaus Ehrwald has to be taken seriously.'

'I take the point well, Sir John. And, of course, the strategic issues are of the highest import,' the Colonel replied. 'The real value of West Africa being secure rests in maintaining the supply of aircraft to the Middle East. Loss of RAF power in the Western Desert would give Rommel a clear run through Egypt to Arabian oil. My orders are very firm on the primacy of protecting the air corridor from Takoradi. I see this kind of rising would obviously jeopardise that.'

By six o'clock in the morning when the Ibadan party adjourned for baths, shaving and breakfast, all the necessary decisions had been taken and orders issued.

143

Colonel Linklater had sent off his lieutenant (who thereby forfeited an excellent breakfast) with secret signals to Kano Command, alerting the watchers on the desert fringes from Sokoto to Katsina and Maiduguri to the possibility that the Germans might soon attempt to emulate the Long-Range Desert Group, and to Enugu to prepare for internal trouble that might arise most likely in the Calabar-Opobo area, possibly in ten days, The lieutenant was also required to produce whatever revolvers were available and a quantity of matching ammunition. Initially the colonel had demurred at the suggestion army weapons should be handed over to civilians but he was overruled by the Governor who pointed out they were for an operation specifically ordered by Mr. Churchill personally.

'I shall try to see you get them back, Linklater.'

The Governor himself drafted for coding a signal to the senior naval officer in Freetown, alerting him to the forecast of a U-boat attack on ships at Lagos and warning that a captured enemy merchant ship was expected to be on passage from Santa Isabel to Lagos in eight or ten days' time.

'The Navy will wonder how a mere landsman could predict that and probably they won't believe me.'

Another telegram was drafted for coding to be sent to Enugu to arrange for watchers to be put on the paths from Cameroons to Rio del Rey. They would report on any movement of "Klaus Force" towards the ports where weapons would be landed, to report but not to stop the men. Interference too early would be likely to prevent the capture of the ringleaders and jeopardise the operation against the *Duchessa di Lucca*.

Sir John then went back to an unanswered point in Steve's aide-memoire, the whereabouts of von Ehrwald senior, Baron Ludwig. In view of the trouble he had caused in the First World War, a special search had been made for him in 1939 but he was not found.

'The younger son was interned by the French in Duala,' Sir John said, 'and the elder son is serving in the German army, we believe, but there was no sign of the father. Perhaps he too may have been in Germany at the outbreak of war. Obviously the French did not keep a proper hold of Klaus at Duala and we don't know if other Germans escaped who might now be his lieutenants in what you conveniently call "Klaus Force". I wish there was more I could tell you but – No! I do not know about the old Baron.'

144

Sir John judged the cutting-out operation to be even more necessary than before. Chris and Captain Moore were given full backing for recruiting and commandeering the equipment required and the draft timetable was approved. The decision produced immediate results. Robin Kitchener pleaded with his chief to be released temporarily from his appointment so that he might join Chris Wickham's group. He said he would be able to see something of the country around Benin and later report personally to the Governor how the operation had gone. His request was so pressing and so obviously sincere that Sir John did not have the heart to deny him and agreed Kitchener could return to Benin with Steve Lister.

'I hope, Sir,' Philip Denstone said to Mr. Hesket-Bramwell, 'that you will not tell me I may not join Tigger Wickham's team. I certainly want to be there and have surely earned my place by being knocked up at midnight to chauffeur Lister to breakfast meetings half-across the country. Please allow me to join Tigger, Sir; I should be away from Ondo only for a week or so and the place can easily tick-over without me.'

The Chief Commissioner laughed. Jocularly he objected that with one Resident dead and district officers taking local leave in droves to undertake some completely illegal activity on the high seas, he would have no administrative officers left. Without immediately answering Denstone's request, he spoke to his wife:

'Silvia. In view of the gap left at Benin with Grenville-Fletcher's death, I believe I should go to hold the fort there. I shall leave later today, probably about noon if I can clear my desk by then. I don't know what commitments you may have, whether you would care to come with me or not. The timing will be rather open-ended, depending on how we find things, so I don't know when we might get back home, perhaps in ten days when Wickham and Lister here return from their jaunt.'

Silvia Bramwell had nothing that could not be cancelled and made it clear she had no intention of passing up a chance of getting away from Ibadan. She would get the boys organised and attend to the packing immediately after breakfast.

'It will be like the old days, going on tour. Shall we stay in the rest-house or at the Residency, Arthur?'

All agreed the Residency would be preferable, especially as a public indication that the era of the Grenville-Fletchers was finished

145

and there was a new beginning. Since Robert was dead and there was no possibility of Hilda returning, Silvia Bramwell undertook to clear out their chattels and prepare the house for new tenants, a prospect she clearly relished.

Since the Bramwells would be going to Benin, Steve thought it fair to return the favour of Helen's work by stressing how helpful she had been in volunteering her service as a secretary in their crisis the day before. It might get her off on the right foot with Silvia Bramwell and could do no harm.

That settled, the Chief Commissioner turned back to Philip Denstone.

'All right, Denstone. But for Heaven's sake don't end up in a Spanish prison. We need you back in Ondo.'

After breakfast, before leaving again for Lagos, Sir John Robertson wrote a short letter to Chris, saying three things. First he commended Chris' handling of the crisis in Benin; second he told him to continue with the Duchess operation on the timetable outlined by Chris; and third, on a personal note, he told him he and Olivia had just received the news that their son James was a prisoner in Germany. This last had perhaps played its part in brightening the Governor's mood in the night-long discussions and in sharpening his decisions. With the letter to Chris he also handed over to Steve some additional papers he had received from London a couple of days earlier relating to the *Duchessa di Lucca*'s cargo. They also agreed some simple code names to allow clear language radio signals to be sent from the *Duchessa* and the Governor passed on the advice of the radio men about suitable wave bands to use for their communication.

Then it was time for the party to break up, the Governor to Lagos, the Hesket-Bramwells to prepare for Benin, Colonel Linklater to activate the military services and Steve Lister's group, now much reinforced, to head for Sapoba and Santa Isabel.

Silvia Hesket-Bramwell, wife of His Honour the Chief Commissioner Western Provinces and Assistant-Governor of Nigeria, went about her preparations with a light heart, singing softly. So, she had been up half the night but something different had happened and now there was the prospect of business she could handle. Not another bloody teaparty. Not another blooming coffee morning. Not another wretched rubber of bridge. She was an intelligent woman who, given half a chance, would have been quite capable of running a district or

146

managing her husband's secretariat. But not only was the Service male, the abundance of servants almost precluded even housekeeping as an activity. Wives might check the addition in the cook's market book and see the drinking water was filtered and properly boiled. Apart from that, there were coffee mornings and bridge, entertainments that palled quickly since on many stations there might be fewer than half-a-dozen white women all told. The climate made family life with children very difficult: malaria, cholera, amoebic dysentery, filariasis and a string of other ailments all lay in wait and even children's play was severely restricted by the risks of scorpions and snakes. Young wives found themselves torn between providing a home for children at school in Britain but longing to be with the husband, like Philippa Wickham, or living with their husbands on the Coast and worrying about the children. And the war had multiplied the problems and the grounds for concern. Silvia now gleefully contemplated the cancellation of the coffee mornings and bridge parties, and savoured the prospect of travel to Benin.

*   *

The Mercedes reached the road junction at Bansara at five minutes to six and, in spite of the Assistant Commissioner's thought of a last minute escape on the Ogoja road, it turned right towards Ikom. Three miles farther on and in gathering darkness, Klaus saw, just clear of the road, the line of poles carrying the telephone and telegraph wires that connected the rest of Nigeria with this corner, the lines to Ikom, Mamfe and the whole of the Cameroons. He pulled the car to a stop, grabbed a small kit-bag that held ammunition, a spare magazine for the Luger and other important items, and ran to the nearest pole. From the bag he pulled a slab of gun cotton and, in a few seconds, tied it to the base of the pole. He pushed in a detonator, like an open-ended .22 cartridge, and cut off a length of fuse that he crimped in to the detonator and lit. He ran back to the car and drove on for a couple of hundred yards, where he repeated the whole process. While he worked on the second pole there was a sharp report that caused him to nod in satisfaction. Then back to the first pole, now lying broken in a maze of copper wire. He would have liked to cut and remove the

147

wires, in order to delay repair further, but the light was now too poor to make a job of that with the pliers from the car's toolkit, so he confined himself to smashing the white china insulators on the crossbars. The second explosion occurred while he was busy at that. Repair would not be made quickly.

Klaus had no means of knowing whether his action was in time to prevent the police in Ikom being warned of their approach but he had done his best. He was immensely tired. Hilda had been asleep half a dozen times after Enugu so he asked her to drive now and take the car ten or fifteen miles farther. There they pulled off the road and had a scratch meal of bread, bully beef and fruit, before trying to sleep for a couple of hours in the car. Sleep was difficult because the mosquitos descended on them, hungry for a blood meal. Sleep they had to have, however, to make more driving possible. The other worry was water. They had left Benin with only six pint bottles, scarcely enough for one person for a day, given the high temperature and their loss of perspiration. With rigorous self-discipline and eking out the supply with fruit, they had now drunk only three and a half bottles; the remainder must be reserved for the next day.

The pair managed to sleep for nearly two hours before vicious mosquito attacks forced them to move. Klaus checked the magazine of the Luger, prepared if necessary to shoot his way through a road block. Then they drove on, fast and hard.

Ahead of them, at Ikom the police were involved in a routine case of theft. In the Mamfe district to the south cola trees grew well and the walnut-size cola nuts were an important and high-value local product, most being sent to northern Nigeria where people chewed them to enjoy their high caffeine content. Traditionally the nuts were carried north by professional porters who head-loaded incredibly heavy bags over hundreds of miles of footpaths. Recently a store where cola nuts were bagged and held ready for carriers had been broken into and several tons had been stolen, which the police believed would be sent north by truck through Ikom. The superintendent had ordered his men to stop all trucks passing north through the town, to check for the stolen cola.

Consequently, in spite of the Assistant Commissioner's order lying useless in Enugu, a road-block was in place on the south side of Ikom town, manned by a sergeant and two constables. Their concern was in produce lorries driving north but custom was scarce in the

148

middle of the night. They had had nothing to do for more than two hours; they were bored. But here was a vehicle coming out of the town going south. Let us stop that and see what they are carrying. Anything to pass the time; there might be a little something in it for us if we can bounce them into paying a back-hander.

Klaus had been ready for a police point north of Ikom, the obvious place if a warning signal from Benin had been sent before his sabotage of the wires. He had been encouraged to find no block there. The town was grave-silent, a few pye-dogs the only creatures moving. He drove quietly through the streets, to attract least attention. Then, just as he thought they were clear, he faced a red light waving in the road ahead.

This was disaster. All the hard driving and anxiety of the last twenty hours was to go for nothing. In seconds Klaus thought of his beloved Kamerun detachment, the men he had recruited and trained so carefully. He thought of the plans, the thrust into Nigeria, the Ibo rising, reversing the disgusting Versailles treaty that deprived Germany of her colonies, the prospect of disrupting supplies to England's army in Egypt and all that could flow from it.

In that instant the despond signalled by the red light changed to fierce anger lest anything should interfere with these plans, deny that prize. He would fight.

CHAPTER ELEVEN

The soldiers at Sapoba found it hard to settle. They were enjoying pampered idleness but at heart each knew that intense action, acute discomfort and a possible fire-fight were just around the corner. There was a touch of Calvanistic guilt in their idleness: surely they would be made to suffer later for this lotus-living. On the one hand they were keen to push on with the operation they had come three thousand miles for, the planning of which had been snatched away at a tantalising stage on Saturday night after the Oba's revelations. On the other hand, like all soldiers, they were content to take full advantage of any lull: ten minutes for a fag, half-an-hour for a kip, half-a-day – what the hell! – that was a holiday. Life was a tease. On Monday, between meals and sleep, they speculated about ways to steal the ship, reminisced about their Norway experiences six months back, about comrades in the unit and about families back home, and then back to how to steal the ship.

They talked too about the Border country they both knew from boyhood. Langholm in Scotland and Cockermouth in England are not far apart and much of their heritage was shared. Cracker recalled the stories his school-teacher had told, many drawn from Walter Scott's *Tales of a Grandfather*, about the raiding parties that made the Borders a dangerous place for generations.

'Whiles the Armstrongs and the Grahams were on opposite sides but they often rode together, Rob, against the Fosters and the Fletchers. So this trip is maybe a repeat. Mind you,' he said with a laugh, 'for this reiving we've cam a hell of a sight further than they ever did in the old days!'

150

Rob Graham pondered, for the nth time, how the Boss and Steve were getting on in Benin City.

'That bloke Fletcher, the Resident or whatever he's called, he's a real bastard, but you saw him off properly, Cracker. He went away with his tail between his legs.'

'There's no use wondering,' the sergeant replied lazily. 'Enjoy the peace and quiet while we can. I could get used to this life with cooks and servants to bring the meals and wash the clothes but it won't go on for ever, so take it while it lasts. I could go a couple of pints of decent beer, though; beer would make this place perfect. Pity there's no NAAFI. And belt up about old sod Fletcher'.

Armstrong's conscience was still sensitive on his own intemperate outburst which had precipitated the Resident's sudden departure from the rest-house; he had been out of line, although the Boss had taken a remarkably relaxed view of an incident his CO at home would have put him on a charge for.

'Let's have a swim before supper. I wonder when Peter will be back.'

At lunchtime on Tuesday the invasion of Sapoba began. Peter Thorburn drove in with two new men and, far more surprising than the fresh faces, with shattering news: Grenville-Fletcher was dead; the Germans were planning to use the *Duchess* to run guns for arming an invasion and an uprising in Nigeria; Steve had driven to Ibadan to alert the army. The project to capture the ship for Britain had assumed far greater urgency than it had only forty-eight hours earlier.

The two NCOs solemnly absorbed the fact that the Benin Resident was dead.

'I didna take to the manny, there's no use pretending, but it sounds a right nasty way to go,' Cracker reflected, then added jocularly, 'If you'd been properly dressed, Rob, with your shirt tail tucked in, he might not have taken a scunner to you and I wouldn't have shot my mouth off. So it's maybe your fault he's handed in his bloody pay-book.'

Cracker grinned. In truth, what did it matter which way the man's number came up? He was a stuck-up bastard, as Rob had said, and if it took a bit of simple torture by one of the Oba's people to make him spill the beans on the scheme with his German pals, so what? It's war and we can't afford to be squeamish. Pity the Jerry brother-in-law got away; catching him would have saved a lot of sweat. The Boss and Steve were slow there. With the tip from the Oba on Saturday night, they should have gone in hard straight off. I can see why they put it off: senior officer – they'd think surely he couldn't be bent. It would be like a couple of platoon commanders suspecting the Colonel of being an enemy spy. But with the wife's brother a Jerry, they should have gone in fast and said sorry afterwards. Still, we must just make the best of it. "Damage limitation" the CO calls it. Anyway, now we can get down to proper business right away. It will be full steam ahead to get the ship, for there's a lot more at stake now. The risk is folk will be in too much of a rush and will want to cut corners and go in only half-trained.

The men who arrived with Peter were Clapper Bell and Donald McIver. They brought in a massive load of tents and household goods, to equip the rest-house as the temporary base for twenty men and their supporters. Their attitude was typical of the recruits: having been denied the opportunity of joining the armed services early in the war, they were determined to make the most of this one.

George Clapperton Bell was a mild-mannered man of forty, an officer in the Education Department and a very unlikely pirate indeed. He was unathletic and wore thick glasses which caused him to peer about like a hen. The appearance was deceptive, however, for he had determination and mental toughness which went far to compensate for his physical shortcomings and he was an expert raconteur. Clapper had read History at university but his real expertise was in languages. He spoke French, Italian and Spanish well and was an acknowledged expert on Yoruba dialects. An extra attraction of Peter's proposition that he should join the Duchess operation was the opportunity it offered of visiting Benin and hearing the Bini language spoken for a few days. Peter was glad to have a second Italian speaker in the party and, as an introduction to the new language, promised to introduce him to Forest Guard Agbontaen as well as Joshua Oshodin.

Donald McIver was a few years older than Peter and the forest officer in the division to the north of Benin. A week earlier Peter had written cryptically to tell him there was "a ploy afoot, too confidential to be described in a letter but on a par with Wallace's effort at Stirling Bridge". His response was immediate.

The appearance, speech and behaviour of Donald McIver left one in no doubt he was a Scot. His manner was dour, his brogue thick.

He smoked St. Bruno in a rough curly-stemmed pipe reminiscent of Sherlock Holmes. Tousled hair overflowed below his ears in generous side-chops. Habitually he wore the kilt. In the McIver ménage each morning began properly with salty porridge (never satisfactory for most people when taken with tinned milk) and dinner frequently included Scotch broth with plenty of barley, his cook being well trained in the production of these warming dishes which were a sore trial to any guest insufficiently blunt to refuse them. For most people, whether Scot or Ruretanian, neither was attractive in a temperature of 95°F and upwards but failure to empty the plate was apt to draw the question: 'Is there something amiss with the parrich?' or 'Do ye no fancy the brose? I dinna like to see guid meat wastit when there's folk in the warld going wi'out.'

In fact Donald was a Londoner, born of a Cockney mother. Admittedly his paternal grandfather was a Scot; he must have been what geneticists call a dominant character. If one looked beneath the silly caricature, however, Mac was a solid citizen, kindly and generous. Friends and colleagues who knew him accepted the veneer of eccentricity which, after all, provided colourful hilarity in a tiny European community where conformity was the rule. 'Good God, it's only Mac,' they would say. Scotsmen in the Forest Department would gleefully emphasise that Mac was a Cambridge graduate – dating from the time that university offered a forestry degree, a taunt which infuriated some of their English colleagues who would fain have disowned the maverick.

When he received Peter's letter, Mac was working on a forest survey far from his station. Figure of fun he might choose to appear, but the man's response was to strike camp instantly and trek 46 miles on foot in 21 hours, all in a temperature over ninety degrees, in order to join the party, a move which exhausted three successive teams of local carriers.

Bell, the historian, was intrigued and greatly amused by the coincidence of the two soldiers sent on this raid being an Armstrong and a Graham.

'It happened before, you know, Sergeant. Back about 1600 when there was trouble in the Scottish Border country. I am sure the Armstrongs and Grahams were allies in joint operations. But perhaps you know that.'

153

'Aye. Of course,' Cracker replied. 'If there's choice, you don't pick the man to come with you on this kind of trip on five minutes' acquaintance. My gran'faither told me stories of the reiving when the Grahams and the Armstrongs lived and fought together along the whole Border many a long year and the schoolteacher at Langholm said the same. The two families could ride out a troop of reivers mair than a thousand strong. The association goes a long way back, as you say, and that was one reason for me asking Rob Graham to join me for this job. Forby the man himself.'

'I should have guessed you would know the history and that the choice was deliberate. Please forgive me for thinking otherwise', and Clapper reflected to himself that people in the north often had a much stronger folk-memory and sense of family history than the majority in the south of England, where he belonged; he envied them.

He quickly followed his apology by asking the sergeant if he was related to the famous Kinmont Willie Armstrong of the ballad, who was freed from Carlisle Castle in a raid led by Lord Scott of Buccleuch, the Duke's ancestor. Cracker confirmed he was.

'Oh aye. Willie Armstrong of Kinmont was one of my forebears. They say that was the last great reiving in the Borders. It was a raid the Commandos would be proud of today. Buccleuch and his men lifted Kinmont from inside the castle, going over the walls with ladders and so as to avoid retaliation they didn't kill even one of the English garrison under Lord Henry Scrope. And they got clean away! Come to think on it, it'd be a fine model for oursel's for what we are to take on now.' As an afterthought he added, 'I seem to mind there was a man Bell rode with Buccleuch and the Armstrongs that day, so maybe you had a forebear there yourself.'

Clapper Bell's crowning triumph was that, from a far recess of his memory, he dragged the opening lines of the great Border ballad and managed to recite,

'O have ye na heard o' the fause Sakelde?
 O have ye na heard o' the keen Lord Scroope?
How they hae ta'en bold Kinmont Willie,
 On Haribee to hang him up?'

He could remember no more but it confirmed him in Cracker Armstrong's mind as "one of us"; it made the Wykehamist as close as a Liddesdale cousin.

In March 1596 William Armstrong of Kinmont was riding home to Morton Rigg after attending a truce meeting with English officers at Kershopefoot on the Border. Although guaranteed immunity on that day by his position as a truce delegate, Armstrong – a well-known trouble-maker and reiver – was set upon by English troopers and taken to Carlisle Castle where he was imprisoned by Thomas Salkeld, the Deputy Warden of the March. Both Salkeld and his senior, Lord Henry Scrope, knew the imprisonment was illegal because of the truce, as did their superiors in London, but they declined to release him, although the countries were not at war.

Kinmont's case was taken up by Lord Scott of Buccleuch, Keeper of Liddesdale and the senior Scottish officer for that part of the Border, but Salkeld and Lord Scrope both refused his requests. Scrope's insulting refusal, as much as the injustice of the imprisonment itself, so angered Buccleuch he determined to break loose Kinmont from the castle.

The task of freeing the prisoner was fearsome, since Carlisle Castle was regarded as impregnable, and Buccleuch added to the difficulty by making it a condition that none of the garrison should be killed, in order to avoid cause for retaliation: to free Kinmont was legally justifiable but killing in its achievement would forfeit that right. The attack had to depend on meticulous planning and intelligence, its execution on speed and stealth. Surprise was essential for an operation which, because of its apparent impossibility, was totally unexpected.

*   *

Ikom was a close call. Klaus' first and instinctive reaction to the red light had been to stop. Then anger forced him to revolt and he slammed the car into gear in order to drive through the barrier. In the headlights he could see no weapons in the hands of the police there. He would knock down the constable waving the red light, thereby reducing the enemy strength by one at the outset. They would force a way through.

'Für das Vaterland', he mouthed as he prepared to ram the post and, too clumsily in his haste, he let in the clutch.

The engine stalled and, instead of accelerating, the car crawled pathetically towards the waiting police.

Klaus dropped the pistol on the seat beside him, as he busied himself simultaneously with the clutch, gear lever and starter button, desperate to restart the engine. In those moments of distraction, the police sergeant stepped to the car door. He too was off-balance because, in deciding to stop the vehicle, he and his men had not anticipated the driver might be European. After all, it was four o'clock in the morning. They had seen only headlights. The car window was open; he would explain they were checking lorries carrying produce. The sergeant signalled to his man to open the barrier. They could expect to extort no money from a European driver.

Suddenly, before the sergeant could speak, the engine fired and the driver looked up. Klaus grabbed the pistol, pointed it at the policeman and shouted:

'Zurück!' (Get back).

The sergeant did not understand. Completely surprised, he stood. So Klaus squeezed the trigger. Nothing happened. In the stress of the engine dying and being re-started, Klaus had omitted to cock the gun. Hilda saw it like a slow-motion film, farcical. Simultaneously the constable, following his senior's order, raised the barrier and Klaus let in the clutch.

The Mercedes roared away from Ikom, leaving three bewildered policemen. Klaus and Hilda, congratulating themselves on their escape, did not appreciate the extent of their good fortune. The sergeant, having no idea the driver was being sought as an enemy alien and on a charge of murder, nor having understood what had been shouted at him, thought the man's behaviour might have been caused by surprise at being stopped late at night, out of town. Perhaps the man had thought the barrier had been set up by thieves to take money from cars by extortion. (Close to the truth!) That would explain the shouting and waving a pistol, if that was what he had in his hand. The sergeant was unwilling to be questioned on why they had stopped a

156

car travelling south when they had orders to stop produce trucks driving north, especially as the European driver might be a friend of the Superintendent. He told the two constables they would say nothing about the incident. Which explained why no alarm was passed along the road to Mamfe to detain a driver who had threatened the police with a firearm.

At the time of the early morning conference at Ibadan, the Mercedes was climbing the steep road beyond Mamfe into Kamerun-Gebiet. The von Ehrwalds were in the clear and on their home ground.

'Der kluge Fuchs had die lässige Jagdhunde überlistet,' Klaus shouted to his sister with a laugh, (The wily fox has outwitted the lazy hounds), his self-congratulation giving scant credit to Lady Luck.

*　　　*

While the party at Sapoba was engaged in putting up tents on the tennis lawn – more supervisors than workers – three cars arrived with more recruits. Helen Smith came with her husband Gerald, newly returned from the Oil Palm Research Station. Neither he nor his assistant, Roger Trimble, was going to miss the chance of the Duchess trip. Roger was a keen amateur radio ham (a useful skill for the party) and Hilary Trimble had joined Helen in volunteering to organise the domestic side of Sapoba; their friend Jean Leach would come later with her husband Tom, the PWD District Engineer, bringing Eddie Hudson, one of his foremen, who was to serve as the ship's engineer.

Although the group was far from complete, the need for a domestic dictator was already apparent. The number of servants was increasing rapidly as most people brought a steward boy, a few a cook also, and the capacity for conflict increased exponentially with the number, just as the service similarly diminished. Left to themselves no servant would attend to the mundane jobs of fetching water or sweeping the floor but each steward claimed precedence for slicing oranges or arranging flowers on the dining table.

Into this morass of futility Helen Smith cut instantly and decisively. Go and draw water. Show me that the water is boiling. Clean the filter. Bake more bread. So she decreed, with the stewards' resentment steadily mounting at being ordered around by a woman. It

157

worried Helen not a whit and servants found complaints to their own masters were dismissed out of hand.

The showdown came when a steward, conditioned by bachelor employment, was so affronted by the monstrosity of female management that he said he would commit suicide rather than obey.

'Fine,' Helen replied in level tones. 'Do it in the river so your body will be taken away by the water and there will be no untidiness'.

This matter-of-fact response to the threat appealed mightily to the Nigerian sense of humour so that in no-time, as the story was repeated, everyone was howling with laughter and literally slapping their thighs in the extrovert fashion that is good natural African behaviour but appears artificial and mere theatre in Europeans. As was usual in the country, the shrieks of laughter completely deflated a tense situation, everyone happily accepted who was boss and got stuck in to their work. The Sapoba commissariat now began to work smoothly.

Tuesday was, however, an unsatisfactory day, as when one arrives hours too early for an important game: several players still had to turn up so there was futile hanging about and conversation had the hollow ring of false joviality. Everyone was wondering what was happening elsewhere, in Ibadan, in Benin, in Cameroons, even in Santa Isabel. A swimming session in the late afternoon rescued the day.

Captain Panda Moore arrived just in time for dinner, with two friends he had recruited in Port Harcourt. Then, with a blare of horns, three cars drove in well after ten o'clock bringing the party from Ibadan and Ondo: Steve Lister, Philip Denstone, Robin Kitchener and three friends he had rescued from the Ibadan Secretariat. Last to arrive was Chris Wickham, bringing Joshua Oshodin.

Chris had to wait in Benin until the Hesket-Bramwells arrived from Ibadan. They had dinner together at Chris' house and had talked through current issues in the division, by way of a hand-over. In normal circumstances such a transfer of responsibility would have been totally unacceptable but Hesket-Bramwell protested he would manage very well and it would be for only a week or ten days. He was anxious to send Chris off to his other duties at Sapoba and felt that, by holding the fort in Benin, acting as combined Resident and District Officer, he was "doing his bit" in making possible the Duchess operation. The main job for Silvia and himself was to sweep up after the Grenville-Fletcher mess. Arthur Hesket-Bramwell said he was sorry Robert had gone off the rails and got himself killed: bad business, y'know. Silvia went to the heart of the matter with devastating female candour:

'Robert was a weak character and should never have married into that Ehrwald family. He got himself far too deeply involved there and, with the war, was in an impossible position with a wife who did not fit into British society and, as a confirmed Nazi, never had any intention of doing so. Quite apart from that, I never trusted the woman. Her bidding at bridge was unsound, she mistreated her servants and she wore those hideous yellow mosquito boots she had made in Italy. It would have been bad enough to buy the things in a shop but to have them specially made showed poor taste.'

*   *

On Wednesday at Sapoba the briefing and training began. Reveille was at first light, around five-thirty, and breakfast was served as people appeared. Donald McIver, in support of his standard breakfast dish, announced to the unbelievers:

'The great thing about porridge is that the cook makes it the night before and leaves it on the warm stove to mature. I'm weel prepared for the day.' Needless to say, he ate it standing up, with the tinned milk in a separate bowl.

At seven o'clock Chris called everyone to order and introduced himself for the benefit of the few strangers.

'This party has gathered for the purpose of stealing a ship, the *Duchessa di Lucca*, an Italian merchant ship which has sheltered in the harbour of Santa Isabel on the Spanish island of Fernando Po since Italy entered the war against us in June 1940. Spain is neutral and will undoubtedly say that our taking the ship is stealing, an illegal act, probably piracy, but there are pressing reasons for Britain and for Nigeria which make it vital this ship be captured. I shall go into those reasons later. Until two days ago we thought there was no special urgency for this tricky job: suddenly it has become extremely urgent. We have only two days to plan and to train. On Friday we leave here for Fernando Po and we intend to attack probably in the small hours of Monday morning.'

159

There was a rustle of suppressed excitement. Chris saw the nineteen men of his team sitting forward eagerly waiting to hear how he intended to carry out this plan. They were keen volunteers and he felt a great weight of responsibility for them. Could he deliver what was required? Was he leading these men into a trap, encouraging them to take on a task that had looked feasible in London but which was, in reality, a stark impossibility? He saw the faultless fresh African sky above the fringe of forest and heard the gentle morning noises of the birds feeding in the trees, all symbols of freedom. Would the operation he was introducing end with his men at liberty to enjoy these things or would they be in some island prison? Grimly Chris suppressed all these disturbing thoughts; he must show no hint of doubt. He went on:

'I am in overall charge of the operation, having been given the job by the Governor, Sir John Robertson. Since you are all volunteers it is only fair you should be given the full background so that, as far as possible, you know why decisions have been taken. This is the letter which set the whole show in motion. It is from Ten Downing Street and is from Mr. Churchill himself to Sir John Robertson.'

He read out the Prime Minister's letter and continued:

'We have only today and tomorrow to decide the plan of attack and to train for it, so every hour must be made to count. We should sail out the *Duchess of Lucca* early on Monday to a Nigerian port. That is the plan in outline. The attack will rely on stealth and will be as non-violent as possible, since we are basically a civilian force stealing a ship with, as far as we know, a civilian crew – albeit an enemy one.

'I must stress one thing. On every score – for the country's sake and for our personal comfort – it is vital we are not caught by the Spanish authorities.

'As I have said, I am in overall charge of the operation. Captain Moore will command the *Duchess of Lucca* after its capture, to decide all the navigation and safety of the ship as its captain. Training and the detail of the actual attack will be the business of Sergeant Armstrong.

'Anyone who has doubts about coming on this trip should say so now because after we start allocating jobs it will become increasingly inconvenient to lose people. Unquestionably this will be

160

a team job; we shall all be relying on each other and we must quickly shake down as a team to play the agreed game-plan.' He paused. 'Are there any questions at this stage? If not, I suggest we each introduce ourselves – name and department or station. Most of us know each other but we must fill in any gaps straight away.'

Chris began. Panda Moore followed, then Clapper Bell, Cracker Armstrong and Rob Graham. Joshua Oshodin would have kept silent until all the white men had spoken; his youth – he was the youngest by a year or two – and the diffidence of being the only Nigerian in the party would have decided that. But after Peter Thorburn had introduced himself, Joshua felt his arm squeezed by Steve Lister who was standing close behind him and Steve commanded,

'You speak now, Joshua.' And he did so:

'Joshua Oshodin, Ologbo Trading Company. I live in Benin.'

Philip Denstone followed immediately but his firm voice was insufficient to prevent everyone hearing Eddie Hudson's comment:

'Didn't know we was to have a wog in the party. That's the first bloody mistake. You can never rely on the clowns, not in my experience.'   Seconds later Eddie was aware that Steve Lister had taken his arm.

'Let's have a walk, Eddie. And a little chat.'

And after a few yards, when they were out of soft earshot of the main party, Steve continued:

'You are wrong, Eddie. The first bloody mistake was for you to open your big mouth too wide and let hot air dribble out. When it comes to gauging people's reliability, no-one knows whether Eddie Hudson is going to be reliable or unreliable. We have to take you on trust. All right! Keep your hair on. Remember I am a Yorkshireman and I don't reckon much on anyone who is not. Joshua Oshodin is not here by chance. He is here because he has great experience: he has been to Santa Isabel more than once and has seen the ship, which is more than you have and more than I have. You might also bear in mind his father was the Benin war chief, a general commanding thousands of men. We don't know how reliable Joshua is, but he has a good pedigree. No young man's confidence or reliability in a team is helped by you foul-mouthing him at the start, so if you want to come on this trip you can keep your racist comments to yourself and don't use words like "wog" again. That is an order and a straight warning. Now get back to the group and introduce yourself nicely.'

161

Eddie's first inclination was to bluster and try to justify his outburst but the fierce tone of Steve's warning dissuaded him.

In regard to race Nigeria was a curious muddle. Colour presented no political problem, since Nigeria was a protectorate, not a colony, and only local African people could own property or vote in an election. There was no official segregation although unquestionably there was social division reinforced by the affluence of white officers relative to the mass of the local population (although the wealthiest people were certainly not British). The final retirement age for expatriates was fifty-five and older white people resident in the country scarcely existed. Black-white relations, although not warm, were generally good, aided in part by the personal standards and education of the Colonial Service, so that overt racist rudeness such as Eddie's was rare; on the other hand, black inter-tribal racism was bitter and common, sometimes with only British officers holding the peace.

When the introductions were complete, Chris spoke again.

'You may be wondering what the Prime Minister meant when he wrote about the value of the ship's cargo. Certainly I have been speculating about that. Yesterday Steve Lister collected fresh information from London about the cargo. When she took refuge in Spanish waters, the *Duchess* was on passage from South Africa to Italy and had just picked up four and a half thousand tons of pure copper ingots from the port of Banana in the Belgian Congo. In terms of war production that copper is very valuable to Britain and denying it to the enemy is even more important.'

A murmur of excitement went round the men.

'The papers are also interesting with regard to the passengers. The South African authorities say three passengers joined the ship in Cape Town, all Italians. We know nothing about two of them but the third was Signor Aldo Pasconi who is a well-known diamond dealer and has acted as the Italian government's agent for the purchase of industrial diamonds. From De Beers in Johannesburg we know Signor Pasconi bought a large quantity of industrial diamonds in May 1940, just before Italy came into the war. On the face of it, it appears strange that a highly valuable consignment of small bulk should have been sent in a slow ship like the *Duchess of Lucca* but with war imminent they would want it in an Italian vessel and there may have been no choice. Added to that, Signor Pasconi may have thought the sheer

162

improbability of the *Duchess* provided a good security cover. We do not know whether Signor Pasconi is still on the ship but from Joshua Oshodin here we do know there is at least one passenger aboard and that he seldom goes ashore. Joshua has an advantage over the rest of us because he has been to Santa Isabel and has actually seen the ship quite close to. If there are industrial diamonds on board they will presumably be locked away safely and they can be "rescued" later.'

'Seems a pity the Admiralty no longer pays prize-money for captured enemy ships, Chris. We'd be in clover!', a comment that brought general laughter.

'That's true, but to us right now, this paper Captain Moore has just brought along has a value comparable to those diamonds. We have to thank Panda's good memory for its retrieval.' He held up a brochure advertising the *Duchess of Lucca* as a passenger ship, which had been filed away, pre-war, in the Port Harcourt Marine Department office. Vitally, the brochure contained a deck plan of the ship's accommodation, a key to devising the plan of attack.

'Before handing over to Captain Moore, to describe the general design of the *Duchess* and to tell you how we shall go to Fernando Po, I have something more important to say about the cargo. The reason for the sudden urgency is that in the last couple of days we have discovered that the Germans have sent a large quantity of arms to Santa Isabel in a South American ship. Those weapons have been transferred to the *Duchess of Lucca* and we know the plan is to sail them to a Nigerian port to arm a force under German command to make trouble here, especially in Eastern Provinces.'

His audience was well able to judge the seriousness of the threat and there were many sharp expletives.

Chris went on, 'The Governor and the Army have been alerted and are preparing counter-measures ashore but the best defence will be to intercept the ship and take her over ourselves. In view of the nature of that cargo it will be best to hand over the ship at Lagos where the Army and the Royal Navy will be ready to deal with the arms and ammunition. All being well, that is likely to be late Wednesday or Thursday next week, according to Captain Moore.'

This produced a ripple of speculation among the men. Chris went on:

'Looking forward to that hand-over, you may recall that Mr. Churchill in his letter said the British government will claim to have

163

known nothing about this operation before the ship appears in Lagos harbour. The Spanish government will no doubt make a huge fuss about the stealing of the *Duchess* from their waters so it would be inconvenient for our government to know officially who has been responsible, as they would have to admit if we were recognised by the public. I plan that we will anchor the ship and disappear ashore, just before the Navy arrives. No explanations or reports afterwards!'

To himself, however, Chris was thinking: But that presupposes we succeed. There will be a diplomatic incident if we are caught, volumes of reports, rafts of explanations demanded by the Spanish government. Not to mention what will happen to this group.

'No names, no pack-drill,' interjected Cracker.

'Exactly,' Chris continued. 'It will be a secret operation. There will be no record of what has happened and we shall all deny having been involved in any such action. That is the way it must be; it will be our own bit of war work and a lot less than some others. Do we all agree?'

'Quite right, Tigger' ... 'Of course' ... 'That's why we're here' ... 'Absolutely' ... 'Agreed, Chris.'

'Thank you, chaps. Later we can discuss plans for what happens when we reach Lagos. Meantime, over to you Captain Moore!'

Panda's voice commanded attention as he described the target ship; people realised the group's success depended on grasping the information he was providing.

'Right. The last edition of *Lloyds Register* shows the *Duchessa di Lucca* to be a steel ship of about eight thousand tons gross, built at Trieste in Italy in 1922 by Stabilimento Tecnico Triestino and refitted by them in 1930. She is a cargo-passenger ship with single funnel, slightly slow by modern standards but very attractive. The bridge and all her accommodation are mid-ships. She is a big ship, four hundred and seventy-five feet long, fifty-eight feet in beam and, loaded, she draws twenty-five feet. She has oil-fired boilers with triple expansion steam engines developing about one thousand horse power, also built by Stabilimento Tecnico. She's designed for the African trade and has four very conspicuous lattice masts supporting the derricks, essential for working cargo where there are no dockside cranes. For'ard some of the hold space is refrigerated for carrying perishable food, fruit and so on. She appears rather low-

164

powered for her size, which may give her a speed of about eight knots. If that is a fair estimate, it would be slow for a modern passenger ship. The brochure I found does not give her speed but the schedules we know she kept seem to confirm the point. Anyway, I hope the deck plan will help Sergeant Armstrong in designing the attack. I shall talk later about the allocation of duties on the *Duchess* for the passage from Santa Isabel to Lagos. As Mr Wickham has said, seven or eight knots implies fully two days' passage to Lagos, apart from any necessary diversions.'

Moore knew well this was a risky operation but to him it was also enormously attractive. It represented the means of command, a status he had been denied for ten years. In that time he had enjoyed the title of Captain but had always been conscious it was honorary, hollow. Now he had the prospect of professional standing and the element of danger in earning it added to the savour.

'Now, about the passage out. I have arranged for the tug *Mungo Park* to be at Bonny on Saturday. We shall take passage in her to Santa Isabel. It will be around a twelve-hour voyage and fairly uncomfortable because she does not have accommodation for an additional twenty men. However, needs must when the devil drives and, although she is not a regular ocean-going tug, she has the great advantage of providing the power to pull the *Duchess* off her moorings and get her under way without waiting for us to raise steam from cold, which would be time-consuming and tiresome – to say the least – when she is lying only a couple of hundred yards off the beach.

'Since it is not clear the *Duchessa* will have steam raised – it's likely she will not, we cannot rely on being able to operate the winches so we can raise the anchors. We must be prepared to slip or cut the anchor chains or mooring cables with a small explosive charge. And I believe that is in hand.'

Chris nodded his agreement and the captain continued.

'The *Mungo Park* will be our vessel for the final approach, from Bonny to Santa Isabel. To avoid the long run by road from here to Port Harcourt and Bonny I have arranged that we can take passage in the *Alexander Holt*. Obviously she is of the John Holt Line which some of you may know. She is discharging cargo at Warri now and will sail on Friday at noon, to allow her to go down river in daylight. She is to load cargo at Port Harcourt but will drop us off Bonny to trans-ship to the *Mungo Park* around 5 o'clock Sunday morning, just at dawn.

'The *Alexander Holt* has berths for only twelve passengers so it will not be luxury but I have no doubt we shall manage. It should be better than going by road and a lot less conspicuous. The passage Warri to Bonny will take about thirty hours steaming, allowing for the slow section down-river through the creeks. It may appear rather a nuisance having to trans-ship but it would have been quite unacceptable to take twenty extra men on the tug for the whole voyage of nearly fifty hours; twelve hours will be long enough as you will discover for yourselves.

'That is perhaps enough for now; I shall have more to say about preparing for the passage out and duties in the *Duchess* after her capture but the allocation of those duties may depend on the decisions about the attack, so I shall keep them till later. The passage in the *Alex Holt* will give us time to practise new sea-going skills necessary for getting the *Duchess* under way; that training will be important and explains my choice of transport. The actual attack is essential but so also will be the voyage to Lagos.'

Reference to crew duties raised a question in Philip Denstone's mind, which seemed relevant to the attack.

'How many of a crew may there be on the *Duchess*? Do we know, Chris?'

'We do not know, Phil. Some may have slipped away or been paid off since June 1940; some may have gone ashore to live. Captain Moore has estimated the normal crew might be around thirty to thirty-five, including extra stewards for the passengers – that is officers and men all told. Then there may be some passengers in addition, perhaps up to three. My aim is that we intimidate them into surrender, using minimum violence.'

'What do we do with the Italian crew after they surrender? Do we put them ashore or take them with us to Lagos?'

'There simply won't be time to let them debate that and pack up, because we shall have to hurry away from Santa Isabel before the Spaniards wake up and start interfering, as I am sure they would if given half-a-chance. So if some Italians choose to leave by jumping overboard I would not stop them, but I think the bulk of those aboard will have to come to Lagos, willy-nilly. No more questions for now? Then let us have a word from Sergeant Armstrong about the attack and training for it. Cracker.'

166

The sergeant took a deep breath and tried to remember the clear and logical way that briefings were given to him by his officers before a Commando attack. Being keyed up for the occasion, his Borders brogue was a little broader than usual but the clarity and logic were there, well justifying the Colonel's choice of the man.

'Ye ken the tairget: the *Duchess of Lucca* ship. We intend to take her over and make her available for Captain Moore to sail back to Lagos.

'Information about the enemy: we must plan on finding around thirty men on the ship. We need to assume they will be armed, maybe with pistols but heavier weapons seem very unlikely. We'll jalouse the Spanish people ashore to be hostile; I know nothing of their strength or arms, so we must aim to avoid them. As far as we know there are no Spanish naval ships in the port.

'Information about our own force: We are twenty men. We have two Sten 9mm sub-machine guns, two rifles – more if we want them – and eight Webley revolvers. We shall have knives and clubs. As a mostly civilian group tackling a civilian Italian crew, we reckon we don't need firepower: instead we must achieve tactical surprise. We go in silently, very fast and intimidate the enemy into surrender, above all without attracting the attention of the Spanish authorities ashore. If at all possible, there will be no shooting. No guns to be fired.

'Timing: We shall attack late Sunday night or early Monday in the dark. We shall need full darkness for the approach to the target to achieve complete surprise. The exact time of the attack will be decided by the Boss when we know about the speed of the tug and so on, but we aim to go in when the Eyetie crew will be asleep. We should sail the ship out of Santa Isabel before 0500 hours Monday.

'Now then. Method: The plan is this *Mungo Park* ship will take us to about eight hundred yards from the target, where we get into small boats for the final approach. We go in with tactical surprise and that means approaching and boarding in complete silence. To achieve the slickness and quiet needed for real surprise, we must train for every move now so there'll be no need for talking on the night and so every man knows exactly what he is to do and how to do it.

'The exact job of each man will depend on the study of this deck plan Captain Moore has brought; that may show where the crew and passengers will be bedded down. Subject to that, I see us approaching the target in three boats, the first with four men to take the bridge, the captain and the wireless room, the other two, with eight

167

men each, to secure the crew and passengers on the lower decks. Captain Moore and Oshodin here tell me there should be a fixed accommodation ladder in place on the starboard side of the ship, that is the side next the shore as Joshua saw it, but we can't use that because it would be too obvious, in full view of the shore. In any case, the crew may lift it clear of the water at night for security. All three boats therefore will have to carry boarding ladders to be sure of getting into the ship. I understand from Oshodin that the ship is anchored bow and stern, parallel to the shore and bow to the east, so that it will not swing with tide or wind. Since the ship is only two or three hundred yards from the shore, we shall attack on the side away from the shore – the captain tells me that is called the port side – so the ship screens us from the town as we paddle in on the final approach.' Cracker held every man's attention. He went on:

'The attack will begin by securing the bridge and radio room, capturing the captain and any crew on the bridge. That should take out the enemy commander and headquarters, and we must prevent the enemy sending out a radio call for help. We must also prevent them sounding the ship's hooter or making any other distress signal. The following two groups will take the crew quarters and cabins in turn, overpowering and tying up all the occupants. As far as possible the method will be to enter each cabin in silence and intimidate the men so that those in neighbouring cabins are not wakened. The method of entering the cabins and frightening the enemy into surrender will have to be practised today. They must be tied up and gagged.

'Before we can decide the exact plan of attack and method of entering cabins we will have to make a close study of the deck plan. We have to decide how each man will be armed, with pistols, knives or clubs, maybe two with rifles. We need to know about the boats that'll take us in; we have to find boarding ladders. At least those men to carry pistols have to be trained in loading and firing, although we don't want any shooting if we can avoid it because the attack will be much easier if we can get into each cabin with the men still in bed asleep. Corporal Graham and I will be armed with our Sten guns.

'Now, because it's to be a night attack there is danger of confusion between ourselves and the enemy, especially with neither them nor us in uniform. I reckon, Boss, we need some kind of easy identification, so that we can recognise each other and don't knock the wrong man on the head.'

168

Now that the job was active, and in front of the men he regarded as raw recruits, Chris was "the Boss" and Rob was given his corporal's rank.

'Boss,' Cracker continued, addressing Chris directly, 'I want six men training on pistols with Corporal Graham. We want someone to make a drawing, as big as can be, of the deck plan, showing each cabin, to instruct each attacking section. And I would like Captain Moore to tell us how long ladders we'll need to get from boats up to the deck. Then where do we find three ladders that length?'

Rob Graham gathered the first group of six for weapons training, taking them through an abbreviated version of the regime to which he had been subjected and had in turn subjected recruits to many times before: naming-of-parts, stripping the weapon, safety, loading and firing. The drill ended with the practice firing, four or five shots each down by the river. Then there was a change of men and the course had to be repeated.

Robin Kitchener and Donald McIver were set to the task of drawing an enlargement of the deck plan from the brochure on two sheets of double foolscap paper. Donald's pocket lens for his interest in botany proved invaluable in deciphering the tiny plans of the ship's cabins. Robin did the drawing and the working plan was soon taking shape, with Panda Moore advising on the technical aspects.

The picture on the front of the advertising brochure showed the *Duchessa di Lucca* in profile. From it and the papers received from London, Panda, Chris and Peter estimated its freeboard, the height from sea level to the rail. With the ship fully loaded this distance appeared to be only about nine feet to the well-deck, thus fixing the length of ladders required. They would have to be light-weight. It was impossible to believe they could find three suitable ladders ready to hand even in the commercial stores in Benin. This, however, presented no problem since there were abundant materials available from which excellent ladders could be produced. Peter and Joshua discussed the merits of various designs and materials, finally agreeing on the dry mid-ribs of raphia palm fronds for the styles of the ladders and rungs of the very light musanga wood. The mid-ribs were used for roof construction by forest people, light and very strong.

The design agreed, Forest Guard Agbontaen was summoned to supervise a team for gathering the necessary materials: a dozen dry mid-ribs of palm, more than required to allow the best to be chosen, a few dozen short branches of musanga, several forked branches to make hooks for the tops of the ladders and a large quantity of climbing palm which would be split and twisted into rope-substitute for tying the rungs and hooks to the styles. In the late morning the materials were gathered and a small team of men from the Sapoba camp began to assemble the ladders under Agbontaen's direction. The Bini forest workers were highly skilled at this kind of craft and the final product was both strong and light. Cracker checked the first ladder to be completed; he asked for a small pillow of bundled fresh palm leaf to be fixed on the inside at the bottom of the ladder so that the wood should not make a noise against the ship's hull. The hooks at the top were tried on the handy branch of a tree and found to support two men without difficulty. The boarding ladders were ready by mid-afternoon. They looked rustic but were designed for the job and lighter than aluminium.

Panda was worried about boats. Space would be at a premium on the *Mungo Park* and he believed it would be impossible to carry three boats in addition to the tug's own lifeboat. It was a good bet that the boats used in the attack would have to be abandoned which meant that the tug's lifeboat should not be one of them. Approached on the subject by Cracker, Rob Graham thought the canoe they had used on the Jamieson River would be sufficient for the first assault party of four, provided the sea was calm – indeed, given calm weather, it would be ideal since a silent approach could be achieved more easily than in a boat with oars.

'But the crew will need practice in handling it over the next couple of days, Cracker, especially if they have to fix a ladder in position and that means standing up. Could be a wet mess and noisy into the bargain,' Rob said with a guffaw.

Panda had already commandeered two small open boats at Warri. He thought the bother might be to train eight men, four for each boat, to handle the oars at night, for which the time would be very short – probably only a practice session at Warri before going aboard the *Alexander Holt* on Friday morning. As it turned out, enough men had rowed at public school and for college boats at university, or simply messing about in boats at home. Fortunately the boats were already fitted with rudders and tillers, thus avoiding the need to use the oars for manoeuvring. Panda himself would cox one boat and Rob Graham the other.

Meanwhile groups were busily engaged in other preparations. Captain Moore's two recruits joined Robin and Donald in producing the enlarged sketch plan of each deck. The result showed there was accommodation for more passengers than they had anticipated and also that the crew members were better housed than in the average British ship of the period, many having their own cabin or sharing with only one other man.

'The bother is we cannot be certain they will be in the cabins marked on the plan as crew quarters: by this time, those who were sharing originally may well have taken over an empty passenger cabin, for privacy and for airier conditions. More than that, we cannot be certain all the crew will be sleeping in cabins; they may be bedded down on deck. The fact is, we can't rely on the crew being in any place.' Cracker and Chris pondered on this worrying thought.

Clapper Bell, when not interrupted by those copying the brochure requiring some technical term there to be translated, was busy preparing a phrase-book for pirates.

'How about "I want to book a room with a sea view for two nights for my wife and myself"?'

'No. no,' Steve replied. 'Stick to essentials like, "Bring me a large dry Martini with plenty of ice." Panda told us the ship had a refrigerated hold, so they should be able to manage that.'

Clapper grinned and promised not to forget the postilion struck by lightning, but in fact his list began:

"Silence my friend: Surrender ... then we shall not hurt you:"

"Come": "Go there": and more.

Copies of the list were typed out by Helen, one for each man; Peter and Clapper gave lessons in pronunciation.

'Everyone must memorise these words by tonight,' Chris ordered, 'and must be thoroughly convincing in using them. There's no point inviting the man to surrender in the same voice as you might ask a girl to join you in a slow foxtrot!'

Aside from organising the meals, Helen and her two friends were devising a simple uniform. Every man had been told he must wear khaki shirt and khaki shorts or trousers for the attack, but it seemed that in any rough and tumble that developed confusion might arise between Italians and Brits who happened to be similarly dressed. This was resolved by two of the wives driving down to Sapele and buying twenty yards of post-office-red cotton cloth. Nigerian women

171

love really bright colours for clothes, so there was plenty of choice. They cut this into squares, one for each man, to be used as a head-scarf or neckerchief, like so many boy scouts. It seemed unlikely this combination would be duplicated among the Italian crew and the risk of confusion would be practically eliminated. At the same time, the women also bought a supply of khaki drill cloth and, at the tailor's shop, had this sewn into twenty bags the size of pillow-cases. The men would require some minimum luggage for the voyage to Lagos but there was no way they could take twenty suitcases on the small *Mungo Park*: small kit-bags would be a workable solution. Amongst other purchases on Cracker's orders were thick twine and small electric torches.

Periodically the morning peace was torn by a fusillade of shots as each of Rob's small arms training sessions ended with firing practice down at the river. Blocks of wood floating downstream provided targets and the wild unlikelihood of the film gangster's phenomenal accuracy with a six-shooter as shown in Hollywood westerns became evident to everyone. Hornbills objected to the disturbance and responded to each volley with a cacophony of raucous honking.

As soon as the deck plan sketches were ready, Cracker and his Boss began an intense study of the routes to be taken by the three attacking groups. The planning had to consider the full range of possibilities: if an accommodation ladder on the port side was rigged and if it was not; if deck lights were on or off; if cabin doors were open or closed; if men were sleeping in cabins or on deck; how to cope with the radio room, a watch-keeper on the bridge, the captain's cabin and so on.

The essence of the attack was that the first small group, led by Cracker himself, should make straight for the top deck of the ship, quickly to take the bridge and the wireless room and then to enter the captain's cabin and incapacitate him. As his companions in the canoe, Cracker proposed to take Joshua, Clapper Bell and Steve Lister.

'I want young Joshua as my Number Two, Boss.'

Chris was surprised Cracker's first choice was Joshua but pleased at this display of confidence in the young man. Cracker pointed out that two men would be required to be sure of taking the radio room and the two radio operators in separate cabins, before taking the bridge where a watch-keeper must be expected, and the captain's cabin.

172

Later the sergeant took his group down to the river to investigate the feasibility of four men operating the canoe with a ten-foot ladder aboard and particularly hoisting the ladder vertical to hitch on to the ship's rail, without turning the craft and its crew into the harbour. A method of working was discovered and the canoe was soon speeding up and down stream, giving each member a turn of steersman and practice in bringing the craft alongside the jetty without a bump and without any splashing of paddles.

'All very well in daylight,' the leader pointed out, 'but that has to be done in complete silence in the dark, so we had better come down here again after dark. When we paddle in from the seaward side, the ship itself will prevent any glow of light from the town reaching the port side, so it will be pitch dark in there close to the hull. Even if there are lights on the ship itself, it should be deep shadow close alongside. We will have to be prepared for the worst; it will probably need two men to paddle quietly to keep the canoe against the ship, one man to hold off against the ship's side to avoid noisy scraping and bumping, and one man to hoist the ladder and hook it on the ship's rail.'

The difficulties and realities of the operation were now apparent to all the volunteers. The sergeant was a hard taskmaster, insisting that every man should practise the drill of overpowering an enemy seaman represented by a play-acting colleague. When Robin Kitchener showed reluctance to go through full-force with subduing Gerald Smith who acted as a sleeping Italian matelot, Cracker bawled him out in the fashion horrid and miserable army recruits knew only too well.

'That is no bloody use at all, Sir. Do it again. You wouldn't frighten the skin off an over-ripe tomato. Put some guts into it. You are threatening to cut the man's head off, not kiss him goodnight.'

The experience of shooting practice convinced most people that the pistol, although useful as a threat and as a last resort, was not ideal for the job they had before them in which silence would be vital. Coshes and knives were probably more practical and both were ready to hand. The Forest Department store had a large supply of machetes, the most suitable being those supplied to forest guards, complete with black leather scabbards; there were ten in store and all were taken for the attack.

'It will be an interesting Board of Survey to explain to Benin NA how ten forest guard cutlasses have vanished from store,' said Peter with a grin.

173

Cracker thought the effect on an Italian of being wakened with the cool steel of a forest guard's machete against the throat would be at least as effective as a Commando's fighting knife but he insisted that they be equipped with leather thongs to slip on the wrist when they were drawn.

'Then you don't lose the thing in a fight in the dark and you don't have the fiddle of putting it back in the scabbard in a tight situation. For most people, including those with the Webleys, we want some truncheons – not as long as a pick helve but longer than a copper's at home.'

A prototype cosh was soon whittled for approval and Peter gave more instructions to Agbontaen for their production at the camp of dry gedulohor mahogany, with crocodile skin wrist-straps.

*   *

Late that evening, while the main party was relaxing after dinner, going over the lessons of the day and catching up with the gossip of other stations and other departments of the extended family which was their service, a small worried group sat in the office round a set of deck plans. Chris, Peter, Panda, Clapper and the two soldiers had studied the drawings until they knew the ship as well as having sailed in her. Helen sat with them; she knew the whole story of the operation, having typed the reports and telegrams. She had an almost proprietorial interest and in truth longed to be going with the men to the island; at the very least she wanted to know what would happen next.

Cracker was repeating a theme he had already developed; it was a reprise without variation.

'I dinna like it, Boss. The risks are ower high. There'll maybe be the best part of thirty men spread through the ship and we dinna ken where. As Captain Panda says, they're mair likely to be in the upper deck cabins or sleeping oot on that deck to get the cool night air, but we canna be sure. So there's a hell of a big area for us to sweep. It would be a hefty job for a fully trained squad.' He hesitated and went on, 'Our group here are shaping up fine, they're keen and promise great but, let's face it, we're not yet a crack team. The big risk is we fail to find some of the crew in the dark, surprise is lost, they

174

start a fight, there's shooting, the Spanish come to help and the fat is in the fire. If Rob and I had this group for another week or ten days, I would back them against anybody, especially the Eyeties, but we havena' the time.'

Chris smiled at finding Cracker identifying so quickly with his new team and at his evident loyalty to these rookies, but he recognised the professional warning. Common sense told him this was a well-founded objection. It reinforced the reservations he had from the start, that he might be leading his party into spectacular failure, and wiped the smile from his face.

'Right, Cracker. I accept that. We shall have to do something to shorten the odds. The problem is: What?'

In the silence that followed Helen laughed: 'You are like a punter at a shady race meeting who wants to nobble the favourite in the three-thirty.'

'It's not that simple, Helen. If only it was! We have about thirty runners to nobble. The fact is our operation looks to be beyond the power of our present numbers and the tight timetable. We have no time to recruit more chaps and the *Mungo Park* has no space to carry more in any event. It is an impasse.'

'Since it's our ignorance of the Italians' sleeping arrangements that is at the back of the problem,' Panda reflected, 'we may be wrong in thinking the best time to attack is when they are asleep. Perhaps a mealtime would be better, if only we knew when the crew would get down to eating their nourishing spaghetti Bolognese in the evening. It would have to be well after dark, of course, to allow the *Mungo Park* to approach the island undetected.'

'By-the-by,' Panda went on, 'I might have mentioned earlier, the regular Spanish steamer to the island will call at Port Harcourt today and leave late tomorrow for Santa Isabel. I don't think it interferes with our plans at all. She will dock at Santa Isabel on Friday and sail on Saturday for Benito in Spanish Guinea, so she should be out of the way when we are going in.'

This news sparked interest. In response to questions, the Captain explained that the *Reina Astrida* was a small cargo-liner, taking about ten cabin passengers. She sailed on a regular schedule between Valencia in Spain and Benito, calling at Las Palmas in the Canaries, Port Etienne in Morocco and other ports, including Santa Isabel. The call at Port Harcourt was a regular one, every two months.

'Perhaps that is how Joshua travelled to the island,' Chris said. 'I should have asked him earlier. But, as you say, Panda, it seems neither to help nor hinder us with our present problem. '

After a quiet moment, Peter Thorburn spoke slowly.

'Tigger, what Helen and Panda have said has given me the beginnings of an idea. As you may remember, I grew up in Italy where my father worked, until I was eight. Then in 1938, my last leave before the war, I spent time there, going round galleries in Florence and so on at just this time of year. It coincided with the anniversary celebration of the Fascist Party's foundation or some such event; I remember the date, the 13th, next Sunday. It was an excuse for boozing and parades.' And he went on to outline a plan.

'I believe I can make it work,' Peter insisted, 'because it depends on speaking some Spanish which I can just manage and on speaking and writing colloquial Italian, which I do. Furthermore, it was my idea and it has a fair chance, as Helen put it, of nobbling the favourite.'

'Hold on a bit,' Chris said. 'Think about the timing. Port Harcourt tomorrow; on board in less than twenty-four hours! Could it be done? For one thing, you would need your passport.'

'It's sitting in the office safe in Benin; getting that will be no problem.'

'The Spaniards will want more than a passport; they will be looking for a visa, surely,' said Chris. 'That may mean Lagos which would be impossible for time. We dare not hold up the ship's sailing and you cannot risk going without a visa because either would attract attention to you – probably fatal to your plan. At the very best you would be conspicuous since Colonial Service officers visiting Fernando Po must be as rare as hens' teeth.'

'There is a Spanish consul in Port Harcourt,' Captain Moore volunteered calmly. 'He is Swiss, manager of the Swiss trading company. I imagine we might lean on him sufficiently to provide a visa in no time flat.'

Helen said, 'You would need a cover story. What earthly reason could there be for you to arrive unannounced in Santa Isabel?'

'I might be investigating the possibility of importing timber sleepers for Nigerian Railways,' Peter suggested tentatively.

'Oh! Come off it and pull the other one,' Chris said. 'No-one would believe that. Nigeria has hundreds of times the timber

176

resources of Fernando Po. What does your passport say is your occupation?'

'Forest Officer.'

'In that case, you should be seconded immediately from Forestry to a new Department of Industry and Trade which I have just invented, and you are being sent to investigate conditions for the export of Fernando Po rubber to Nigeria, since the UK needs all the rubber we can buy for the war. It is only a story for the Spanish immigration officers and they wouldn't have time to check. You shouldn't be there long enough to get into trouble, like having to buy real rubber.'

The cover story was agreed but Chris Wickham was uneasy about Peter going alone to the island. One person would be vulnerable to a surprise crisis, perhaps something quite trivial. Clapper Bell wanted to go but Chris forbade him on the grounds the main group must keep one of its Italian and Spanish speakers.

'We cannot volunteer him for it,' Peter said, 'but it seems Joshua Oshodin would be the strongest candidate. He has been there before so he knows something of the lay-out of the place and already has some contacts. Furthermore he really is trying to import Spanish rubber into Nigeria and must have some basic knowledge of it.'

Chris agreed to put it to Joshua but insisted he must not be coerced into going if he had any misgivings. The main problem, however, was time.

'OK, Peter. Get Steve to drive you to Benin now for your passport and whatever else you need, and the pair of you get papers for Joshua at the same time. Then get back here, fast. Meantime I shall speak to Joshua and sleep on the plan. If Helen and the rest of us can't think of anything better by breakfast tomorrow, you can go. From Benin please phone Charles Allison to lay on transport for you from the ferry at Onitsha to Port Harcourt and passages on the ship. It will be a hell of a rush, but everything is. Before you leave here in the morning we should have to agree exact plans for the attack on the ship itself. Good grief! Is there enough time for that?'

Peter grinned and, rather deliberately, replied, 'When I passed you the ball you always had time to do something, and when we really tried, we won. I don't believe I ever gave you a "hospital pass" in any of our games and I shall not now. If the opposition break through too fast, I shall do something on my own and link up with our forwards!'

177

Peter's reference to their past playing relationship underlined for Chris the true cost of the gamble in allowing his former team-mate to go ahead with his plan. And, as the meeting ended, there were further worries for the leader. The three Admin. officers from the Ibadan secretariat showed signs of dissatisfaction with the dining arrangements. The small group was led by Charles de Mangold.

'It is undoubtedly necessary for twaining purposes for us to have instwuction from the sergeant and cawpwal, but I question whether we must mess together. Might there not be a Sergeant's Mess? Hudson and Oshodin could eat there also.'

Before Chris had a chance to reply, there was a blunt response from Peter, backed by an equally indignant Donald McIver who overheard.

'This is a Forest Department rest-house and as FO Benin I shall invite whomever I choose to it, and on my terms. Armstrong and Graham are my guests, I am proud to have them here, they eat with me and if you don't approve you can bloody well take your food out ....'

'No, Peter!' Chris overruled. 'It is your rest-house and what you say about guests is correct. But at this party no-one will take meals anywhere but in the diningroom. There will be no separate messing in tents or anywhere else. There is one mess and it will remain so. We have so little time to work up as a team, every hour counts. We cannot afford anything which creates division, so pocket your pride, Charles; I do not want you or anyone else going off in a private party.'

Charles was surprised at the vehemence of the response. 'Oh, I thought they might be happier ...'

'Wheesht!' Mac interrupted. 'Did ye no hear? The man said "No", so just tak tent. Least said: soonest mended.'

Chris wished the suggestion had not been made; it balanced Eddie Hudson's remark earlier in the day and put colour prejudice into context. Locally, social division was at least as strong as racial. Typically the instinctive rejection had come from the foresters who were a department notably less conscious of class than his own. Perhaps the solitary life in the bush bred tolerance. Common sense too.

Peter remarked to his friend later, 'For the same reason, there is good sense in my taking Joshua with me on the Spanish steamer.

178

His value lies in his contacts with the people on the island. Here, he is a distraction and maybe a source of irritation for some of our group; they may gel better without him.'

Chris could only agree, reluctantly. Apart from the immediate matter of social barriers, he was disconcerted to find how easily the attention of his team could be diverted by trivia from the main issue. Sense of purpose appeared to be disappointingly weak, at least in some of its members.

*   *

Hilda and Klaus had reached a "safe-village" in Kamerun and the Mercedes had been hidden by the simple process of building it into an empty traditional farm produce store. In a couple of days the wet clay on the new wall would be dry and the car would be undetectable, save in a most rigorous search. It was glorious to be free from the sticky heat of the Niger and Cross River delta, to heal nerves stretched almost intolerably in the hectic drive from Benin City.

On his return Klaus immediately questioned his assistants closely on events over the past week, especially orders received by radio and the movement of their troops. The reports were generally satisfactory. Admittedly the desert column was a day behind schedule but it was moving and the commander of the para-troops was confident they could make up time for their attack; the ship was ready to sail, *Alles in Ordnung*; their own men were already in transit, if anything slightly ahead of programme. The attack plan was progressing well.

Hilda had relieved one anxiety by confirming Klaus' memory that he had not mentioned the port for unloading the arms when he had spoken to Robert, so even if his brother-in-law under stress had revealed what he knew of the German plans, that essential element could not have been compromised.

The restoration of contact with Friedrich and Karl fed Klaus' ego since he now had juniors to whom he could issue orders. Sleep in the cool freshness of the highlands restored his well-being as the operational commander so that both in appearance and self-belief he had grown appreciably. In contrast, Hilda was doubtful, sometimes apparently positive and confident, at other times nervous and inadequate. She was sharply conscious of being the only woman in this six-hundred strong male operation. There was no womanly role for her and the men's cultivated politeness, bordering on patronising, made it especially difficult for her to find her feet. Their nomadic life style was hard, constantly hiding from the British authorities, and sharply at odds with Hilda's memory of her privileged life in the area before her marriage.

Nevertheless things were moving to the crisis. Only a few days to go until the attack. Klaus was confident of success.

CHAPTER TWELVE

The release of Kinmont Willie Armstrong in 1596 depended critically on intelligence from within Carlisle Castle itself and on the cooperation of the Grahams who occupied much of the English land between Carlisle and the Scottish Border.

Young Lord Scott of Buccleuch, having decided to raid the castle on a Sunday, spent the previous day at the horse races at Langholm, a favourite pastime which provided useful cover for his presence close to the Border. He had recruited a picked force of eighty troopers, mainly Scotts and Elliots from Liddesdale, with Armstrongs – including Kinmont's four sons, all experienced riders.

The party gathered on Saturday night at Kinmont's house of Morton Rigg to collect their ladders and tools. Then very quietly they rode south towards their objective a dozen miles away.

When Peter Thorburn and Joshua Oshodin stepped ashore at Santa Isabel on Friday morning after the short voyage from Port Harcourt, Peter felt in a whirl. They had only just caught the ship the previous evening. Joshua appeared relaxed, although in fact he was excited and apprehensive at the deception they were engaged in. He carried a travel document which said he was employed by the Nigeria Department of Industry and Trade as Mr Peter Thorburn's assistant. Typed by Steve late at night, it was impressively stamped in both the Benin District Office and the Provincial Office, and for good measure

*See pages at back end paper

181

was countersigned with a flourish by Arthur Hesket-Bramwell as Chief Commissioner and Assistant Governor. ('Since the Chief Comic is handy in Benin, he may as well earn his crust and perjure himself like the rest of us,' was Steve's comment). Sapoba transport had taken them as far as the head of the queue at the Niger ferry. Charles Allison, the DO at Onitsha had been engaged by the "old boy net" to meet them off the ferry and drive them to Port Harcourt. There the net had alerted the local DO to have the Swiss businessman ready with his rubber stamp to visa their papers and also have passages booked on the *Reina Astrida*. Even so, they had almost missed the ship owing to the slowness of the manager of the Bank of British West Africa in issuing a letter of credit for Peter to draw cash in Santa Isabel; admittedly, the man had a point when he protested it was irregular to conduct such business out of banking hours for a man he had never seen before. Nonetheless they had caught the boat and, although this was a neutral Spanish island, Peter had the exciting feeling they had entered an enemy citadel; they were successfully "behind the lines" but it had been a hell of a rush.

The Spanish immigration officer accepted their travel documents and cover story of rubber trade promotion without the flicker of an eyebrow. Nonetheless Peter wished he had a firmer grasp of the business he was supposedly representing and better understood the qualities which made some rubber tradeable and other not. Nevertheless he took the opportunity of asking the officer's advice about the best place to eat in town, since this was his first visit.

'Beyond doubt the Hotel Granada. Señor José Rodríguez keeps an excellent table, especially if you have a taste for Andalusian food.'

Engaging a taxi, decrepit but the only one available at the quay, Peter quizzed the driver also about hotels. It seemed there were two used by Europeans, the Granada and the Isabella. They drove first to the Banco de España Ultramar to present his letter of credit and lift local currency.

They dismissed the taxi at the Hotel Isabella. Joshua left to contact his friends in town and to make certain vital arrangements with them; he was to rejoin his leader in two hours. Peter then entered the Isabella to check in, displaying his passport and by his language and demeanour establishing himself clearly as British. He booked his room for three nights, paying a cash deposit and giving a good tip to the receptionist as an investment. He also chatted freely to the man about his supposed mission, trotting out the cover story of the rubber trade with Britain, airing a little of the information he had gleaned from his work in Benin and from Joshua during their journey.

It was now time to go into action. Peter had noted the location of the Restaurante del Hotel Granada as they drove along the waterfront from the bank; it was only a couple of blocks from his hotel. He would walk. Now nearly noon, it was steamy hot, so he walked slowly.

The town was laid out on a simple grid system, with four main east-west roads running parallel to the base of the bay. The harbour was magnificent; two narrow spits of land, a thousand yards apart, ran out from the north coast of the island to form a deep bay, with the town filling the whole of the landward side. To the east was the Pinta Fernanda, a narrow curved spit, almost a thousand yards long. Off the point of the western spit, the Pinta Cristina, were small islets, the Isoltes Enriques, which helped to give further shelter to the massive anchorage, the Bahia de Santa Isabel.

In that bay, straight in front of the hotel entrance and close inshore, was the ship. Panda had said the chart showed a depth of thirteen fathoms – about eighty feet – only two hundred yards from the shore, and here was the proof of that; the ship was anchored very close. Their target was streaked with rust and altogether rather shabby after a year at anchor, but easily recognisable from Panda's brochure as the *Duchessa di Lucca*. Peter resisted the temptation to gaze at her, lest his special interest be noted. Instead he pulled on his wide-brimmed felt hat, imagined himself into the role of an Italian businessman and walked slowly along the waterfront road, la Avenida Marítima, trying to take note of conditions and activities, knowledge of which might be useful in the next forty-eight hours. This commendable action, however, was disturbed by a vivid memory as he saw the distant view.

Looking to the north, past the anchored ship, he could see the hazy blue humpback peak of Cameroon Mountain forty miles away across the sea. The sight triggered a flashback to his time at school, sharp in every detail. It was of a classmate reading, while old Ledingham stood with his back to the roaring fire, his black gown hitched over his arm to get the full benefit of the blaze on his bottom. The story was of Neco, the king of Egypt about 600 BC, sending

Phoenician ships down the Red Sea with orders to sail round Africa and return through the Straits of Gibraltar, the first circumnavigation of the continent. Among the wonderful tales the men brought back of their three year voyage, they reported sailing between two volcanoes in full fiery eruption, one on an island and the other on the adjacent mainland. The only place that could have been was right here, between the volcanoes of Cameroon Mountain and Mount Clarence – Pico de Santa Isabel the Spaniards called it. Peter swallowed hard with rising emotion at the thought of those hardy Phoenicians who had rowed round Africa, rowed through this very patch of sea over two thousand five hundred years ago. What men! He had not recalled old man Ledingham for years but now every detail of that class came back without conscious effort.

Although Santa Isabel was Spanish-African, it had a curiously cosmopolitan appearance, like many West Coast towns. The Portuguese, the Dutch and the British had all been here, as well as the local Africans, and each had contributed something. Foreign traders and local entrepreneurs had run up buildings at different times and in different styles, few with the services of an architect, most on inadequate budgets, none with the benefit of skilled artisans. The result was a hotch-potch of facades, almost all whitewashed, with a jumble of red-painted or red-rusty corrugated iron roofs behind. Peter decided some of the newer Spanish municipal buildings were handsome, the post office and the spired cathedral especially, in ornate Hispanic tradition. Regularly spaced along the seaward side of the Avenida Marítima were palms, an attractive feature which provided a distinctive air, like some place on the Mediterranean coast of Andalusia. A glimpse down a side street broke the illusion; this was an African town, down on its uppers. Behind the buildings, less than a mile away, the ground rose steeply to the slopes of the volcano which dominated everything on the island; the British had called it Mount Clarence, the Spanish Pico de Santa Isabel and Joshua had told him the local African people called it Basilé. This would not be an attractive place for an Italian seaman to be stranded months on end, short of spending-money. The thought gave him encouragement as he came to the Hotel Granada; the crew might be willing guests. At the last moment before entering he sought to disguise himself by the simple amateurish procedure of putting on dark sunglasses.

The hotel design was a curious mixture of Moorish, Art Deco and African-concrete; it was clean and painted in patches. To the enquiry of the African clerk at the reception desk, Peter asked for el Hospedero, Señor Rodríguez. The owner proved to be a middle-aged Spaniard, short, with a smooth oval face and somewhat obsequious. He was obviously very keen to see some trade coming to his house, long hit by the civil war at home and now by the war in all Europe. Peter addressed him in voluble Italian, then apologised profusely and repeated his story in deliberately halting Spanish, excitedly offering French if his poor Spanish was not understood. It was good acting; in language and extravagant gestures the man would never have been taken for a phlegmatic Britisher.

Peter explained he was a visiting Italian businessman, newly arrived in the island. (Could he please have a glass of white wine and soda water, and would the Hospedero care to join him? *Salúte.*) He was anxious to arrange an evening meal for compatriot friends, Captain Palma and his officers and men of the *Duchessa di Lucca.* They were very isolated by this war and, as a fellow Italian, he would like to provide a little hospitality, especially as it is the season for remembering Il Duce's accession to power and therefore a time of national celebration. Would this be possible? *Eccellente*! Two evenings hence, on Sunday evening? There should be twenty people. Say two or three bottles of an aperitif – ginebra? *Eccellente*! And some *vino, naturalmente,* for that number of guests perhaps two dozen bottles of Rioja? You will decide what dishes are possible, but perhaps a rich *olla de carne* or *olla podrida*. And fresh fruit or a *torta di frutta* to follow, with good coffee which you grow so well on the island, and brandy. He would pay a cash deposit now, say two thirds of the probable cost with the balance on the night. Would that be acceptable to the Hospedero?

Señor would be welcome. The party could have the main dining room; other guests would eat in the small sitting room that evening. On Sunday evening, at nine o'clock? Peter knew this was the earliest the Spanish restaurant could be persuaded to receive a group for the evening meal. To eat before ten would be regarded as quite eccentric.

'Assuredly. I shall give you the estimated cost in two minutes. It is a pleasure to do business with you, Señor.... And what is the name for the reservation? .....Señor Garibaldi. A famous Italian

name, Señor.... Allow me to offer you a coñac, Señor......*Salute*......
Until Sunday, then.'

It proved surprisingly simple, so far.

Back in privacy of his room at the Hotel Isabella, having shed the dark glasses, Señor Thorburn, himself again, began the difficult task of composing a letter. It was surprising how the Italian came back to him after all these years; he suddenly thought of Lucia the maid in Turin and Mamma Pati, the cook, who, without him realising what was happening, had taught him the language. It had been easy to pass himself off as Italian to a Spaniard; it would be a different matter convincing a native Italian. The letter had to be persuasive, the tone right, the idiom perfect. He had discussed the content thoroughly with Clapper Bell before leaving Sapoba and the half hour conversation with the hotelier at the Granada had helped by starting him thinking in proper latinate fashion; now he must take real care.

```
             from Hotel Granada,
                   Santa Isabel.


To the Captain of the steamship
                'Duchessa di Lucca'
     Please forgive my writing to you
without formal introduction. I am
travelling on Italian government
business and have just arrived in Santa
Isabel. I expect to be here for a few
days only. I give you my greetings as a
fellow Italian.
     From my official contacts I know
of the unfortunate position you and your
crew are in, forced to remain in this
foreign port for so many months when, I
am sure, you and your men would have
preferred to be at sea. I trust (and I
have good reason to believe!) that the
long waiting period may now soon be
ended and I want to wish you well.
     I should like to make a small
acknowledgement of indebtedness to our
```

186

famous national merchant marine by entertaining you, your officers and the whole crew of your ship to dinner on Sunday evening at the Restaurant of the Hotel Granada. Sunday will be (I am sure you will recall) close to an important Fascist anniversary ordained by Il Duce, so there will be an additional reason for a celebration. I hope the whole crew and your remaining passengers will come as my guests. The dining room has been reserved at 9 o'clock for an Italian evening; the food and wine are commanded, so we may eat at 10.

Before Sunday, I shall be engaged in official business out of town and thus unfortunately unable to visit you but the restaurant arrangements are made and I trust you will do me the honour and give me the pleasure of joining me at dinner.

Arrivederci,
Ricciotti Garibaldi

Peter was satisfied with his effort and thought the mixture of floweriness and formality might pass muster but he knew better than to send the letter in his own handwriting. It would have been recognised instantly as not the work of an Italian, just as he dare not meet and speak to the Captain. While he had been at the Granada, however, Joshua had contacted one of the town's professional letter-writers who had a passably efficient typewriter, and had brought him to the hotel. Loyal to his trade, the man was most reluctant to allow any fingers other than his own to caress the keys of his precious machine, while Peter had no intention whatever of allowing a third person to know the content or recipient of the letter. As there was a handsome cash incentive on Peter's side of the argument, however, the man joined Joshua across the room while Peter typed. The Imperial had seen better days and the ribbon was well worn but they sufficed; with a few mistakes, he hammered out the Italian text on

187

some plain paper, as if from the Granada Hotel, together with a matching envelope to Captain Palma. Taking care that the letter-writer did not see the product, he packed up the machine and dismissed the man, well rewarded.

The next step was to have the letter delivered to the ship. The arrangements were left to Joshua who engaged a canoe boy. A small sum was handed over, with the letter and a receipt. The return of the paper, signed by the recipient, justified the payment of a second and larger instalment. This was much faster and a thousand percent more reliable than the local postal service.

All they could do now was to wait until the trap was due to spring. Peter took the opportunity to instruct Joshua in detail what was to happen and the parts they would play on Sunday evening.

*   *

The initial training was over and the kit-bags packed. The wives had been kissed and the Sapoba camp broken up. The servants were left to strike the tents, so the tennis lawn looked like a village park after the summer fete: trampled, tent-peg torn and sickly green in patches.

The *Alexander Holt* was anchored midstream at Warri, two hundred yards from the cluttered untidy shore of this tired little town. To the bewilderment of her regular crew, eighteen men had boarded the ship just before she sailed, laden with a variety of awkward and unlikely luggage, including a fifteen-foot dug-out canoe and two heavy gigs which had to be swung aboard and tied down, inverted, on Number 2 hatch cover. The party was in high spirits, for the training led by Cracker and Rob had the effect of bonding the men into the beginnings of a unit. They had gone to Sapoba as keen volunteers, several known to each other, so the unifying process had been rapid. Now they were raring to go, focused on the single operation.

Before their embarkation, a touch of comedy was provided by the whole group taking to the water in the small boats. The men knew this was simply part of their preparation, but the locals at Warri never had such good communal entertainment provided by the whites: this must surely be one of those curious games that white men play at certain times ("the Cambridge-Oxford boat-racing game", one

188

rumour said). Seven or eight men entered each rowing boat and (what delight!) three white men were in the canoe; the two boats were white-man design but surely the canoe was a Jekri craft. Depressingly, for the onlookers at least, no-one fell in the water and the racing, if it was a race, was boringly slow. The white men were ponderously competent and rowed sedately half-a-mile down the creek and back before the boats were hoisted aboard the Holt Line ship.

Everyone, but Chris especially, was relieved that the trial with the boats had gone so well. The coxes had called a slow and very steady stroke, so no-one caught a crab or even made a noise.

Few of the party had seen Warri before that day and no-one yearned to stay. It was not a place commending return visits. Towards the end of the nineteenth century, European trading companies, the Royal Niger Company the largest, set up trading posts on the branches of the Niger delta, Koko, Forcados, Brass, Warri and others. Set on mangrove-fringed sand-bars beside sluggish creeks, backed by miles of mosquito-breeding swamp, they were among the most depressing and unhealthy places in Africa. The atmosphere was that of a steam laundry where the ventilation had broken down. There was nothing to regret in leaving Warri. The party had more on their minds: they were going to war.

Once aboard, the group split up, at Captain Moore's insistence, to learn some of the special tasks for the period after the attack when, if fortune smiled, they would have an eight-thousand ton ship to sail. Under the second mate and bo'sun of the *Alexander Holt*, one team was given instruction in handling the winches for the anchor chain and the mooring wires. Steve Lister led them, still retaining some knowledge from his whaling days in South Georgia. Since Panda Moore would have command of the ship after the attack, Chris volunteered for the engineroom party which, of course, included Eddie Hudson. This group, sweating in a temperature which made the outdoors ninety degrees seem pleasantly cool, struggled to acquire sufficient seamanship and technical competence to ensure success. They became painfully aware of the enormity of the task they had taken on. Having disposed of the Italian crew, they would have to get a massive ship to sea, quickly, unobtrusively and in the dark.

In the race to gain skill there was one non-runner. Eddie Hudson was silent and unquestioning. At first Chris put this down to the belief everything must be familiar to him and questions were unnecessary. The Holt Chief Engineer had been told Hudson was expected to take over the *Duchess'* engineroom; he was a plain-spoken man from Govan who did not hesitate to question Eddie bluntly about his experience. Many of the replies were vague; some appeared to surprise the Chief and Hudson became resentfully silent. The Chief knew the success of their operation would depend in large measure on the effectiveness of the engineroom (no ship's engineer is in any doubt about his greater importance than any deck officer), so he persisted in trying to establish contact with Hudson, in fact achieving greater truculence and separation.

With alarm, Chris came to suspect Hudson's silence did not indicate a wealth of knowledge but poverty and an awareness that his ignorance was about to be exposed. Urgently he sought the Chief Engineer when he came off watch to ask for his expert opinion.

'The man's a fuil. He's no genuine. He's maybe been a stoker but that's the limit. He has no experience, no experience at all and I wouldn't put him in charge of the engines of a Clyde puffer.'

This damning reference confirmed Chris' worst fears; although not unexpected, it was nonetheless devastating news. Coming so late in their programme, the loss of such a key man would throw the whole operation into jeopardy; without an engineer, the *Duchess* was very unlikely to sail anywhere. Chris would have a thorny interview with Hudson in the morning. To dismiss him as unreliable or to support him? For the present, he would try to sleep on the problem and devise an alternative scheme; in his bunk he tossed restlessly as he viewed the breakdown of the operation.

Saturday morning was a perfect tropical day at sea: they were now away from the steaminess of the Warri creek, the heat was tempered with the freshness of the breeze out in the Bight of Benin, the sky faultlessly blue, the porpoises diving and wheeling on either side of the ship's bow. Occasionally a flying-fish skittered across the placid sea. There was special interest too, as Panda pointed out the different colours of the water they were sailing through, now clear blue of the open ocean, now muddy brown from the River Niger; even twenty miles out from land, the two waters were reluctant to mix.

Captain Moore's black eyebrows twitched alarmingly as the preparations went ahead. The job of Port Superintendent in the Nigerian Marine Department was all right in its way, comfortable and safe; he had been fortunate to get the appointment at the time and was

190

grateful. But it did not come within a mile of having one's own command. Day in, day out, he was on board ships, John Holt Line's, Elder Dempster's, Palm Line's, but always as a visitor. Now there was a prospect of walking his own bridge again and, even if it was only for two or three days, that was an excitement to put a spring in his step, psalm tunes whistling through his teeth and dark eyebrows twitching. In a couple of days, all going well, he should have a command. In his kitbag he had packed a large Union Jack, in anticipation of success.

*   *

Chris Wickham awoke with a start, heart racing. In darkness he lay in his bunk and listened to the ship noises: the constant thump-thump-thump of the engines, the hiss of the forced ventilation, the occasional quiet creaks and somewhere in the background he thought he heard the swish of water beyong the steel wall. These had not wakened him. Instinctively he knew the alarm had sounded within himself.

Unwilled, a thought welled up about the Oba. A little worry. Had the Bini king passed on all he knew? Might he have held back some part of Grenville-Fletcher's confession? Surely the Oba could not have been a partner in the Resident's ambitions? No! What possible advantage could he gain by keeping back information? He told us about the German plans. He was the source of the vital intelligence. I am worrying about nothing.

Wait a bit! That was the rub. Everything we know rests on what the Oba told us. All our plans depend on that. All our dispositions. Suppose he has got us committed the wrong way. Chris felt the sweat run down his chest: the cabin was hot and his thoughts harassing. What if he is playing a double game? Playing Germans against British, Ibo against Hausa. That was the kind of power-balancing act England played in Europe long enough. We could hardly object if Benin plays it now; it would be a kind of irony. And yet......Chris recalled the Oba's open revulsion at Grenville-Fletcher's treachery, his indignation at the murder of the driver; these were genuine. And their developing friendship over months, the games of

191

snooker, tennis, serious discussions about economics .... Surely it was not in the man to play false in that way? Gradually the fears subsided.

Chris turned over with a positive decision to put all that out of his mind and go back to sleep.

But, hang on! Now wide awake, Chris remembered the thought that had wakened him. Back before the Resident's confession and death. Before Klaus von Ehrwald appeared on the scene. It was last Saturday back at Sapoba, the Oba spoke about *"an Italian ship, in which I also am very interested"*. Surely those were his words. Why on earth should the Oba of Benin have any interest in an Italian ship at Fernando Po? It was bizarre! He came all the way to Sapoba to tell us about cargo being loaded into the ship – rifles we now believe. That news of the loading so gripped our attention, it blinded me to the strange fact the king had any interest in the ship.

What did the Oba want to achieve? Did he want the rifles? How could he get them? Perhaps the ship is not to go to an Eastern port as we imagine but is to land somewhere else. Has the *Duchess* already sailed? If the Oba has played us false, he has succeeded in shipping off most of the senior administrators in this *Alexander Holt:* me, Steve, Peter, Tom. What if there's a rising in Benin?!

The anxieties rushed round and round his mind, adding to the concern about Eddie's reliability. Wild thoughts of the sort that cannot be quieted even when one knows they are nonsense. Of course it was nonsense. But why was the Oba interested in the Italian ship? Rifles? He had encouraged us to go.

Why?

*   *

Chris Wickham was not alone in having a disturbed night. In his cabin aboard the *Duchessa di Lucca*, Mattia Palma was depressed and wakeful. Months ago the ship's supply of his favourite dry vermouth had run out and the nearest Spanish substitute was not near enough. In itself it was a trivial loss, one of many more important, but it was personal, rankled and continually reminded him of all the others. In one way Palma was glad of the vermouth's triviality: it provided a counter-irritant to the real worries he accepted as captain.

192

There were worries a-plenty. Keeping a crew cooped up in a ship at anchor month after month was a recipe for trouble. There was simply not enough work to keep the sailors occupied and idle sailors get bored, no matter how good a crew normally. And bored sailors quarrel. There had been fights, fortunately only one resulting in a serious knife wound. Although he could not tolerate indiscipline, the captain did not blame the men entirely; it was enforced idleness that was at the root of it.

The lascars and the Portuguese members of the crew had been paid off and had sailed in other ships, so they were now an entirely Italian complement. That helped. All but one of the passengers also had gone, the Portuguese to Spain and two of the Italians to Argentina. Only Pasconi remained and he had a very special reason for staying with the *Duchessa*.

Stores, oil fuel, food, water, everything was a worry because everything cost money and money was a worry because they were kept short, getting credit through the Italian consul who was a Spanish businessman. That did not help. Spain had hardly recovered from its disastrous civil war and Palma felt the consul was one of its casualties. He was not a man with whom troubles might be discussed, let alone shared.

All the troubles of idleness, shortages and poverty melted to nothing, however, with the arrival of the latest orders. The work of loading the extra cargo from the Argentinian freighter had been a blessing in making idle men busy but when the sailing orders had come there had been severe indiscipline. It was as close to mutiny as he had known in more than forty years at sea. His young officers had sorted things out in ways that avoided their captain having to take formal action, but in truth Palma himself had grave misgivings. The orders called for him to take his ship into an estuary that was extremely hazardous and the operation would probably result in the ship being stranded. It was all too easy for office people, drawing lines on small-scale maps, to order a ship to go "there"; they did not have to sail the vessel. *Dannazione e inferno*, he was the captain, a professional, and he had never run a ship aground in his whole career. They were asking too much. At high water he could sail in but six hours later they would be sitting on the river bed, and they might never get off again.

This letter and invitation from the businessman Garibaldi was a real blessing, offering a distraction that should raise the spirits of the men. It had seemed almost too good to be true but when Secondo Costanti had returned from making enquiries at the hotel, he reported the whole thing was genuine enough; the meal was ordered for the whole crew and had been paid for in advance. Rodríguez at the Granada had described their host as small, dark and very businesslike; 'typically Italian' he had said. Palma wanted to meet this man Garibaldi; he would allow Costanti to head the party for the meal – Palma did not want to leave the ship at this stage – but he would invite Garibaldi to come aboard for coffee and cognac afterwards. There was a hint in the man's letter he knew about the coming operation. He might be a government agent and, if so, he was a man Palma needed badly to talk to. It was the one bright prospect.

Captain Palma writhed in the bunk and made a conscious effort to put these thoughts away so that he might get to sleep.

*   *

Oberst Otto Eichel was also wide awake, struggling with star-charts and tables of logarithms to fix their position; 'Like some damned naval officer in the middle of the Atlantic Ocean', he groaned. The fact was they had wasted time today. The man charged with reading the sun-compass in the lead vehicle had fallen down on the job – the closer they travelled towards the equator, the more difficult it was to maintain direction in the middle part of the day. Eichel blamed himself for not supervising him closely enough but the wretched result was they had driven in a great arc, almost a semi-circle, and were kilometers off-course. They could not miss Lake Chad – all they had to do was drive south – but the bother was to be sure of avoiding the French posts and local settlements, so that their entry to Northern Nigeria would be unannounced. As soon as he had fixed their position, he would order the column to make up time by night driving. They were late already and must not lose more time.

*   *

Saturday was to be a rest day for Joshua and Peter. Everything had gone smoothly on Friday, so the essential preparations had been made and all they could do was lie low and keep their fingers crossed. Accordingly, Peter rose later than his wont and breakfasted lazily, reflecting on the fact that the Sapoba contingent should now be on their way to join him. He spent some time covertly observing the *Duchessa* but there was no obvious activity and the business became boring. In his supposed role of a trade-promoting civil servant he might have been expected to be knocking on the door of some Spanish produce marketing officer (since Saturday morning was a work day) but he dared not expose his relative ignorance of rubber and other trade products. Nor could he risk strolling round town lest he be seen by the proprietor of the Granada and pointed out to members of the Italian crew who might well be ashore on Saturday. He had agreed with Joshua they would not meet until next day; Joshua was quietly gathering some local gossip about the ship and preparing for their part of Sunday night's work. He would come to the hotel today only if something extraordinary happened. Peter was bored and restless, denied the lively conversation Joshua would undoubtedly be enjoying in the family home of his African friends.

The hotel receptionist broke the tedium of the morning by tapping on his bedroom door and delivering an envelope addressed to "Mr Thorburn, Isabella Hotel". The enclosed letter read:

Dear Mr Thorburn,

Today I hear from the owner of the Isabella Hotel that you have arrived in Santa Isabel.

I am an Englishman who has lived here for nearly ten years, trading in Coffee and Palm Oil. Very few English-speaking people come to the Island and I feel very isolated, especially since the beginning of the War. It would be a great Kindness if you would give Time to join me today for the mid-day Meal at my Home so that I could hear your News. Also, I could speak English, instead of always Spanish.

My Driver carries this letter and he will wait to bring you to my House, which is a little way up the Mountain. Please come for some hours and for the

195

Mid-day Meal. That would be a kindness. I look
forward to your visit.
　　　　　Yours truly,
　　　　　　Richard Forrest

Here was a fellow-countryman whose homesickness he could well understand in this dull town. They probably had very little in common but this visit was something to do to pass the time and a gesture to a fellow-countryman. Forrest might well have some snippets of information that would be helpful in the *Duchess* operation. Peter had time on his hands and it would be a charity to call on the man. The way Forrest's note was written suggested he had indeed become a stranger to his mother tongue; he was probably not a well educated man, for – Peter noted – the writing was somewhat irregular. He would go to the man's house; if nothing else, the visit would let him see more of the island, which would be interesting.

Peter scribbled a note for Joshua to explain what he was doing, dropping it at the reception desk and, at around half-past eleven, he left the hotel. As he did so an African wearing a brass-buttoned blue drill suit rose from a shaded bench and put on a peaked cap. Forrest dressed his servant smartly, it appeared.

'Señor Torbun? I am your driver,' he said in Spanish. 'This is the car.' Peter was shown into a Renault tourer with a radiator bonnet shaped like a snowplough. He settled himself comfortably in the back seat and enjoyed the fresh breeze as the car picked up speed.

After a mile they were clear of the town which lay along the margin of the bay. The roadside vegetation showed this was an even wetter climate and a richer soil than Benin Division. On the lowest land there was a profusion of lush vegetable crops, casava and yams growing in dark red earth under the open shade of hundreds of oil palms. Even a mile or so from the town the road was rising steeply and views were opening up over the sea to Cameroon Mountain. The road was narrow and in poor repair, so that Peter was glad he was not driving and relieved it was not his car. Patches of maize appeared in the farm crops and higher still, five miles from the town, coffee bushes under the shade of trees with attractive pink flowers. Then the car turned into an unsigned side road. Half a mile further they stopped at the steps of an attractive white bungalow. Neatly cut grass sloped down steeply for fifty yards to a coffee plantation, allowing a magnificent view down the valley they had climbed. Far below was the sea, with a glimpse of Santa Isabel.

At the top of the steps stood a large man, apparently in his late-fifties, clean-shaven, his close-cropped grey hair revealing a head shape which instantly categorised him as a "Beaker Man". The face was strong, the aspect grim rather than the welcoming one which might have been expected on a host greeting a specially invited guest. Peter was somewhat taken aback.

'Come in, Mr Torburn,' the man said bluntly in English as he turned ahead of him and led the way into the house.

The area they entered was, in fact, a large square verandah built out from the front of the house, facing the superb sea view, the sides open and the roof supported on pillars only. It was welcomingly airy and cool. Invitingly low armchairs and carved drinks stools were the only furnishings. His host waved a hand to indicate that his guest should be seated. Then he shouted in Spanish for his steward who came with drinks. It was not the welcome Peter had expected but rather the preface to a business meeting; little warning bells were ringing in his head. Confirmation of trouble came immediately.

'I must say to you, Mr Torburn, that my name is not Richard Forrest. That small deceit was simply to bring you here because I vant to talk vith you.'

Peter was not a winner at poker-dice for nothing; he did not blink but waited silent for the hand to be played.

'For many, many months no Englishman travels from Nigeria to Fernando Po. There is no interest. Now suddenly you come, I believe without any correspondence to the authorities here. My friends at Customs Department tell me your passport says you are of the Forest Department vich appears very curious. Vill you not say to me the reason for your coming, Mr Forest Officer? Vy do you come at this time?'

Peter did not reply immediately but gazed up at the roof of the verandah. This man was European but not Spanish. He was not part of officialdom (evidence the bother of bringing him so far from the town) although he had friends who were officials. Peter thought of the letter that had brought him here, with capital letters at various nouns; he had regarded it simply as an idiosyncrasy or the result of infrequent letter-writing but now he realised it was the lifetime habit of another language. The manner of his speech suggested the man was

197

German and this was confirmed by the content of the letter, German being a language in which all nouns have initial capitals. The deception which brought him here could not be a coincidence; there must be a connection with his own mission, in which case he must not reveal either his own hand or his having perceived an enemy. He cursed his stupidity which had put him in this vulnerable position.

'I don't believe it is any business of yours,' he said, 'but in fact it is very simple. Fernando Po produces several natural products Britain wishes to buy, including wild rubber. I have been seconded from Forestry to the new Trade Department and sent to enquire about possible purchases. Do you have rubber or palm oil to sell from this farm?'

'No! I do not,' was the spluttered reply, 'And I do not believe your stupid story. If it was true, you would have written letters enquiring about these things first, before you would come. Vat price do you pay for rubber you buy here?'

'Two hundred and twenty pounds a ton,' said Peter immediately, inwardly cursing that he was probably mixing up pounds per ton with pesetas per hundredweight.

'Ridiculous. I knew you were not a trading officer. The price is too high. I believe you come for some other reason. Tell me your real purpose.'

'I am afraid your market information is out of date,' Peter replied calmly. 'There is a war on and the price of rubber has risen dramatically. Also the United States has entered the market and its buying has pushed up the price. You are out of touch.'

To himself Peter was admitting how thin was the ice he was on but he rejoiced to see that his opponent was now less sure of himself; in fact he was looking worried. It was interesting how similar this situation was to a game of liar dice in the Benin Club: what he was passing as a full house, kings and queens, was really a pair of nines. Why should this German "Forrest" be worried? The little language robot in his head automatically translated the name into German and Peter nearly blinked! "Forest" could be rendered as *Forst* but it could also be *Wald. Wald!* Ehrwald! He had met Hilda several times, although not her brother Klaus, but now, looking more keenly at the man in the other armchair, he reckoned he might be meeting their father, Baron von Ehrwald. His age was right, late fifties or sixty, undoubtedly German, speaking good English, as he would from living nearly twenty years in British Cameroons. His presence here – if it was he – explained why they had lost sight of him at the start of the war.

If this was von Ehrwald, that would explain the man's concern. He must be in charge of the island end of the German operation. We were naive not to guess there must be a controller here. They have everything complete, the ship just about to sail. Then, right out of the blue, I arrive, a British Colonial Service officer, the first for months or years, with no prior correspondence to the Spanish authorities. My coming must appear very threatening, suggesting their plans have been compromised. That is why he picked me up, lest word of the ship sailing should leak out. He does not want me loose but, on the other hand, he cannot be too direct in his questioning lest that draw attention to the operation which at present I may know nothing about.

Continuing the liar-dice analogy, the stakes had immediately increased a hundred-fold. He had the full detail of the British plans to attack the ship, if the Baron could worm or beat them out of him. And the Baron, he was sure, knew the full extent of the German operation and equally must guard his tongue. On either side, the penalty for blinking and letting slip a clue was now vastly increased. Around thirty-three hours remained until the Duchess attack; Peter was committed to a long game and must keep his opponent guessing if he was to be around for the end-play.

'I do not believe a word of your precious story,' said the Baron.

In poker terms, Peter did not want to be "seen", so the correct thing was to raise the stakes still further.

'So be it', he replied, 'but on Monday when my colleague and I go to negotiate trade terms with the Spanish Agricultural Director, you will find that what I say is true.'

'Your colleague? I vas told you arrived alone with only your servant boy.'

'Then I am afraid your information is inaccurate. I did arrive with a colleague and, as the management of the Hotel Isabella will confirm, I do not have a servant with me. My colleague will be expecting my return to the hotel.'

The thought that there was a second Brit in the town clearly was a facer for the Baron; things were going wrong. In his book (and apparently in his Spanish informant's) a colleague must be a white

199

man; Joshua was a "boy". Peter was confident, however, that Joshua, living in the town with his friends, would be too well hidden to be at immediate risk and was beyond Ehrwald's easy reach. He was hopeful too that Joshua would have the confidence to carry out their plans alone, even if he himself continued to be held by the German. As things stood, it looked as though Joshua might well be on his own. For the present, however, introducing the idea Peter had not come alone considerably increased his chances of survival by making a quiet murder less effective.

'Now I should like to return to my hotel, if you will have the goodness to call your car,' he asked.

'No. I invited you for *Mittagessen*. First ve shall eat and then ve shall consider.'

Lunch was a silent, unfriendly meal, each man busy in his own thoughts. The universal tropical weekend food was served, curry with rice, but Peter was too concerned to savour it. Rough Spanish wine was served but both drank sparingly, conscious of the need to remain alert, which was difficult enough in the moist heat and eating heavy food.

Glancing covertly at the German, Peter weighed his chances of making a break. Although twenty years his senior, von Ehrwald was tough physically and was backed by two or three African servants; fighting or running, Peter would very probably lose. Further, his base at the hotel was known and vulnerable; by car von Ehrwald could reach it far ahead of himself on foot. Whatever he did, he must achieve by guile. A prime concern was that he should not be taken back to Santa Isabel by von Ehrwald himself. His approach to the Granada restaurant had been stupidly open and amateur. If anything of that connection was exposed, as it was almost bound to be if he was seen in the Baron's company, the fragile plot to entice the Italian crew ashore would crumble. Worse, the revealing of the scheme to bring the crew ashore and the timing of the meal would expose the time of the British attack and would mean his friends would find an enemy fully warned, alert and armed. It would be a disaster.

Come to think of it, if von Ehrwald himself goes to the ship and hears from the captain that the crew have been invited ashore by an unknown benefactor, it will be almost as bad, given that his suspicions have been aroused by the arrival of a British officer. He would probably check the arrangement at the Granada and would see

200

through the ploy. I must not let slip my knowledge of Italian and somehow I must keep the Baron here at the bungalow. That is easier said than done.

These thoughts were interrupted by the man himself.

'This statement you make that you have a companion I shall investigate. If you tell the truth, perhaps I vill turn you over to the Spanish authorities so that you may negotiate trade in rubber at your stupid prices. But I do not believe vat you say and this I shall test. If I find you have no companion, then I shall know you are lying and then I shall find out the real reason for an English officer coming to Santa Isabel.'

Peter sensed that remonstrance in the face of this clear statement of action would be futile and could be worse since in argument he might inadvertently give some clue to his real purpose. He toyed with the idea of protesting that he was a Scot, not English, but rejected it as being beyond the German sense of humour or tolerance.

'You vill remain here for now. Then ve go to town and I make enquiries at the hotels and vith my friends. But first I have some business in my study,' the Baron looked at his watch, 'for about one hour. It would be possible to lock you in a room so that you do not get to mischief but that would be very hot, so – since I am very kind – I propose to leave you in the command of my servants. They vill have orders to keep you here and prevent you from leaving. You may valk in the garden if you vish. But in case you have thoughts about the car, I must tell you the keys are in my pocket.'

Peter was relieved that action was not immediate but he tried to show neither pleasure nor concern at the announcement; he inclined his head, in a formal acceptance of the sentence. He resumed his seat and, under the watchful eye of the steward, carefully reviewed what had been said. A quarter of an hour later, in the silence of the afternoon heat, he became aware of an irregular clicking which suggested his captor's business in the study involved radio transmission, perhaps a regular schedule with his son across the water in the Cameroons.

It was time to reconnoitre the bungalow and its environs. He rose and, followed by the steward, made for the garden. The grounds were not elaborate, a half-acre of hand-cut grass, dotted with hibiscus, plumbago and other flowering shrubs; frangipani and lagerstroemia trees framed the view of the sea. Twenty yards beyond the bungalow

201

and slightly to the rear was a large open-fronted motor-house which sheltered the Renault from the sun and the weather; at the side of this building, making use of its shade, an African carpenter was busy hammering together some boxes. Peter was drawn to watch, admiring the man's dexterity and amused at the neat way he kept a ready supply of nails thrust into his tightly curled hair. The box of stout three-inch nails lay on the ground behind the man and the germ of an idea formed. After the man had taken another half-dozen nails from the box and turned back to his hammering, it took only a second for Peter also to reach down, scoop some up and slip them into his pocket. His guard was a dozen yards away and did not appear to have noticed what had been done.

*   *

Eddie Hudson did not appear at breakfast. Steve Lister finally went to rout him out but found the task beyond him. The man was sprawled insensible on the floor of the cabin, with an empty whisky bottle rolling gently at his side with the vibration of the ship. As there were also the remains of the lead foil which had originally sealed the cork, it was a fair assumption he had consumed the lot, which was supported by the depth of his unconsciousness.

Steve broke the news to the Boss. 'Tigger. The raiding party is now nineteen-strong and you need a new engineer. No question: Hudson will not be with us.' And he described the position in detail.

This blunt announcement came as no real surprise and the finality of the verdict was something of a relief. Chris immediately put the problem to Captain Moore who brought in the *Alexander Holt*'s Chief Engineer. Panda explained Hudson's incapacity.

'As we might say at home in Orkney, he's ill with the no-weels.'

'Well, you could take my Third, John Balman. He's from Plymouth and he's no bad. He would do the job for you.' Panda correctly interpreted this technical reference as meaning Balman was exceedingly efficient and the Glaswegian thought the world of him, even though he was an Englishman.

Chris was concerned about young Balman being pressured into a dangerous job but the Chief said he would jump at the chance

202

and would probably rate the danger at Santa Isabel as less than sailing in the *Alexander Holt* in and out of Liverpool at the current rate of U-boat sinkings.

So it turned out and Chris' spirits rose sharply from their low as he saw the competent way John Balman handled the new challenge, He read the rather scanty notes London had sent about the *Duchess*'s machinery, asked his own Chief's opinion on the likely design and best routine, then gathered his scratch crew of amateurs and instructed them rigorously on their duties and the likely problems they would face. It was sensible and methodical. Balman was mildly concerned about how he might return to the *Alexander Holt* after the attack (confidently he assumed it would be successful) and this was solved by Panda promising he would be ferried out from Lagos to meet his ship on her homeward passage from Port Harcourt.

The hours of Saturday were far too few for their needs. There was the drill for dealing with the moorings; the drill for getting the *Mungo Park*'s tow connected; instruction on steering; how to launch a lifeboat (just in case!); signals to communicate with the tug and so on it went. Chris, Captain Panda and Engineer John Balman tried to plan for every eventuality; if there was steam up in the main boilers, that would be fine; but if there was not, how long could they wait after a successful attack that had not alerted the authorities ashore? After the evening meal, Chris chased people to their bunks since they would have to be up by four in the morning and they would certainly have no sleep at all the following night. Excitement was mounting and for many people sleep seemed unlikely until it took them unawares.

*   *

Up at the farmhouse on the mountain, the sun was now low in the west and the air was cooling, but Peter was far from relaxed. It would be two hours at least before he could make his move, yet somehow he must ensure the Baron remained at the house for that period. He loitered in the garden as long as he could but eventually the Baron's booming voice summoned him.

'So, Engländer, my office business is now finished. Ve shall have a small drink and then go to town.'

203

Drinks were served and Peter began a conversation of great difficulty and enormous importance. He began by thinking he was talking for his life; then he realised he was talking for his friends' lives also. In the event of talk failing, as a final move to delay the departure, he was prepared to make a run for it into the country but he recognised that would almost certainly fail when chased by the local servants and must finally confirm the Baron's worst suspicions. It would surely expose him to severe questioning, even torture, to reveal the British plans.

So Peter talked. But even in that he was restricted: he did not want to reveal he had guessed von Ehrwald's identity or even his nationality, since that might tend to confirm von Ehrwald's scepticism about his story. Peter used a slight clumsiness of the steward in dispensing drinks to make a patronisingly racist comment about the man, a bait to which the Baron rose: the English "had no proper understanding of the black man" was the general theme. All Peter had to do was make the odd provocative remark or question to keep the tirade going. When that appeared to be flagging, he had a sudden inspiration and mentioned the name of Grenville-Fletcher as the senior officer in "a neighbouring province" who had died the previous week apparently at the hands of African medicine-men. The temptation was too much for the German but the subject required both men to walk tightropes: von Ehrwald lest he reveal he already knew of the death and especially that he was the deceased's father-in-law, although he was desperately keen to know if the death had led to a leaking of the German plans; Peter that he should not reveal he knew of the men's relationship while continually hinting there was more to the death than first appeared, as a way of prolonging the talking.

So the time passed until the servant came out with a roaring Tilley lamp and suddenly it appeared dark. The Baron immediately recalled his intention of going to town and began to issue instructions prior to his departure; the lamp should be taken indoors before they were besieged by moths and flying ants, arrangements for dinner and so on.

Waiting until the servant was carrying the lamp and the Baron was in full voice with orders, Peter suddenly announced he needed a pee and would "visit Africa", the normal arrangement and euphemism where all sanitation was dry. As if unusually modest he strode out of range of the light from the house, then raced on tip-toe to the car. He was confident the Baron would not see anything should he try to look from the bright room but the danger was that the driver might be around the motor-house, preparing for the journey to town.

He was in luck – there was no-one there – and it was the work of seconds to prop the carpenter's nails under the tyres in such a way that, as the car moved, punctures would be inevitable and instant. Peter put nails both before and behind the two rear wheels, before one front wheel and behind the other, reckoning that three punctures should be caused even if the driver perversely decided to move initially in reverse. He thought destruction of all four tyres could not be put down to ill-fortune and the carpenter's careless scattering of nails (three was pushing it) but he dropped the few remaining nails on the ground to lend "artistic verisimilitude", and hurried back to the house ostentatiously buttoning his flies.

Five minutes later the Baron called for the driver to bring the car and Peter tried not to hold his breath. He thought: I am passing you a pair of kings, old boy! as he heard the Renault's engine start. If the nails simply fall down with the car's vibration, the hand will be a broken straight. No! The engine suddenly died and the chances rose it was at least a pair of aces – one puncture. And whoopee! Confirmation came as the driver hesitantly shuffled forward with his unwelcome news.

'Uno pinchazo, Señor.'

'Maldito! Do not stand there. Change the wheel immediately. I want to drive to town. Put on the spare wheel.'

And the man left at the run.

So far, so good. A pair of aces for sure, but with luck the man has not looked at the other tyres yet. In the dark would he notice as he walked round the car or would he have another surprise only when he re-started the car? What were the values of the five dice under the cover? As the minutes dragged by, Peter the dice-player was delighted to see patience fraying on his opponent, always good in a poker game. And here was the driver, infinitely more reluctant than before to break his unpleasant news to the irascible boss. Oh joy! It wasn't a broken straight or even a full house; it was a royal flush!

'Dos màs! Two more punctures! Verflucht! Der Teufel ist los. Hol dich der Kuckuck. Nicht zu glauben! Das ist die Höhe.' The torrent of German was produced under the stress of the occasion and finally removed all pretence about the man's nationality.

Peter feigned complete surprise.

205

'Are you German? I am quite astonished. You speak such good English.' He was the model of the patronising Englishman, guaranteed to inflame any self-respecting Teuton.

The prisoner had undoubtedly won the day. Unless he walked, there was no possibility of the Baron visiting Santa Isabel tonight. The repair of the punctured inner-tubes would take several hours, although it was unlikely the tyres themselves would have suffered any lasting damage. Furthermore, the Baron's options on the Sunday would be much reduced. On Saturday evening von Ehrwald might indeed have enquired at the hotel about Peter's imaginary companion and aimed at tricking him into revealing himself, but he must expect any companion and the hotel management to be alarmed and alert by noon Sunday when Peter had been missing for a whole twenty-four hours. It seemed unlikely von Ehrwald would risk taking Peter into town in daylight when there were people about to whom a prisoner could appeal for help. If only he could keep the charade going until darkness on Sunday. What he feared most was crude torture that might induce him to disclose the piracy plans and timing. There was also the unpleasant possibility of a quick bullet, simply to dispose of him; he remembered how Klaus had dealt with the inconvenience of the Resident's driver.

Perhaps Peter's best strategy now might be to risk his own position and admit there was no accomplice and, therefore, no point in going to town. That decision could be held over to Sunday morning. The shrilling cicadas accompanied these disturbing thoughts as he lay hot under the mosquito net on the strange bed in the bungalow; the bedroom door was locked and there was heavy expanded metal fixed over the windows. He must wait for Sunday.

In his dream Peter eavesdropped on Father Francisco, his friend and liar-dice rival in Benin, confessing to the Baron he had sinned by passing a full house, aces on kings, as a pair of tens; the Baron gave him absolution for two pairs, Hail Marys and knaves, which made the Baron laugh so uproariously that he changed into Joshua who did not think it funny at all because he was a Catholic, so Peter and Father Frank wept a little, which was making the pillow hot and wet. Peter turned over the pillow to the cool underside and went back to sleep.

'Fifteen hours to go,' was Peter's first reasoned thought on waking and looking at his watch. His next, as he reviewed his prospects as a captive, was to wonder what treatment he might receive. In fact a generous supply of water and the use of a safety razor were soon provided by the steward, before coffee and fruit; the Baron, or perhaps the steward, appeared to set high standards for prisoners, at least for white men.

That set Peter thinking about Joshua, in particular whether he might have the self-confidence and determination to act without Peter's lead in the key moves to mount the attack on the ship. You paid your money and took your choice in regard to success. He was young, one black man in a white man's project and had never been briefed specifically on "You may have to do this entirely on your own", so it might be asking too much to expect him to carry the whole show. On the other hand he was intelligent, ambitious to show that a Bini could succeed as well as a Scot and obviously he had been well briefed by his father and the king not to fall down on the job. To his credit, Peter's misgivings concerned his own stupidity in falling for the simple trick which left Joshua exposed, rather than on Joshua's ability.

Peter was undecided how to behave towards von Ehrwald. He did not want to be taken to town, since he feared that might lead to the disclosure of the British plans, but he felt that an innocent prisoner would be expected to object strenuously to his detention and would demand immediate return to town and to his hotel. There would be no harm at present in making that fuss for return, since the car was out of action, so Peter objected loudly and asked to be taken to Santa Isabel. He emphasised that, since it was now daylight, he would be recognised and would be able to call for help against his illegal detention. The Baron made no answer and, needless to say, did not comply.

By mid-morning, impatience drove the Baron to investigate progress on the puncture repairs. He did not speed up the car's roadworthiness but his absence from the house and inattention by the steward gave Peter an opportunity to enter the study. Pride of place on the desk was taken by a radio receiver-transmitter in a metal case and, linked to it, a morse key and a battery pack. Peter thought it highly desirable this communication link should be broken but, apart from crude and noisy destruction likely to bring him immediate trouble, he had no idea what to do quickly to achieve it; he had no knife and no tool was ready to hand on the desk. The only prompt action was to switch over the positive and negative terminals on the battery pack; Peter hoped that might cause trouble and that the Baron might not notice the substitutions. The cable connecting the morse key to the set was cloth covered and, logic said, must contain two cores, probably rubber-covered from the feel of the cable. Peter carefully pushed an office pin diagonally down the cable so that it appeared to pass through both cores; he would have cut off the pinhead had he had pliers but had to be content with pulling the cloth cover over the head to make it less obvious, although there was a very pronounced bump and kink in the wire. With luck the key would be shorted. Finally he lifted the heavy radio six inches above the desk and deliberately let go so that the set crashed down. It was treatment he would never have given to his own precious wireless receiver and he hoped it might cause a valve to fail. Reluctantly content with that, he quietly left the study back to the verandah just before the Baron returned from his futile supervision of the car repairs.

The German was in a foul mood because the repairs were taking longer than he found convenient. Peter attacked again by expressing eagerness to go to town so that he might call for help and achieve his release. The bluff worked, for the Baron responded angrily that there would be no opportunity for rescue since they would arrive in town after dark, which was precisely what Peter was aiming to achieve.

In the afternoon, as quite usual at this time of year in the Bight of Africa, the sky became heavily overcast and there was rain. Great wreaths of cloud wrapped round the Basilé peak, lightning flickered and sudden squalls of wind lashed the shade trees in the coffee plantation below the house. Peter noted with satisfaction that, even outside the squalls, visibility over the sea was poor – much of the time he could not see Santa Isabel, which removed one major concern they had at the planning stage, that from high on the mountain in the afternoon people might see the *Mungo Park* heading for the target.

At the Baron's command, Peter was locked in his bedroom. With no book, he was left with his own increasing worries about the operation due to begin in a few hours. From the barred window, he watched the antics of a beautiful slaty-blue-bodied lizard with a bright orange head doing press-ups on the verandah to the obvious delight of his admiring harem of small green-headed females. He had no worries. For Peter every passing minute was a gain towards success, countering anxiety about the operation. Best go to bed and relax. So he was content to lie quiet, perspiring in the humid air.

After a couple of hours, his rest was abruptly broken by von Ehrwald bursting into the room. 'You lie, Engländer. You are an English Intelligence Officer; this I have proved. You try to destroy my radio and, as I suspect, you must be responsible for putting nails in the car punctures.' A stream of threats and grim forecasts followed, which Peter decided to interrupt. Standing in front of the Baron, an erect but not very impressive scrum-half beside a burly second-row forward, he spoke firmly, using the man's name for the first time.

'I am not in the British Intelligence Service, Baron von Ehrwald – as I believe you are called, but the Forest Officer, Benin Division; I think you would say *"Oberforstmeister"* and I must ask you to give me my title, as I shall use yours. And incidentally, I am not English as you keep suggesting; I am a Scot. As for the car tyres and the radio, I must remind you, Baron, that Britain and Germany are at war and it is my duty as a British officer to do all I can, even as your prisoner, to upset and delay Germany's war plans. If you do not like the result, hard luck! As we say, "If you do not like the heat, you should leave the kitchen".'

And, imitating what he thought might be formal German behaviour in such circumstances, he gave a stiff little bow; from the small man, it verged on the ridiculous but the effect on von Ehrwald was to make him even angrier.

CHAPTER THIRTEEN

As they rode south from the Border, the Armstrongs were spread as a screen of scouts, with supporting riders behind. The men carrying the ladders and tools followed and finally Lord Buccleuch with the main troop.

They crossed the frontier at nightfall, close to the point the River Esk enters the sea, and made their way carefully through the moss and marshes directly south towards Carlisle, riding quietly at a steady walk. Their route was to Stanwix Bank, the cliffs screening them from the castle, then across the River Eden downstream from Carlisle Bridge and thence to the meadow west of the city. The night was pitch-dark and misty.

It was still quite dark when the triple beat of the *Alexander Holt*'s engines slackened. Four-thirty on Sunday morning and they were on station, ten miles south of Bonny. The team members were ready, kitbags packed with their few items of personal gear; they carried their assorted machetes and clubs self-consciously on this friendly ship, apologetically among the men who had welcomed them aboard only on Friday and had helped to train them for their mission.

Chris blessed Panda's foresight in arranging this transport and the essential training it afforded; without it, he realised, they would have been lost. Quietly they thanked their hosts for their hospitality and their patience in imparting some of the skills of a seaman to a motley crew of amateurs.

There was an embarrassing episode when Eddie Hudson, weakly shaking and grey in his partial recovery, tried to argue his case for coming with them, protesting his fitness. Chris blamed himself for failing to spot the basic inadequacy of the man, which resulted in his hitting the bottle. At heart Eddie wanted to go on with the operation; he had tried to improve his credentials by exaggerating his experience and had then realised, not for the first time in his life, he was saddled with responsibilities he could not handle and expected to provide a service he did not know how to deliver. The Boss decided there could be no reprieve; the risk to the others was too high, so the sick man wept the bitter tears of the alcoholic. He would be taken on to Port Harcourt and from there could return to Benin City.

The grey of first light revealed a lonely, gloomy morning, cool almost to the point of being cold, a thin mist clinging to the surface of the sea's oily swell. With the combination of nervous tension and the chilly dawn air, men shivered. As the greyness brightened, navigation lights appeared and later a little ship, the *Mungo Park*.

"Little" was the essential word. This was no great ocean-going tug for towing between continents, but a harbour tug, its normal service to bring ships over the sandbars which block most West African ports and to tow them up the long creeks which were the arms of the huge Niger delta. By the time the gigs and the canoe had been deposited on the deck aft and twenty men had come aboard with their kit-bags, truncheons, rifles, ladders and machetes there was no space left. The clutter was increased by the inclusion of a pair of spars to serve as sheer legs for launching the boats, a crate of bottled water and a huge box of fruit and sandwiches supplied by the *Alexander Holt's* steward, rations for twenty men for two days. The man took a gloomy view of Italian food: 'With it being an Eytie ship, Sir, you may find nothing there but macaroni.'

The *Mungo Park* was both uncomfortable and unattractive, the hull dull black, the upperworks dingy brown. Her tiny bridge, stumpy mast and tall thin funnel were well forward, her after-deck dominated by the gigantic spring-loaded towing hook, her tool of trade. The crew was racially mixed, the two officers – the skipper Tony Robson and the engineer Matthew Consett – both Tynesiders, and the remaining eight men all African from the Niger creeks.

Pithy Geordie cracks and broad African grins marked the embarkation. The number of passengers and the unlikely nature of their luggage caused hilarity. West African languages are rich in greetings, many half-sarcastic; one shouted by the coxswain produced renewed shrieks of laughter; when Chris asked for a translation he was told, 'Welcome for coming with plenty fine presents, Sah' but he suspected it was a good deal saltier. All the crew were excited at the prospect of a voyage away from their base, out of the creeks and out of their routine.

It was full light when everything was transferred and they had time to look back at the *Alexander Holt*. She appeared huge, seen from this midget. The change of scale and the over-crowding quickened pulses and brought the imminence of the attack into focus. At Sapoba the whole project had been a lark, fun but unreal. The scale of the job and their urgent need for proper training became clear on the *Alexander Holt*; that was the size of ship they were aiming to steal. Now another phase was behind them, as they waved goodbye to their friends of two days' voyage, who were heading for Port Harcourt to load palm oil and groundnuts. The intensity of their initiation meant that the memory of these short acquaintances would remain especially vivid; in weeks to come, men would wonder how that particular Holt Line ship and those special people were faring as they joined the homeward convoy out of Freetown, whether they would get past the U-boats to reach Liverpool or suffer the torpedo-fate of so many others. For the present, two plumes of steam, two hoots and they were off on opposite courses, the *Alex Holt* up-river to PH, the *Mungo Park* southeast for Fernando Po.

The climbing sun gave point to the rigging of the tarpaulin awning on the after-deck; they would have to spend the whole day in the open. There was no larking; talk was quiet and purposeful; gathering in their attack teams was natural, almost instinctive. It was sobering to see the soldiers loading the Sten gun magazines slowly and methodically, and to have Cracker distributing the revolvers and their ammunition. Suddenly the whole show stepped up another gear: before they could steal the ship, they would have to fight.

As the sun burned the mist off the lazy swell, the distant view cleared and the horizon hardened to a firm line. They had the ocean to themselves. It was a hot loneliness. The scorching sun, at noon to become directly overhead, added to the greasy roaring heat of the engineroom. The funnel and every piece of the tug seemed to pulsate and glow. Chris blessed Panda's wisdom, founded on long experience, in ordering the *Alex Holt*'s steward to send aboard what appeared, at

212

four in the morning, to be a quite ridiculous volume of bottled water and lime juice. He appreciated the Captain's statement: 'Eight pints a day minimum and a lot more for the men in the engineroom.'

By late morning the raiders had wilted with the heat and were clustered in the small areas of shaded deck, by the wings of the bridge and under the scanty awning. Noon was approaching when skipper Tony Robson made the comment which brought every jaded warrior to his feet to stare directly ahead.

'There's Mount Clarence showing now, fine on the sta'board bow.'

The ten-thousand foot mountain danced as a silvery blue shimmer fifty miles ahead. Each man visualised the map of the single volcanic peak forming the whole island of Fernando Po, a rough triangle with sides each thirty miles. Most of the coastline was precipitous and unsheltered save in the centre of the north side where two promontories a thousand yards apart formed the deep bay of the Santa Isabel anchorage. There was the target. Now that they could see the wispy peak, the operation racked up another gear and tummy muscles tightened a notch.

The two captains agreed they would probably have some rain and thundery squalls in the afternoon.

'Ideal for cutting visibility and preventing our approach being seen from the shore, so long as it doesn't get too rough. Don't want the lads to get seasick!'

Chris' concern was elsewhere: 'I am worried about Peter and Joshua,' he admitted. 'It was a hell of a risk, going in ahead like that.' Visions flitted through his mind of his friend languishing for years in a Spanish jail or even worse if they were caught.

*   *

Von Ehrwald was now even angrier. His identity had been disclosed, which he had not intended, and he suspected – correctly – that Peter's pompous behaviour, bowing and clicking his heels, was not genuine but a caricature to poke fun at a Prussian stereotype. It did not help when he realised he could counter neither the argument itself nor the caricature without losing face as a German officer and reinforcing the fun.

The Baron was also extremely anxious. For eight months he had been living a lonely and precarious life here in Fernando Po, trying to respond to the mounting demands from Berlin and lately from Afrikakorps Headquarters in Tripoli. The High Command expected miracles of organisation, making no allowance for the fact he was on his own, unable to rely on subordinates to carry out an order. He was reduced to asking people to act for him. The *verdammte* Italians appeared quite content to spend the whole war swinging at anchor in the safety of a neutral port. Captain Palma might be a good seaman but he was extraordinarily reluctant to move when the *Oberkommando* called for prompt action. These supposed allies were sick-scared at the prospect of leaving their sanctuary to sail to Calabar. There had been a near-mutiny when the arms arrived from Argentina and they realised this was the end of loafing about. They were like the Spaniards – there was nothing to choose between them, except the Spaniards were more money-grubbing. It was sickening to think how many good Reichsmarks he had been forced to shell out in bribing officials to do what should have been done as a duty. The Führer and German aircrews had brought Franco to power: now Franco's people should pay the score. Instead the Baron was paid with half-truths and slow service (like the information on this little *Engländer*: I still don't know if he has a colleague in town – probably not). And this just when the ship is due to sail and Germany has the prospect of taking over the whole of West Africa.

In spite of having to use the lethargic Spaniards and the damned Italians, he had things moving. In fact fortune was smiling. Klaus and Hilda were lucky to get back from Benin to Kamerun – that was a close-run thing. We have the arms and we have the men, if only we can put the two together by persuading Palma and his lily-livered crew to sail to Calabar. *Verflucht*! It's only a hundred and fifty kilometres – like Berlin to Leipzig – and England has nothing to stop us closer than a destroyer at Freetown two thousand kilometres away. We must succeed.

Klaus has done well enough, though I wish I had been in Kamerun to see things were properly ordered. He should not have made that risky trip to Benin City to collect Hilda. We did not really need Hilda's husband: he's dead now, which just proves the point. He was slow-witted, *dumm*! I shall become *Kommandant* myself and will appoint deputies of my own choosing at the time. Klaus has done well but I wish we had Helmut and a company of his SS. When one considers the prize, it would surely be worth committing far more than that by way of resources. We shall cut off Britain's supply of aircraft from Takoradi in Gold Coast flying to Egypt; without their air cover, Egypt and the whole Middle East will fall. Arabia: oil: India! Everything hinges on getting these *ganz fürchterliche* Italians off their backsides to deliver the rifles to Klaus at Calabar. And at the last moment there arrives this little Englishman – no! he says he is from Schottland, like a Bavarian except they wear the kilt instead of *Lederhosen*. He makes much trouble, coming so near to our attack but I admire him a little because he is active, not like the Spaniards and Italians. I may have to shoot him, but perhaps he would be useful as a native English speaker when the ship approaches the Nigerian port. I shall keep him alive until then, if he makes no trouble.

'Ve shall drive by auto to town, leaving very soon. You will not become free. For you I have other plans. But if you misbehave, I shall shoot you.' And with that he left the bedroom and locked the door.

It was well after seven o'clock in the evening when Peter was summoned to the car, a time which made him quite content. Certainly he was keyed up wondering how his friends' operation was proceeding, and he was hungry, since the Baron had failed to invite him to the evening meal. But in the circumstances that was a small penalty.

The journey to town was slow and precarious. The damp cloudy night swallowed the headlights, making it difficult to identify the edges of the road which, even in good visibility, was unsuited to fast driving. Peter's main concern was that he might be taken somewhere he would be recognised as Garibaldi and linked to the booking of the Italian party at the restaurant. Arriving in the town, however, they drove steadily through the main streets down to the eastern end of the Avenida Marítima, to the base of the stone pier. The driver jumped out, leaving Peter in the car with the silent Baron.

As they waited, an African walked towards the car, the movement catching Peter's attention. To his horror, he realised the man was Joshua. This was disaster! All he could do was slowly shake his head and will the man not to greet him and thereby reveal their relationship.

Just then the driver returned, accompanied by two scantily dressed men who briefly bargained with the Baron in pidgin Spanish,

215

from which Peter deduced that the party was to be continued on board ship. The Baron issued dire threats against Peter attempting to escape, backed by a short-barrelled Luger, and the group went quickly down to a canoe, leaving Joshua bewildered on the jetty.

*   *

Shortly before sunset the *Mungo Park* was on a due easterly course and twelve nautical miles north of Santa Isabel. The awning had been dismantled and the sheer legs rigged. With the last of the daylight Captain Robson and his coxswain supervised the launching of the two gigs which were streamed on either quarter, each with a crew of two men. Now only the canoe lay on the afterdeck, left there because of doubts about how she might tow. In gathering darkness, the ship then altered course due south, directly towards the target, steaming quietly at five knots, completely blacked out.

The raiding party's mood had changed again. Now there was obvious nervous tension. There was little talk. A scratch meal of sandwiches had been eaten. A tin of cigarettes was passed round.

'I don't mind if I do', came in the darkness, in blimpy imitation of Tommy Handley's Colonel Chinstrap.

'We have missed hearing ITMA this week. Pity! Other things on.'

'There's a repeat on Sunday night. Might hear that.'

'This is Sunday, you clot. We've missed that too.'

'No matter! Press on regardless!'

'Get right down low when you are using that bloody lighter. We don't want to get spotted at this stage.'

Ninety minutes later and seven miles from the target, Tony Robson cut the speed to bare steerage way to allow the crews to man the boats. Chris and Panda thanked Tony for his part so far, shook hands and left. Cracker Armstrong gripped Rob Graham's elbow as in a vice, the closest intimacy there had been between them:

'Watch how you go, Corporal!'

Now only Clapper Bell, Steve and the Sergeant remained on board with the *Mungo Park*'s crew. Quietly Tony Robson called, 'Slow Ahead', and resumed the course towards the port. Navigation was no problem, with the town's lights twinkling faintly ahead and the lights on the eastern promontory and the islands at the west side of the bay.

An hour later the Captain again cut the tug's engines and the ship drifted slowly to a stop. Ahead, less than a mile distant, the pin-point lights of Santa Isabel sparked in the velvety darkness and, against the lights, the vague silhouette of a ship could be seen. Their ship: the *Duchess*.

Tony Robson turned to Steve who was with him on the bridge.

'We are in position and on time: nine o'clock, twenty-one hundred. Time for you chaps to get aboard your dug-out.'

'Right. Thanks, Tony. I don't know if you have spotted it, but there's a fire apparently on the beach in about the place one might expect. OK; you have seen it. That may be them. Give us the wire if there is a signal. Bye now. We'd best get going.'

The low freeboard of the tug made launching the canoe easier than they had feared, especially with the manpower of the tug's crew to heave and lower it. Five minutes later the last three raiders were afloat, steadying their craft in the gentle swell, waiting for the signal, if any was to come.

Suddenly there was a flare of crimson from the shore, obvious even to those in the boats. The party was on. Then another .... and another. The canoe crew dug in their paddles, passing close to Captain Moore's boat. Chris gave the order.

'Go in now, Sergeant! Peter has given you a clear run, it seems. We shall be five minutes behind you.'

*   *

When Joshua Oshodin awoke on Sunday morning he was mighty pleased with life. As planned, he had spent Saturday night noisily and enjoyably with his local friends. They were happy people, very like his family back in Benin, full of fun, and they treated him as an important guest. Although young, he had status here because he had travelled from far away and was a businessman, able to talk – almost as an equal – with father who was head of the family. Last night had been a good party with the people of his own age, plenty to eat, a little local beer and exciting dancing. To admiring girls he had talked about Benin City (Well! What if he had dressed it up a little? The girls liked it that way!) and about Lagos where he had been once (when he was only six years old – but he didn't tell them that) and Ibadan where one million people live (that is fifty times all the people in Fernando Po island!).

Relaxed and in good spirits Joshua arrived at the hotel, as arranged at eleven o'clock, to meet Mr Thorburn: and the gilt began to rub off his day. Soon he was a worried young man. A letter, handed him by the hotel clerk told him Thorburn had gone by car to see another white man on the island. He felt Thorburn was letting him down; this was the big day when there were plenty things to be done but the white man goes off enjoying himself. He questioned the clerk: When had the white man left the letter? Yesterday noon! Has he not come back? Has he eaten breakfast this morning?

Joshua was in a confusion of resentment and anxiety. He liked Thorburn and knew this matched the opinions of his father and the Oba, both of whom said Thorburn was straight. For almost an hour he fluctuated between concern and resentment. He imagined Thorburn involved in a motor accident. He condemned the white man's neglect of their plans in some pleasure-taking which casually left the African to wait. Then the thought of another aspect came: the jobs he and Thorburn planned for tonight were part of a much bigger operation. Indeed they were critical and Joshua began to worry that the main operation would fail because their part would be missing. Thorburn would not have risked that lightly. Something serious must be keeping him.

What if he was delayed much longer? Joshua's anxiety sharpened with realisation that the critical tasks basic to the attack on the ship would fall on him. And on him alone! It was not fair! It was not fair he should be left to do everything. If they failed, as a black man he would get the blame! But training, tradition and pride gradually took over: the Bini tradition, the Oshodin family pride, confidence flowing from the trust shown by his father and the Oba in sending him with Thorburn. If Thorburn was unable to return, he would have to be prepared to act alone. He could: he must.

There were things in Thorburn's luggage he would require and by mid-afternoon he could wait no longer. At the hotel he told the clerk he had instructions to pack up Señor Thorburn's luggage. The man recognised Joshua as having arrived with the guest and thought he must be his assistant or a servant of some kind. The guest had paid his bill in advance so that was no problem; he handed over the key.

By sunset, Joshua's arrangements were in place. Two teenagers of the host's family had been pressed into service, only too willing to be in-spanned to help this exciting visitor from Nigeria; Joshua urgently impressed upon them the need for secrecy and exact obedience. They were now on the beach at the far west end of the bay towards the Punta Cristina. Before them they had a fire burning briskly which they kept supplied steadily with fuel; their anxiety was that the rain squalls of the afternoon might return and dowse the flames, but local experience told them this was unlikely. Nearby on the shingle a small canoe was drawn out of the water, just sufficient to take three people. They waited for Joshua who had said he would come one hour or two hours after sunset.

A half-mile away, Joshua was loafing unobtrusively near the stone pier, the landing place where the town's main group of canoes was drawn up. As far as possible he avoided conversation with the locals who were curious at the presence of this stranger, but he appeared to be interested in the movements of the canoes and boats, and in the arrival of any motor car. He carried a small parcel wrapped in oil-cloth. *(*See map of Santa Isabel at rear end paper)*

Some time after seven o'clock there was a noisy interlude, as a dozen white sailors from the *Duchessa di Lucca* disembarked at the quay. The men, carefully counted by Joshua, were talking excitedly in what he guessed was Italian, as they walked away across the Avenida Marítima into the town. The motor-launch which had brought them returned to the ship nearby for a second load and the performance was repeated.

Half an hour later, just as Joshua was about to leave the quayside, his interest in cars was finally rewarded when a Renault tourer stopped nearby. Two white men sat in the back; one was Thorburn but instinct told Joshua not to rush forward to greet him. There was something artificial about the two.

With some care, Joshua slowly walked towards the car. While he was still a few yards away, Peter Thorburn turned in his direction and instantly there was eye-contact. The white man deliberately shook his head and Joshua received the message he should go no farther, although he could see no reason for the change of attitude. Was Thorburn denying their acquaintance because he was in the company of another white man? Was he suddenly too proud to acknowledge his black companion? That would be a massive change of character, a rejection of the Oba's assurance and his own recent experience, but he wondered. Another glance at the men in the rear seat of the motor car told him these were not close friends, whatever Thorburn's reason for not wanting to acknowledge him; there was tension between the two men in the Renault.

The African driver had left the car briefly and now returned with two burly locals who were canoe-men. The white men came out of the car and went to a canoe; Joshua was thrown momentarily by the fact that Thorburn appeared to be going off quite willingly, thus abandoning the plans they had drawn up together. Although he was unsure about the white man's action, he was clear what must be his own. He watched the canoe with Thorburn and the other white man until it was well out towards the ship. Then he set off at a brisk pace westwards along the Avenida, past the cathedral towards Cristina Point. It was a sultry overcast night; he hoped the boys had the fire burning well and had protected the fuel supply in case of rain.

It was a relief to see the fire sparkling down on the stony shore, with the two lads lounging near it. Time was pressing and, after giving them the proper greeting for sitting idle, he ordered all the available dry fuel to be added to the fire. Five minutes later there was a roaring blaze lighting up the rocks, enough to attract the attention of passers-by on the road at the top of the beach.

The effect of the bright fire was to deepen the darkness beyond. Out to sea there was a black nothing; the shower clouds had blotted out the stars to leave no distinction between sea and sky. Joshua had to take everything on trust and he felt desperate indecision. It was now almost four days since the plans were laid at Sapoba. Were the arrangements to go ahead as planned then? Was there really a ship out there in the night, with Mr Wickham, Mr Lister, Sergeant Armstrong and the others? There was no sign and, although he knew there would be none, he longed there might be something to reassure him. For him to go ahead with the scheme, not only without Thorburn's approval but immediately after his white colleague apparently having walked out on him, required a lonely kind of determination, what Sergeant Armstrong would have called "bloodimindedness", although Joshua did not know the word.

He had been told what should be done. He took one of the small envelopes he had removed from Peter's suitcase and threw it into the fire. Instantly a brilliant crimson sun-burst flooded the beach to the tops of the palms fifty yards away. The fireball held for a few seconds, then died, leaving Joshua and the boys temporarily blinded by its intensity. Joshua repeated the spectacle with a second packet, being careful this time to look away, and then with a third. The packets had worked as they had practised at Sapoba on the previous Wednesday evening, when the contents of a marine flare provided by Captain Moore had been divided and tested. His three red beacons signalled to the attackers that men from the *Duchess* had come ashore; three beacons meant more than twenty.

The boys now abandoned the fire and launched the canoe. After the brilliance of the flares, their blind darkness was so complete that every action was fumbled, but fortunately the sea was smooth, only a lazy swell hissing rhythmically on the pebbly beach. With Joshua a passenger amidships, the two boys paddled straight out to sea for almost a quarter mile, then turned east, parallel to the shore on a course to bring them directly to the stern of the *Duchess*.

Cliff-like, the great black bulk of the ship towered above them as silently they came under the overhang of the stern. Everything was magnified by their view from the very surface of the sea, their tiny canoe fragile as a bubble. The minutes dragged to a quarter-hour, Joshua periodically shivering with suppressed excitement and growing panic that the whole operation had failed and he was abandoned, so that he would be left all night holding to the barnacle-encrusted top of this ship's rudder plate. Were they in the correct place? Was this the wrong ship?

Night-vision was fully recovered when, suddenly, he was aware of something darker than the sea resolving itself twenty yards away, ten yards, to seaward. The far-travelled Jekri canoe, fashioned from good Benin *ovbiache* on the banks of the Jamieson River, grew from a shadow to something solid, close, tangible; three figures became friends and the huge worries of the last twelve hours evaporated. Steve Lister's whisper was urgent.

'Peter? Are you there? Joshua! Thank God you are there. Where is Peter Thorburn?'

Rapidly Joshua told the surprising turn of events, that Peter had gone on board this very ship an hour before, accompanied by a big white man. Asked about the movements of the crew, he replied that twenty-two men had gone ashore earlier.

'No matter how this operation goes from now on, Joshua, you have done a great job. Well done', Steve said quietly. And Cracker added solemnly, 'Aye, you've done weel, laddie,' which was the Borderer's acme of praise.

Cracker then ordered Joshua, with his baggage, to join them in the larger canoe and to dismiss his friends. The transfer, in darkness, from one fragile craft to the other was not easy. Quietly Joshua slapped the hands of the two black youths who then back-paddled and slid away silently over the oil-dark water.

Steve in the bow and Clapper Bell in the stern gently paddled along the black wall of the hull, while Joshua fended off so that no scrape or bump should sound an alarm. Cracker, seated amidships, was holding the ladder along the port gunwale; even with the top hook of the ladder resting on the edge of the canoe, it was not easy to keep the thing stable. A new problem now emerged: they had not appreciated how difficult it would be, in darkness and close alongside, to judge their position. If they went too far, they would miss the after well-deck and their ladder would not reach the rail. Cracker hissed a halt. Now the ladder.

The drills at Sapoba paid off. Three men tried desperately to hold the canoe steady, while Cracker, crouching low until the last moment, slowly raised the ladder hooks to the ship's rail. All his upper body strength was needed to place the ladder there without a noise. Then he gave a gentle pull to ensure it was safe, tapped Steve on the shoulder, hitched the Sten on its sling out of the way and swung himself carefully on to the bottom rung.

Cracker's first glimpse through the rail at deck level told him they had done not badly in judging their position; only a few yards away were the steps giving access to the upper deck. That was their route. Nothing moved. He waved a hand to bring up the others, raised the Sten to the ready, then quickly up and over the rail. Into the cover of the steps and scan the after deck carefully for movement. Much lighter here than overside. Dim deck lights are on. Wait for the other three. Joshua's a good lad; has an advantage for night-ops – doesn't need to blacken up like the rest of us. Now, up these steps. Across the deck here. More steps, just like Captain Panda's plan showed. We'd have been lost without that plan. The guys are moving well, as I told

222

them; quietly too. Half way up the steps: look along A-deck. No-one in sight. This block must be the radio-room and wireless operators' cabin. There's music coming from inside; that's a help.

Cracker signed to the other three for a drill they had practised: two men to take each of the two doors simultaneously. The doors opened together, within a second. Steve and Clapper found the sleeping cabin empty, with bunks for two men, so they immediately went next door where they found Cracker and Joshua beginning to tie up a terrified Italian radio officer. Steve, armed with a Webley, was left to guard the radio room, just in case any free crew member tried to get off a distress signal.

The other three crossed the length of A-deck, using the cover of the funnel and ventilators, to reach a door at the back of the bridge. Here they paused and Cracker slowly raised his head to glimpse the interior through the glass panel. One man was seated on a high stool, looking forward.

*   *

The Baron's threat to shoot Peter if he resisted transfer to the canoe and thence to the ship was wholly unnecessary. Nothing suited Peter better; he recognised it was too late for him to play any part on shore – he must rely on Joshua for that – and moving to the future centre of action was next best. For form's sake he protested mildly as he was led down steps to a large canoe. Ehrwald followed, with drawn pistol; he was contemptuous of the prisoner's lack of resistance to his forced embarkation ("*dekadenter Schotte!*"), being blissfully unaware that yet another game of poker-dice had begun. The two paddle-men took only a few minutes to bring them to the bottom of a ship's accommodation ladder and Peter, first of the pirates, stepped aboard the *Duchessa di Lucca*. At the head of the ladder they were met by a single member of the crew who saluted the Baron, obviously recognising a frequent visitor.

As he was marched along, Peter looked around. Thank Goodness it is the right ship; it would have been bloody silly if it had been another. There is the name in big letters but, more important, I recognise it all from Panda's sketch; I bet I know the lay-out better

223

than the Baron. Our use of that starboard ladder shows Cracker was right to ignore it for the attack and to concentrate on the dark port side. My God, Cracker and the others may come any time now; let's get off this deck and out of their way. Only one member of the crew around so far; it looks as though our diversion plan must have come off. I hope the Italian lads are having a good party right now at the Granada Restaurant; I wish I could be there at least to have some *olla di carne* because I am damned hungry; not to mention I paid for all the chop and the vino. Still, those at the party will miss the ship, with any luck. What is the penalty for a seaman missing his ship? Probably dire in the old days, keelhauling, clapped in irons or something worse. Up another flight. Yes! We are heading for the captain's cabin. But what about Joshua? Has he made the signals? Will the attack be able to come in on time? I was bloody silly to fall for Ehrwald's trick. Thought I was clever sending the Italian a fake letter! If Joshua has slipped up, it's my fault.

Captain Palma was standing in his day cabin, dressed in a loose white open-necked shirt and white trousers. With his neatly trimmed beard he looked like a fifteenth or sixteenth century Venetian merchant-explorer, which was exactly what his ancestors had been. It became immediately apparent that the common language for the German and the Italian captain was English.

'Good evening, Baron. I did not expect you until tomorrow but I am delighted to welcome you aboard tonight. You have brought a visitor?'

'Ja. I introduce him. He is my prisoner. An Englishman, Torburn. He is an English spy, I am sure.'

'I am not a spy. I am not English. I am Scottish. My name is Thorburn and I am a Forest Officer in the Colonial Service in Nigeria.' Peter stepped forward and shook hands with the Italian captain; by this move he aimed to establish a sympathetic relationship with Palma and thereby create a tension between his two enemies.

The Baron, however, was in no mood to allow such civilities. He asked the Captain to produce the hand-cuffs which he knew were available and Peter, loudly protesting, suffered their indignity; threatened with the Baron's pistol, there was no escape. He sat down heavily on the locker seat at the cabin wall.

'For you I have plans. Vether you are a simple *Forstmeister* or an English spy, you will remain in this ship. Soon the ship will sail

224

to a port in Nigeria and it will then be useful to have an English speaker, since by the authorities the arrival will not be expected. You will be a little insurance for a good reception.' And he laughed unpleasantly. Abruptly his mood changed and he demanded, 'Vy is the ship so quiet? Vere are your officers and men? Are there no preparations?'

Palma's explanation came as a relief to Peter but no surprise. He had given most of the crew shore leave; it appeared sensible in view of the impending sailing. The men were stale after their long and depressing inaction; the opportunity for a break to improve morale had been provided by the generous gesture of a visiting Italian businessman offering to entertain the whole ship's company and passengers to a meal at the Granada. 'It was too good to miss: I am only sorry I could not go myself but I decided to allow First Officer Costanti to head the party. We have only a harbour watch tonight.'

'Has Pasconi attended?' the Baron asked sharply. Peter recalled the name as the passenger whom London had reported as having had business with de Beers immediately before the ship sailed from Cape Town.

'Yes, he has gone ashore. He was anxious to meet Signor Garibaldi, this evening's host, as a fellow Italian businessman and a man of culture. From his letter to me, it appears Garibaldi may be an agent of the Italian government, which finally decided Pasconi to go.'

'I am surprised he allowed himself to be separated from his precious "cargo"', the Baron laughed mirthlessly. 'But perhaps he took them with him?'

Palma shook his head. 'No, no. they are secure in the safe.' And he pointed to the key-ring on the table beside him.

For a little time the Baron appeared to be considering a new situation. Finally he made up his mind and again addressed the Captain.

'In view of the plans for the ship', and he glanced meaningfully towards Peter, 'it is obviously undesirable that Pasconi's goods should remain on board. The ship will sail into enemy waters, in effect into battle, and ve cannot be certain about the result even though ve are confident of success. Such goods must be safeguarded for the Reich's war production – or for Italy's', he added as an afterthought on seeing Palma bristle. 'It is better I take charge of them to make them safe while the ship is away, so I suggest you bring them out now.'

225

Palma's reply was immediate and unhesitating. 'No. Those diamonds belong to the Italian government and any proposal that they be removed from the ship must be agreed by Pasconi. And already you know that Pasconi does not want them taken away from the Italian sovereignty of this ship into Spanish territory, even to the bank, because the ownership may come into question. He has personal responsibility; that is why he will not take them ashore and why he refuses to remain here in Santa Isabel but insists on coming with us on this operation to Nigeria.'

'Pasconi is a fool to think of allowing such valuables to be taken into a battle area.' The Baron spoke slowly and moderately, as if holding himself in check. 'I can look after them. I would not allow the Spanish authorities even to know about them, certainly not to hold them. They will be safe with me.'

It was Peter's own opinion, and he judged it was Palma's also, that diamonds or any other valuables taken into the Baron's keeping were most unlikely to be returned to Pasconi or the Italian government ever again.

Palma was adamant. 'The stones are Italian property in Pasconi's charge. They are in the ship's safe for security and I cannot release them to you or anybody else without Pasconi's explicit agreement, which I am sure he would refuse. So I will not hand them over. That is final.'

As he finished speaking there was a dull thud, very audible in the quietness of the ship, as if something heavy had fallen on deck.

'What was that?' the Captain asked and walked across to the cabin door. Opening it, he raised his head to peer up the stairway immediately opposite, which led directly to the bridge and called out,

'*Pietro. Cosa e questo chiàsso? E tutto a posto? OK?*' (Pietro. What was that noise? Is everything in order? All O.K?)

Peter Thorburn tensed. He guessed the British attack had started and feared it had gone wrong – the bridge was to be attacked immediately after the radio room. But a reassuring Italian voice replied.

'*Si, si! E niente.*' (Sure! It's nothing.)

Peter relaxed, then glanced at the bulkhead clock which showed 9.35, and realised the operation planned by Chris and his friends had been scheduled to begin twenty minutes earlier. They must be late; something had gone wrong. Had Joshua sent no signal? Weather? Breakdown of the tug?

Captain Palma was not entirely satisfied by the reply shouted from the bridge and stepped out of the cabin to look at the deck himself. As he left, Baron von Ehrwald acted swiftly. He swept up the bunch of keys from the desk and in two strides was in front of the bulkhead safe. The safe key, far longer and slimmer than the others, was obvious. One turn of the key and the handle was free to open. The door swung back and the Baron was rummaging through the contents. Peter saw him reject the two upper shelves which carried only papers and books, and then bend down to take a leather packet, like a lady's evening bag, from a lower shelf. The door swung to, the handle and key were turned and the bunch of keys went quietly down on the desk.

As Palma reappeared in the doorway of the cabin he called out again to the man on the bridge above,

'*Pietro, vieni qua giú.*' (Come down here.) And to the Baron said, 'There was no-one at the ladder. I thought it might be some thieving locals. But I shall tell Pietro to keep a sharp lookout.'

Peter reckoned he had been silent long enough. This was the critical time to cause some diversion, even if only to delay the sharpening of lookouts or hold the captain's attention. Minutes might be vital now if his friends were in the final approach in the canoe and the gigs. Palma's last thoughts about thieving natives gave him his lead.

'*Scusi, Capitano. Forse il ladro è tedesco, non un negro del luogo.*' (Excuse me, Captain. But the thief is German, not a local black man.)

Palma and the Baron turned open-mouthed to the man on the seat. The Baron shouted in English, 'You speak Italian. *Gott im Himmel!*'

'Yes, of course. Why should I not understand Italian? I lived in Torino for several years when my father worked there.'

Palma turned to Peter and said in Italian, 'Are you telling me he opened the safe while I was out of the cabin?'

Peter faced him squarely: 'Exactly so. He took a black bag which I assume holds the diamonds you were speaking about.'

Palma followed Peter's nod towards the keys on the table. They lay on top of an open type-written letter. An instant too late, Peter recognised it as his own, the invitation to the party at the Granada. This vignette, coupled with the fluency of Peter's Italian flashed an awful realisation in the captain's mind.

'*D'mio!* You are Garibaldi, offering the party ...'

Before he could say more, the quietness of the night was shattered by the clang of something heavy striking the steel hull. Following the first noise, this could not be ignored. von Ehrwald and Palma looked at each other for a second and then collided as they squeezed through the cabin door, von Ehrwald leading, leaving the handcuffed Peter seated on the locker.

Clear of the door, the Captain, as a matter of habit, raced up the steps to the bridge where, in semi-darkness, he failed to notice his watchkeeper Pietro lying on deck in one corner, tied and gagged. Instead he found Clapper Bell who confused the captain by shouting a stream of Italian. For a vital few seconds Palma thought this must be some other member of the crew who was asking questions:

'What was that noise? Has someone fallen overboard? Is it something in the engineroom?'

He had come from his cabin unarmed and the confusion of the questions in fluent Italian allowed the other man to get close. Clapper suddenly changed from the garrulous questioner into a very decisive enemy. Laying the blunt back-side of his machete against the captain's throat (Clapper was a gentle man and meant the captain no harm), he spoke, now crisply, in Italian.

'This knife is very sharp. Do not force me to use it. Stay silent and very still so that no harm comes to you. Kneel down slowly. Now put your hands on the deck, slowly.'

The heavy knife lay cool against Palma's carotid artery. He did not feel inclined to question whether it was blunt or keen, and still less to test it. As he obeyed the instructions and changed position, he felt the individual hairs of his beard move against the steel blade, so he lay quietly while Joshua tied his elbows and his ankles. The tightening knots caused him to reflect on the full extent of the plot which was robbing him of his command: the letter from "Garibaldi", Peter Thorburn from Torino, the party for the crew at the Granada; all these he accepted as *un astuzia di guerra*. But it choked him that the Baron, his supposed ally, had stolen valuables from the ship's safe, like a common thief; *un bastardo tedesco*.

Meanwhile, the said German Baron had raced along the companion way towards the stern, seeking a view overside whence – logic told him – the noise had come. He was not aware that the captain had headed straight for the bridge and he thought the pounding steps close at his heels were Palma's. The captain's cabin was on the port

228

side of the ship and thus on the side the British party was attempting to board. Down one flight of stairs, three steps to the rail and, by chance, he was precisely at the point where the ladder had been hooked on by Rob.

The place the Baron looked down was unlit but there was enough reflected light to show a small boat crowded with men and, on a rough wooden ladder only an arm's length away, a man in the act of climbing aboard. Rob's head was just below the rail, his machine-pistol uselessly slung against his chest. The significant linkages of the *verdammt* Peter Thorburn's lies, the punctures, the *dummer* Palma falling for the cafe invitation to get his crew out of the way, all flashed across his mind in milli-seconds as he raised his pistol to kill the first of the *Schweinhund Engländer.* He would shoot the men in the boat like sitting ducks, *kein Problem,* and then at leisure – *mit Vergnügen* – he would go back to the cabin to shoot *Forstmeister* Thorburn, but first he must shoot the man on the ladder. Rob, looking up as he climbed, saw the Luger and knew what was coming; instinctively he cringed into a ball, as if that would make any difference at point blank range.

Cracker's left arm whipped round under von Ehrwald's chin and jerked back his head. The slim Commando dagger point thrust upwards into his back just below his left shoulder blade. Unfired, the Luger fell from the Baron's outstretched hand into the sea at the rowing boat's bow. Cracker felt the straining body go limp and lowered the dying man to the deck. He bent over him for a moment and then turned to the rail to address Rob urgently.

'Get up here fast, Rob. And don't make such a bloody great noise about it. You could have got hurt, letting the buggers know you were coming, like that.' And as Rob climbed over the rail, he continued, 'The knife worked just as that instructor said at battle-school. Get your lads up here and crack on. I'm going back for Peter.'

To Rob, this was the first news Peter was aboard. As Cracker left, Rob signalled his team to join him and they began the methodical search of their sector of the ship.

Fifteen minutes later Chris Wickham and Captain Moore stood on the bridge of the *Duchessa di Lucca* and received the vital reports of success. The whole ship had been swept by the raiders and five crew members, plus Captain Palma, had been captured without a fight. The Acting Chief Engineer John Balman reported the boilers were fired and he could have full steam pressure in an hour.

Improbable though it had appeared at the start, the ship had been captured, apparently without people ashore being aware of the fact. At least as important, no radio message had been sent, so Klaus Ehrwald should be unaware of the cutting out of the ship which was to deliver his weapons.

Now began a nerve-stretching interlude. They could call in the *Mungo Park* immediately to tow the *Duchessa* off her moorings but that might be a slow process for the small harbour tug, working in the dark, with a scratch crew on the big vessel and little or no help from the *Duchessa*'s engines. The Spanish harbourmaster would surely have time to intervene. But delay in getting under way meant risking twenty Italian crew trying to come back aboard, their party over, and calling in the protective power of the Spanish authorities.

'The ship is yours, Captain,' Chris said formally. 'We shall do our best for you as a crew. Make your own judgment when to sail. You have more experience of ships and the sea than the rest of us put together and I trust you to weigh the pros and cons.'

'Very good, Chris. I shall wait as long as possible in order to have steam for the main engines. Chief, get steam pressure up as fast as you dare and let me know progress with that every five minutes so that I can order the tug when it's needed. Chris, put the soldiers out of sight but handy to guard the sta'board side accommodation ladder, and men ready to raise it immediately if the Eyetie crew come out from shore to get aboard. You have the charges being laid on the anchor chain?'

'Yes. Tom has that all in hand'

'Good, but we sha'nt blow it until I'm ready for the tow. And we want Steve Lister's fo'castle party standing by for immediate duty on the moorings and the tow cable the instant that is needed. Two men to secure the small boats and the canoe right now and quietly bring those and the ladders inboard; boats drifting in the harbour would be bound to attract attention. No noise, and keep people off the upper decks where they can be seen from shore.'

'Now, Mister Signaller,' the Captain continued, addressing Roger Trimble, the oil palm breeder whose hobby was radio, 'Make the first signal to the tug with that screened lamp for Success and Wait" – that is six dots, then pause and repeat that six or eight times. After that, Chris, we put two good men ready to deal with the aft mooring lines; they must be slipped soon after the tug brings her head to sea. Who will you detail? McIver and Smith? Right.'

After a pause, the Captain went on:

'The bother, Chris, is that the Chief's effort to rush firing up the boilers is bound to create smoke and someone ashore is almost sure to spot it. We saw the problem right at the start in Sapoba and it hasn't gone away: we don't have power to get under way right now, it will take us the best part of an hour anyway to raise steam pressure by which time the Italian crew will either have had their supper or will have twigged Mr Garibaldi is a phoney, and the longer we wait the more power we have but the greater the chance of being seen and of the damned Spaniards interfering.'

While he was speaking he used the ship's binoculars to scan the jetty area ashore.

'Aye! Just as I said. Look at the smoke young John Balman is making. Keep watching for that ship's motorboat Joshua mentioned and the front of that cafe where Peter Thorburn booked the party. What I aim to do now is bring the tug in quietly to lie close alongside to port. If Robson brings in the *Mungo Park* very slowly with no lights, he's unlikely to be noticed. We can then pass the wire without any hurry and we shall be ready for a quick getaway whenever the need arises, whether we have full steam pressure or not. Let's get that going.'

As part of his studies in civil engineering, Tom Leach had attended lectures on the handling of explosives and thus was accounted a demolition expert by his fellow pirates who knew nothing of the subject. The bother was the university course had been theoretical and had said nothing at all about cutting anchor chains. Tom's lecture notes were quite explicit about blasting rock for quarrying and even dealt with some nice problems of tunnelling, but the flat ground and deep sand of Benin where Tom worked offered no opportunity for practising these dark arts.

Tom had to guess how to cut the chain. Before the boats were hauled on board, Rob and Phillip rowed quietly to the ship's bow to let the "peterman" do his worst. The rusty, slimy, weed-festooned thing was as stiff as a stone column but it provided no obvious place to attack. Each link was a copy of its neighbours, one place as good as any other. Tom chose the link immediately above water level to tie on the charge and the fuse was led back to a colleague on the fo'castle. It worried him, however, that with nothing to contain the blast, to concentrate its effect on the chain itself, the explosion would simply expand into the air – so much easier than cutting the steel.

Luigi Costanti was an unhappy man. He had been looking forward to the evening ashore, the chance of a good meal at someone else's expense and meeting a new face. When the Captain had shown him Signor Garibaldi's letter, he thought the Old Man would accept the invitation himself and he, Luigi, would have to look after the ship. After all, the businessman must be an important guy and interesting to meet, quite apart from the prospect of the supper party, so it was a surprise, a real bonus, when the Captain said he would stay on board and allow Luigi to go. He was to suggest to Signor Garibaldi he should go out to the ship after supper to meet Captain Palma.

Now a string of things was conspiring to steal all the enjoyment. Naturally, as First Officer he was responsible for the crew's behaviour, nothing out of the way in that, but the circumstances and the environment were unusual. Even the arrangement of tables in the Granada dining room could not remove the tension that was bound to exist when the whole ship's company sat down together at a social engagement, officers, deck-hands, stokers, a passenger, stewards and cooks. There was an artificial quietness at some tables, a false "best behaviour", contrasting with peals of raucous laughter at the boatswain's bawdy jokes. Nostromo Manatti was taking full advantage of the free wine and would have to be watched lest he became tiresome. He was unlikely to start fighting (that could be dealt with very promptly) but would probably become homesick and maudlin if he went on supping up the wine as he was doing now, and that would upset others. It was part of the penalty of sitting idly at anchor for eighteen months. Confidence and discipline have suffered. The men know we shall be sailing soon – *Madre di multissimi!* only the day after tomorrow. That is putting everyone on edge; no-one can tell how this voyage will end and the men are nervous.

The men are nervous? I am nervous too. This voyage could be a bloody disaster. The old German is doing the scheming but we have to sail the ship and no-one needs a crystal ball to see we shall be sailing into a heap of trouble when we are supposed to deliver a load of guns and bullets. And the men know that is the deal.

Where is our host? Signor Garibaldi is very late. I thought he would be waiting here when we came ashore. It's embarrassing,

232

drinking his wine without the man himself being here. The hotelier has been generous in filling the glasses but it's a ridiculous situation, twenty-odd guests waiting for an unknown host who is more than an hour late. I wish the Captain was here instead of me. Any minute now the hotel people will want to begin serving food, making things even worse. Not that food wouldn't be welcome: the Spaniards overdo the business of late eating and I need more than these nuts. Where is Garibaldi?

All the window shutters were open to allow maximum ventilation but the room was very hot with more than twenty men smoking and perspiring freely. First Officer Costanti was restless and needed more air; he could not sit still a moment longer. He walked out on to the front terrace of the hotel, weaving his way among the pavement-tables where a few customers were sipping coffee. Automatically he glanced at the ship. *D'mio!* Even against the night sky he could see the wreaths of oily smoke belching from the *Duchessa*'s funnel. He could smell it too. Surely the Captain would not order the boilers to be fired up like this. Had the watchman in the engineroom lost his head?

When called out by Costanti, Engineer Officer Fabbro became excited and indignant; the man left on watch in the *locale macchina* would never have opened up like that without orders and assuredly the orders had not come from him. Fabbro's questioning of his juniors seemed mainly to convince Costanti the blame did not lie with the engineering staff. The Mate was more concerned to get someone on board quickly, while Nostromo loudly pointed out that stoking the bloody fire was the job of the greasers and they should sort out their own bloody problem. They had mucked things up as usual. He wanted his supper.

Meanwhile the hotel staff hovered, ready to begin serving food but hesitant until the host arrived and while this discussion was going on. Where was Signor Garibaldi? In the end Costanti decided he, Fabbro and a couple of men should make a quick trip out to the ship in order to satisfy themselves about the rapid firing up of the boilers. Pasconi insisted on joining them; Garibaldi's absence had robbed the dinnerparty of its attraction and all kinds of doubts were rising in his mind.

233

Costanti and his colleagues were cutting things very fine but all was not yet lost. Captain Moore had just given the order to bring in the *Mungo Park* and pass the tow line.

'OK. Fo'castle party make ready to pay out the towing cable as the tug moves out into position off the port bow and make ready to blow the anchor chain for'ard.

'Chief: we shall slip the moorings in three or four minutes, as soon as the tug takes the strain. Do we have power on the steering engine now? Right, we shall test the wheel, full lock, starboard to port and back. When we get under way, give me whatever power you can manage on the main screw.

'Mister Wickham, double check that McIver and Smith are ready to slip the aft mooring wire when I give the order. They have power on the winch now. I shall leave you to deal with the Italians and any Spanish who come off.'

After looking round the deck and checking with the engine room, the Captain gave the order to fire the charge cutting the anchor chain. ...... Half a minute later there was a flash off the ship's bow and an impressively loud explosion.

Steve shouted the disastrous news : 'The bloody chain is still solid. We're still stuck to the flaming island!'

The seriousness of the failure was obvious to all the raiders. The walls of the Spanish prison loomed in the moments of stunned silence, broken by Donald 'Mac':

"As bees flee out wi' angry fyke," he laughed, 'And if that doesn't bring the B-s out, nothing will!'

*   *

When the Italian group arrived at the jetty to recover the ship's motor launch from the charge of the local boat-minder, they found two agitated Spanish officials of the harbourmaster's department already there discussing what was happening aboard the *Duchessa di Lucca*.

'What is going on, tell me that? There are harbour dues to be paid and you Italians are trying to slip away to sea without paying.'

'Nonsense,' Costanti began. 'We are just as ...'

'There's no use denying it. The evidence is there for us all to see. You are raising steam and there is only one reason for that. We require the money to be ...'

'For pity's sake! Stop going on about the damned money. The crew are all ashore at the Granada. Fabbro and I are just as much in the dark about the steam-raising as you are, and he's the Chief Engineer. We are on our way to find out. Come with us in the launch, if you want. I think Old Man Palma must have flipped his lid.'

But even before Fabbro had the engine of the launch started, there was the flash of the explosion by the ship's starboard bow.

None of the party grasped the truth.

'That was a bomb. It must be an English air-raid. We are being attacked.'

'That must be why the Captain is raising steam. He must have heard.'

'No! You must be wrong. There's no noise of aircraft.'

'What was the explosion, then? Tell me that.'

'For pity's sake, Fabbro, get the engine started. We must get out there.'

Aboard the *Duchessa*, Steve raced along the foredeck to speak urgently to the Captain.

'I guess we don't have either enough steam or enough time to raise the anchor in the ordinary way ....'

'Correct on both counts. And its likely the explosion has so distorted a link it would foul the windlass if we did try to hoist.'

Steve went on, 'We can get into the chain locker, Panda. I've been in myself. So if the Chief could give us enough power on the for'ard winch to pull even one or two links over the windlass, we could knock out the big steel spike that stops the chain pulling through the locker bulkhead. Then the whole damn thing could run out and join the anchor on the bottom. I've never done it but I was warned about it solemnly down in South Georgia. I am game to try – always supposing the Chief can raise us a sledge hammer.'

'Right, Steve,' the Captain replied. 'Thank goodness you know about that. It was my best option but I doubted if anyone here would know how to do it. I'll get the Chief to give you all the steam he's got, and a sledge. Then do your best. And be sure to get your chap out of the chain locker and keep all your people clear when that anchor chain runs clear 'cos it'll thrash viciously. It would certainly be quicker than trying to set another explosive charge, which might or might not work. Smartly as you can.'

Two minutes later Steve set the foredeck winch so that the anchor windlass was engaged and began to open the valves to put power into the winch motor. A deck below, Tom Leach was sizing up the task and making a practice swing with the massive hammer.

Clank!

Wheeze. Cla .. Wheeze.

Clank-clank. Clank-clank.

'That's enough. Hit it, Tom!'

With the sledge hammer Tom Leach cleanly knocked out the pin which, for nearly twenty months had held the ship securely on its anchor chain.

Satisfied Tom was safe, Steve disengaged the windlass so that the chain was free to run clear. His signal to the bridge was unnecessary. In an ear-splitting metallic clattering din the whole chain poured out seemingly never-ending to those close-by until, in sudden blessed silence, all that remained was as a great cloud of rust.

'Well done, Tom. Praise be the chain didn't snag as it went out. Now watch how the strain comes on that tow cable. The tug should be able to pull us clear.' Steve waved all set to the bridge and the Captain acknowledged.

From the wing of the bridge Chris reported to the Captain,

'Here comes the motor launch. Six or seven men, I think.'

'The *Mungo Park* is the weak spot,' the captain said. 'If they are armed and have the sense to go straight for the tug we could be in real trouble. It's a tricky business handling a tow and Tony will have his hands full as it is, without holding off a boarding party. Fortunately we have some power up ourselves so we don't depend entirely on the tug.'

'If they do attack the *Mungo,*' Chris said, 'we must intervene.' He urgently called up the two soldiers: 'Sergeant, there's a tricky situation developing. It looks as though the crew and the Spanish harbour police are on their way out to us in that motorboat. We should easily keep them out of this ship with the ladder hoisted but the tug is vulnerable. They know the danger and we shall hope to

236

keep their attention here. If they try to board this ship we must push them back with fists, but no guns or knives unless our people's lives are threatened. As a last resort you may fire the Sten guns to scare them but for goodness sake aim to miss because we are not at war with Spain and you will lose your stripes and more besides if you are the cause of changing that.'

The sky had fallen in on Costanti and Fabbro. They were beyond rational speech. Captain Palma was a rock, utterly dependable, highly experienced; he alone had brought them through the past eighteen months while they were prisoners in this miserable place. He must have gone mad to act like this; there could be no other explanation. The two Spaniards had no such illusions. They thought the Italian seamen were an untrustworthy bunch and here was the proof: the captain was trying to slip away without paying.

The idea had not yet dawned on either the crew or the Spanish officials that the ship was being moved by *force majeur.* The bulk of the *Duchessa* still hid the *Mungo Park* on the port side pulling to seaward. Even as they approached, the accommodation ladder was raised and men – strange men with red scarves – appeared at the rail. The grim fact was evident: the ship had been stolen.

Costanti shouted, 'Holy Mary! She's under way. They have dropped the bow anchor. She's swinging to port. Quick, Fabbro! We must get aboard.'

Pasconi was distraught: 'That German count must be behind it. I've never trusted him. He's a twister.'

'Look! There is a tug-boat. It's not Captain Palma's doing.'

'No. Surely it must be the British Navy.'

'Stop them! Use your pistol,' the Assistant Harbourmaster ordered his man.

With this direct instruction from his senior, the member of the harbour-police, the only man aboard carrying arms, rather reluctantly drew his pistol. His hesitancy arose in part from sensible disbelief that pistol shots, his or anyone's, would have any effect in stopping an eight thousand ton ship, and in part from a lack of confidence in himself as a marksman.

The launch party spent valuable minutes under the starboard accommodation ladder swinging tantalisingly many feet above their heads, this being their usual point of entry. Late, they realised it would have been better to have gone straight to the tug. Meanwhile the two ships were gathering way. Shouting obscenities at the ship's bridge achieved nothing; there was no reply, not even a rude gesture. Firing the pistol was equally futile since, in accord with Chris' orders, no-one now showed himself at the ship's rail. Pistol bullets at the steel hull were no more effective than peas. Finally Costanti decided to overtake the *Mungo Park*, although by now he realised it was a forlorn hope since he could see that the *Duchessa*'s screw was turning.

Tony Robson saw them coming and was prepared. He handed over the wheel to his coxswain, picked up a rifle from the corner of the bridge and stepped out on deck. He was confident of taking on the launch crew with his Winchester .375 magnum which hitherto had been fired only at crocodiles in the Niger creeks. With a smile, he reckoned that a couple of lucky shots on the waterline 'and I could sink the buggers, if only I could see the waterline!'

He waited until the launch was some thirty yards away, pointed the rifle at the sky and fired one shot as a warning. An impressive flame flashed from the muzzle and Costanti immediately realised there was no chance of overpowering the tug as a precursor to the recovery of the larger ship. He knew they had failed and reluctantly he spun the wheel to head back to the harbour.

The Assistant Harbourmaster continued to shout rude words at the ship, interspersed with demands for money.

Sadly the real losers Costanti and Fabbro watched their ship and their precious personal possessions being sailed away.

Pasconi was weeping, incapable of speech.

*   *

Dawn found the *Duchess* and the tug thirty miles west of Fernando Po, heading into the fresh trade wind from the south-west. Early in the night they had abandoned the tow as unnecessary and becoming something of a problem since it involved keeping the ships strictly in company. Now the *Mungo Park* was a few hundred yards on the starboard beam, ready to come to the larger ship's assistance if necessary, although that seemed unlikely. In the *Duchessa*'s engineroom, Acting Chief Balman was glorying in his responsibilities

238

with an excitement that kept him awake although his assistants were visibly wilted in the pulsating heat. Above decks, the story was the same: Chris Wickham and Captain Moore were alert but many others were cat-napping after two sleepless nights and the stimulus of piracy now gone. Steve was at the wheel, half his mind contrasting this warm and placid sea with the icy roaring ocean off South Georgia where he had last steered a ship, and half comparing this pleasant activity with his routine as an administrator in Benin.

Chris commented to Panda that the first part of the operation had gone better than he had feared; all that was needed now was to sail to Lagos. Panda saw no reason to doubt that could be done, 'provided the boys down below can keep the kettle boiling.'

Peter and Clapper came on the bridge from the captain's cabin.

'We have discovered on Palma's desk the full plans for the ship to land the arms, all written out as a timetable. The ship was due to sail from Santa Isabel tomorrow, Tuesday, and head for Calabar, to arrive there at dawn on Wednesday with the load of rifles for Klaus and Co. It is difficult to know whether Klaus will have any means of discovering their plan has been blown away by our pinching the ship. From the routine at the bungalow, I guess his main communication was through his father. Now the old man is dead, Klaus may be in the dark, so the insurgents may be sitting at Calabar in blissful ignorance of their scheme having aborted.'

'We must try to get word to Port Harcourt or Lagos for a reception party,' said Chris.

Roger Trimble was roused to send a signal to the Governor in Lagos. Using the simple cover previously agreed, it read:

TO OLIVIA MESSAGE BEGINS WEDDING TO TAKE PLACE AS EXPECTED AT MARYS CHURCH ON WEDNESDAY 0600 STOP SUGGEST FRIENDS OF ROBINS BROTHER ATTEND IN PLACE OF THE NOBLE LADY STOP ALL FRIENDS HERE WELL STOP TIGGER

All messages addressed to Olivia were to be passed to the Governor personally. The code referred to Calabar as Mary's Church, after Mary Slessor, and, as the Governor knew, Robin Kitchener's brother was a Royal Navy officer.

The Captain commented, 'I hope they do fix for the Navy to flush out Klaus Force. We do not want to take this ship in there because there's always a risk, albeit remote, that some disaster might allow the weapons to reach the enemy. But it would surely increase the chances of catching the enemy off guard if they were to see some ship – almost any ship – coming in to Calabar at the arranged time.'

*   *

Chris, assisted by Panda Moore and Philip Denstone was investigating the events which had led up to Baron von Ehrwald's death. It was more than likely the violent death of this man (at least nominally civilian) in the British attack on the Italian ship in Spanish colonial waters would subsequently attract attention, so it was sensible to record what had happened. Reverting to his profession, Chris was writing a magistrate's report.

Peter described what had happened in the captain's cabin to the moment the Baron and Palma had rushed out, leaving him handcuffed on the locker seat.

Cracker reported leaving Clapper Bell and Joshua to deal with the watchkeeper on the bridge while he approached the captain's cabin. He had been able to listen to the conversation and realised Peter was being held there. He heard the noise of Clapper and Joshua overcoming the man on the bridge and feared it might bring out the Captain; he just had time to hide in the doorway of the next cabin before Palma had indeed come out into the companionway and shouted up to Pietro.

'I thought the Italian on the bridge was already secure and guessed the captain would go up there when he got no reply. Clapper and Joshua would deal with him so I had to be ready to take out the German who was armed. But in fact a whole lot of Italian came back shouted from the bridge. At first I thought Clapper had fallen down on the job, but then I twigged it might be Clapper himself 'cos I remembered he spoke Italian. It was a good job Clapper was in my team. The captain told the German he wasn't satisfied and he went to the other side of the ship, I guessed to look at the official boarding ladder there. I didn't want to start tackling the German on my own with the captain free behind me, so I waited a minute. That was just as well because he came back almost at once. When he went in, Peter said something to him in Italian which surprised both men, because the German shouted something like "God in hummel".

'At that second there was a crash, which was Rob's boat misjudging things in the dark and ramming the side of the ship. The German and the captain ran out of the cabin; I plastered myself against the wall by the door and neither saw me. The Italian captain headed straight up for the bridge where I guessed Clapper Bell and Joshua would cope with him since they would hear him coming. The German rushed down the alley for the stairs leading to where Rob should be coming aboard. I ran after but he didn't seem to realise I was close behind. I saw the hooks of Rob's ladder on the rail and the German must have seen them too. He went straight there, leaned over and raised his pistol to shoot the man on the ladder that I guessed would be Rob. I could have shot him before but we had agreed there should be no shooting except as a last resort. As I ran down the alley I had drawn my knife and at the rail there was nothing else for it. He had raised his gun to shoot Rob so I hooked him with my left arm and pushed in the knife as we were trained to do. I'd never done it before. I pulled him back from the rail and I think he was dead when he hit the deck.'

Rob agreed; he was halfway up the ladder, his head almost at deck level when he had heard running steps and saw a man lean over the rail. To his horror the man pulled out a pistol.

'I thought I had had it and must have crouched away, but no shot came. I heard a gurgle, something fell past me and the guy had disappeared. Cracker told me to get going and we found the man dead on the deck.'

It was only some time later, when Chris was talking to the Italian captain, that Palma asked what had happened to the packet of gemstone diamonds which he then described. The Baron's pockets yielded nothing, as did a careful search of the safe, the alley and the deck where he died. Peter confirmed the German had taken the leather pouch from the safe and had left the cabin with it, although whether in his hand or in his pocket – as seemed more likely – he could not recall; it was all in a rush, but certainly the diamonds had been taken from the safe and had left the cabin.

Cracker repeated that the Baron had run at full speed from the cabin to the ship's rail. They had been only two or three yards apart the whole way.

'After that I was too busy stopping the man from shooting Rob on the ladder and the guys in the boat to see what he had in his hands, forby the gun. I know the gun fell in the sea but whether there was more, I canna say. It was gey dark, you know.'

Rob and the men in the boat agreed. They heard the splash or splashes, as the gun, and presumably the diamonds also, fell into the sea. It was the only explanation. Palma was more concerned at losing his ship than someone else's diamonds but was loud in his condemnation of the thieving German Baron. Pasconi might have cared more deeply but he was probably more worried at being stranded in Santa Isabel. The Italian government, owners of the diamonds because they had paid de Beers, did not know they had been lost.

After full questioning, Chris Wickham was satisfied that the jewels were irrecoverable. Their loss was undoubtedly due to their theft from the ship's safe by Baron von Ehrwald. Fortunately, the strategically far more important industrial diamonds were secured for Britain.

Rob was ordered to take charge of the revolvers, now no longer required by the British crew. Meanwhile Cracker personally attended to the unloading of the Sten gun magazines, including one carried by Joshua, his Number 2. Surprisingly, he not only unloaded that magazine but removed the platform and spring before covertly reassembling it. Although it seemed unnecessary with the action over, Cracker then returned the long box magazine to Joshua who, in the hurried disembarkation at Lagos later, had no difficulty in failing to return it to his Number One.

During the night Cracker Armstrong casually dropped an empty leather pouch over the ship's side.

CHAPTER FOURTEEN

Just before midnight in Monday, Sergeant Armstrong, Captain Moore, Peter Thorburn and Chris Wickham were in the captain's cabin for a meeting hurriedly called to consider a radio message. Chris waved the transcript and announced:

'Change of plans, chaps, I fear. Roger has just brought me this signal. It is from the Governor, signed "Johnno", the private nickname Lady Robertson gives her husband.'

> TO TIGGER MESSAGE BEGINS FRIENDS OF ROBINS BROTHER UNAVOIDABLY DELAYED AND CANNOT KEEP APPOINTMENT STOP NOW ESSENTIAL YOU SHOW UP AT MARYS CHURCH TO ENCOURAGE CONGREGATION SINCE NOBLE LADYS ALTERNATIVES LACK HER DISTINCTIVE APPEARANCE STOP PLEASE ATTEND BUT DO NOT REPEAT NOT JOIN THE PARTY MESSAGE ENDS JOHNNO

'So the arrangements,' Chris went on, 'for the Navy to go in to get Klaus Force have fallen through. They want us to go to Calabar, if that is possible Panda, not directly to Lagos as we planned.'

'Captain Palma's papers give the rendezvous as Calabar at 0600 Wednesday,' Peter said. 'Off the Southsea Factory, below Mission Hill at Duke Town to be precise. Can we make it in time?'

'Yes, I believe we could, if we must go,' Panda replied. 'I guess we are twentyfive or thirty hours steaming from Calabar, so there should be time if we alter course without delay. I must study the chart to check that and make sure there is sufficient water for this ship. I should want the *Mungo Park* to come too, to help us in the creek which could be very tricky. If you are fully settled on the change of plan, Chris, I will signal the tug and order the new course immediately.'

As he spoke the captain pulled out the large-scale chart of the Cross River estuary. He ran his finger up an area closely covered with figures. He explained:

'These are fathoms and feet, 4.3, 3.2 and so on, so 3.2 means 20 feet of water. No question, there is insufficient depth for the ship at Calabar itself and the devil of it is there is really not enough even off Duke Town, a mile downstream. At the top of the flood we could get up past Alligator Island, at this last bend here, but without a doubt beyond that bend in the channel the ship would settle on the bottom with the ebb tide. We should be stranded and at risk of being boarded. I strongly advise against going in there, Chris, It would be hazarding the ship.'

The boss pulled the lobe of his ear, caught undecided between the new request from Lagos and prudence in carrying out his original orders.

'Alter course for Calabar in any event, please Panda, while we think and talk this through.'

And when the captain returned to the cabin, Chris went on:

'Look! Could we sail in past Parrot Island and James Island as far as the sharp bend in the channel at Alligator Island? The chart shows that should bring us within easy sight of the Southsea Factory and we could make ourselves obvious there, sounding the ship's siren and what have you, to make sure Klaus and Co know we have arrived and brings his chaps into the open. That should be enough to flush out the enemy and there would be no need to go farther up the narrow channel.'

'Much better, Chris,' the captain replied. 'We shall try that. The whole Cross River estuary is very treacherous. You can see for yourself the channel up past Parrot and James Islands is narrow, shallow and twisty but it is marked with light buoys and should be just possible for this ship. Right! As far as Alligator. It is a good thing we have Tony Robson in the *Mungo Park* to lead us in and, if needs be, to pull us off. He knows the place well.' With a laugh he added,

'Captain Palma would not have had Robson as a guide and I'll bet he wasn't happy at the prospect of going up there in the dark.'

'I hope the Governor and the Army have made a proper job of organising the reception committee at Calabar,' Peter said with feeling. 'If Klaus has men for even half the number of rifles on board this ship, we could be in real trouble. After all, we climbed aboard without too much ....'

'They must not be given even half a chance, Peter. We sail in just so that Klaus and Co. commit themselves by coming into the open. Then we back out fast, head for Lagos and leave it to the lads on shore to mop up the enemy, which should not be too difficult for them since we have the enemy's rifles.'

*   *

Hilda stood silent and still, close by the Southsea building on the waterfront at Duke Town by Calabar. She was dressed in a khaki drill bush jacket of her brother's and khaki trousers; in contrast to the style in Benin, her blond hair was now tied tightly back in a pony tail, giving her a purposeful look, although no-one was there to see it. At four o'clock in the morning it was dark, for the moon had set and only the stars showed; Calabar had no streetlights by the waterfront. There was not a breath of wind but here by the sea the air was fresh, although moist and tropic warm. The velvet darkness and utter silence made Hilda more aware than usual of the special smell of Africa, a hot, damp and earthy sweetness, difficult to describe, a little like wet wool, unique and wonderfully evocative. It was that near-silent hour, just before first-light, when even the night animals rest. Suddenly far away in the town a dog howled, a lonesome sad noise. Hilda remembered from her teenage days in Bamenda that Kiari, her Fulani horse-boy, insisted whenever a dog howled like that in the night someone was dying. Sad, maybe true. Then quiet again.

Must stop dreaming about Kamerun and Kiari and the warm smell of African earth: must concentrate on the task in hand – *meine Pflicht* – one's duty as a German and member of the Party. Hilda gripped more firmly the stock of the Schmeisser machine pistol slung from her shoulder and tried to peer down the estuary. Then logic told her it was much too dark for the ship to enter such confined waters; they would never risk it yet. Klaus said to expect them at dawn. More than an hour to wait; he should be back before that. Instead she turned to look along the waterfront; a couple of hundred metres away more than two hundred men were resting, also waiting for the ship. They were quiet, mostly asleep, she expected; sensible to sleep when there was nothing to do but wait. But she was the lookout, the armed sentry, so she must keep awake, alert.

She wished Klaus were here to give her his confidence. He reckoned the move from Kamerun had gone well, better than expected. Thanks to good organisation, the two lieutenants Karl and Friedrich had started moving the men early, so there had been no last-minute rush, no crowd to attract attention. They appeared to have lost only sixteen men on the trek, say three percent, which Klaus said was quite acceptable. The men had travelled by three separate routes to gather outside Calabar last evening and it seemed the pathetic British administration was entirely unaware of the storm about to break. Local village heads had shown surprise and curiosity at the sudden influx of so many strangers but money handed out as a "dash" by Klaus had quietened their fears and shut their mouths, which was all that mattered.

Now it only remained to get the arms ashore from this Italian ship and the preparatory phase of the operation would be complete. The real task could then begin. Father was in charge of the shipment, so there would be no mistake there. *Ein afrikanischer Blitzkrieg* was what Father demanded. That was the order.

Father would be on the ship. She had not seen him for – let's think – more than three years. It would be exciting to have him around again: he was a great man, he made things happen. Klaus had been in regular radio contact with him; that's how the orders came from Berlin.

Klaus and she had travelled together from Buea, joining up with Karl and Friedrich only two days ago. Concentrating their forces should have made them stronger but, because of the shortage of weapons, in fact it had made the group more vulnerable, more liable to detection. This was the time of greatest danger, when interception by the British would have been disastrous, with nearly six hundred of our men unarmed. Right now there were only twenty-four Mauser rifles, three Schmeissers and half-a-dozen pistols for the whole group.

246

Tomorrow every man would be armed and they would take Calabar. The town would provide transport and recruits too. Fortunately the British were asleep!

Even with the shortage of weapons, the preliminaries had gone well. Already one patrol had cut all the telephone lines out of the town and had stolen a couple of motor cars. True, it had been necessary to divide the force and weapons for these few critical hours. Klaus had taken fifteen riflemen to cover the central police barracks where the police arms were held; it would be from there the British force would come if the alarm were raised but if fortune should hold, we should get the rifles off the ship before any alarm; then a hundred of our men will attack the barracks and overwhelm them.

The two lieutenants had also taken small parties of riflemen to the European reservation, to cover the homes of the Resident and the senior police officer. Those two would be shot when they emerged in the morning, so that the British capacity to react would be weakened. Klaus thought their death would paralyse their response but that was questionable: to take command in an emergency at Benin, Christopher Wickham would have been more effective than Robert, it had to be admitted, and Wickham's assistant Lister might have been even better. No matter: removal of the Resident and the police chief would be helpful. They must be still asleep. Klaus should be back soon, whenever the men were in position; he would organise the unloading.

From the nearby side-street there was the hum of a car engine and the reflected glow of lights, quickly doused. Two minutes later Hilda was aware of someone approaching.

'*Halt!*' she said softly.

'*Glatter Sieg,*' (Complete Victory) came the reply; she recognised her brother's voice. 'The men are in position'. And after a pause, 'Look! The sky is lightening in the east. Not long now.'

*   *

In response to orders from Enugu and Lagos and contrary to Hilda's belief, the police at Calabar barracks had been paraded at ten o'clock the previous evening and issued with arms. The Kamerun riflemen under Klaus' command were outside a stable door from which all the horses had gone and the chief of police was not asleep but very much awake with his men. News of the enemy's movements had been brought back from scouts who had shadowed them for the past several days. Before midnight a detachment of police had been put in position at the foot of Mission Hill to cover the probable unloading quay. Inspector Daggash and his men had heard Hilda and her great party arriving; the big risk was Klaus Force might accidentally stumble on the police position but fortunately they appeared to have settled down two or three hundred yards away along the waterfront.

Daggash had kept his men close together so that he might control them more easily. They would probably have a long wait; no ship could come up the creek in the dark. Dawn would be action time. His orders were clear, to wait for the arrival of a ship and, following the orders to be given by the Assistant Commissioner who was nearby with other police and soldiers, to intervene when the enemy would be concentrated, criminally involved and largely unarmed. The Assistant Commissioner wanted to act when it was light in order to get the white men who were the leaders out in the open but before the rifles could be brought ashore from the ship to arm the rebels. Keeping the men quiet and alert was Daggash' main problem.

Constable Orumi hitched himself uncomfortably and thought about the orders he had been given by the inspector. When ordered to do so (but only when ordered), he was to open fire on a group of Germans and troublemakers from the Cameroons who were armed and landing rifles for a rebellion. He had never been on such a duty. He was tired, staying awake all night.

To open fire when ordered! Orumi went over what that would involve. The rifle was loaded. The sergeant and Inspector Daggash had supervised that. Ten rounds – nine in the magazine and one up the spout. All that was required was to release the safety catch and squeeze the trigger. You either pulled the safety catch back with your finger or you pushed it forward with your thumb. In training, the sergeant-instructor had laid great stress on how to operate the catch. You push it back with the thumb and pull it forward with the forefinger. Or was it forward with the thumb and back with the finger? Orumi tried each in turn. Both ways worked. The safety catch was quite stiff. The bother now was he was not sure whether the safety catch should be forward or back. Was it on or off? If he fumbled

248

moving it when the order came he would be late opening fire and would be in trouble. Surely the catch must be at "safe". If he squeezed the trigger gently now nothing would happen and that would confirm it was safe.

Flash! The bullet struck the hard road just five yards ahead of Orumi and ricocheted away through the night like a whining banshee. The sudden crack of the shot echoed back from the warehouse walls, shattering the peaceful dawn.

Two constables beside Orumi who had been dozing guessed they had missed the order to fire and obeyed that command. Three others who were fully awake were sure there had been no order but copied their neighbours and opened fire as a nervous reaction. None aimed at anything in particular: firing was the thing. Within ten seconds the whole detachment was firing, with the exception of Inspector Daggash. Moments later, neighbouring sections of police joined in.

The grey half-light was just sufficient for the police to make out the mass of Klaus' men two hundred yards away but it was too poor to see the foresight blade clearly, so aiming was difficult. Nevertheless two or three of the huddled Cameroon men fell wounded almost immediately. With no means of returning fire or of defending themselves in any way, the men promptly tried to take cover. The discerning among them quickly assessed the new situation: the white man Ehrwald had promised a ship would bring rifles; no ship; no rifles; no revolution and now they are firing at us; this white man is not successful and therefore not worth fighting for; we had best go home. So the discerning ran. As usual, the less discerning followed their lead.

When Orumi's bullet went whining over their heads, Klaus and Hilda momentarily failed to appreciate what it was. Even as other shots came in, they found it hard to accept that the British could have comprehensively pre-empted their move at Calabar. It surely could not be. But the delay was enough to allow the spillage of their unarmed force, running, gone for ever. The show was over.

Police Assistant Commissioner Kennedy swore long and loud at the indisciplined firing but, even as he strove to regain control of his men, he saw the enemy break and run. He guessed that few of Klaus' men were armed, so he stood up and ordered his police to advance.

249

Quickly Klaus faced the bitter truth this was a battle already lost; his unarmed men had fled and he was utterly outnumbered or at least outgunned. Cruelly, at this critical moment, the throaty roar of a ship's siren drew attention to the grey shape and navigation lights of the *Duchessa di Lucca* in the pearly morning haze, down the estuary at Alligator Island. It had been as close as that. The light was growing every minute. There were police advancing along the waterfront towards him now. Urgently he shouted to his sister,

'Hilda! Stay in the doorway under cover while I start the car. I shall reverse down the side street to this corner and call for you to come. We must try to collect Karl and Friedrich. Obviously the English were ready for us. It is finished and all we can do is get out if we can. I hope Father can hear the firing and get away with the ship.'

'Yes. Get the car. I have the Schmeisser and I can hold them up until you are ready.'

Klaus sprinted forward to the street corner and was gone.

The whine of bullets and the coughing splutter of shots were almost continuous. Suddenly Hilda thought of her elder brother Helmut, a vivid communion in spirit. This, on a small scale, was what it must be like on the Russian front. Married to Robert, she had felt helpless, as if she was traitorously consorting with her country's enemy. Klaus had rescued her. Now she saw the enemy face to face and she was free to strike against them. Anger welled up as she saw the wrecking of Klaus' plans, more than that – Father's plans, the Führer's plans for the occupation of West Africa and the recovery of the Fatherland's colonial empire.

There in the street before her were the wreckers of those plans. All fear gone, she was at one with the SS at Leningrad, suddenly and utterly passionate in her belief in the rightness of her country's cause, armed and ready to fight for it. The light made it difficult to judge distance but she saw with alarm that the advancing police might well reach the end of the side street before Klaus was ready with the car and able to escape. She checked the two spare magazines in the left hand pocket of her bush jacket, slipped the Schmeisser safety-catch to off, gripped the gun firmly in both hands and, in a half-crouch, stepped forward towards the line of threatening police.

Rasping half-second bursts of fire ripped from the Schmeisser, alive in her hands. She checked her stride to fire three more short bursts. Already her immediate objective had been gained: the nearest policemen had stopped, some flat on the roadway to shelter from the angry lash of her bullets. Two men were down obviously hit, screaming with pain. Hilda saw one man kneel down to aim his rifle at her. She checked her stride again to take better aim and fired a long burst deliberately at him. The gun suddenly died in her hands, so she unclipped the magazine and slipped in a fresh one from her pocket, worked the cocking handle to reload and fired again. And again.

Constable Orumi was one of those wounded, hit in both legs and bleeding profusely. He lay on the road, clasping his hands round his smashed knee. Inspector Daggash dropped down close beside him and picked up the rifle Orumi had dropped. With the same cool determination he would have shown on the range, Daggash lined up the sights and squeezed the trigger of the Lee-Enfield, intent on making every round tell. Here was no excited explosion of shots; this was a sober marksman firing at seventy yards. He intended and expected to hit the bull.

The first bullet hit Hilda on her arm, up near the shoulder. Instinctively she clutched the place so there was blood on her hand when she changed the next magazine, her fingers slippy as she worked the bolt. Her bursts of fire were longer, less controlled. When Daggash's next bullet slammed into her body, the clenched fingers of her right hand fired off the whole half-magazine in an automatic roar of agony.

Klaus had reversed the stolen Alvis tourer to within five yards of the seafront road and, leaving the engine on, had run to the corner to bring Hilda to safety. Instead, he arrived in time to see his sister fall and hear the long burst of fire from her gun. He knew it was the end and, looking beyond the fallen body, he saw the police running towards him. There was no point in delaying further – Hilda was beyond his help, so he vaulted back into the car, slammed it into gear and drove hard up the street, his foot heavy on the accelerator as he went through the gears. In anguish, he realised he had led his sister to her death and was abandoning her. And what of his father? What of the ship? Could that be saved or had the British struck there also? His only course right now was to rescue his two lieutenants on Government Hill, if that was possible. They were the only remnants of his force.

In a grey mist, Hilda was aware of a black face close to her own and thought she was looking at Kiari, her Fulani horse-boy in Bamenda. She tried to tell him to saddle up Red Fox because she wanted to ride over the mountain grassland above the homestead. It was her last thought.

*   *

Aboard the *Mungo Park* and the *Duchessa di Lucca*, at the sharp bend in the channel half-a-mile from the Duke Town wharves, they heard the popping of the rifle fire and the occasional whine of the ricocheting rounds. Chris Wickham had no hesitation.

'They don't need us here to flush out Klaus' people,' he said to Captain Moore. 'They have a full scale war going on already, with no encouragement from us. Let's get to hell out of here and head for Lagos, Panda. Whatever happened, we have arrived late and by hanging about we should only prolong the risk of some counterattack on the ship.'

Promptly Captain Moore gave the order to turn the ship back towards the open sea and with a megaphone repeated the decision to the *Mungo Park*. He turned to Chris:

'Praise be for that! I have never run a ship aground yet and I didn't want to start today. It was a dead certainty if we had stuck around there.'

*   *

Late on Thursday afternoon, without the service of a local pilot, Captain Moore brought the *Duchessa di Lucca* slowly over the Lagos bar and into the anchorage close to the Marina, the fine seafront roadway and promenade of the Nigerian capital. The port bow anchor was dropped, all they now had. The bridge rang "Finished with Engines" and a deep silence settled on the ship. Both port and starboard accommodation ladders were lowered and a series of well planned moves then followed in rapid succession. Their duties done,

252

the whole raiding party hurried down the port-side ladder, screened from the Marina crowds by the ship itself, to the two boats used in the attack, which had now been relaunched. Close on their heels, a Royal Navy party entered the ship by the starboard ladder, in full view of the interested crowds on the Marina. Thus the Navy could report, with almost complete truth, they had boarded the *Duchessa* in Lagos harbour after she had been abandoned by those who had sailed her from Fernando Po. The reception drill suggested by Chris in the paper to the Governor had worked faultlessly,

Chris and his friends came ashore, unnoticed, half-a-mile along the Marina at a private commercial jetty, whence they travelled to the Bristol Hotel in the city centre. While the men relaxed in the lounge bar, they gazed with considerable satisfaction and some awe at the ship they had stolen, now anchored in the channel in front of the hotel. The setting sun intensified the colours of the bright funnel and glittered on the lattice masts and derricks. Like a salmon in the eyes of the angler, the ship was larger than life and the men marvelled at their success. In order to keep their secret, they kept their voices soft and low, but the talk was joyously and proudly excited, for they had succeeded against heavy odds.

'My God! We did it.' ...... 'Good health' ...... 'Cheers!' ......'I didn't believe we could.' ...... 'Lucky they had started to raise steam before we arrived.' ...... 'If they hadn't, we should have been in queer street.' ...... 'Up the bloody creek without the proverbial paddle, what!' ...... 'Yes, I didn't fancy life in a Spanish prison.' ...... 'It was worse than prison our boat faced when that damned Baron leaned over the rail with his pistol levelled at Corporal Rob!' ......'It was a bad moment when that charge didn't cut the anchor chain, Tom.' .....'I thought we had had it' ...... 'We were damned lucky, let's face it.' ...... 'A lot of that supposed luck was thanks to Peter here. When I saw the mass of cabins, it was obvious we should never have succeeded if the whole Italian crew had been on board.' ...... 'We got the ship but I wonder if they caught Klaus and his sister.'

In the midst of the delight, Chris took the opportunity – because it would be brief and possibly the final chance – to go round his team to thank each man personally and arrange travel back to his station. The effect, quite unintentioned, was to dampen the party. His words made men realise they had played their last match. This operation, these problems and especially these companions had so filled their lives for the past week, nothing else had entered their focused minds. Now Chris was recalling them to other realities, forcing them to face the fact they would probably never meet these two soldiers again, perhaps others also, The transition from civil servants to amateur commandos had been swift enough: the reverse move was brutal. The stimulating experience had been wonderful: it was as fleeting as a beautiful sunset. The mood swung violently from ecstasy to sobriety touched with sadness.

Soberly, Clapper Bell shook Sergeant Armstrong's hand and thanked him for his training and leadership of the first assault party.

'I wouldn't have missed this trip for anything! Quite simply, it is the most exciting and most important week of my life. And I believe our success in taking the *Duchess* at least matches the springing of your ancestor Kinmont Willie from Carlisle Castle: I'll bet Johnny Armstrong himself would be proud, and perhaps a little jealous too.'

Cracker was touched by the compliment but said:

'Na, na! The boot's on the other foot! It's for me to thank you. You all made the training easy and we've made a great team. All you folk have been right good to Rob and me, and we've seen a bit of Africa into the bargain. I am only sorry we can't keep the squad together, for you have the makings of a fine Commando group.'

Panda Moore was despondent at having to give up his temporary command so soon, but his depression was not simply self-centred as he showed when speaking to Peter and Steve.

'I feel real sorry for Captain Palma: terrible to be violently robbed of command in a couple of minutes and made prisoner. He was dropped suddenly from master to nobody. And, you know, the chances are he may not be offered a ship again at the end of the war. Someone then is likely to say he'll be too old – like me! If I had a bottle of Highland Park, I'd split it with him because we are in the same boat, but unfortunately I don't have a bottle to hand. More's the pity!'

*   *

Chris Wickham came to Government House quite unobtrusively in a taxi. The African lilies were still in bloom. The vermilion hibiscus and the magenta bougainvillaea clashed as before. He was again depressed at the sight of the dismal croton in the porch. A great deal had happened since his last visit but nothing appeared to have changed. His entrance was unobtrusive but there was certainly nothing half-hearted in Sir John's welcome.

'By all that's holy, Tigger, I am glad to see you back,' as he wrung the younger man's hand. 'The sight of you is a heavy load off my conscience because after your last visit I had the guilty feeling I had sent you on a mission that was quite likely to land you in a Spanish jail. I'm damned glad to have you back. How did it go?'

'Thanks to the team, it went well, Sir. There is the ship, as you can see for yourself, parked off the Marina, all in one piece, plus four and a half thousand tons of copper bars, four thousand Mauser rifles, a hell of a lot of ammunition and what should have been Italy's war supply of industrial diamonds. We lost a packet of gem quality diamonds, I am afraid. I don't know what value they amounted to but they must have fallen overboard after being stolen from the Italians by Baron von Ehrwald. He was the only casualty in the operation, killed by Sergeant Armstrong on the ship, just as von Ehrwald was about to shoot Corporal Graham.'

'My God! You caught up with the old man! And he's dead, you say?'

'Yes. It was self-defence of the group, either Ehrwald or Graham and others in his boat who were defenceless. We buried him at sea on Monday. I have written up the circumstances in a proper report in case of a come-back. The Baron was in charge of the Fernando Po end of the German operation, with a radio link to his son in the Cameroons.'

'That explains a lot, Tigger. Incidentally, we heard from the French that a German column was spotted in the desert north of Lake Chad. With surprise lost, and the operation apparently running late with the difficulties of Saharan travel, they retired north back to Libya, so the threat to Kano never materialised and never became public knowledge. And you have succeeded in grabbing the ship. I hope you got your chaps ashore without being spotted.'

'I know there can be no recognition for the team, Sir, but everyone did frightfully well – Peter Thorburn, Captain Moore, Tony Robson in the *Mungo Park*, the two Commandos, Robin Kitchener your ADC – everyone. The success of the show really hinged on Peter

255

Thorburn and Joshua Oshodin going to the island ahead of the main party and inveigling the Italian crew ashore; that was away beyond what the rest of us did.'

Sir John frowned. 'You mean you took a Nigerian in the party? I distinctly recall speaking against that,' he said coldly.

Chris said, 'Oshodin had special local knowledge of Santa Isabel, Sir, which the Oba of Benin brought to my attention. As it turned out, Oshodin's contacts were crucial to our success. We should probably have failed without him.'

'My concern is he won't keep his mouth shut,' Sir John replied tartly. 'There will be hell to pay if news of what really happened gets into the *West African Pilot* or the *Lagos Times*, both in its effect here and in relations with Spain. My line and HM Government's is that the first one knew of the affair was when the ship dropped anchor off the Lagos Marina and unfortunately the pirate crew slipped ashore and escaped. This man is in a position to give us the lie and to name names.'

'I stake my reputation he will not do that, Sir, and the fact Oshodin is answerable to the Oba makes me doubly sure the story is safe.'

Inwardly Chris was far more upset by Sir John's doubts than he cared to show. The Governor had given him a free hand for a difficult task which the old man had admitted he did not know how to tackle but after its successful completion he was carping about Chris' judgment, doubting the reliability of a Nigerian who had risked all in the operation and discounting the word of the Bini king. He recalled Eddie Hudson's objectionable remark when Joshua had introduced himself at Sapoba; there seemed precious little to choose between the basic racist attitudes of Eddie and the Governor. An idol was falling. Chris changed the subject.

'What happened at Calabar, Sir? Did we get Klaus Ehrwald?'

Sir John Robertson reluctantly admitted Klaus and his lieutenants had avoided capture and, against the odds, appeared to have got clean away.

'It seems our chaps cornered the leaders, including Klaus, before the *Duchessa* came up the estuary. Unfortunately a policeman gave the game away by loosing off a shot without orders and far too early. Klaus and some others escaped thanks to one of their group giving covering fire. As a result there was a shooting match before pursuit could begin and then, it seems, we were too late and never caught up. The rearguard who sacrificed herself was Hilda Grenville-Fletcher. That allowed Klaus to get away and I hope he appreciates it. Several police constables were severely injured but fortunately no Calabar people were hurt and those arrested were all from the Cameroons. So we told the press, and they duly reported, the affair was Cameroons migrant workers in a mellee when a ship came into port. It is very satisfactory we have been able to prevent the real thing reaching the press.'

To Chris it appeared sad the main consideration concerning a brave action by the German woman was that no word of it should appear in the papers. From his knowledge of her over a couple of years in Benin, he saw past her prejudices and petty concern for position, and guessed that, at the last stand, she had given her life out of loyalty to her country and her brother. That deserved better than convenient suppression and it added to his feeling of anticlimax.

Sir John spoke again. 'By the way, Tigger, Arthur tells me that, while you were away, a PWD chappie in Benin, Eric Somebody – no! – Eddie Somebody – committed suicide. He hanged himself from a tree in his compound. A foreman, I think. Sad business always. Curious thing, his name was on your original list for special local leave but obviously he didn't go with your party.'

As the Governor continued to talk, Chris considered the irony of this death and the others around the operation. The *Duchessa*'s Italian crew and the attacking force were entirely unscathed, if one overlooked some hurt feelings among the Italians. But fate had pointed its bony finger at others: the Resident's driver, a simple and innocent bystander; Grenville-Fletcher himself, not innocent but ironically not given time to become guiltily involved; Hilda Ehrwald who, however inadequate as a person, had lived according to the rules of Nietzsche and had died heroically in true Wagnerian fashion; Eddie Hudson who had wanted to be heroic but could not face his own inadequacy. (Would Eddie have been better off had he read Nietzsche or had known about Siegfried?) And Baron von Ehrwald whom, alone of these dead, Chris had not met in life; fighting his corner, he had died a soldier's death at the hands of a soldier and Chris reckoned the man would not have complained at that. The casualty rate had been far greater among "support staff" than in the front-line troops, but perhaps that was the fashion in this war.

257

Peter and Steve, his friends of long standing, Panda, Joshua, Clapper and the others whom he had known only for two frantic weeks had put out intense effort and had succeeded mightily against the odds. Now they must all trundle back to providing village water supplies and stopping illicit tree felling. He knew that was how it must be, for the rules had been set by Churchill and the Governor. Nevertheless it seemed hard on Peter who had chanced more than his arm, hard on Joshua who had shown initiative and dedication far beyond what might have been expected of a young man who did not have the support of a great service behind him, hard on Hilda Ehrwald who, as an enemy, had given her life for her cause. Sir John had trivialised the affair; soon it would be completely obliterated.

Tomorrow the team would disperse, almost certainly never to meet again as a full squad. John Balman would be taken out by tender to rejoin the *Alexander Holt*. Robin Kitchener would be back in the Lagos Secretariat. Others would be on the train to Ibadan, there to break up to Ondo, Benin and elsewhere. Cracker Armstrong and Rob Graham would be posted and would disappear into the war's mass of soldiery.

Chris found it all quite depressing. He had known from the start there would be no publicity, no acknowledgement, but the cynicism was a disappointment.

*   *

El Señor Felipe Alonzo Hernández, His Excellency the Spanish Ambassador to the Court of St James' sought an immediate audience with the Foreign Secretary, which was granted. In the strongest terms, the Ambassador conveyed to Mr Anthony Eden the Spanish Government's complaint at Britain's apparent involvement in an act of piracy which had occurred on the previous Sunday night and Monday morning, the thirteenth to fourteenth January, in the Spanish colonial territory of Fernando Po. In that incident the Italian registered ship, the *Duchessa di Lucca*, which had been at anchor in the harbour of Santa Isabel, had been illegally boarded, her captain and crew members made prisoner and the ship forcibly sailed out of Spanish territorial waters in spite of the repeated objections of the harbour

258

authorities. Reports from the island strongly suggested that the perpetrators of this criminal act came from the British Protectorate of Nigeria, a view supported by the fact that the ship had been sailed to the harbour of Lagos Colony and remained at anchor there.

The Spanish Government demanded that the pirates should be arrested by the British authorities and should be handed over to Spain for trial. The Ambassador was instructed to make clear to Mr Eden personally that the Caudita took the gravest exception to this flagrant violation of Spanish sovereignty.

Mr Anthony Eden expressed His Majesty's Government's sympathy but assured Señor Hernández that his Government knew nothing of the incident until the *Duchessa di Lucca* anchored in Lagos harbour. He regretted to say that those who had sailed the ship there, who were presumably the same people who had illegally removed it from Spanish waters, had fled and were not identified. He assured the Ambassador categorically that no Royal Naval personnel or ship had been involved in removing the vessel from Santa Isabel. The matter was undoubtedly serious. Had any Spanish citizen been injured in the incident or suffered any material loss? No? That was indeed a blessing. The Foreign Secretary expressed his relief and deep satisfaction at that assurance.

His Excellency the Spanish Ambassador then requested that the ship should be returned forthwith to Spanish territorial waters in order to restore the *status quo ante*. In reply, Mr Eden pointed out that, while the ship had enjoyed the protection of Spain as long as it had remained in Spanish waters, it was not a Spanish vessel to be returned on that account. Undoubtedly it was an Italian ship and a state of war had existed between Italy and Great Britain since June 1940 when Italy, entirely without provocation, had declared war on Britain. Irrespective of how the vessel had arrived in British waters, he submitted there was no cause for His Majesty's Government to send the *Duchessa di Lucca* back to Santa Isabel. In accordance with normal practice and international convention, the enemy ship would be seized and its cargo forfeit.

Señor Hernández informed Mr Eden that the Spanish Government would send a written complaint concerning this violation of their territory, holding Great Britain responsible for that violation and demanding the surrender of those involved to face trial on charges of piracy. The Foreign Secretary, on behalf of His Majesty's

Government, courteously agreed to receive the note when it was delivered and, following His Excellency's present verbal complaint, would immediately instruct the Governor in Lagos to apprehend any known pirates operating from British colonial or protectorate territory. Indeed, if His Excellency had any information or suggestion concerning a base from which pirates might be operating in Nigeria, this would be followed up vigorously and expeditiously ....*et cetera.*

CHAPTER FIFTEEN

AN EPILOGUE FROM THE DEBATABLE LAND based on a letter by G.C.Bell, CB.

The springing of Kinmont Willie was the perfect raid, a model of its kind: meticulously planned, skilfully executed in darkness by expert marauders under an inspiring leader. There was no deviation or distraction from the single, simple objective. The raiders deserved good luck and enjoyed it.

Although no-one knew it at the time, it was the last great raid of the Border country. In only seven years the frontier disappeared, as the kingdoms of Scotland and England were joined. Some people described Kinmont Willie as the last of the reivers.

Some years after the events described at Santa Isabel, I returned to Britain on leave prior to retirement. At the end of the war I had gone to the Far East on promotion within the Colonial Education Service and later had been busy setting up a new radio and television station there. It was an absorbing and demanding job which may explain (although it does not excuse) my failure to keep in touch with former colleagues in West Africa. I regretted the loss of contact and aimed to make amends during this leave, which was why I was in the Border country. I left the main road north of Carlisle and drove to a farm near Canonbie to meet the Armstrongs. I had telephoned ahead to ask if we might talk about the fate of the *Duchessa di Lucca*, to enquire if I might visit them and to ask directions to their home, so Cracker and his wife Margaret were expecting me.

I was mildly surprised at the apparent affluence of the place. The buildings were neat, painted and, even to my inexpert eye, well equipped. My first impression of a modest prosperity was confirmed when we went indoors, through the farm kitchen to the comfortable sitting room decorated with some nice watercolours and good porcelain. This seemed far removed from the small hill farm I had associated with the family. I said something about expecting the farm to be nearer Langholm and more in the hills.

'Na, na. That was my faither's farm. I went back there when I was de-mobbed and we were there when Marget and I first married. But this farm cam on the market just when I could afford to move and I couldna' see past it. It's good land down here, sheltered too compared with the old place. I always had a notion for this bit of country.' As if it explained the point, he added, 'That's Morton Rigg you see by yon clump of trees.'

'Just be straight,' his wife interrupted. 'Jimmy is a romantic softie! The Armstrong clan fought and reived for a hundred years and more, always with an eye on the few miles hereabouts called the Debatable Land. A heap of men must have died for meddling in it. The Armstrongs aye coveted it and Jimmy here is no different. When it came on the market, he had to have it. And, to be fair, it was a good move.'

'I was lucky at the time, to have the cash to put in the right bid. And it's a fair farm. But you wanted to talk about the *Duchess*.' That was said with such finality I sensed James Armstrong would say little more about moving from the hills to this richer land.

Accordingly I asked what had happened to him after the *Duchess* had reached Lagos. Cracker told me he had gone on to the Middle East to join a desert-raiding group in Libya and then on to Italy.

'I even ended up in Trieste and saw the shipyard where the *Duchess* had been built and the offices of the firm that owned her. She survived the war, you know, sailing as one of the *Empire* ships; the British Admiralty renamed all captured enemy ships that way. She was a fine ship, very nicely fitted up; Captain Panda liked her,' he said reflectively. He was sorry to have to go back to his job at Port Harcourt.'

'And what about Corporal Graham? He came through the war safely, I hope.'

'Rob? Oh, aye; we were together for quite a while before he got his promotion and we see the Grahams pretty often now. He has come a long way from the shop in Cockermouth. He has two supermarkets in Carlisle and big shops in other Cumbria towns too. He's shaping to be the biggest grocer in that part of England.'

'He is a good businessman and keeps top quality stock,' Margaret put in. 'He deserves to get on.'

'That is a big change of scale from the old family business,' I said, surprised because my notion of the man did not fit this picture of an emerging tycoon.

'Och, he managed; there would be his demob gratuity.' And again I sensed the curtain coming down. Rob's demob grant of a few pounds seemed an unlikely capital base for even one supermarket, but with scarcely a pause Cracker went on, almost as if was the same topic.

'We keep in touch with the Oba, you know. His son came to stay with us, the first time at the Langholm farm only a year or so after I was demobbed; he was going up to Cambridge, like his father. Nice lad. It caused a wee stir in Langholm, that first time he came; there wasn't many black men to be seen there then. Now no-one looks twice.'

Somewhat enigmatically, Cracker went on, 'I aye got on well with the Oba. I played straight with him: his secret society seemed to have too long an arm for anyone to do otherwise. He is a good man, a real gentleman.'

Speaking of the Oba sparked memories, for Cracker abruptly turned to his wife and spoke nostalgically about Sapoba: the majesty of the trees; the purity of the Jamieson River; above all, the tranquillity. 'I would like fine to go back there and let you see it all, but only if it was like what it was when Rob and I stayed that weekend.'

Turning to me he said, 'Forest Guard Agbontaen and Joshua Oshodin have asked us, as well as the Oba, and I am sure they would give us a great time. Agbontaen became Chief Ranger and later he got a university degree. Then, last year, he got Peter's old job as Forest Officer, Benin. But I am afraid the place would be far more commercial, sorely changed, and it would spoil the memory of how it was. Rob feels the same. We often talk about the fruit bats and watching the canoe-builders, but it doesn't do to go back, you know,

263

not there or to the Western Desert. All the same, I would like fine to see the Benin folk. They were genuine, nice people – like Borderers in many ways; for one thing, they had been bonny fighters. Joshua would have done fine in the Commandos.'

There was a hint of wetness on the cheek of the tough Borderer and I knew Africa had imprisoned Cracker Armstrong, as it has so many others. To save his embarrassment, I changed the subject.

'What about Klaus Ehrwald? Was he ever captured?'

'No it seems he got clean away. Rob and I asked if we could chase after him from Lagos, although we would have been several days behind, but we were sent straight to Cairo instead.'

'How did he succeed in escaping,' I asked.

'It was surmised Klaus trekked north on the route the cola-nut porters used and that the porters covered for him. Maybe he lay low in Cameroons until the end of the war or he may have got away across the desert to join Rommel. Who knows? He was a bright lad and a tricky one. If he did walk out with the cola porters he was a tough lad too, because it was a coarse road by all accounts. Peter Thorburn told me the Cameroons people said he escaped and was still alive. Peter left the Colonial Service, you know; he is the senior manager with the South Scotland Forestry Company and lives in Melrose. We see him whiles. He keeps in touch with Chris Wickham. Peter tells me Chris lives in Surrey now.'

Margaret Armstrong poured more tea and there was no more talk of the *Duchess* operation until just before I left. On the mantelshelf, looking quite incongruous, stood an empty Sten gun magazine. Cracker saw my interest.

'Aye. That's the magazine Joshua carried. The Oba's son brought it on his first visit. His father thought I might like it as a keepsake.'

The large solitaire diamond set in Margaret Armstrong's handsome engagement ring flashed red and sparkling blue in the firelight. The notion that Kinmont Willie Armstrong was the last of the reivers was just silly.

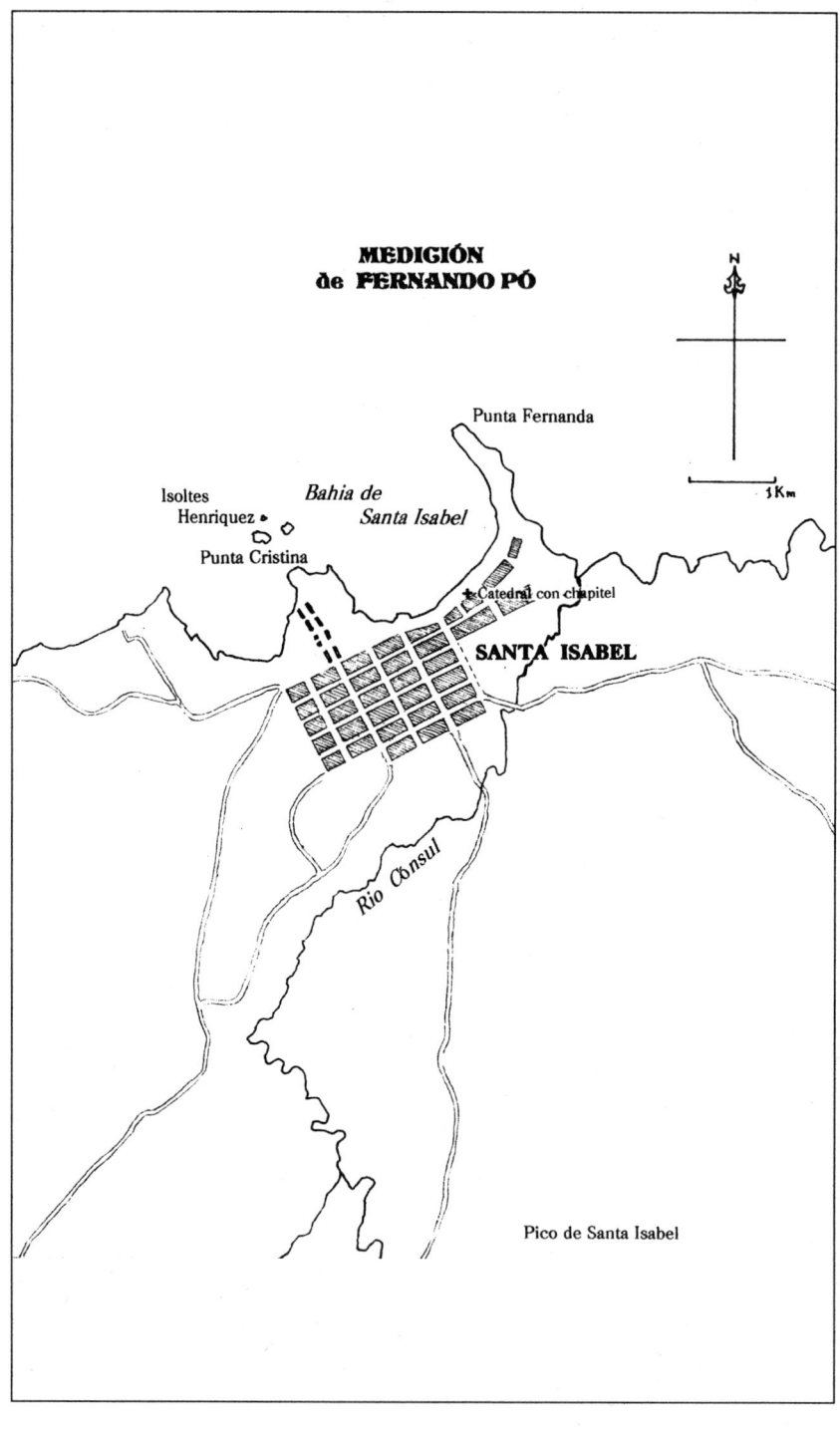

MEDICIÓN
de FERNANDO PÓ

N

↑Km

Punta Fernanda

Isoltes
Henriquez •
Punta Cristina

*Bahia de
Santa Isabel*

✝Catedral con chapitel

SANTA ISABEL

Rio Consul

Pico de Santa Isabel